THE POSER

THE POSER

DETECTIVE PAT NORELLI SERIES

DAVID E TEMPLE

82 MERCER PUBLISHING

THE POSER

Published by 82 Mercer, Inc.

Third Edition

Cover & Interior Design: David e Temple

Edited by Barbara Ann Temple, Ph.D.

ISBN: 978-1-7330913-7-4 (Paperback)

Published in the United States of America

Connect: DavideTemple.com

A NOTE ON THIS THIRD EDITION

The Third Edition of *The Poser* features a newly revised opening chapter, refreshed front and back matter, a new cover design, and updated author materials. While the core story remains unchanged, the presentation has been thoughtfully updated for this release.

A sneak peek of *The Impostor*, the next novel in the series, appears at the back of this book for those readers who enjoyed this and wish to continue Detective Norelli's story.

For more about this series and other books by David, including his nonfiction memoir, visit DavideTemple.com.

ALSO BY DAVID E TEMPLE

Standalone Thriller:

Dark Hunger, February 2026

Book & Film:

Chasing Grace

Non-Fiction

LIFE IN TWO COLUMNS:

Shit That Matters. And Everything Else.

THE POSER
DETECTIVE PAT NORELLI SERIES

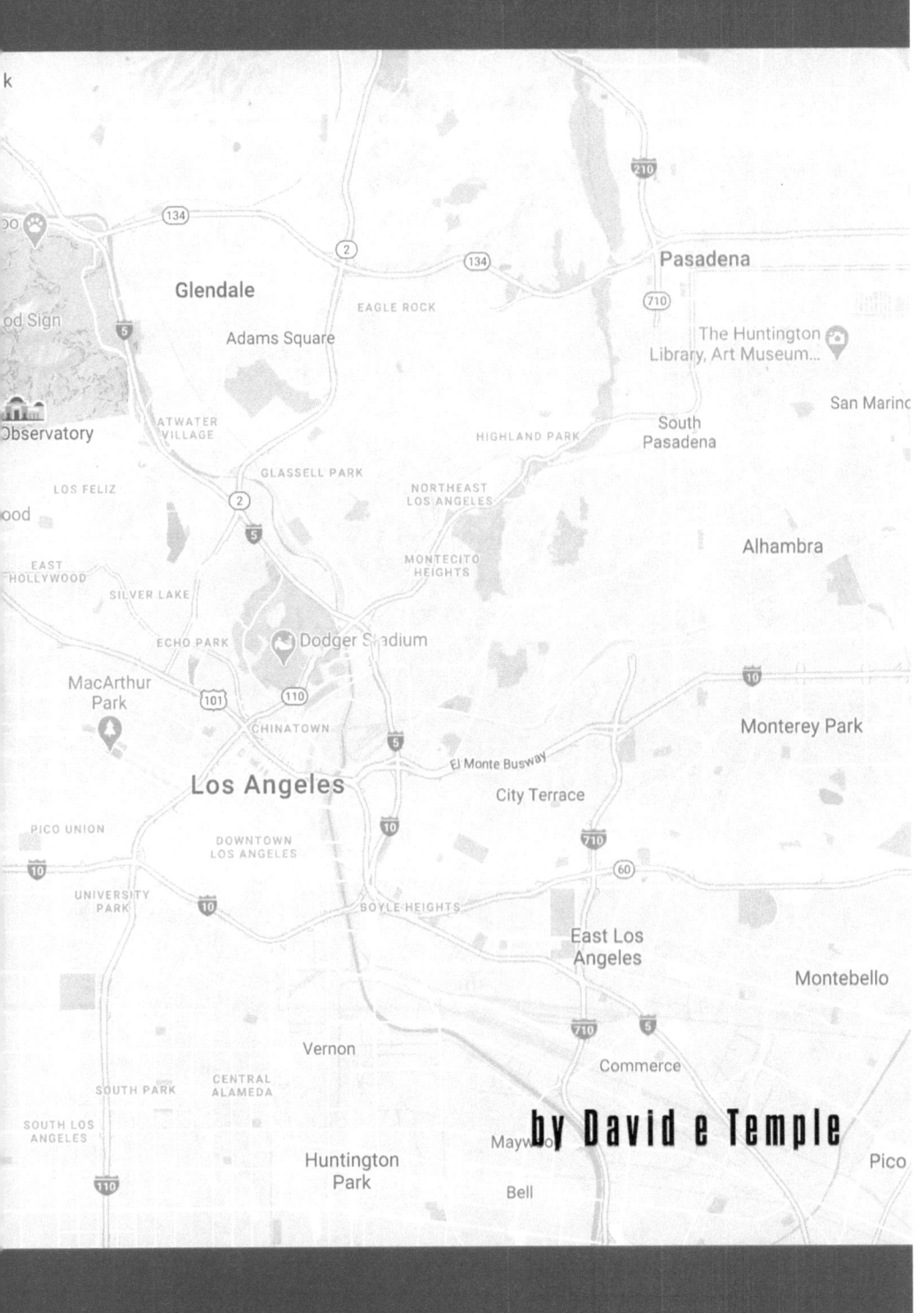

by David e Temple

For Tammy—my inspiration, my heart

It is impossible to suffer without making someone pay for it; every complaint already contains revenge.

— FRIEDRICH NIETZSCHE

1

CRIMSON SHEETS

S tanding over the bed, he watched the erratic bursts from his lover's neck slowly subside. He always savored this instant—when the body surrendered and the world went quiet. Leaning closer, he saw the light leave her eyes and captured the moment in his mind like a polaroid.

Reaching for his smartphone, he began posing her body like Hollywood starlets who graced past magazine covers. He took great pleasure in orchestrating his art, capturing images from multiple angles. Halfway through, his glove slipped on a smear of blood—minor, but enough to irritate him. He reset his grip, took a steadying breath, and resumed.

Minutes later, he put away the phone in one jacket pocket and removed a folded letter from another, placing it in the center of a nearby writing desk. Taking out a pen, he placed it in her hand before returning both to the desk. Pleased, he began gathering his clothes.

A faint noise snapped through the quiet.

He froze.

Listening.

Nothing.

On alert now, he made his way down the hall. He thought he heard another sound and stopped. The only noise came from the splashing fountain next to the pool in the backyard.

He continued creeping through the long corridor to the rear of the house. Moonlight cast long shadows across the marble floor. Stopping, he scanned the room until his eyes landed on a door in the corner of the great room. It was cracked open. He stepped outside, scanning the grounds.

Nothing.

Still keyed up, he returned to the master—checking the hallway clock en route. It was 4:26 a.m. He had less than an hour.

Picking up his pace, he returned to the bedroom, finished dressing, and wiped down the suite with practiced efficiency. In her home office—the control room lit by dim monitors—he saw a bank of cameras covering every angle of the property.

The panel clock read 4:44 a.m. Two more stops.

Entering a password, he tapped a series of keys—erasing the hard drive and shutting the system down. Satisfied, he killed the lights and moved to the kitchen, loading dishes into the dishwasher. As a final precaution, he wiped down anything he recalled touching and was about to leave when something tugged at him: her cell phone.

His pulse ticked up.

He checked the kitchen, dining room, and office. Nothing.

Returned to the bedroom—writing desk, dresser, bathroom. Nothing.

His breath thinned as he checked his watch: 5:02 a.m.

Moving faster now, he swept through the bar, great room, and library.

Still nothing.

A memory surfaced—her purse on the foyer table. He found it, pulled her phone, swiped. Locked.

Jaw tight, he carried it back to the bedroom and held it in front of her face. Open.

He erased specific photos, deleted several texts, then returned for the final touch. Retrieving the bloody razor, he wrapped her fingers around the handle—careful, deliberate, ritualistic. Her bedside clock read 5:21 a.m.

From his pocket he removed the souvenir, placed it in her other hand, and closed her fingers around it. He admired the symmetry. The story he'd built. The signature no one else understood.

One last photo. A quiet whisper: "Sweet dreams, love."

Gathering his things—and the remnants he always took—he exited the back door and moved through the pool area before closing the gate and heading down the driveway. At the end of the street, he spotted his rental.

Reaching into his bag for the keys, he didn't see the speeding car rounding the hairpin curve behind him.

High beams flashed.

He staggered back as the car swerved, missing him by inches.

The engine's throaty roar and a blaring song tore through the stillness as the driver downshifted into the next curve and vanished into the night.

2

COLD CASE

I t was late and the precinct was unusually quiet—especially odd given it was in the center of Hollywood. I had spent little time working overnights since the Academy, but I was currently working to put a period at the end of a sad story. Though the particular bloody headline had faded nearly a decade ago, I had been tasked with closing it for good.

Finishing up paperwork, I flashed back to my days as a *boot* working alongside my then-teacher, now-partner Detective Stuart Brown—a veteran cop and a good man. He started in The Graveyard like everyone else and was fond of saying it was a place to begin or end a career—depending on whether you were a new uniform or knew your time had come. I was glad to be working in the daylight these days.

Fortunately, fate smiled on me because someone on the ninth floor felt I showed promise—something about solid instincts and good chemistry—so I got a boost to Detective Third Grade and was partnered with Brown. Moving from nights to days, the two of us had been joined at the hip since, but I was now more than eager to make Detective First Grade.

I had spent enough time on the job to gain almost enough respect to be treated as an equal. I say almost because in the all-boys club of the LAPD, it was next to impossible to break through that ceiling. Besides, I was too stubborn to quit. Having a brother as a Police Captain and a father as Circuit Court Judge, I had been provided as much leg up as was possible without fully tipping the nepotism scale.

Closing the file in front of me, I caught myself smiling, finally putting to sleep a cold case that napped in Hollywood back alleys for half a decade. Lucky for me, the answer had been in sight—it just was not plain.

It involved a fresh out-of-high school wannabe named Rebecca Strong who had come to Hollywood by way of Atlanta in search of fortune and fame in a town of glitz and glamor. According to sources, her career lasted all of eleven months. After dozens of acting classes and hundreds of commercial auditions, her sparkling smile but average talents were bashed along with the back of her head. Blunt Force Trauma—or BFT as we called it—put her dreams to sleep for good.

She was attacked in the middle of the night in the middle of Hollywood without any witnesses. Stuart had been *this close* to closing it before it was buried in the Cold Cases file. I had just happened to stumble across a record of one of her old acting teachers and connected him to an arrest linked to another unsolved case.

Long story short: the tiny needle fell from the overwhelming haystack when I unraveled the case with reverse engineering, a technique I learned early in life from my father.

Fresh eyes and dogged tenacity helped.

A loud cackle from the coffee room snapped me back. Checking my watch, I saw it was past midnight. Stretching a stiff back, I gathered my things as my tired eyes landed on a picture frame on the corner of my desk.

The first photo was me graduating from the Academy. I was standing alongside my parents and brother Peter. It was about the same time my only sibling left Hollywood as Sergeant to become Captain in New York's First Precinct. My father, Judge Samuel P. Norelli, had both arms around his two suits in blue and a hand on our mother's shoulder.

In the second one, I was holding my daughter Shay just minutes after she was born. I had purposely folded the photo where my ex-husband crowded the happy scene.

The third showed Stuart and me the day I was promoted to Detective. And the last photo was of my black Lab Lucy who died from cancer last summer.

Heading for the door, I heard Officer Patrick before I saw her. She had more bravado than most guys I knew, and she sounded in rare form.

Catching my eye, she shouted, "What'n the hell are you doing here on the weekend, Patty?"

"Closing cases, girl. And keeping an eye on rookies like you, *Patty*. Be careful out there," I waved over my shoulder.

"Will do, Detective," she laughed, disappearing from sight.

Few people called me Patty and only my parents called me Darcy. My boss used Patricia when he was serious, and most friends called me Pat— or just Norelli.

3

QUIET TOAST

P assing through several beautiful and exclusive neighborhoods in the hills above Los Angeles, the man in black blended into the awakening traffic halfway between the murder scene and his home.

Miles away in a nondescript strip mall, he pulled up to a dumpster in the back. It was a procedure he had rehearsed earlier in the week. Double-checking for wandering eyes, he saw none. In fact, the only thing of note was a sign on the metal bin confirming pickup service in a couple hours. He tossed all bloody evidence and cleaning supplies in the oversized bin, then quietly disappeared.

Several dozen blocks later—in another string of repetitive shops— he approached a Goodwill dumpster. Its large mouth yawned open, waiting to devour a deposit of clothing. Thanks to the more-than-ample population of homeless in the neighborhood, he was confident all remaining items would disappear quickly and without a trace.

Once home, he poured a drink, slid open a wall of glass, and approached the pool which clung to the side of a cliff.

His eyes reflected the light shifting from night to day as he savored a vintage Scotch.

He replayed each step of the deed, meticulously analyzing the orchestrated chaos. Confident everything went as planned, he finally relaxed.

Staring into the Pacific, he inhaled the cool air, lifted his glass, and whispered, "Cheers, Mum."

4

CRISPY START

The next morning I arrived at the precinct to a day warmer than most and at a time later than usual. Fortunately, a strong cup of coffee kick-started my brain, and while soft around the edges because of fatigue, my head was entering the game.

"Morning, Detective Sunshine," Detective Stuart Brown said as I entered the office.

"What's up, Sparky?" he asked with a frown creasing his forehead.

Dropping things on my desk, I looked down at myself, then up at him. "What is it?"

Without even trying to suppress a grin, he said, "Not to be rude, but why's it look like you've been up all night?"

Stuart and I were close. Brother-sister close. Whenever we spoke our mind, it was done from a place of love. And highly unfiltered.

Rolling my eyes, I smirked. "Because I have."

Dramatically ignoring him, I took out a folder and tossed a file on his desk. In big red letters it read: CLOSED.

"Now, that's what I'm talkin' about," he grinned, leaning over for a high-five.

Slapping his hand, I said, "Somebody had to put a nail in it," making a gesture for *mic drop*.

"Copy that. And nice work," he toasted his mug to my paper cup—just as our boss entered the room.

Captain John Nelson had been with the LAPD for approaching twenty years and had recently hinted at retirement. He was the last of the old guard and still too sexist for his own good. He operated like most any Police Captain: played by the rules, did not bend them, had a bigger bark than a bite, and genuinely enjoyed helping detectives better understand crime scene photos.

"What's the celebration all about?" he barked.

Nelson was not as angry or cantankerous as he appeared. It was his way of ruling with an iron fist. Fact was, he was a pussycat underneath.

Winking at Stuart, I said, "Morning, Captain. Brown and I were just laughing at a joke. Go ahead and share with Captain what had you choking on your Krispy Kreme."

As Stuart's expression said, *I'm gonna get you,* my eyes darted to the clock on the far wall.

It was 9:20 a.m.. Policy dictated we begin at 8:30—Captain preferred 8.

"Could give a shit," Nelson said, looking me up and down. "You're late, Norelli, and why does it look like you haven't slept, but did so in your clothes?"

"Good eye, sir. Actually, I was here late but by the time—"

"Can it, Norelli," he dismissed with a wave. "Wanted to make sure you weren't sleeping one off in the parking lot. Again."

The Captain didn't drink and had no patience for drinkers. Besides impairing judgement, he felt it made people fat and lazy. And while I was known to tie one on every now and again, I tried to keep it under wraps. The Captain liked to bark at me, but I think it was his way of looking out for me.

"There's been a murder—or suicide. Hell, it's up in the air right now, but I do know the victim is Meredith Johansen. An anchor on one of those magazine tabloid shows." He sat on the corner of my desk. "And evidently a documentary filmmaker, too."

He tapped the folder he was holding against his leg—as though wondering what he was going to do with it. "It's a freakin' conundrum, if you ask me," he said, glancing around the room.

Stuart and I eyeballed one another, and I leaned forward. "Captain, let me have it. Us, I mean," I said pointing back and forth between Stuart and myself. "Conundrum's right up our alley."

He shook his head like it wasn't a good idea and scanned the room like he was looking for a better offer. "Yeah, about that..." he sighed. "You still got a long way to go before—"

"Captain," I said, waving for Stuart to hand me the closed file on his desk. "As you'll see, I finally put this one in the vault. Signed, sealed and—"

"Yeah, I see that, Norelli. Thing is," he checked his watch. "This one's gonna take some finesse," he said, looking at my wrinkled outfit. "With all the hub-bub on this one, the ninth floor wants it handled fast. And quiet," he dropped his voice. "Not sure why the push, but—"

"But that's good. I wrapped this one quick. Well, okay it took a couple years, but once I got my hands on it—"

"Norelli," he barked, waving me back like I was too close. "Pump the brakes. I get it. You're on it. But like I said, this one's, well, it's high profile. Gonna get a lotta heat."

Stuart stepped in. "Boss, she's right. After she put her mind and our resources to it, the pieces fell into place. Fast."

The frown on Captain's face confused me. I wasn't sure if he was having a hard time seeing Stuart, hearing what we were saying, or making a decision. But he was still in front of me and that was good enough.

"Look Captain, I don't wanna say I'm begging you, but c'mon, what's a girl gotta do to—"

He held up a hand. "Woah, Nelly," he said, looking around. "We don't need anyone—least of all you—working that 'me too' shit."

Cocking my head to the side, I looked at him like, *Really?*

A rookie quickly entered the room. "Sorry to interrupt, Captain, Detectives, but you've been summoned to—"

Not waiting for the rest, Captain waved the newbie aside and headed for the door, barking over his shoulder, "Norelli, Brown. My office in ten."

Stuart's exaggerated shrug punctuated my snort, "That went well."

5

PSYCHO BABBLE

Nine minutes later, Stuart and I arrived at the Captain's office only to have his secretary tell us he got sidetracked but should not be long. She pointed to his office and I suddenly felt like I was in the principal's office. Stuart scanned headlines on his cell while my hands mindlessly fidgeted with a bottle opener attached to a key ring.

I had a good view of the executive offices and saw Nelson through a partially open door. He stood at attention getting his ear chewed by Police Commissioner Christopher Miller, a boss whose tolerance for bullshit registered zero.

I was reading over Stuart's shoulder when Captain Nelson entered and sat on the corner of his desk. Stretching his neck from side to side, he popped it loudly several times.

"Here's my challenge, Detective Norelli. There's some scuttlebutt going around from people who think you don't have what it takes to do your job."

My stomach fluttered, but my face remained neutral.

Captain leaned forward—too close for my taste—and let out a deep sigh. His aftershave and coffee breath were fighting for fragrance domination. The aftershave was losing.

"Maybe it's because you like to dial it up a few notches on those two-for-one nights at the pub with your pals. Or, how you like to keep banker's hours while the rest of us grunts bang it out according to regulations."

He went to his credenza and poured a coffee from an old thermos.

"You do realize your coworkers know how your brother moved up the ranks so fast, right?" Not waiting for an answer, he added, "Word is they take issue with your similar advancement. Me? I think it's just old baggage that keeps you from getting ahead."

I was not sure if his dramatic slurp was due to frustration, levity, or both.

"Sir?"

"Maybe you're depressed, or pissed. Hell, maybe you're overcompensating for something," he stared into his coffee mug. "So your husband left you for someone else. *Waaah*," he mocked. "Shit happens, and yes—"

I started to speak, but his raised hand stopped me.

"A lot's expected of you…" he looked inside the folder, "And such a high profile case could be a game changer."

"Could be a *career* changer," I said.

Frowning, he looked from me to Stuart to the folder in front of him. Skimming the pink sheet, he half-mumbled, "Doesn't make sense. This gal's on top of the world, just snagged the biggest trophy of her life, was loved by the public and what, goes home to party with some friends and stare at her gold statue….only to *off* herself sometime in the night?"

He rubbed his entire face like it itched.

"Yes, sir. Bizarre."

Eyeballing me over the top of his cup, he took another slurp. "Hell, could be a copy-cat. Of those Strip Killers years back. Who knows."

Doug Clark and Carol Bundy, aka The Sunset Strip Killers, were a whacked-out couple from the early '80s who traveled Hollywood, killing randomly. The legendary case had several inside the system wondering when a repeat performance might surface. Serial killers were often cyclical, and several inside the force were betting sooner than later. To me, this didn't feel like that.

"Captain, I *really* want a chance to change the game. Sir, let me lead this case. And if I don't solve it in the time you think is fair, hell, I won't go back to the graveyard shift….I'll *quit*."

Stuart looked at me like I yelled fire as Captain's eyebrows raised.

"That's an interesting idea," he said—eyes darting between me and Stuart, then kept moving like I hadn't spoken. "Could be just a high-profile bimbo who got murdered for fucking the wrong studio exec. You know how this town is."

"Or, maybe a nut-case killer with an axe to grind," I shrugged.

Stuart finally spoke. "Sir, you said suicide."

"Seems so." He smoothed his tie. "I'm thinking differently."

"Makes little sense," I mumbled.

"Murder rarely does, Norelli."

As much as I wanted to push, I waited.

This was one of those opportunities that came along every once in a while that could do big things in moving a career forward. I knew it. Stuart knew it. And the Captain knew it. Plus, the fact it was downgraded from murder to suicide so quickly had my skin crawling.

After an entirely too long of a pause, followed by an overly dramatic sigh, punctuated with a final slurp, Nelson spoke.

"All right, Norelli, it's yours. Take the lead. But Stuart," he tossed his chin at my partner. "You watch her back. Every step of the freakin' way, you got that?"

"Yes, sir," he saluted mockingly as we stood.

I took the folder from Nelson's hand and nodded, then Stuart and I were both out the door when he shouted, "Norelli?"

Spinning around, we returned to the doorway.

"I need you to close this sooner than later. Copy?"

We both said, "Copy."

Squinting, he said, "Brown, go grab a coffee. She'll catch up in a second."

"Yes, sir."

Nelson motioned to close the door.

"Listen, I don't care what you do on your own time. What I do care about is how you perform your duties, protect our community, and that you at least *attempt* to show up on time. You don't want your coworkers saying shit behind your back like you're the teacher's pet, do you?"

I shook my head and he stopped chewing the inside of his cheek.

"Do us both a favor and talk to someone."

"Sir?"

"You know, a professional. Someone you can dump your...you know."

"A therapist?"

"You know the drill," he said. "Maybe go outside. Off the books. Draw less attention."

On one hand, I was shocked he was suggesting this. On the other, I guess I understood—for any number of reasons.

"I can do that."

Whether I really needed one was anyone's guess, but if I could get this case and prove myself to my peers, my boss, and my father—especially myself—it would be worth it.

"Hell, there are more shrinks per capita within five miles of here than anywhere else on earth."

"Have you been seeing one?"

He swatted the air. "Hell no. My wife," he barked, making a spinning gesture to the side of his head. "Bats in the attic."

"Right."

"Not certifiable." He looked ashamed for saying such. "Just depressed. Anyhow, I'm doing this for your own good. Pull it together, okay?"

"Yes, sir. Got it."

"Now, get the hell outta here and show this precinct you've got the goods."

"Copy that," I said, opening the door to leave.

"Last thing, Norelli?"

"Sir?"

"I'm on your side. But how this ends is all up to you!"

6

BLOODY MESS

Driving to the crime scene, Stuart stopped at a light and stared at a helicopter overhead, shaking his head like he was arguing with someone. Looking over at me, he said, "Sorry to be nosy, but I am your friend."

"Huh?"

"Yeah, while you were with the Captain, I kinda hung around. And kinda overheard your conversation. Just wanted you to know...if you need, I've got a friend in the program."

"What? No, it's cool."

I could feel my armpits steam from the embarrassment and wondered why everyone wanted me to get my head checked all of a sudden. "I'm... kinda fine, really," I winked.

"Cool."

Stuart turned onto Beverly Ridge Terrace. As we approached our destination, he chirped the siren to grab the attention of a TV news videographer blocking the driveway.

After showing our credentials and donning the appropriate crime scene garb, we approached the impressive Bel Air Mansion. I couldn't help but gawk. The house had to be 10,000 square and in addition to the four garage bays, the compound had a pool and cabana, tennis court, and an English flower garden on a lower level that reminded me where I grew up in Pasadena.

The area was taped off with two black and whites and a Coroner's vehicle. Local TV and radio station vans sat along the ridge overlooking Franklin Canyon reservoir.

"What's up, JayCo," I said to the Chief Medical Examiner who was unloading her van.

"What up, girl? And my man, Stuart."

She and I exchanged a quick hug. Stuart got a fist bump.

Jackie Corazon had grown up in LA and was well-known as a ball-breaking, get-it-done ME. She had the knowledge of a professor, the demeanor of a bouncer, and a stomach of steel. She's the only person I knew who could slice open the belly of a dead body while eating a sandwich.

As we made small talk, I scanned the gathering crowd. It was common for perps to circle back after committing a crime. The only odd thing I saw was a woman with her hair up in old-fashioned rollers walking a tiny dog —not something you see everyday. The rollers, not the dog.

"What's it look like, Jackie?" I asked.

Heading toward the house, she looked over her shoulder and waved us to follow, "As my Brit friends say, 'A bloody mess.'"

7

PANIC ROOM

E ven dead, Meredith Johansen was beautiful. Lying atop blood-soaked sheets, her body was twisted at the trunk and arms spread wide, as if to say, *Ta-Dah*.

The amount of blood was disturbing.

"That's some trajectory," Stuart said—his eyes following a path of blood across the headboard.

"Arterial spray. Either force or exertion. Maybe both," Jackie said. "And under extreme duress? Could be *yards*, not feet," she continued, aiming a device the length of the spray. "Distance laser saves a lot of time."

Stuart pointed to the device. "May I?"

She spoke several details into her smartphone, then handed the laser to him. "What is it with boys and their toys?" she asked, grinning.

"Looks like he just discovered fire," I deadpanned.

It didn't take me long to spot something across the room. Crossing to a nearby writing desk, I picked up a note with tongs and read it, then handed it to Stuart.

He read it and frowned.

"Yeah, right," I mumbled. "With a cut like that? No way."

"Exactly."

Just then, Jackie's phone rang. "Be right back."

Approaching the victim, I got a closer look at the depth of the gash across her throat. I wasn't sure if it was because I had not eaten enough breakfast or had consumed too much late night wine, but my gut did a somersault. I waved for Stuart to follow me out the French bedroom doors for some air.

Stuart flipped through his notepad while I watched the crowd. "Do you think for one second—"

"A woman? To herself? No *effing* way," I snapped. "And why the rapid downshift from murder to suicide from upstairs. Just because of a note?"

"Seems odd," Stuart said.

"True. Just too…I don't know."

Stuart returned to scribbling something when I noticed a dark-skinned and bearded man across the street. For whatever reason—one I could not put my finger on—he seemed out of place. I watched him take a case from a van with an Arx Security logo. While his overalls matched the color of the van, his shoes didn't match his outfit. Just then, our eyes met and he swiftly made his way down the street.

"What is it?" Stuart asked.

"Just watching that guy," I said, turning to see Jackie heading back in. She waved for us to follow.

"What guy?"

As I looked back, he was gone.

"Never mind."

BACK INSIDE, Jackie examined the victim's limbs while Stuart checked the windows for entry and I took out my cell phone, dragged a chair to the side of the bed, and waved to Stuart for help.

"What are you up to?"

"Hold on," I said, taking several photos before stepping down. Pulling up Google, I typed a quick image search. Within seconds, I turned the phone toward him. "Read the caption at the bottom."

"*Playboy* magazine debuted in 1953, starring unknown Marilyn Monroe. Hugh Hefner published this as his first centerfold." He looked at me and grinned. "Nice pull."

Additional crew entered, we stepped aside, and I continued snooping through drawers while Stuart continued scouring the room and scanning books on a nearby bookshelf.

I heard someone clear his throat behind me and turned to find a rookie named Chavez standing in the center of the room with a short, thick Hispanic woman. She was dressed in a maid's uniform, reminiscent of maids from the '50s. Her dark hair was pulled back and she wore little to no makeup. I could tell by the size and condition of her hands that she had worked hard most of her life.

Her eyes were teary, but she had a lovely, welcoming smile.

"Detectives, this is Gabriella Flores, Miss Johansen's housekeeper. She found the victim this morning when she arrived for work."

"Thanks, Officer. Miss Flores, my name is Detective Norelli. This is my partner Detective Brown."

She turned from the bloody scene, still fighting tears—a pink handkerchief clutched in one hand.

"Let's step into the living room," I said, taking her by the arm.

Forcing a smile, she whispered, "It's so sad. I just saw her Friday."

"Can you tell us, Ms. Flores, what did you do the *moment* you arrived?"

"And when was that, exactly?" Stuart asked.

"7:40 a.m., just like everyday. I get here every Monday through Friday between 7:30 and 8:00."

"And you didn't touch anything, right?"

"The door handle. And the security panel to turn off the code."

Stuart began to speak, but she interrupted, "No, sorry. That's what I *usually* do. But this time, the little box didn't beep."

"Didn't beep?" I asked.

"Usually when I show up, I unlock the door, come in, and I hear a beep. That means the alarm has been set. Then I unset it with a code."

"Of course," I smiled. "Which means Ms. Johansen wasn't here, right?"

"Yes."

"What time is she ordinarily gone?"

"Miss Meredith is an early riser. She's gone by 6:30 every day. She tells me, uh, told me she liked to be at work before anyone else," she said, suppressing tears.

Stuart and I looked at one another, then he asked, "Miss Flores, my colleagues and I noticed the home was spotless when we arrived."

A nod and a faint smile.

"However, it's the Monday after a weekend, and I don't know about your family, but my home's a wreck come Mondays," he grinned.

"Yes?"

"What I'm getting at is your job starts at 7:40, and yet, it looks as though—besides the bedroom—your job was already done."

She looked confused, so I jumped in. "I think what Detective Brown finds particularly strange is how this past weekend was a time of celebration. And we both imagine she would be partying with friends. But the home is spotless."

"Ah, yes," she smiled. "That's something funny about Miss Johansen. She would clean the place before I arrived."

"That's peculiar," I said, "Why do you think she did that?"

"She told me she was too self-conscious to leave the place messy for any visitors. And I would tell her it was my job not hers. She was funny that way."

We shared a smile. "So, I would show up, it would be clean, but my job was to clean this home, top to bottom, every Monday through Friday."

"Gives new meaning to the word neatnik," Stuart mumbled.

Flores whipped her head in his direction and said, "Yes, that's what she called herself. A neatnik."

"Miss Flores, we're almost done," I said. "Before you leave, can you tell us all of your duties?"

She took a deep breath. "I vacuum the entire home, including the garage, wash the floors in the entryway, the kitchen, and the bathrooms. I dust the house, wash any laundry left for me, including bed linens. Miss Meredith wanted clean sheets every night. I also wash the windows, but only on Friday. She entertains...entertained on weekends and wanted everything spotless."

"What about outside?'

Turning to Stuart, she said, "She had me let the pool man and yardman in at 8. That way, we're all here at the same time. She liked to keep it in the family."

Touching her arm, I asked, "Keep it in the family?"

"The pool man is my cousin," she smiled, "And the yardman is my brother. She didn't have family, so she called us her family."

I made a mental note to check into family members and saw Stuart write the same thing in his notepad. "That's nice. Family's important," Stuart said.

Flores looked across the vast living room to where two men stood outside. Holding hats in their hands, they stared at the ground.

"They don't speak very good English," she said.

Stuart nodded to me then asked, "Miss Flores, can I ask you just one more question?"

"Si."

"Do you know any secrets about Miss Johansen? That no one else knows?"

Frowning, she pursed her lips.

I knew where he was going, so I added some support. "It's safe to tell us anything you might know. This is a very important police matter," I smiled. "And I'm certain Ms. Meredith would want you to help."

"Anything at all, Miss Flores. Maybe a secret hiding place?"

She shook her head, "Well, she liked privacy. And security was *muy importante*. Which is why Ms. Meredith has...had...four cameras."

Stuart and I exchanged looks. Checking his notepad, he said, "We only counted three. One at the front gate, the front door, and the back door."

"Where's the fourth?" I asked.

She pointed behind us. "In the backyard. In that tall tree beside the pool."

We made our way to the patio area, and I instantly saw it. Looking back at the house, I saw how a camera in that location would allow for a wide shot of the entire back and both sides of the house.

"One night when she was drinking a lot of wine, she told me she was scared of photographers and wanted to be able to see everything from her..." she stopped and frowned again.

"Her what, Gabriella?" I asked.

"What did she call it? Her *panic* room? That way, she could see anyone coming."

I eyeballed Stuart. "Where is this panic room?"

"I don't know."

"But you said you cleaned the *whole* house," Stuart pushed.

Shaking her head, she said, "She always told me she would take care of that room herself."

8

HARD DRIVE

It took several sets of eyes, but Stuart, a forensic tech, and I located the panic room. The hidden door was located inside the master closet behind a wall of shoes. The clever entry point was a button hidden beneath a shelf. Once tripped, the wall sprang open several inches which allowed us to open it further. Inside was a soundproofed, well-ventilated smaller room. It had no windows, but it did have a two-way mirror that looked into the master. There was also a single Murphy bed folded into the wall, a nightstand with lamp, and a small fridge. We were standing in the grand foyer when Jackie came around the corner.

"You two follow me."

Joining her at the foot of the bed, she took Meredith's outstretched arm and opened her fist. "Look familiar?"

In Meredith's hand was a miniature gold-colored Oscar statue.

"Nice find, Jackie," Stuart said.

"Crazy, right?" She said, waving for a forensic photographer to shoot it before placing it in an evidence bag and handing it to me.

"It certainly changes things."

ON THE WAY back to the station, I continued to read about the famous Marilyn Monroe photograph. The photographer was Tom Kelly.

"I knew I'd seen that picture before. So many photos had her lying on a red velvet background," I said, taking a pack of gum from the glovebox. "That shot launched Monroe's career and made Playboy a household name."

"Quite the professor of porn, huh?" Stuart grinned.

"Curious is all. You see how—"

"Or should I call you a Pornistorian?"

I looked at him sideways. "As I was saying, look at the similarity between my shot and his."

"And?"

"Not sure. Let me see your notepad."

He took it from his jacket.

"Please and thank you," I said, comparing his notes to the ones on my iPhone. "How can you read this shit?"

He looked at me from the corner of his eye. "You kiss your momma with that mouth?"

I ignored him with a mumble, "Why the elaborate pose?"

"Start with the obvious," he said, looking in every direction of the Beverly, Sunset, and Crescent intersection before pulling into traffic and passing the Beverly Hills Hotel.

"Anchor at *The Hollywood Mole*, documentary filmmaker, part-time actress, Meredith Johansen, 35—" I tried to read a scribble off to the side. "Not to be confused with Scarlett Johansson?"

"Keep going," he grinned.

"Throat cut ear-to-ear. TOD between midnight and 5? No forced entry, theft, or sexual…wait, why do you have misconduct in quotes?"

"You heard Jackie say there were signs of sex, but likely non-violent. I'm assuming consensual. Just a note to dig further."

I said, "In depth. I get it."

"Snarky."

"When I mentioned blood in the carpet, she said she'll go back to scan the room with her CrimeScope."

"Make a good name for a TV show."

Ignoring him, I said, "I want to know if the killer was right or left handed. Also, how about tire casts of the driveway."

"Pea gravel," he frowned.

"Never hurts," I said, putting my spent gum into a wrapper. "Ever seen such a hardcore neatnik?"

"Not unless we're talking about you and your car."

I slapped his arm. "It's called pride of ownership."

He nodded toward his pad.

"Right," I said, still trying to decipher his shorthand. "What's this say about cameras and herd—"

"Hard drive. I got a tech to boot up the computer and looked around the hard drives. All empty. Blank. As in, either a new computer—which it isn't—or new drives—which they aren't."

"Or, erased," I added.

"Bingo."

"Finding the panic room was key."

"Ya think?"

"Clever way to hide…your hideaway," I said.

"Plus four main cameras to watch the house. Front gate, security panel, front door, and overlooking the pool."

"I saw you looking at something else while I was chatting it up with Jackie."

"Yeah, I noticed two *additional* ones," he scanned his notes. "One in a carbon monoxide detector in the garage. And in the chandelier over her bed."

"How'd you—"

"You know I love gadgets."

"I get the garage, but—"

"Voyeurism at its best," he grinned.

WE MADE it back to the station in good time, and while Stuart unloaded an evidence box from the trunk, I answered my vibrating phone. "What's up, Jackie?"

"We found something after you left."

"Talk to me," I said, putting her on speaker.

"Meredith's cell phones. We found one under her mattress, just beneath her head. A second was in a kitchen drawer."

I stopped a second to process. "Love to get our mitts on 'em."

"I'll ship them over. And you owe me a beer," she laughed. "Or three."

"Like that'll be a problem."

As we headed down the hall, Stuart chimed in. "Hey Jackie, I see the hard drive for her monitoring system had been erased."

"Right?"

"Yeah, with all the cameras, I'm sure we'll have a goldmine. Probably on a loop every 24 or so."

"Well, that's for you detectives. I'm just the scientist."

We thanked her and rang off.

Unwrapping a candy bar, Stuart said, "Two phones, huh?"

"Lots of people like to keep work and personal separate."

"I suppose."

"What do you make of the letter?" I asked, holding up the bag.

Taking it, he read aloud: *I simply can't take it anymore. The pressure, the politics, the insecurity, and the bullshit. I'm tired of phony friends, this phony town, and my phony boyfriend. To my family, I'm sorry. Love, MJ.*

"I don't know this person, but it doesn't feel...authentic."

Flipping through notes, he said, "And is it me or does that pose seem...coincidental?"

"And since we don't believe in coincidences, let's take a look at the other goodies."

Taking Meredith's laptop from the evidence box, Stuart said, "Time we crack this puppy open."

9

TIGHT BOX

A dark-skinned man wearing a jumpsuit entered his handsome and well-appointed home. Setting down a tool chest, he picked up a remote from an oversized coffee table and pushed a single button. A piece of exotic art on the wall quietly moved aside, disappearing behind a thin panel over the fireplace and exposing an enormous flat panel television.

Clicking another button, he initiated the surround sound system that bellowed headlines from a local television station. He adjusted the volume and began removing pieces of beard while making his way down a long hallway toward the back of the house. The disguise was nearly gone by the time he turned on the shower.

Minutes later, his damp hair was lighter than before, his eyes were bright blue instead of dark brown, and dress slacks and a pressed shirt replaced the jumpsuit.

In the sleek living room, he divided his attention between local news and an encrypted iPad he had removed from a floor safe—deftly camouflaged by a pattern of squares cut into the concrete floor. With no visible handle, it was opened by pressing a button hidden under the lip of the fireplace mantel, making the floor door open pneumatically from below.

The hidden space was roughly the size of a large trunk and contained a variety of electronics, money in several currencies, and an assortment of weapons. He took a seat and loaded a photoshoot onto the iPad.

Pressing the remote, he revealed his handiwork on the television.

He became aroused at the sight of Meredith. Even amidst the blood, he found her intoxicating. Moving his attention to an original Tom Kelly photograph of Marilyn Monroe on an opposite wall, he compared the two.

"Nice," he said aloud.

An image on the television grabbed his attention. A news bulletin showed a view from a helicopter. He turned up the volume: ...*All we know for now. Again, at approximately 7:30 this morning, a housekeeper arrived at this Bel Air home to find the owner, Meredith Johansen—documentary filmmaker and television host of The Hollywood Mole—dead in her home. Neighbors told Channel 8 she was a kind person and a humanitarian who served her community. The cause of death, according to authorities, appears to be suicide. We'll have more details...*

Muting the sound, he returned to his recent artwork.

"Oh, she served many of us," he said, smiling.

Checking his watch, he shut down all the electronics and returned the iPad and camera to his secret space. Sliding on shoes and a jacket, he was in his car and down the road with little wasted motion.

10

DARK WEB

The forensics lab at our precinct wasn't like the well-known NCIS labs—all lit up with hip brick walls and shelves of super nifty, new equipment. And the primary forensics scientist wasn't a sexy, smart-mouthed, pigtailed gal named Abby.

Instead, our lab was drab with boring concrete block walls and random shelves of not-so-nifty, old equipment. And our forensics scientist—while somewhat sexy and sort of handsome—was a baldheaded guy named Oscar Gonzalez. Ozzie, for short.

As we arrived, he was bent over a keyboard, staring at a large monitor and sipping green tea.

"What's up, Ozzie?"

"Diagnostics," he said without looking up.

His was a less-is-more vibe.

"Sounds fun," Stuart responded, trying to engage.

"Necessary."

"Ozzie, if you've got some time, we'd love to ask a few questions," I said, making my way to a stack of materials labeled *Johansen.*

Checking the clock, he said, "Lunchtime."

Looking at one another, I shrugged and Stuart said, "I'm buying."

"Sushi?"

"Done."

Twenty minutes later, we were sitting at the counter of Fish, a tiny pristine space behind the Arc Cinema at Sunset and Ivar. With every sort imaginable, ninety-nine percent of the selections were raw. We each ordered a spicy tuna poke bowl and got to it.

"Ozzie, we've only just started, but several things have come to light that require our moving quickly."

Ozzie lifted his face from his bowl. "Why?"

Stuart jumped in, "Ticking clock with a suspect who's twitchy. Plus, I'm due vacation."

"Okay, shoot."

"We've discovered two hard drives on the victim's home security computers have been dumped."

Ozzie shook his head. "The cloud. Pretty much SOP these days," he said, devouring more fish.

"Our hunch is that while the killer—" I began.

"Or possible suicide—" Stuart interrupted.

"*Not* suicide," Ozzie raised his chopsticks with a deadpan expression.

"Yeah, we're good on that assumption," I added.

"Not assumption." Ozzie wiped his mouth and methodically placed his chopsticks on a napkin before turning to face us. "A fact. Lateral cut, left to right. Deep enough to cut the carotid, not just the jugular. Sliced clean through the larynx. And finished on the other side. Murder one. Nothing else."

Expressionless, he waited to be sure we got the message.

"So what you're saying…" Stuart said, drawing out the last word.

Ozzie stopped him with a single finger in the air and a sip of tea. When he finished the sip, he continued the explanation.

"The cut was *left to right*. Telling me she's right handed. She couldn't make that cut unless she was ambidextrous. And I doubt that. Calluses on her left middle finger knuckle tell me that when she writes—and as a journalist she does—she bears down hard. There's also a faint tan line on her right wrist —from her watch. Next, her muscle tone—while showing me she was in *yoga* shape, not weight-training shape—says the depth of that cut took strength she didn't likely have. At least not the kind this *particular* cut would take."

"Interesting," Stuart interrupted.

"Third, the carotid makes you bleed out fast—not the jugular, as most think. The fact she caught both the carotid *and* jugular on *both* sides, tells me—once again—it was someone much stronger than her. And fourth, someone *self-inducing*," Ozzie emphasized, "Wouldn't have the stamina to cut through her own larynx."

Stuart and I nodded without expression.

"My opinion?" he began.

"To kill her *voice*," I finished.

His first expression: a grin. "Yes, between the bruising on her forehead —right at her hairline—the fracture of the C5 vertebrae, *and* the rupturing of the spinous process of the C4."

"English?" Stuart smirked.

Ozzie slid on his Zouri sandals and stood behind Stuart. "May I?" he asked—and without waiting clamped down his left palm on Stuart's forehead while slowly and simultaneously pulling it slightly to the left.

"Feel that? Right here," he said, pressing a finger deep in the middle of Stuart's neck.

"Ow. Yeah, got it. Can you let go now?"

"Sorry. But see how the left hand pulls the head back, fully exposing the neck? That move makes for a fracture of the fifth and rupture of the fourth vertebrae."

"Because of the force," I said.

Removing his sandals, he returned to his poke bowl and nodded. "Exactly."

BACK AT THE STATION, we flanked Ozzie at his desk, watching as he stacked photos of Meredith and placed them in an envelope. He handed it to me.

"That's yours. I have my own."

"Thanks," Stuart and I say in unison.

We were heading out when I stopped and spun around. "I almost forgot. About the cloud, do you think—"

"No, I *know*," he instantly shook his head. "She's a Mac user. Busy with no time. Needs order in her chaos. She'll have a backup."

"All we need is her sign-in," Stuart said.

"Save your time," Ozzie said. "Ring McCloud."

11

MAGIC CLOUD

When we arrived at Groundwork Coffee on Sunset less than two blocks away, we spotted Stan in the back corner talking to a server. He waved, held up two fingers, and mouthed, *two minutes.* I gave a thumbs up and Stuart headed toward the order line.

Stan McClintock, aka McCloud, was a hacker with an obsession for information retrieval. His specialty: hacking cloud-based services. Legal? Perhaps. Necessary? For us, yes. And having him on the payroll as a "semi-permanent *surveillance* contractor" proved to be convenient.

Standing in line, I said, "We need to do more business in our backyard. Save all that drive time."

"No doubt."

"Should we pay him for this?"

Stuart eyeballed me. "Doesn't he owe you something?"

He was referencing some under-the-radar work Stan had done for us a while back. We often called on him when backlogged in bureaucracy. On more than several occasions he provided background checks where we drew blanks. Other times, he unearthed nasty leads on something he called The Dark Web—something I was aware of, but knew little about.

"True," I mumbled. "But let's see if we can't sweeten the pot this time. Thoughts?"

"I'll *brew* on it. Get it?" He laughed like he was on stage at The Laugh

Factory. I ignored him, looking instead for Stan's beckoning wave. Not yet.

Stan's resemblance to Buddy Holly was uncanny. While he wore the same outfit—the signature sport coat, tie, and glasses—they were all black. One of the perks, he told us in the past, was the tips he made walking down Hollywood Boulevard. On a good day, he would sign two or three dozen autographs for tourists before calling it a day. He called it "coffee money" because he didn't like beer.

I got the wave while Stuart got the coffee.

"What's up, Detective Norelli? Besides beautiful as always," Stan said, holding the back of the chair for me.

"So polite, *Mr. Holly.* But you can save that for the tourists; we've got serious shit to cover," I said, playfully batting my eyelashes.

"You're hilarious," he said, opening a nondescript yet oversized laptop with a small box attached to the side that had a row of miniature flashing lights. He saw me checking out his hardware and said, "Heavily encrypted and *very* secure personal Wifi. Never trust coffee shops," he winked as Stuart joined us.

"Detective Brown, welcome to one of my many offices."

"Professor McClintock, welcome to one of our backyard playgrounds."

"Right. Oh, and nobody calls me by my real name, you should know that by now."

"Okay, *McCloud*," Stuart grinned.

"Cool. Okay, what do you kids have for me?" he said, rubbing his hands like they were cold.

We spent the next several minutes volleying information back and forth, getting McCloud up to speed with the investigation. He listened intently without expression and when we were done and he had the big picture, I opened my backpack and handed him a hard drive along with Meredith's cell phones.

He plugged one phone into his computer and the hard drive into a small black box inside his metal briefcase. He tapped several dozen keys before taking a long, deep breath.

"Okay, I've got the website," he said, looking at the phone. "And my laptop is searching the cell phone. Now, all I need are the passwords," he said, looking us square in the face.

"Uh…" Stuart began.

McCloud laughed, "I'm fussing with you. Pat, give me something. Some place I can start."

Stuart retrieved his notepad and I grabbed my iPhone.

"Let's start with her name, address, birthdate. And any pets," he said.

I started with the basics before Stuart filled in the rest with way more than I expected. He had researched Meredith's parents' names, her pet's name, high school mascot, and name of her college as well as her astrological sign, social security number, and even her three-digit body dimensions.

"Holy shit, Sherlock," McCloud chuckled, "Nice work. Now, gimme a minute. If I can't crack this in the next fifteen minutes, it's on me."

MINUTES LATER, he had a connection to Meredith's Mac account and was unlocking her phone. Turning his laptop in our direction, he said, "We're in."

"How'd you—" Stuart began to say, but stopped.

"It's not that hard. People use the same passcode for pretty much everything. Even their bank accounts. They hate memorizing codes. And worse? Most people use a variation of that same passcode."

I leaned forward. "So, what's the passcode?"

"The hard drive for her security computer is her street name capitalized and her birth date in the standard six digit configuration. So, Beverlyridge plus 040484."

"And her phone?" Stuart grinned.

"That took a little longer because she put the numbers first—a slight rarity—followed by her cat's name capitalized, plus the last four digits of her social, followed by the pound sign that happens to be the most popular symbol used. So, 3926Bogart#."

As Stuart and I grinned at one another, McCloud said, "According to those smiles, I'm guessing I could crack your phones right now."

We laughed.

"Okay, what am I looking for?" McCloud asked, turning the laptop back and hitting dozens of keys at twice the speed I could think.

IN LESS THAN AN HOUR, we were able to view all the contents of her business and personal phones. Both were nearly identical. Both were full of selfies—thousands that included famous or very recognizable people— and just as many appointments. While the calendar appeared to be duplicated across both phones, only the personal phone had a consistent two-letter code.

The business phone—for nearly every day including weekends—was littered with appointments, most of which followed a routine description: name, title, time, and meeting place. The personal phone had pictures of people I assumed were close friends and family; the business phone was clearly work related with several trailers for her documentary film and several dozen amateur interviews. The calendar with two-letters in the corner of each day ran for weeks.

The suicide note created a different tone to the case, and discovering the type of people who were her associates would eventually provide good insight. Once we waded through the vast number of men with whom she had been involved over the past two years, we would know more.

Next came the video from the security system from her home.

The good news was the service had been set up to record on a looped basis and stored everything in the cloud. The bad news was her account had lapsed last month after she had failed to renew two months in a row.

We made a call and learned the security company had given her a grace period twice before finally cancelling service. I assumed with the pressure of the approaching Oscars, those details had undoubtedly slid through the cracks.

Bottom line: the last month or so went unrecorded, and the last 48 hours—our most important window of time—were nowhere to be found.

The three of us sat in silence, staring at the screen.

"Well, shit," I finally said.

"No doubt," Stuart added.

"On the bright side?" McCloud chimed in. "You at least have the phones."

"True, and we were super lucky," I said. "One was under the mattress. Why there is anyone's guess. Perhaps she was in the middle of something. Or someone. Before her date arrived."

McCloud was smiling at the photo on the screen. "Cute kitty. And exactly how I broke in so quickly. I mean, who puts a picture of a pet *with* the pet's name on the cover and *not* expect me to crack it?"

Stuart leaned into my face. "Good thing I don't do that."

Taking my phone from my purse, I swiped the screen and turned it toward McCloud. It was my Lab holding an oversized custom rawhide bone in her mouth with *Lucy* printed across it.

"Let me guess," he smirked, taking out a pen and scribbling, "L-u-c-y—"

Stuart added, "1-0-2-6-7-7."

"Nice," I blushed.

McCloud pocketed the pen, checked his watch, and slapped his thighs. "Okay, gang, don't know about you, but I've got other clients to see."

As McCloud packed up, I said, "I owe you."

"Save it," he grinned. "I want a handful of deposits in my favor bank before I make a *big* withdrawal."

12

THE CONUNDRUM

Circuit Court Judge Samuel Norelli paced his office, stopping every few moments to stare out the window at the City of Angels he helped build. He tried to recall how he had gotten into a sticky situation that involved the mob, especially in the closing months of tenure. His spotless reputation of honesty and integrity was legendary. Now in the eleventh hour, he was faced with heavy decisions that, win or lose, good or bad, would decide if someone lived or died.

Rubbing both temples, he shook his head, trying to knock out his headache. Thoughts tormented him as he pictured what he would be remembered for in the end. His biggest fear was that his legacy would be one of corruption.

"I might beat this guy," he mumbled, feeling sweat form beneath his expensive suit. "But will my family be destroyed in the process?" he asked aloud with no one to answer.

Staring at the phone on his desk, he considered whether or not to call his son—the other Detective in the family. He had raised both children to be strict enforcers of the law. Patricia was strong, but Peter was stronger. Patricia had the best instincts he had ever seen but was impatient and often distracted. Peter, on the other hand, was extremely patient and had an uncanny power of focus. Patricia had proven to be a good cop and was on her way to becoming a good detective. Peter had grown into higher ranks quickly, destined to be one of the greats. Patricia could have the same success if she kept her eye on the ball.

His gaze left the phone and settled on a wall of photographs reflecting past decades. He had enjoyed the unique opportunity to meet movie stars, authors and screenwriters, and politicians and world dignitaries while working alongside the best police men and women from across the country.

The judge had arrived especially early that day to get a head start on preparing for a robust roster of cases. It had been a busy month, the week had been busier, and today would prove to be particularly taxing. Yet now, in the quiet confines of the office, with a barely touched chicken salad sandwich, he had neither the appetite nor the drive to face the oncoming storm several floors below. All he could focus on was keeping his family safe.

He reached for the phone, thinking he would check in on his wife of nearly 50 years, but he decided not to spook her.

Daphne was a demure woman, full of grace and stamina. She had to be strong raising two precocious, overachieving cops and being married to a hard-nosed, bulldog of a judge. Nothing much ruffled her feathers, and she faced life with a fearless determination. That is what had kept her going all these years. Smiling, he admired a photograph on the corner of his desk that was taken at their tenth anniversary party.

When the phone intercom buzzed, he jumped.

"Yes?"

"Judge, you've got a call on line two from a man who would only give his first name, but he said you'd want to take it."

"The name?"

"Frankie."

His stomach dropped. He could feel his palms begin to sweat.

"Thanks, Evelyn. I'll take it."

The reason he was twisted up was because of a call he had received several days ago from Frank Simoncini. "Fat Frankie" was the right-hand man to LA's most notorious mobster Nicholas Michelini, aka Nicky the Crusher. Together, both men had made Judge Norelli's life a living hell the past half year. Nicky was set to do a long stretch in California's securest prison. However, an extremely valuable piece of evidence stood between a life in prison or freedom.

Judge Norelli was the only person who could make that decision, and while he was neither weak nor easily intimidated, he knew Nicky could make or break a career—not to mention erase someone from the face of the earth.

Taking a deep breath, he said, "Judge Norelli."

"No, Hello? No, how-rya? Aren't we still pals, Judge?" Frankie snorted.

"Hello. And no. What's up, Frankie?"

The long silence made him more nervous.

"Remember our little chat from last week?"

"Of course."

"Well, you don't think I'da forgotten, do ya?" Frankie breathed heavily.

"No. But as you said, it's only been—"

"Don't be a *mook*. You know what I'm saying. I figured I'd check in to see if you'd made time to, you know, start putting your...plan of action together. The one to help my boss, you know, stay put with the ones he loves."

Judge Norelli paused, knowing matters were in his control and would be put into motion soon; however, he was not sure when those pieces would actually fall into place.

"I've made some calls. I'm working on it," he said.

"Uh huh."

"Do you *think* I'd purposely put my family's life in danger if there were anyway I could keep from doing so?"

A long silence. "Judge, you're a smart man. Way smarter than me. But the biggest difference between you and me? The way we were brought up. You follow?"

"I think so."

"I was never afraid to get my hands dirty. I'm sure *you* never had to concern yourself with it—what with your impeccable reputation and all. But that's about to change real soon 'cause you're about to experience a whole new level of dirty."

Physically distanced from his enemy, Judge Norelli felt more confident.

"Listen, Frankie, I don't need you—"

The line went dead—along with his hopes of buying any extra time.

13

BIG SHIFT

B ack in the office, Stuart shuffled paperwork while I stared into space, pondering how it had become increasingly clear no one was buying suicide. Nursing a coffee, I stared at a map of the neighborhoods where Stuart and I had met characters over the years. There was Hollywood: notorious for being a dark hole that swallowed souls. The volume of talentless people who geared up and failed, then gave in and bailed, far outnumbered those who actually achieved a shot at notoriety.

Next door was Beverly Hills. Their reputation for overpriced plastic surgeons and overhyped tiny restaurants was the stuff of legend. There was more synthetic reality inside a scant six square miles of semi-perfection than most any place on the planet. With its own police and fire stations, its own governing body, and a population of less than 35,000 people, the 90210 was a perfectly polished piece of municipality.

"Hey, partner, what's up," Stuart asked, coming up from behind without a sound.

"Just thinking. You know, about what the Captain said about my getting some help," I said, dropping my head.

"We could all use some," he said, propping his feet up on the corner of a desk. "What's the plan?"

I considered how—as much as I enjoyed living my life large—I didn't like the idea of people talking behind my back or thinking I was a lush who could not control her own life.

"Just considering options."

"Good for you," he smiled. "As for the case, where you wanna go next?"

I knew I could count on Stuart for quiet support. "I say we see about our Hollywood trinket."

WE WERE WELL on our way and knee deep in traffic when Stuart asked, "Where's your head? You've been mighty quiet...for a change."

"Well, Mom and Dad are retiring—which means a move. My only child's disappearing—time for college. And that means I gotta move—which means a change."

"And seismic at that."

"Yeah, right?"

"But you like change."

"I guess," I said without looking up. "Making this big a shift is going to require real estate assistance. I think I have the person—a realtor who sold my parents our current house."

Patting my knee, Stuart whispered, "You'll be fine—you always are. Call and settle your mind."

He was right, so I figured it could be a good time to reconnect with my old friend Angie and googled her number as we drove. Then, I shot Shay a short text: *Hi daughter. Plan on dinner w/ fam. Spago@7. Don't be late.*

"How long before we land at Meredith's place?"

"15, maybe 20 minutes," he said, checking the GPS.

Angie answered, "Your Beverly Hills Realtor Angie Myers! Let me find *your* next home!"

"Now that's a greeting. Hi Angie, this is Detective Patricia Norelli. My father—"

"Pat, are you kidding me? How in the world are you? Oh my God, I haven't seen you in entirely too long. What are you doing calling little old me?"

"I'm good. And it's true. Been too long—since I got married."

"And how is the good doctor?"

"Well, *therapist*. Didn't really have the grades to be a doctor. And I don't know how he is; what with his younger, prettier girlfriend."

I felt my BP climb and opened the window.

"Sorry, and never you mind, we can discuss another time. What can I do to help?"

"Angie, I'm in the middle of a murder case and walking in to talk to the victim's boss, so I'll make it super fast."

"I'm all ears."

"I just learned Dad and Mom are moving. And my daughter will be graduating soon."

"Shay's already graduating? Holy moly."

"Here's the thing. When they move, we'll be moving too. Dad and I turned that three car garage into a two, adding an apartment on top. That's where Shay and I've been living since I got divorced."

Stuart tapped my leg, pointed ahead, and mouthed, *almost there*. Angie and I dialed in a place to meet before my family dinner and rang off just as Stuart and I headed in to play our own episode of Good Cop-Bad Cop to the people of *The Hollywood Mole*.

14

HOLLYWOOD MOLE

T*he Hollywood Mole* was a notoriously mid-to-low-brow tabloid show with more credibility than *TMZ* but less than *Entertainment Tonight*. We had arrived within minutes of our appointment and while waiting in the lobby, we couldn't help but chuckle at the enormous byline on the wall, *Every Minute Counts*.

Personally, I thought they took themselves too seriously because they were more tabloid and less news. Their reporters had model looks and had won awards, but as we quickly learned, many had less than admirable reputations.

Julia King, aka The Gatekeeper, was the second in command and moved about with an air like she owned the place. Greeting us in the enormous glass lobby, we made pleasantries, agreed to a speed tour to get a feeling of the heft of their organization—her words not mine—then settled into her office.

"Meredith was a talented young woman. Perhaps the most talented of our entire staff. Everyone on our team loved her. The community loved her. She was an amazing person."

Julia looked from me to Stuart to her desk then out the window and back to me. Her body language said nervous—which wasn't unusual, just distracting. It took me a moment to understand her expressionless face. It was then I realized she was squeezing in covert peeks at a wall of television screens behind us.

"So, what you're saying is the two of you didn't get along that well?" I asked.

Stuart nodded—knowing where I was going—and her furrowed brow told me we got her attention.

"What? I just said she was admired by everyone here. That includes me," she frowned.

"Sorry. Didn't catch that."

I was counting on her next expression. "Detective Norelli, I don't know what you're inferring, but let me assure you, she was a force to be reckoned with. In fact, I have it on good authority that had she lived, she would've soared to the top—perhaps courted by the Big 3."

"Mrs. King—"

"Ms.," she instantly said. "I'm not married."

Big surprise, I thought. "Right. *Ms.* King, can you think of anyone who may have wanted Meredith dead?"

"Absolutely not. As I said, everyone loved her."

Stuart removed a pad and pen from his breast pocket—a move to either draw out questioning, intimidate interviewees, or scribble a note to me. My money was on all three. Looking across the room at a wall of awards gave me a chance to see his note.

"You have quite a cachet of awards, Julia. Very impressive."

He had written: *Competitive bitch.* I tried not to laugh aloud.

"Thank you," she said, crossing the room to the display wall. "I've been here a long time. Was one of the first reporters and moved my way up the ladder," she said, pointing like a model on *The Price Is Right.* "Soon, I became a first rate producer, then moved up as EP. That's Executive Producer."

Stuart and I nodded like matching bobble-heads.

"And when the chance came along to be VP, well, as you might imagine, I jumped on it."

I'm sure you jumped on a lot of things to get ahead. "That's amazing. And in just a few short years?"

"Yes, actually—"

Staring at me for a long moment, I couldn't tell if she was having a stroke or admiring my wit. "Detective Norelli, I think we're done here. I'm much too busy to entertain your snobbery," she said, walking to the door.

"I'm sorry, Julia. We completely understand. It must be something running a little studio like this," I said with a plastic smile.

"Ms. King, thank you for your time," Stuart intercepted. "We're sorry to have taken so much of it. Before we go, we need to speak with one or two of Meredith's coworkers. It would be a tremendous help. Can you do that for me?"

Looks like my boy's soft approach was exactly what we needed.

"Come this way," she snorted while taking his arm and stepping in front of me.

15

THE PITS

Moving through a large room they called "The Pits," we settled on two of Meredith's closest coworkers, Carrie Montgomery and Jessica Conrad. Between the photos plastered over their cubicles and the red eyelids, it was easy to see they missed their coworker. We sequestered them in Meredith's office that was twice the size of her coworker's offices. And while it wasn't twenty paces from their own cubicles, her retreat had a door, a window overlooking the studio floor below, a couch, make-up room, and a walk-in wardrobe closet.

"I'm just sorry I was never able to catch her show."

They both nodded, smiling politely. Carrie and Jessica were smart, attractive women, both in their mid-to-late twenties and looked perfectly suited to replace Meredith. Judging from the enormous company photographs adorning two of the four walls in her office, I ventured a guess they saw themselves holding court in this very office, giving Ms. King a run for her money. I began seeing an All-Girls Club with several contestants—or, were they competitors?

Carrie spoke first. "She was like an older sister to me. Always there with an answer, no matter how busy she was."

"Yes, and she was always busy. I mean, besides hosting the seven o'clock show, she co-hosted a weekend countdown show and volunteered with several organizations..." Jessica said, stopping to wipe her eyes and blow her nose. "Sorry."

"Take your time," I said. "Tell me, Carrie, were you working with her on the documentary?"

As the girls stared at one another, I bounced a tiny nod to Stuart.

"Detective Norelli, do you mind if I interrupt you for a moment," he asked, taking out his pad and pen. "I have some notes and just want to be sure I'm saying the right things."

"Of course, Detective Brown."

Jessica gathered herself. Carrie stood a little taller.

"Ms. Montgomery, may I call you Carrie?"

"Of course."

"Thank you, Carrie. Let me see," he said, flipping a page. "According to *Ms.* King, Meredith had just won an Oscar for best documentary called, *The Other Hollywood Elite: Women in the Wings But Not In the Spotlight.* Did I get that right?"

"Yes," Carrie said. "Meredith liked long titles."

"Yeah, it was like a trailer in a title," Jessica chuckled.

"Meredith was not a big fan of *The Hollywood Mole.* I mean, she liked it," Carrie said, "But in my opinion, I think she felt better than us, ya know? And then, when word spread that she would likely win an Oscar, well, let's just say, we all doubted she'd stick around for very long."

"Between her human interest pieces and her documentary, I think she felt it was going to be the sort of material that got her into *60 Minutes,*" Jessica said, turning to Carrie. "Right?"

"Pretty much. Oh, and you can bet," Carrie said, "JK was *not* going to have that on her watch."

"Why's that?" Stuart leaned in.

"Besides King being an outright bitch?" Carrie spat.

Jessica laughed.

"There's that. But more because King wanted so desperately to land a job with CBS, but they, well, word is they slammed the door in her face because she spent too much time working at a shit-shack like this."

As Carrie and Jessica fist-bumpedd, Carrie checked her watch and looked at Jessica.

Just then, our attention shifted across the room when a very tall and extremely muscular young man entered through the studio door with an attractive woman in tow.

"That's not what I said if you were listening to me," he shouted.

When the high volume of his voice clashed with the restrained level of our group, the disparity was obvious. He stopped abruptly, sized up Stuart and myself, then quickly diverted our stares, heading in the opposite direction. The buxom blonde scurried behind like a lost puppy.

As our two interviewees looked at one another, Jessica rolled her eyes and Carrie shook her head as they simultaneously said, "Douchebag."

I accidentally snorted before saying, "Not a fan, huh?"

"Ya think?" Carrie chimed.

"What's his deal?"

"His deal?" Carrie echoed, "You mean besides being a DB?" She sneered at Jessica. "Someone you want to talk to."

"Yeah, right?" Jessica said. "He's the Director of the show."

"That Meredith hosted?" I asked.

"Yes," they said in unison.

"His name is Bobby Shapiro. His stepdad is Robert Shapiro."

I look at them expressionless.

"Of the *CBS Evening News*. Robert directed that show for something like 45 years before retiring," Carrie said.

"Since TV was black and white. Not like I was around for it," Jessica giggled.

"So, son is following in Dad's footsteps?" I smiled.

"Kinda. His real Dad was a fuck-off. But he upgraded to a new Dad and landed a better job," Carrie said.

Stuart and I shared a glance before I said, "Ladies, just one more question and we'll be on our way."

"Whatever you need," Carrie said without conviction.

"So, here's what we know. And while I can't be super specific with the details, I can say her murder was not a nice one."

The girls looked at one another, and Carried gasped, "Wait, I thought it was a suicide."

Stuart jumped in, "Let's just say that it's officially *unofficial*."

This got a short nod and two long stares between the girls.

"And it appeared to be violent," I said quietly.

"It would also suggest malicious intent which leads us to believe someone was against her or perhaps didn't want to see her succeed," Stuart paused for reactions.

Eyeballing one another, they remained silent.

"There's also the possibility someone broke into her home, robbed, and killed her," I said matter-of-factly.

"She was damn rich for someone her age and position," Jessica mumbled.

I watched Carrie for reactions.

"Maybe someone didn't like what she was uncovering in her documentary," Carrie said, tossing her chin toward the door.

"You think so?" I asked.

"Could be," Carrie said. "There were people who didn't like that she was shining a spotlight on—" she looked to Jessica for support. "People who didn't get the credit they deserved."

"And some 'me-too' shit," Jessica mumbled. "Working both sides of the fence."

I had a good idea where this was going; however, without anything more substantial, I was looking at two disgruntled girls who had reasons to get Meredith out of the picture, but I doubted either had the balls to do anything about it.

"Speaking of violence," Jessica said, looking at her shadow for approval. "Talk to Bobby. He and Meredith used to be a thing."

"Yeah, who wasn't, with that *thug*?" Carrie said.

"For five minutes, anyway," Jessica smirked.

"Gets around, huh?" I leaned in.

"Yeah, he and Meredith were off and on—"

"And on and off," Jessica said.

"Guy looks like a gym rat," I mumbled.

Stuart went in for the push. "You think he has a violent side? Our only exposure so far makes me think he's a—"

"Bully?" Jessica said, "He is. Ass thinks he's a big shot. Like he owns the place. Partly because of his dad."

"And partly because King wants so desperately to be at *60 Minutes*, she can't stand it," Carrie said.

The room was suddenly and oddly silent as though the cubicles were awaiting the next sentence. Within seconds, a flurry of noise wafted through the area.

"We went out once," Carrie said. "Was all I needed."

"Why's that?"

They looked at one another, then in the direction we saw him last.

"When he drinks? Like he does. A lot. He gets really mad. Like, stupid mad."

I waited. Evidently, Carrie liked being milked for information.

"Did he hit you?" I asked quietly.

Looking around, she gave a barely visible nod.

"Looks like my partner and I may have another person to chat up," I said, "Like you suggested."

Leaning forward, Stuart said, "Ladies, you've been very helpful. Let's do this…" he hands them both a business card. "If you have anything else that comes to mind, run into anyone who may be able to help—besides Mr. Bully—or want to share anything at all, please don't hesitate to call."

They looked from his card to one another, nodded in unison, and put on an overdone smile. "Okay."

Carrie had the first look of fear on her face since we arrived. "Um. So. Can you, maybe not mention what I said just now? You know. When you talk to Bobby?"

"Of course," I said, reaching to shake her hand. "It's all on me. And *our* secret."

"Thanks," she said with a genuine smile.

Stuart buttoned it. "We'll see ourselves out. But if you think of, or need anything, please don't hesitate to call either of us."

* * *

Weaving our way through the serpentine cubicle hell, I looked at the faces of those working in the pit. Their eyes were glued to blue screens, no doubt searching the world for insipid fodder for their mindless show.

"What a waste," I whispered to Stuart.

"No shit."

"As for Bobby? I say we—"

Just then he came barreling through another door—this time, heading toward the front door.

"Speak of the devil," I said, tossing a phony smile at Julia King as we passed through the lobby.

We made it out to the parking lot just as Director Boy backed out of a parking spot and peeled away.

"Dammit."

"No biggie," Stuart said, reaching for his pad and writing down, "R-D-Y-1-T-K-1."

I felt sure my clueless expression said it all.

"Director speak for ready one, take one," he smiled. "Clever."

"*Whatever,*" I responded.

16

SLAMMING PINKS

S tuart and I had little time to get back to the station and look into this director who just skipped us. En route, we did a snatch-and-grab at a greasy LA institution. Pink's was a side-of-the-road hot dog stand that made the best dogs around. Stuart never missed an opportunity to stop no matter when he had eaten last. The last time I recalled supporting the habit was several months back after a late night of shots. It had been the perfect remedy.

"Now *that* hit the spot!" Stuart said, failing to suppress a man-sized belch.

"More like bitch-slapped it," I said, waving away the double-onion cloud of his *Planet Hollywood Dog* belch.

My phone vibrated with a text from Shay, telling me she couldn't make tonight's family dinner. I responded with another text: *Call me. Please.*

Maneuvering traffic while digging through the console for breath mints, he said, "What's up?"

"The daughter. I'm trying to dial in a dinner with my parents. She's not coming."

He shook his head.

"See what you have to look forward to?"

"Not my girl. She'll do exactly as I say."

I cut him a look and snorted, "Good luck with that."

After he stopped shaking his head, he said, "Shit, I can't control my wife—a grown woman— what makes me think I can control a young girl?"

I caught myself smiling at his reality dampened enthusiasm. "Oh, you're in for a good long trip. She'll be your little girl, you'll do every-thing together, then you'll blink one day and she'll hate you and want nothing to do with you. But just be patient; she'll eventually come back around and act nearly human."

We arrived at the Precinct, parked around back, and were crossing the parking lot when my cell rang. It was Shay. I waved Stuart on.

"Hey, baby girl."

"Hi, Mom. Before you start climbing down my throat—"

"Wait a second. I'm *not* going to climb down your throat. You're a big girl and can make your own decisions."

After a long beat, she said, "Thanks."

"If you aren't able to join us, so be it, but it's about the *only* time the four of us will all be together, enjoying a nice meal, *especially* knowing there's a significant change coming our way. And it's important for your grandparents to share it face to face with the both of us."

Sure I was pushing all the guilt buttons, but sometimes it was the only way I got her attention.

"What do you mean significant change? Grandad's heart acting up again?"

Dad suffered an occasional flutter. Doctors said it had to do with too much Scotch and too little relief from the stress of his job.

"I don't know that much, but one thing about your grandad—once he makes up his mind about something, there's no changing it. It's likely retirement which means they'll be moving. And that tells me they'll want to liquidate assets to make the next place exactly what they want."

"What the hell?"

I could hear fear in her voice. I had heard it throughout her childhood, especially after her father and I split. It usually came whenever big changes were in the wind. She had always worked hard to appear indepen-dent and strong, but deep down, she was still my little girl, and I knew this was going to change things a great deal.

"Honey, I have to run but we'll talk more. Just know that you and I can make our own plans."

"Okay."

"And who knows, maybe it's all for the best. It won't be long before you'll be in college full time and—"

"Mom, I want to move out anyway. To live at school. Like everyone else."

Strong emotion suddenly washed over me as her childhood flashed before my eyes.

"Mom?"

"I'm here," I said, trying to remain calm. "Weren't you just asking where *we* were going to live?"

"Yes, but I was more concerned about you. Besides, it was just a matter of time. And time for me to get into the right college. It just makes sense."

"What school are you thinking?"

"UCLA. School of Law. I know it will be expensive, but it's the best. Look, that's why I've been taking all these classes to get ahead. Besides, it will keep me in town close to you."

She was working it, but she was also right. At least I'd stand a better chance of seeing her than if she moved away.

"I like that idea. The cost will be—"

"I'm going to get a job. And maybe Daddy will—"

"NO! That deadbeat hasn't been there for us up until now. I'm not expecting him to surprise us with any grand gestures."

Silence.

"I'll do everything possible to help you."

"I know, Mom, and c'mon, with a 4.1 average? There are plenty of scholarships and grants. I'm sure we'll find something."

"You always were the smartest one in our bunch."

"And just so you know, Dad and I speak from time to time. Between therapy and real estate, he's doing okay."

"If I recall, his front desk girl became his back room girl—"

"I don't know about all that, but I do know you're both better off the way it is."

As much as the reality stung, I knew it to be true. We were a mismatch from the get-go. My mind was trying to drift to better days when two squad cars lit up their sirens and tore out of the parking lot.

"What was that?"

"Standing outside the station. Okay, so you'll come tonight, right? It'll be nice, Shay."

"Yes, Mother. I'll be there. 7 sharp, just like Grandad likes."

"Good. See you then. And kid?"

"Yeah?"

"It's all gonna work out."

17

RAP SHEET

Entering the squad room, I passed Marjorie, the Captain's secretary, and two rookies who had just joined the precinct, along with a man who was either homeless or a new undercover guy. They were all making faces like a dead body was nearby. Inside our office, I would have said they were right because Stuart's stink slapped me in the face. He spun around from his computer and grinned just as Captain Nelson rounded the corner.

"What in the hell died in this office?" Captain barked. With squinted eyes, he got in Stuart's face. "It's gotta be you, Brown."

Swallowing the rest of his breath mints, he said, "Yes, sir. I can't help it. Wife's got me eating so much—"

"I don't give a wheelbarrow full of shit—which, by the way, smells better than your breath about now. Just tell me you have a suspect."

Stuart stood—towering over the Captain by a good six inches—and walked to the whiteboard, waving for the Captain. "Join me over here, sir. I think you'll like what we've accomplished so far."

As the Captain approached the board, Stuart looked at me, then nodded toward a folder on his desk. Looking inside, I found Bobby's rap sheet. Evidently, he had pulled it while I was on the phone. I quickly learned Shapiro had two assault & battery charges, a minor drug possession, and a concealed weapons charge.

"Okay, Captain," Stuart said, looking in my direction. "Norelli was largely responsible for finding this lead. I'll turn it over to her."

I joined them at the board. "Well, I wouldn't say I was *largely* responsible because Stuart has such a keen eye for detail, but here's what we have."

I ran down Shapiro's sheet. While the charges were not earth-shattering, they certainly gave us probable cause. The Captain listened intently, chewing the inside of his mouth, scratching at his chin, and rocking back on his heels.

At the conclusion, he told us to follow up because he didn't feel it was enough and that we needed to spend more time with the coroner. He had a meeting upstairs, so he wrapped by saying we needed to consider scouring the scene multiple times, then disappeared with a wave.

"That went better than expected," I said.

"Couldn't expect much from the drug charge since it was just a few ounces of pot and a first offense. And as much as I had hoped the concealed weapons would do more, he somehow has a license to carry. Just expired is all."

I felt deflated. "Tell me more about the A and B. Bound to offer some probable cause."

"Yeah," he said, taking the file. "Two charges of assault & battery with one happening two years ago—a Lauren Carnegie of Brentwood suffered bruises and a sprained wrist."

"Trying to get away," I mumbled.

"Yeah, my guess too," he said looking up. "Bruises on her arms and neck plus a sprained left wrist. Second one was Rachel Woods. A model living in Santa Monica."

"I'll show him how fast a sprain can become a compound fracture," I said, feeling heat rise in my chest.

"I've seen your handiwork. Best watch himself," he winked.

Looking at the clock across the room, I said, "It's gonna be too late to do that today—with the haul back across town and so close to drive time."

"We'll get to it tomorrow," he said, placing the folder in our TO DO rack, then shoving another handful of Tic Tacs in his mouth. "A few more couldn't hurt."

"Ya think?"

. . .

I WAS in the car and a mile down the road when I remembered telling my father I would swing by before he left for the day. Ringing his office, I told his secretary I would be there in minutes if he could wait for me. Flipping on my concealed lights, I hit the gas and cranked the stereo as Bruce belted out "Born in the USA."

18

TWIRLY BALLS

After attending all the best schools, Judge Samuel Norelli went off to the Army and in short order became known as a man who did not take guff from anyone. His tenacity catapulted him to the highest ranks in record time. He became a decorated soldier and, immediately upon exiting the Army, landed one of the best jobs in law.

The hours were long and thankless, but as a clerk and eventually a District Attorney, his quick mind and dogged determination paid off. Displaying a natural acumen to spot the good guys from the bad proved him a worthy foe, especially in a city as corrupt as Los Angeles. And for forty years, *The Good Judge* held his head high, enjoying a spotless record for honesty and justice. However, that impeccable record was about to be tested.

Staring out the window, he looked over Century City, rubbing his chin with one hand and twirling Japanese baoding balls in the other. The ornate gift from a visiting dignitary helped him relax because the tinkling sound distracted his mind. Fixated upon the ebb and flow of traffic several dozen floors below, he felt a twinge of fear creeping through the center of his belly.

The intercom buzzed. "Judge Norelli, your daughter is here."

"Thank you. Send her in," he said, putting away the baoding balls and approaching a nearby mirror to straighten his tie. "Show time."

Hi, Judge," I smiled, entering my father's office with a hug.

"I'm so happy you're here. Have a seat, sweetheart."

Crossing to the bar, he poured two glasses of thirty-year-old Scotch in lead crystal glasses, adding a splash of water. Over the years, I had watched my father interrogate brutal foes, bending them to the point of breaking. He could crush a man's spirits by the slam of a gavel—an act exercised on hundreds of occasions. And while he could be the kindest and most sympathetic man on the planet, he could likewise annihilate adversaries with equal ease, especially anyone who maneuvered outside the lines of justice.

Suddenly, and for no reason, I felt like one of those saps.

He handed me a drink and I asked, "What's on your mind?"

"Can't I have a drink with my daughter?"

"Sure, but it's kinda funny, don't you think?"

A mischievous grin spread across his face. "What's that?"

"I haven't been in your office in who knows how long, and I don't recall you once offering me a drink. Especially during the work day."

Leaning against his desk, I enjoyed his smile that was as warm as the Scotch sliding down my throat.

"Really? It's quitting time, hon," he said, before his smile dissolved and eyes darkened. "I'll cut to the chase. You're too smart for bullshit." After another sip, he set down the glass.

"A dash of courage before I ask you something."

Now, I set mine down. "What is it, Dad?"

"Darcy, you know how crucial it is to me for you to respect my position."

"Of course. And given you've started this conversation with my first name, well, it makes me a bit nervous."

"Right," he snorted a nervous chuckle. "But you know I wouldn't ask you for a favor unless it was supremely important."

I nodded.

"And you know there's nothing more important to me than my family —to be sure you all are always out of harm's way."

"For the love of Pete, Dad, spit it out."

"Spoken like a Norelli." Pulling a chair next to me, he asked, "Remember last year when Nicholas Michelini was in my courtroom?"

"Nicky the Crusher? Uh, yeah—only one of the biggest cases of your career."

"*The* biggest. As you'll recall, I sent him up to Pelican Bay State Prison on a laundry list of offenses. Racketeering, gambling, prostitution, pornography, drugs—you name it."

"Biggest mob boss in LA."

"In the country, actually. Set to do life. And given the jail is classified *Supermax*, he would never walk."

"Right."

"Except, he must."

The heat began as a bubble in the center of my chest—the kind that appears when I'm about to explode from anger or fear. Or both. "Why? You had all the evidence you needed, right?"

"That's just it. I need that evidence to—*not* be had."

We stared at one another for much too long for comfort.

"Not be had?" I nervously chuckled. "I'm pretty sure that's the worst use of English I've heard you use."

His smile was more nervous than genuine.

"Are you telling me that you need the evidence to—" I leaned forward and raised my eyebrows, leading him to finish the sentence.

"Disappear."

"Disappear," I whispered with a nod. My palms began to sweat, so I stood and began pacing. I suddenly had the feeling that inside the next several moments my father and I might enter territory we had never traversed. "Given I'm in *Homicide* and what you're discussing is in a different division—"

"Except there *were* multiple homicides involved in his case—"

"True, but *I* was not on the case," I said, hesitating just long enough for the quarter to drop.

"Darcy, Michelini's going to have me killed."

That heat bubbling in my chest was working up to a slow boil. My vision narrowed as I blurted, "WHAT?"

"IF...I don't make certain *vital* evidence disappear. For good."

Even with all the blood leaving my head, I managed to say, "But he's already in prison. And, it's public record—"

"Honey, he's only being held *temporarily*. Awaiting his transfer. The case isn't a hundred percent closed yet." He leaned forward to place a hand on my knee. "And his number one guy, Frankie Simoncini?"

"Fat Frankie?"

"Called to tell me he has an order from above that *if* things don't go their way…"

"I can't believe what I'm hearing."

"It gets worse."

"How could it get worse, Dad?"

After a deep breath, "He's not going to kill me *first*. He's going to kill me *last*."

"What?"

He slowly swallowed. I quickly inhaled.

"The hit will be on your mother first."

"My head's about to explode. This can't be happening."

"Then Shay."

"Oh my God, Dad."

"Then your brother, Pete."

"No!" I shook my head, trying to make it all disappear.

"Then you, and finally…me. That is if you and I don't do something."

I sat frozen in silence.

He walked to the bar, poured a glass of water, and handed it to me, "I'm sorry. This isn't supposed to happen to people like us."

"No shit," I said, emptying the glass before rolling my neck from side to side. My father was the best example of all that was right and good in the judicial system. He had always stood for justice and truth. Yet, here he was preparing to throw all of it out the window—potentially tossing my integrity with it.

"Dad, this cannot be happening. It won't happen. We *will* find a way out."

A long silence passed before he said, "Trust me. If there's a way, I know you and I will figure it out. It's just a matter of time."

"Speaking of—how much do we have?"

His next two words crashed in my ears like a cymbal.

"One week."

"Oh, shit."

FOR THE NEXT TWENTY MINUTES, we discussed a variety of plans that included heightened security for the entire family. We role-played different angles, imagining all the best and worst case scenarios, and we contemplated the long term effects of our actions. Therein was the conundrum:

we do the right thing—we die; we do the best thing—we live. One is legal; the other is not.

"Guess we shouldn't have started with the booze. But frankly, I needed it."

I could see the shame on his face and I felt for him. But I also felt for me. This put me in a precarious position. "Dad, I've got to run this past Stuart, he's got a good—"

"NO!" he blurted so loudly I jumped. "Sorry, Darcy. You can't tell *anyone*."

I could feel my world closing in. "Dad, this won't solve itself. I'm going to need my partner."

"Darcy, you understand the ramifications for *both* of us if we tell anyone else?" Then, shaking his head, he began quietly, "I'll never forget what a pal of mine in the Bureau told me a long time ago, 'Sam, if you ever want to get away with something—murder, theft, whatever— there's only one way to do it.' He said that 100% of the time, the secret was to tell *no* one. Not a pal, not your lover, not your spouse—nobody—but I've now told you."

"Got it."

"I'll have to take this to my grave."

"Me, too, Dad."

I'm gonna need a bigger Scotch.

19

DON'T LOOK

After leaving Dad's office in shock, I made tracks to the Coroner's office. It was at the corner of North Mission Road and Marengo Street in the shadow of the LA County and USC Medical Center.

On the drive, I pictured the LAPD Headquarters, a 10-story, half-million square foot epicenter of justice where I imagined my potential clandestine operation would take place. That is *if* I chose to help. Thinking of doing anything illegal made my head pound and my survival instincts shift into overdrive. I would have to come back to that because I had a meeting with a dead body.

As I arrived, Stuart was watching Jackie maneuver the naked and formerly beautiful Meredith Johansen. Seeing her on the stainless steel table with her chest cut open was unnerving. Jackie was cutting through her sternum with a tool that looked like my grandfather's hedge shears. In fact, the sound it created was not much different than his cutting thick branches from my grandmother's heirloom rose bushes.

Watching an autopsy was like watching someone about to be hit by a car: you know you shouldn't look, but you couldn't help it. Once again I found myself in that similar situation as Jackie was sawing open both sides of Meredith's rib cage so that the breastplate that included the sternum and ribs were no longer attached to the rest of the skeleton. In seconds, internal organs were exposed and I was about to lose my lunch.

Stuart, on the other hand, had a steel gut like Jackie. Many summers ago when my brother Pete was working the beat as a detective and I was a boot just out of the academy, I saw my first stiff in the morgue. I arrived with my brother to find Stuart and Jackie standing over an overweight black man shot multiple times. His lower gut had been blown apart, yet they were eating sandwiches and discussing what his life's diet must have been.

I nearly lost it then, and I was *this close* to losing it now.

"Hey, Norelli. C'mon in and let me share some homework with you two."

I found it best to look in short bursts—thinking if I avoided staring, it might keep my last meal from landing on the floor.

Jackie moved from one end of the table to the other, stopping to adjust the overhead microphone and speaking both technically and conversationally—perhaps in order to save time and energy.

"While it's evident her vagina and anus have been penetrated repeatedly, she's devoid of semen. There *could have been* some in her stomach; however, it appears she had a cream-based dish for dinner along with white wine. So, between the sauce and alcohol, it's hard to get info on the cum. The only other specific thing I found was a blood blister inside her bottom lip, suggesting she may have enjoyed being bitten by her sexual partner."

Stuart and I shared a shrug.

"There is bruising around her neck—specifically at the base of her trachea—telling me she may have been into erotic asphyxiation."

"Could it have been from an earlier escapade?" I asked.

"Likely. And according to the bruising that would make sense. By the way, and for what it's worth, we're seeing more and more of this erotic stuff."

"I'm as kinky as the next gal, but the thought of having to do something that extreme just doesn't do it for me."

"To each their own," Jackie said. "I found something else."

"What's that?"

"Two things, actually. First, yellow chips," she said, turning off the recorder and laying down her tool. Picking up a baggie, she motioned me over. " This is dental floss—not a mystery; however, there are several little yellow chips of—not sure at the moment—looks like paint. We're running it through Chem to check the makeup."

I watched Stuart as he got entirely too close to the body.

"Hey partner, whatcha think?"

He reacted like he was getting caught at snooping girlie magazines. "Uh, yeah. Could be. Not corn or squash?"

Jackie shook her head, "No, hard. Like paint or wood."

Snapping his fingers, he said, "Old number 2's. Probably Dixon or Ticonderoga."

"Good call," Jackie said, "And the second were imprints. Whoever the neatnik was he—or she—missed brushing three small indentations in the carpet when he vacuumed. The dents were a few feet from the foot of the bed. Guessing a tripod…which is nowhere to be found."

"The cleaner's a photographer," I mumbled.

"I'm almost done here," Jackie said, taking out a large saw. "You'll probably want to—you know—be somewhere else."

"Right, thanks. I think we've got enough."

"Talk to you later, Jackie," Stuart said as we started for the door.

"Oh, one last thing."

At the door, we turned back to her.

"She was pregnant. 10, maybe 11, weeks."

20

POUND IT

Pulling up to the front entrance of the Montage Beverly Hills, I felt self-conscious—partly because Beverly Hills made me feel that way and partly because I wasn't pulling up in a Bentley or a Rolls. Then again, my new Camaro ZL1 was nothing to sneeze at. With a 650-hp 6.2 liter supercharged Corvette V8 under the hood, the 6-speed convertible was an eye-catcher. After my ex and I split, I cashed in my divorce settlement and bought my dream car as well as set my daughter up for a great education —another topic for tonight's agenda.

Getting out of the car, I flashed a charming smile, working it like an informant. The valet—a kid who looked barely old enough to drive— flashed an equally handsome smile and matching physique. With one hand, he gave me a ticket, and with the other, took my hand to help me from the car like a real gentleman.

The fragrance of expensive perfume and exotic flowers filled the entrance. The enormous containers of cascading flowers and immaculately dressed hosts were impressive. Making my way up the thickly carpeted sweeping staircase to the second floor, I paused a moment at the top for my eyes to adjust to the dim lighting of the paneled bar.

Ten Pound was located on the second level of the hotel in the heart of Beverly Hills. The handsome building had entrances on both Canon and Beverly Drives and took most of the block just north of Wilshire Boulevard. To call the bar elegant would be an understatement. It welcomed true connoisseurs of the world's most precious whiskey, The Macallan Single Malt.

Friends who drank with me knew I enjoyed a good Scotch, bourbon, gin, or tequila. I was also a fan of red wine and felt right at home with a craft beer. All in all, if it wet my whistle, softened the pressure of The Job, or killed the pain of broken relationships, it was my friend.

My drink and date arrived at the same time.

"Darcy Patricia Norelli," Angie began, looking me up and down like she wanted to lick me.

"Angie Myers. You look fantastic!"

"Oh, shut the hell up, girl. You're the one nobody can take their eyes off."

A waiter arrived and flashed a Rembrandt smile.

"Whatever. Sit your sweet ass down and let's get you a drink. I'm having an Old Fashioned. "

Looking up at the waiter, Angie winked. "I'll have a Tequila Sunrise, handsome man."

"Coming right up!"

Angie watched his ass walk away before whispering, "I could hurt that boy."

———

AFTER GETTING CAUGHT up on old times with hearty laughs, we ordered a second cocktail and a small snack, then got down to business. We discussed how business had treated her well over the years. She asked where I would like to live, and we settled on several nice places near the water: Malibu, Santa Monica, and Manhattan Beach. The first would have to be last because of cost; the second would have to be next because of availability; and the last became my first because it was in her wheelhouse.

"I've lived in Manhattan Beach for some time and just love it."

"Who doesn't?" I laughed. "Just doubt I'd ever be able to—"

"Stop it right there. I have just the place. I'm on the *southern* side. Imagine that," she laughed. "Close to Hermosa Beach, which is right next door. The place I'm thinking about is tucked up on a hill with a great view. It's not big, but certainly workable."

In our remaining time, I learned Angie had been married and divorced three times. We recalled how the very first home she sold was to my father —thirty years ago. The last thing on our chat list was the best.

"You can imagine I know all the General Contractors in the South Bay —the guys who get the work done. In fact, one in particular—Steve Owens—is a GC with his own biz. Had a nasty divorce not that long ago —she got the house; he got the boat. And when he grew tired of LA traffic and Hollywood airheads, he told me all he wanted—besides building unique homes—was to spend his time surfing and living on his boat."

"And?"

She stopped sipping. "And what?"

"How is he?"

Winking, she said, "Oh, he's handsome all right. And as much as I'd like for him to toss me around his boat, I'm too old for that man."

We laughed and I waved to the waiter for the check.

"No way in hell, little Missy," Angie said, smacking my hand. "It's my treat, for goodness sake. Old friends who've been out of touch for much too long."

"Hey, I asked you—"

"Please, Darcy. You get our next outing, okay?"

"Ha! The only people who call me Darcy are Mom and Dad."

"Right, Patricia. And here's how I'm going to leave it," she said, whipping out a platinum card. "My opinion about Steve? He's like most men: wants low commitment and high entertainment value."

"Sounds like a dream come true to me," I chuckled.

"That's a conversation for another time."

"Where are you headed now?" I asked, standing to leave.

"Girl, I get my head shrunk every Thursday. Lord knows I've got some issues," she said as we made our way toward the hotel lobby.

"You know, I've been looking for a shrink myself."

"Really? Well, look no further. I'm serious. Call my guy. Name's Dr. Darius Tercel. Has an office not far from here. He's a good listener, has good insight, and bonus—he's easy on the eyes."

As we were making our way down the curved staircase toward the entrance, Angie stopped, smiled at the doorman, then turned to me. "He's a little pricey, but you get what you pay for. Anyway, I'll text you his info. Just book a session. You'll thank me."

As her car arrived, she gave me a big hug. "Last thing? We think the Doctor has a permanent girlfriend. Which is good."

"Why's that?"

Getting into her Benz, she shot me her hundred watt smile and said, "Because it keeps all us *single girls* from climbing aboard his couch!"

21

SPAGO SHOWDOWN

Arriving at Spago, I immediately spotted my parents across the restaurant. He was working the room, shaking hands like a politician. They were one of the original power couples in Los Angeles, thanks to my father's reputation. Governor Jerry Brown had appointed him to the LA Superior Court over 40 years ago, and his profile had remained high ever since.

The anxiety I felt earlier was somewhat diminished, but only because now—watching him schmooze—I realized his days in the spotlight were numbered.

I was gawking at the ostentatious show of wealth by a gaggle of celebrities when an extra thin and ridiculously tall hostess approached. I couldn't help but stare because she had more plastic work than a Lego factory.

"May I help you?"

"Yes," I said, motioning toward my parents. "I'm with them, and…" I hesitated, looking around for Shay.

"Hi, Mom," came a voice from behind.

As I spun around, I got a big hug.

"Hi, love bug," I said, ignoring the hostess over my shoulder who no doubt was awaiting her next exhausting duty.

"I see the grandparents are working it," Shay said.

"As always," I smiled, waving toward Dad who was waving for us to join them. He had reserved a prime location with curtains for privacy, a fireplace for ambiance, and two personal waiters for excessiveness.

Spago is everything one would expect in a fine restaurant: elegant, overpriced, and busy every night of the week. The most impressive element—besides a remarkable art collection—is the 30,000 bottle wine collection running the length of the main dining room: impressive in a "died and gone to heaven" sort of way.

After hugs and kisses, we sat and ordered drinks. And while Dad and I periodically exchanged glances, attempting pleasant smiles, we peppered our conversations with small talk. When the chatter lulled near the end of our first drink, Shay cut to the chase.

"So, Grandad, what's the big news?"

As he looked to my mother, I wasn't sure if he was searching for permission or support.

"Okay, good idea. First of all, thank you for joining us for dinner. I know your lives are demanding, so Shay, thank you for setting aside a school night to be with us. And Darcy, for taking time from your cases."

"Sure, Granddad, but it's not like we don't see you, like from *your* backyard," she chuckled.

"I know, but when's the last time we sat down to eat together?"

We shrugged, knowing he would recall the exact date. "It was three and a half months ago. We all decided on a day-trip to Malibu. I believe it was—"

"Your father and I are moving to Palm Springs," Mom interrupted, clearly excited about the change.

"Actually, Palm *Desert,* southeast of Palm Springs."

"That's cool, Grandad. When are you moving?"

"Maybe a month, or so—to coincide with my retirement."

"Won't you miss LA?"

"We'll miss being closer to you, but we've spent pretty much our entire lives here," he said.

"Do you have a place picked out yet?"

"Shay, it's called Bighorn," Mom said. "It's a nice retirement community in the foothills of the Santa Rosa Mountains."

"Nice, Gramps. Your digs big enough for me and a couple girl-friends?"

He laughed, "Plenty of room for you, Shaylene, anytime you like."

Dad checked on me with a look. I faked a smile.

"What is it, Darcy?" Mom asked.

I could feel heat in my chest and tried to understand why I was getting so rattled.

"I'm happy for you both. I mean, I think it'd be nice if we had more time to figure things out, but it'll work."

My parents looked at one another like most do when trying to tell the kids they are getting a divorce.

Mom said, "Darcy, you know we don't want to disrupt your busy life."

Looking at her, I slowly shut off the sound of her voice.

"It'll all work out," Dad said.

"And you know you're welcome anytime like your father just said to Shaylene."

"It's *not* Shaylene—it's Shay!"

By the stares from nearby tables, I would say my small sentence was big on volume. Shay looked at me like I had flashed the dining room.

"Sorry. I think I've had—"

"Honey,…" Mom began.

I held up a hand to stop her. "Excuse me a minute."

As I left the table, I heard her say, "Enjoy your drink, dear, we'll be back in a moment."

"SHAY, does your mother know yet about your plans to move?" Samuel smiled, patting her hand.

"Not exactly. I was going to tell her. Soon."

"You may want to sit on that a little while."

"Ya think?"

They both sipped their drinks.

Samuel checked his watch. Shay checked her phone.

After a long moment, he said, "And have you told your mother about your…preference?"

Shay nearly spat her tea across the table. "My what?"

"Preference. You know what I'm saying."

Shay could feel herself flush. "When, uh, I mean, how did you—you know—know?"

Smiling, he took her hand. "Shaylene, I may know you better than my own daughter. And while not *obvious*," he winked. "I just know."

They laughed.

"You're funny, Grandad."

"I'm glad you think so," he smiled, patting her hand. "And another thing?"

"Yeah?"

"You'll want to sit on that for—"

"A while. Yeah, I know."

IN THE BATHROOM, I was leaning over splashing water on my face, trying to sober up enough to make it through dinner. "And you think he's been doing what?" I asked my mother, checking to see if anyone else was in the room.

"I don't know. Just the way he's been acting. Something's different. I guess I've started to wonder, you know, if he's been seeing anyone."

"Mom, that's ridiculous. He loves you. Always has. Always will."

"Well, it's just he's been so distant, working later and going in earlier."

"Mom, Dad is NOT having an affair. He's *retiring*."

The look on my mother's face was priceless. That's when I realized she could be feeling as unsettled as I was, so I took her hands and said, "Mom, he's just under a great deal of stress, what with his career winding down, and at the one place he's been for his *entire* professional career."

"You're right," she sighed, hugging me. "I feel silly."

As she let go, I kissed her cheek. "He's saying goodbye and preparing for that place called retirement. Trust your detective daughter. I know."

"I do. You're right, and Darcy?"

"Yes," I said, motioning for us to make our way back to dinner.

"You and Shay will be fine."

We returned to the dining room, complete with fresh lipstick and pleasant smiles. When Dad squinted at me, I took a deep breath and pulled the biggest smile out of my ass.

Mom said, "Us girls got it all worked out."

"I'm sorry, you two," I said. "And I'm happy for both of you. I'm sure your new home, and new life, will be everything you've dreamed of."

Taking Shay's hand, I said, "As for me and my girl, we'll be fine. After all, we're BFF's. Right, kiddo?"

Smiling, she looked to her grandparents, then slowly slid her hand away and took a sip before saying, "Just one thing, Mom."

"Yes?"

"I, uh, really want to go to Stanford."

I wasn't sure if my spinning head was the booze, the news, or both. "What?"

"Yeah, the Law School."

"I thought you wanted to go to UCLA. To save money. And be closer…to me."

"I know, Mom, but Grandpa said Stanford has one of the best law schools in the country."

I looked to find him with a sheepish grin. "I think it's time for your little girl to spread her wings, Darcy. It's a good thing. I went there, your mother went there. Hell, *you* should've gone there."

"Yes, so I've heard," I responded after a deep breath.

"And see where my law degree took me? The same could happen for Shay. I'll help open some doors. And help in her first year. Then—"

"I've always told her I'd cover her first year, no matter where she wanted to go."

"Mom, that was when we were talking UCLA. Stanford's *way* more expensive."

"What say I cover the *second* year," Dad interjected. "I'd love to be a part of her education."

"It'll be the *best* thing for her. You'll see," Mom said.

I caught my breath, trying to keep my face from revealing my pain. "That could work," I said to Dad before turning to Shay. "Maybe he's right, and if that's what you want, it's what I want."

Her frown slowly grew into a smile. "Now, that calls for a celebration."

Perfect. My home's breaking apart, Dad and I are scheming with the mafia, and my boss has me seeing a shrink.

"And the perfect time for some champagne," Dad stood, waving to the staff.

"Yes, it is," Mom chimed in.

He raised his glass. "Here's to my three gals and one perfect night."

Bottoms up.

22

TRIPLE PLAY

O n my way to the office the next morning, I stopped to grab five shots and a splash of foam. I liked to call my post-drink therapy "crack in a cup." Driving down Sunset, I was feeling good about beating Stuart to work. Wind blew my hair, caffeine coursed my veins, and my mind raced back to last night.

In the light of day, watching Dad share his news was laughable. And while I was probably too hard on him, it was only because I was going to miss living in the house where I had spent a big part of my life. On top of that, learning Shay was going to leave me for the Bay area nearly broke my heart.

I hung a quick right on La Cienega and scooted down to Santa Monica Boulevard, hoping to miss the construction of a new mega-structure. Sitting at the Cahuenga light, I had an idea hit me like a starburst—*Why the Oscar statue? Because she was killed on Oscar night?*

The light cycled back to red. I exhaled deeply as another idea struck— *A disgruntled actor who got shunned by the Academy?*

The light turned green and I was off. I was still lost in thought when my familiar inner voice whispered, *Think outside the box.*

Within minutes, I snagged a parking spot up front and was walking down the hall and into our office, glancing at the clock above our desks. It was 7:20—*Sweet Jesus, I'm more than an hour early.*

Dropping my things, I grabbed my favorite mug and headed to the break room. Just as I rounded the corner, there he was, sitting at a table, stuffing a fast food biscuit into his mouth.

"Are you kidding me?" I shouted, ready to throw my coffee.

Grinning from ear to ear and wiping greasy crumbs from his chin, Stuart said, "Ya gotta get up pretty early in the morning to beat your partner, Detective."

"I was so sure I was gonna beat you."

He laughed as I shook my head and heated my coffee in the microwave. Opening the fridge, I looked for fruit, settled on a too-ripe banana, and at the ding, grabbed the cup—now hot enough to melt my gun —and returned to the office.

Stuart followed behind. "Sorry, DP. If I'd known it was going to piss you off, I'd have drug my feet. The wife certainly wouldn't have cared."

"Whatever," I mumbled, peeling the banana with my teeth.

"Such dexterity. Use it often?"

"You know it."

"C'mon, I wanna show you something that'll cheer you up."

At his desk, I hung over Stuart's shoulder, staring at the screen as he cued up a video on his computer. Considering the source, I was surprised at the graininess of the image.

"You'd think—" I began.

"Yeah, for a broadcast company, right?" he finished. "So, watch these two coming out of the building. That's Bobby," Stuart explained, tapping a greasy finger on the screen.

I handed him a napkin.

"Now, watch that person next to him."

"Copy."

SMACK!

"Whoa!" I shouted, "What the—?"

"Right?" Stuart said, stopping the video right after Bobby smacked one of the women to the ground. The image was frozen—showing him in mid-swing—as the woman was trying to get back up.

Staring at one another, I growled, "That really pisses me off."

"Me, too, partner."

"Whether or not he's our guy, we could use this video to—"

"Accomplish other deeds."

Nodding, I said, "Any way to enhance that image?"

"Not really, but look…" he said, making the image progress frames at a time. "There's just enough light coming from the streetlamp that the shadows are washed out."

"Hmm."

"You remember the girls we met at the station? Either one make you think of—" he nodded to the screen.

"You mean Carrie and Jessica?"

"Right. Now, think," he said, rewinding it a third time.

"Could be either one. Both about 5'5", both some version of bottled blonde."

He stopped the video just after the knock to the ground and before the arm swung for a second hit. Seeing it again made me just as mad as the first time. "If I get my hands on that fuckwad, he'll wish he never hit a girl."

"You tell 'em, *Dirty Patty*."

I stood up straight, stretching. "But you know who else it could just as easily be?"

"Meredith," we said in unison.

"Here's something else I found," he said, reaching for a folder. "He's been written up, not once or twice, but *five* times for sexual harassment."

"What? How can that douche get away with it? Isn't there a limit to—"

"It's part the system and part his position, or more accurately, his step-father's prestige that got and *keeps* him in the Director seat."

"Pompous, entitled nut-sack."

"Get this. He's dated nearly a *third* of the women in that network."

"You're joking."

"Yet they all still rat him out."

"You'd think if someone knew what an ass he was she'd share it with their coworkers."

"It's Hollyweird, man."

"So many suck-up wanna-be's trying to get ahead."

"In more ways than one."

"Right. Anything else?"

"Funny you ask. Wanna guess why he got fired from his last job?" Stuart asked, stopping to check his notes. "A low-rate show called *Hot Gossip Tonight*."

"Sexual harassment."

"And drinking on the job."

"What a screw up," I snorted, then drained my coffee.

"They managed to keep his drinking problem on the DL if he agreed to community service and got into a program. According to this, he's been clean and sober ever since."

I made a mental note because I was pretty sure there was more muck stuck to this idiot's shoe. "Can I see that? I wanna do something before we head back to see Mr. Personality."

"Sure," he said, tossing the file on my desk, then returning to the video.

"By the way, where'd you get the video?"

"I don't actually have it. As much as I have *access* to it."

"What?"

"A pal—somebody I play ball with on the weekend—needed a favor. Parking ticket. I took care of it and he said if I ever needed the return, just ask. And I remembered that conversation watching a game last night."

"Yeah?"

"So, he works in the IT department at none other than—"

"Nice luck, Stuart."

"So, I called to see if I could check any security footage from the weekend. He got all squirrelly before saying he could give me a private login, but he couldn't officially let me see it—you know, without a court order—blah, blah, blah."

"And so you—"

"Exactly. The game was over, my girl was down for the count, so I logged in to the cloud and started scouring footage from this past weekend. I started with Sunday. Nothing. Watched Saturday. Nothing. And keep in mind, it wasn't like you could shuttle at high speed. So, by the time I hit Friday, I told myself just one more. Then, about the time I was gonna call it—boom."

"That's gold."

"Copy that."

Tapping my fingers on the top of Shapiro's file, I grew a grin.

"What's that look mean?"

"Just an idea about finding this clown's Achilles heel."

His eyebrows raised.

"Then stomping on it."

He grinned and I plopped into my chair, checking the clock. It was just after 8, and coworkers would be arriving soon.

"What?" Stuart asked.

"What, what?"

"Watching your mental gymnastics. Where's your head?"

"You mean besides my being here an hour already—which is about the time I usually drag in?"

"Yeah, try *another* hour."

"Whatever. Three things have got me chapped."

"Here we go," he mumbled.

"First, that pisses me off." I pointed to the computer. "I wanna jam my .45 up his ass and—"

"Got it. Two?"

"I've got my first date today with—" I looked around and lowered my voice, "The shrink. Remember?"

"Good idea," he nods. "And three?"

"I've got to find a place to live. Alone, I might add."

Stuart frowned. "What? I thought—"

"More later, but I've got 30 days to make something happen. Starting now."

"Sounds like a full day."

"And that doesn't even include the last two things," I said, pulling my things together.

"What? You said three."

"That's personal shit. The last two are all business."

He rolled his eyes.

"Track down the manufacturer of that Oscar statue. And pay a visit to Bobby Doucheroo."

"I'll meet you back here after your appointment," he replied with a wink.

23

DEEP DIVE

D r. Darius Tercel sat at his desk—almost in a meditative state—contemplating his accomplishments. After spending his college years studying psychology, then doctoral work focused on behavioral modification, his passions grew to include dissociative identity disorder, previously known as multiple personality disorder. He had spent enough time in school to know several things with certainty. He was smarter than most of his colleagues, was obsessed with learning everything he could about the human mind, and possessed an extraordinary photographic memory and encyclopedic knowledge base.

A car horn honked outside, snapping him back to current time. He checked his watch.

Two manilla folders were on his desk: Angie Myers and Patricia Norelli.

Angie had been Tercel's patient for nearly a decade—long enough to get to know her, long enough for her to trust him, and long enough for both to learn from one another.

Since Detective Norelli was referred by Angie, he would send Angie a handwritten *Thank You* note—a personal touch he knew meant a great deal in a town like Beverly Hills.

He scanned Angie's file: thrice divorced and twice admitted to a center for substance abuse. She bounced back from the failed marriages—gaining handsome settlements two of the three times. She returned to drinking, but left the depression meds behind.

Scanning his vast bookcase, he calculated in which category he might place his new client. He had spent countless hours researching important topics over the years and had carefully selected his favorite categorized books: *Deciphering Archetypal Father Figures, Overcompensating Obstacles, Hypnoanalysis, Games People Play,* and *Men Are From Mars, Women Are From Venus.* He felt confident he would find just the right approach for Patricia Norelli.

He glanced at the mirror to his right, seeing the clock on the opposite wall so that he could see what time it was without distracting his patients —a trick he learned from a former instructor.

24

SHRINK RAP

Arriving at Dr. Tercel's office early gave me a few moments to center myself. I think that's what my old yoga instructor used to call it. I called it "clearing my head." After making nice with the receptionist and signing paperwork, I took a seat in the far corner of the elegantly appointed waiting room and sipped on a bottle of designer water. Smooth Jazz played overhead. After a few moments, I closed my eyes and actually relaxed.

Within minutes, a calm voice snapped me back. "Detective Norelli?"

Startled, I looked up and asked, "Dr. Tercel?"

He extended a hand and waved me toward his office like a game-show model. It played more charming than phony.

OVER THE NEXT SEVERAL MINUTES, we exchanged generic pleasantries—all orchestrated to break the ice and ease tensions. It comfortably paved the way for what would become either a tortuous 50-minute session of introspection or a near-hour of self-enlightenment. Having been in therapy before, I was painfully aware the first several minutes were less than comfortable and more than awkward. After all, just moments earlier we were complete strangers, and now I was supposed to trust a stranger with my innermost thoughts.

"By the way, I do have one question before we begin."

He lifted an eyebrow.

"I heard you're always booked—as one of the heavy-hitters in town—so how did I get in here so quickly?"

He smiled. "Angie gave me your name. Said you were good people and how she had been a friend of your family for years. I suppose it just felt right. And as I mentioned at the start, while I can't ordinarily take on new clients, I've recently lost two to personal conflicts."

Shifting in my seat, I said, "So, ya' wanna jump right in?"

"Is that what you want to do?"

I stared out the window before saying, "That's exactly what my ex used to say every time we'd get into an argument, I mean, *conflict*. They were never *arguments*. Just conflicts. What bullshit."

He followed my gaze out the window. "Is that how you feel about this? Bullshit?"

I shifted my attention back to him and smiled. "Not really. Nervous tension, I guess."

His shirt was crisp—his sport coat, tailored. *Bet it cost what I made last month.*

Glancing at his hands, his nails were perfectly trimmed.

"You're persnickety, aren't you?" I asked.

He burped a chuckle. "That word has always made me laugh," he said. "It's so old school."

"You'd prefer *fastidious*?"

His tanned face spread a perfect smile.

Parents must've paid a fortune on him as a kid.

"I think the cut of a person's attire and how they groom tells a lot about what they think of themselves."

"True," I said, looking at my outfit. "Not terribly fetching, is it?"

"But functional, correct?"

Nodding, I checked my watch. *Twelve down, thirty-eight to go.*

Uncrossing one leg, he crossed the other, shifting his weight.

A passing siren shifted my attention. "Let's start with the basics and go from there."

He nodded.

"In case you hadn't summed it up yet, he was a therapist."

"You're referring to your ex?"

"Oh, right. Yes."

"And you didn't like that?"

"Is that a question or a statement?"

"Right."

"Good one," I smiled. "And a statement. I was putting him through school, working a full time job, *and* taking care of a kid. He wanted to be a doctor but didn't have the grades. Or the stamina, I suppose."

"Understood."

Staring at the weave of the expensive tapestry on the floor, I said, "I always called him a *soft doctor*."

"Soft?"

"Meaning he didn't have what it took to be a *full* doctor."

He kept a tiny smile at bay.

"No offense."

"None taken."

"Fortunately for me, I never sat on his couch. Unfortunately for others, they did."

Exercising a pair of dimples, he said, "Nicely played."

"And to anticipate your next question, it made me feel—disappointed."

"Why?"

"Because I hated *funding* his education—only never to benefit—but hey, at least I was able to rid myself of a psychopath."

As I glanced up from my lap, I caught his raised eyebrow. "Really?"

"Okay, maybe not as much a psychopath as he traveled a path of psychosis."

"Care to explain?"

"Let's just say he put in enough hours to obtain the power to *self-prescribe.*"

"Ah, yes. That can be dangerous."

I brushed invisible lint from my slacks. "You bet. Especially with an addictive personality."

"Yours or his?"

That caught me off guard. "Ouch."

"I apologize. What I meant was did his *self-medication* prove to dull his anxiety or feed the anxiety *you* were feeling."

After pondering that a moment, I said, "Maybe both, actually. He was a narcissist. Which took me a long time to learn. Even as long as we were married. When I finally figured it out, it helped me understand things better. My biggest lesson was—" I hesitated, "That it wasn't my fault."

His confirming smile added to my comfort.

"I just said that aloud, didn't I?"

"You did, indeed."

"That's something I've not admitted. To anyone. Maybe ever."

"Good," he smiled. "That's a *big* step."

"Yeah, that's pretty much it. And it felt good to say that."

"That's a very good observation," he said quietly.

"Truth is, Dr. Tercel, I couldn't decide if I respected him because of his honesty or hated him because he was cruel. So, I left him because of his honest cruelty."

25

SHARING GLADLY

I wrapped with Tercel and met up with my partner. On the way to our next appointment, I shared with Stuart how my appointment went better than anticipated. In true form, he encouraged me with quiet support. We also discussed Meredith's ex-husband as a possible suspect, wondering if he was likely to have had a motive.

Thanks to some scoop from one of Meredith's co-workers, their marriage and divorce lasted no longer than a magazine subscription. Evidently, his attention span was shorter than a seven-year-old and was not aimed at other women.

Given this discovery, she filed and he fled.

Further confirmation came when I learned he couldn't have killed her because he was getting married in San Francisco to his longtime boyfriend on Saturday night, and the two of them were on a honeymoon flight to Paris the next morning.

With me driving, we were across town, up and over the 405, and pulling into the Getty Center parking lot in record time. I found a spot in front, placed my placard in the dash, and headed for the door.

I was pleased because I didn't often impress Stuart.

"Okay, so you got us here faster. However, I feel it's safe to say I lost a month of my life in the process," he grinned, polishing his sunglasses before returning them to his breast pocket.

The Getty Museum—built of stone and glass—was complemented with fountains and parks, creating an impressive architectural marvel. The world-renowned art on display was equally remarkable. Passing through the doors, visitors knew they were in for a treat. We approached the front desk, showed our badges, and shared with the attendant our purpose for the visit.

"I could spend days here," Stuart said. "Reminds me of the Louvre. But less French."

"There you are," a voice came from behind.

Turning, we faced a very attractive woman. In fact, she bore a striking resemblance to Meredith Johansen.

"I'm Sharon Gladstone, and you must be Detectives Norelli and Brown."

We shared pleasantries, then followed her through an elaborate lobby, ascending a dramatic staircase, before arriving at an office the size of my entire apartment. It was adorned with handsome furniture covered in lavish fabrics.

Although I didn't know the first thing about what made some art fine, the art on her walls was notable. I estimated all the furniture in my home cost less than her office desk. The added bonus was the view. In the distance, we could see several skylines of the LA basin—Westwood and UCLA, Century City, and further south, Culver City. Off to the west were the seaside towns of Malibu, Pacific Palisades, and Santa Monica, not to mention the vast blue Pacific.

Stuart and I were actually gawking.

"Breathtaking, huh?" Sharon said, giving us ample time to admire it all.

"Not too shabby," I said, trying not to appear like a hillbilly.

"Quite nice," Stuart echoed, taking out his pad and pen.

Prior to arriving, we had decided to go with our usual routine. Only this time, I would be the nice one and Stuart the A-hole. We thought it may be a nice change from our performance at *The Hollywood Mole*. Besides, my gut about Sharon was every man likely drooled over her, so this would make for an interesting departure.

"Ms. Gladstone, we won't take much of your time," Stuart began, pointing to chairs in front of her desk. "May we?"

"Certainly," she replied, waving to the chairs like a hand model. "Can I offer you coffee, espresso, wine, water?"

"Nothing for me," Stuart said.

"Maybe a double espresso?" I smiled.

She pushed a button on her desk before circling her desk to join us.

"More comfortable this way," she said with a sincere smile. "Now, how may I help you, Detectives."

"Ms. Gladstone, could you please—"

"Sorry to interrupt, but please call me Sharon."

Nodding, he said, "Sharon. Could you please tell Detective Norelli and myself if you killed Meredith Johansen."

"What?"

The look on her face was priceless. Either she was as good of an actress as she was a fundraiser, or she didn't kill Meredith.

"Heavens, No," she said, taking several moments to dissolve the frozen look of surprise from her face.

I caught myself feeling blindsided by her authenticity.

"Meredith and I were close friends. Very close. We were roomies at one time for goodness sake. I mean, I loved her. Like a sister."

Sharon's assistant quietly entered the office, placed a silver tray on the glass table next to me, and then with a quick smile, disappeared.

"Sharon, I think what Detective Brown is trying to do…" I began, giving him a disappointed look, "Is to get the *obvious* question out of the way. Not to be rude."

"I understand," she said, taking a tissue from a silver box that resembled a cigarette case. Dabbing her perfect nose, she added, "You're just doing your job."

Stuart moved in. "Actually, it's a perfectly good—albeit frank—question which needs to be addressed. Which we've done. Now, moving on," he said, scribbling something before flipping a page. "How long were you two involved?" he asked.

"What?"

"As roommates. *If* that's all it was."

"I'm not particularly comfortable with your insinuations, Detective Brown. But to answer your question, we shared a house."

"And boyfriends?"

I was half expecting her to slap him, but instead, she blushed. Then, after a long, dramatic sigh, said, "Only on *rare* occasions. It *is* Hollywood, after all. And we have *quite* the life to live. Even if that means sharing more than purses and a pool."

Her attitude reversal gave me whiplash.

"Sharon, did you know, or do you know Bobby Shapiro?"

Licking her lips, her eyes shifted back and forth. "Yes. And no."

"Excuse me?" I said, looking at Stuart. "I'm confused."

He added, "How's that?"

"Yes, but does anyone *really* know Bobby?"

"Can you elaborate?"

"Bobby and Meredith were the 'it' couple and everyone knew it. And to your earlier inference, yes, Bobby and Meredith and I were very close. Frankly, Bobby and I had a better relationship and understanding."

"Can you explain further?" Stuart asked.

"We shared each other in a three-way relationship. I'm bisexual, she was bi-curious, and Bobby—well—he's just bipolar."

"Is that true?"

"Yes, to all the above. Meredith was being treated for depression—ask her doctor. Bobby should have been treated for his condition—ask anyone at his work. And I don't need treatment."

Stuart and I looked at one another without expression.

"Personally, I think their neuroses are what brought them together."

Stuart hesitated for a moment. "Sharon, where were you on Sunday night?"

Her eyes shot up and to the left. "Where everyone was on Sunday night. At the Oscars," she smiled.

"And your date?"

"Judd Lowenthal. The actor."

Judd Lowenthal was the latest 'it' guy in Hollywood. Drop-dead gorgeous, ripped body, killer smile, and seemed to be in nearly every other film of late.

"Good-looking guy," I interjected with a coy smile.

"Right? And ridiculously talented. As an *actor*, of course," she winked.

"I'm sure, Ms. Gladstone," Stuart said, returning to her title on purpose. "And needless to say, if we were to ask him the same, he could confirm this?"

"Absolutely. In fact, let me get you his number."

She popped up and circled her desk. "I would ordinarily send you to his manager or agent, but since this is a police matter—I'm sure he'll be happy to cooperate."

After several scrolls through her phone, she scribbled on a notepad and handed it to me. An interesting move, given it was Stuart who asked. She winked at me again.

"Just another question or two, and we'll be on our way," Stuart said, flipping a page in his pad. "Were you aware of—"

"Sorry for interrupting, Detective Brown, but wasn't her death ruled a suicide? That's what I heard on the news, anyway."

"That's the preliminary assumption. But as you can imagine, we have to examine her case from every angle." Smiling for the first time, he said, "Things are often not what they seem."

"Indeed," she practically sneered. "Proceed."

"Were you aware she had been depressed lately? Anything about her behavior that confirms that suspicion?"

Smoothing her skirt, she didn't answer right away and let out a long sigh before continuing.

"While she did have a stressful job—one she loved more than anything else—I don't know I would say she was suicidal. I mean, we had talked, you know—girl talk—about how this business and this town can get to you. It has its own way of wearing one down. She also shared with me how her father's recent passing had a significant impact on her. Frankly, it may be a better question for her therapist."

Stuart stopped scribbling and looked up. "And who might that be?"

"Same one we all use. Therapist to the stars. Dr. Darius Tercel."

26

PINK TACO

We approached Beverly Hills in short order and pulled into *The Hollywood Mole* studio lot. Stuart ran in for a snack and a soda at the 7-11 next door while I stayed put chomping on a Bonk Breaker Bar and sipping Fiji water. I turned on the radio just in time to catch the Eagles singing "Hotel California." I found it interesting how we were parked on Sunset Boulevard facing Chateau Marmont, a hotel that had always made me think of that classic song.

Watching construction trucks enter and exit the lot, I tapped the steering wheel to the beat of the song. According to a small billboard at the entrance, the studios were in the middle of a major renovation, transforming the recent Pink Taco restaurant into a state-of-the-art broadcast facility. The building's prior life was Wolfgang Puck's original Spago, better known as the place Swifty Lazar held his world-renowned post-Oscar party.

Scanning the action, I wondered where Bobby's car was parked. From my vantage point, I could see the main entrance where we saw Bobby hit who we assume was a coworker. I spotted cameras in the upper corners of the building entrance and thought of Carrie and Jessica—wondering if either of them were in that video. Observing people enter and exit the building, I was surprised at how many fit the description of the woman in the video.

Not able to suppress my need to snoop, I backed out of the designated visitor section and pulled around to the employee lot. Since the back half of the building was still experiencing renovations, I counted on traffic being increased—not to mention the gate was locked in the up position and the guard looked well over 60 and appeared distracted by a TV screen.

While I was sure I had a good chance of getting in without hassle, I undid my top button for backup.

"Hi, I'm Detective Norelli. Julia King asked me to circle the driveway. Something about a car break-in a couple nights ago. I'll be in and out in a jiff."

As expected, he spent the first ten seconds looking from my eyes to my blouse and the next ten eyeballing my badge. I started a slow roll to show I was not planning on hanging around for long. His lackluster attire and negligent nod told me he didn't give a shit.

Passing several construction vehicles, I circled the lot until I saw our boy's car. A school-bus yellow Porsche Cabriolet 911 was not hard to spot. Being a gear-head, I knew the flat-six twin-turbo 580-horsepower beast redlined around 7200 and cost more than I made in the last two years—or more.

Slowing to a crawl, I checked over my shoulder to see if the guard could see me. A concrete mixer blocked his view, so I parked, got out, and quickly circled Bobby's car. On the front floorboard was a gym bag, empty water bottles, and an enormous tub of protein powder. Checking the side door pockets, I didn't see much and had an idea.

Having previously scanned the lot, I knew there were no cameras covering this area and given the quality of the cameras covering their front doors—the most important part of their security—I had little fear I would be seen. Returning to my car, I retrieved a notepad and small baggie. In order to avoid any attention, I walked around several cars, pretending to take notes, before circling back to Bobby's car. Taking a small knife from my belt, I made an insignificant slice in the edge of the roof on the passenger side. Looking at my cell phone with my left hand, I inserted a bag of evidence into the slit with my right hand and pushed it toward what would be the backseat—if there were one.

In the next second, my phone pinged with a text from Stuart wondering where I was, so I parked and went in—feeling more happy than guilty.

27

MOUNT EVEREST

E ntering the studio lobby, I found Stuart sitting on a skinny, modern couch, flipping through a *People* magazine. He was much too large for such a small couch. The look on his face said pain. As I approached, he tossed the rag on the oversized glass coffee table.

"How's your tummy, pal?"

"It's further south, if you must know. What are you up to?"

"What? Nothing. Waiting on you."

He cocked his head to the side, eyeballing me funny. "You look like the cat who ate the canary."

"That's me. Munching canaries and protein bars."

Making our way to the reception desk, I whispered, "If you must know, I scoped out Bobby's car and made a little insurance plan."

"What?"

"Never you mind. And it's only backup. Anyway, let's get in and work him over. According to our friend, *Ms*. King, HR must be present if we need to speak with him."

"That's gonna complicate matters."

"We'll work around it. Which one you wanna play?"

While he pondered, I planted a sincerely fake smile so the receptionist would know we were ready. She acknowledged and dialed her phone.

"Why don't we mix it up and *you* be the asshole," he winked.

"Perfect," I said, getting a nod from the receptionist.

Within seconds, a buttoned-up and overweight middle-aged school teacher of a woman joined us in the lobby. "Hi, I'm Janelle Everest. Bobby's been informed you're here, and we're meeting in the conference room, if you'll follow me," she said, walking away without awaiting a response.

"Warm bunch, huh?" Stuart said quietly.

I couldn't help but notice how everyone was eyeballing us like we weren't wearing pants. "What's that about?" I mumbled.

"They know you're cops," Ms. Everest said, without missing a beat. We shrugged, following our tour guide into a brightly lit conference room. "Please wait here. I'll be right back. And can I assume this won't take long? We have a show to do."

I bit my tongue as Stuart pleasantly said, "Yes, Ma'am. We don't expect to be longer than 10 or 15 minutes. Thank you."

She grew an instant fake smile and left.

"Can I assume this won't take long?" I mockingly whined, "I have a buffet to devour."

Stuart snorted, shaking his head.

"I know. I'm a bitch."

TEN MINUTES PASSED with no sign of Bobby. I shifted my focus from a large monitor to Stuart who was checking email on his phone. I read every award on their glory wall and was *this close* to counting ceiling tiles when Ms. Everest entered the room—without Bobby.

"I'm so sorry, Bobby's kinda the star around here—being the main director and all, so he asked if you wouldn't mind waiting just a few more minutes," she said, expressionless.

As much as I wanted to be nice, it was not going to be possible. Stepping forward, Stuart instantly anticipated where I was going and took my arm while smiling big for our friend. "Ms. Everette, I think—"

"Everest. Like the mountain? Not Everette."

"Ms. *Everest.* I'm not sure if you understand—or rather, if Mr. Shapiro understands—but we are police officers—Detectives, actually, from the Los Angeles Police Department. He doesn't really get a choice in the matter. He needs to come and speak with us, not in a few more minutes, but now. As in immediately."

I could not take her smug expression any longer.

"Or..." I began, allowing the change in authority and volume to get her attention. "IF Mr. *Shitbag* doesn't get his Neanderthal ass here inside the next five minutes, I will personally see that he's arrested for..." I advance two steps closer, holding up fingers to count off, "One, for obstructing justice. Two, for failure to comply with a *murder* investigation. And three, for possession of illegal narcotics. Am I making sense? Are we crystal clear? Do you understand what I'm saying, Ms. *Ever-Rest*?"

She swallowed hard. "Yes, Officer—"

"No, *Detective*. Patricia Norelli."

"Yes, Detective Norelli. Right away." Another hard swallow and she was down the hall like her shoes were on fire.

Watching her scurry, Stuart said from the side of his mouth, "When's the last time you referred to yourself with your proper first name?"

"Never."

"And illegal narcotics? Is that what you meant by—"

"Yes, and shut it." I nodded to the ceiling. "These rooms aren't private."

"I enjoyed that. Much longer and I'm sure it would have turned into a smack down."

"Oh, boyfriend, she does NOT want to tangle with me. It's been a week of reality bitchslapping me in the face, and—at least for now—we have the only murder suspect in a case we've got to solve sooner than later."

He put up both hands. "Oh, I feel you."

28

BADASS & MOFO

Another ten minutes passed when I saw Ms. Everest coming down the hall—again *without* our suspect. She had a terrified look on her face, and I felt heat simmer in my chest.

"Officer, I mean, *Detective* Norelli, uh, Mr. Shapiro said that he was, uh, busy and couldn't be disturbed right now, but that he could schedule—"

I didn't let her finish. Instead, I motioned for Stuart to follow my lead. Brushing past her, heading down the same hall she had come from, I pushed through a set of double doors with flashing red lights overhead. Seconds later, we were standing in front of an enormous glass enclosed room full of people. Dozens of television monitors covered an entire wall. I spotted Bobby down front in between two guys pushing colored buttons on huge boards. I checked over my shoulder for my backup and kept moving.

Bobby was wearing a headset, waving his arms and calling shots: "Wrap the B-roll. Okay, ready one? Take one. Ready two? Hold it…"

An apparent assistant frowned at me and stood to stop me.

I gave her a look and proceeded with my approach. "Bobby Shapiro? Detectives Norelli and Brown. Can we have a word with you?"

He looked at me, frowned, shook his head, then returned to the screen. "Ready two? Take two. Okay, ready to wipe in lower third."

I stepped closer, putting my hand on his shoulder.

"Wipe. Now, gimme—" he stopped, looked at my hand and yelled, "Cut," without taking his eyes off my hand.

The room stopped. He looked up at me and growled, "What the fuck are you doing?"

"I'm conducting an investigation," I said, turning to Stuart, "And *we* want to speak with you. Now!"

I was not prepared for Bobby's size. As he stood, I estimated him at about 6'6" and about 285. He reminded me of The Rock with hair.

"Can't you see I'm in the middle of a show? I told Ms. Everette I couldn't be disturbed." As he looked in her direction, all heads followed to find her cowering behind the glass door we just entered.

"It's *Everest*—like the mountain—dumbass. And I don't give a shit what you told her. Step outside with us, right *now*, or face a world of pain."

Staring me down, he said nothing.

"Are you catching my drift, asshole?"

Without turning his head, he let out a long breath and said to an assistant, "Take over. I'm back in five."

"Maybe," I said, heading to the door.

Stuart hadn't said a word and, without any expression, motioned for Bobby to follow me.

BACK IN THE CONFERENCE ROOM, Bobby sat at the head of the table, posing like he owned the place. He may have for all I knew, but I didn't care. Stuart was on one side of the table—I, on the other.

"Doesn't even make sense why you're here wasting my time, interrupting my show. We're number one in the market for entertainment, you know."

"Entertainment gossip *bullshit*," I snorted with enjoyment.

Staring ahead, he didn't move a muscle of his hulking mass.

"What we're doing, Mr. Shapiro, is looking at all possible leads into the murder of Ms. Meredith Johansen. And given she's the former star of this two-bit slop shop—and perhaps more importantly for this discussion, your *ex*-girlfriend—we thought we'd start with you."

"I don't know shit."

"That's possible. And evident," I smirked.

"What Detective Norelli means is it's possible you didn't kill Ms. Johansen, but perhaps you know someone who did."

Not a blink.

"Or know someone who could have a motive," Stuart said calmly.

"No fucking clue," he whispered.

"Mr. Shapiro, in our line of work we're constantly looking for two things. You know what they are?" I asked.

Silence.

"Clues and motive. That's pretty much it. And while we may have no clues on you...yet, we certainly have motive."

He slowly turned his head to me, saying nothing. I waited until enough uncomfortable silence had passed before continuing.

"Let's start with the fact you and the victim were an item, on and off for nearly two years. That would be these past two years," I said, checking my notes. "Thanks to Carrie and Jessica—two co-workers who were friends with Meredith and who happen to despise you."

"That's old news," he mumbled, still looking straight ahead. "I dumped her months ago. Besides, she got around." He looked back at me. "A lot."

I looked at Stuart and discreetly scratched my throat—our sign for "your turn."

Stuart took a beat, pushed aside a chair that was not in his way, and then leaned on the table, getting extremely close to Bobby's face.

"Bobby, there are two ways this can go. The easy way and the hard way. Now, you're making me think you're wanting it to go the hard way. However, I'm guessing you're smart enough a man to want to pursue the easy path. Is that a fair assumption?"

Bobby kept staring. Stuart leaned closer.

"I'm sure from your size, age, and strength you could hurt me pretty well. That is, if you wanted or needed to. Thing is Bobby? Although I don't look like much, I'm a badass. And she—" Stuart tossed his chin toward me, "She's a Mo-Fo. Don't let those beauty pageant looks fool you. She could take us both out if pushed into a corner."

Oddly enough, that got Bobby to shift in his seat. It was a tiny shift but enough to let me know we were getting his attention.

"Now, I'm not insinuating anything *illegal*. That wouldn't be cool. But I want you to be aware of something because I have a pretty good hunch the three of us are going to be circling around one another for the next several days—if not weeks. Am I making sense?"

Bobby finally nodded.

"So, how about telling me just two little things. Then, we'll be on our way, okay?" He didn't wait for an acknowledgement. "The first question is, and it's going to sound silly, but you see it's my job to ask you. Did you kill Ms. Johansen this past Sunday? We're not 100% positive, but it's likely to have happened sometime between the hours of midnight and 5 a.m. Did you?"

"No."

"Okay, good enough. See how easy that was?"

Bobby looked at Stuart with an expression of *That's it?*

"Nice work, Bobby. Now, this one's even easier. During the time you and Ms. Johansen dated—those two years together—did you ever once hit or physically attack Ms. Johansen?"

"No."

"You never hit, slapped, pushed, or attacked her? Ever? Not in any way, shape, or form?"

Bobby turned and stared a hole through Stuart. "No. Never. In any form."

As the old saying went, one could hear a pin drop.

"Okay, Bobby. That'll do it. Thank you for being so helpful. We're sorry to have interrupted your little TV show," Stuart grinned.

Without any fanfare, Stuart and I looked at one another, turned, and headed for the door. We were about to exit when I stopped and walked back over to him.

"Bobby, can I ask a personal question? And you don't have to answer if you don't want to. It's just something that's bugging me," I said with my most charming smile. "You're a really big man. And I'm guessing you're crazy strong, right?"

Not sure, but he may have flexed.

"How much can you bench press? Ballpark."

Without hesitating he said, "460."

Whistling, I looked to Stuart. "Holy shit, that's impressive. That's nearly a quarter ton."

For the first time since we arrived, I thought I saw a tiny smile.

"460 is no joke," I continued. "You know my partner made a comment earlier about me being a Mo-Fo," I chuckled. "Not really. I mean, yeah, I can probably knock someone to the ground, but certainly not you. I bet you could knock me to the ground without even breaking a sweat."

"Wouldn't take much," he sneered.

In a flash, I wiped the aforementioned charming smile from my face and said, "I bet not."

That caught him off guard. Just enough. So, I held his stare for the length of time I needed to decide what to do next—basically, to keep him on edge. Frankly, I didn't think he was smart enough to push back. Either way, I returned my smile and reached out to shake his hand, "Thanks for your time."

He reluctantly obliged, trying to mask his confusion.

"Damn, that's a helluva grip. Wouldn't want to get on your bad side," I chuckled, smacking the side of his arm. It was as hard as I had imagined.

"Thanks for your time, Bobby," Stuart said with a smile.

"Yeah, you've been a great help. We'll be on our way and leave you to finish your little TV show."

At the door, I stopped to shake Janelle's hand. She had been silent in the corner the whole time.

"Thank you, Ms. Everest, for your help. You two have a great day."

———————

PASSING THROUGH THE LOBBY, we smiled at people like we were just married. We were out of the building and by our car when I finally let out a long sigh.

"No shit," Stuart said, taking out a handkerchief to wipe his brow. "Certainly a prime. Especially the lie about his never hitting Meredith."

"Hundred percent," I said, sticking out my hand.

"What?"

"Let's double-check it."

"Oh, right." Taking a pen from his breast pocket, he tapped a button. Two tiny beeps chirped before he clicked it again.

"*...happened sometime between the hours of midnight and 5 a.m.? Did you?....No.....Okay, good enough. See how easy that was?*"

Tapping it again, it stopped.

"That'll come in handy later. In the meantime, let's check on those statuettes."

"Copy that, *Mo-Fo!*"

29

PLASTIC TOY

To geeks who came from all over the country to get their fill of tchotchke bullshit, Hollywood was probably utopia. To me, it was capitalistic bullshit. Nonetheless, we wanted to see if we could possibly track down the producer of the small plastic Oscar statuette we found in our murder victim's palm.

We arrived at Hollywood Souvenirs in the La La Land building on Hollywood Boulevard at North Orange. We parked around back in a No Parking Zone, then walked around to the front where we were bombarded by a mass of starry-eyed tourists scurrying along the Boulevard like ants on hot pavement.

Stuart caught me shaking my head. "What's up?"

"I just wonder how we became addicted to so much crap."

"Like?"

I tossed my chin toward the throng of humanity. "Fat tourists wearing T-shirts with obnoxious quotes and baggy sweats with flip-flops, sucking on high-calorie, overpriced drinks of caffeine and sugar, all the while snapping selfies of their every move."

Stuart stared at me a solid beat before saying, "I see you've given this some thought."

PASSING THROUGH THE ENTRANCE, we found our senses were bombarded again—this time with bright lights, loud music, and burnt popcorn.

"Looks like Costco and Target had sex in a Hollywood alley."

Stuart snorted a chuckle. "Where do you come up with that stuff?" He checked his notepad. "We're looking for a man named Charlie Wong."

"Are you kidding me?" I asked in disbelief.

Stuart stopped a clerk to let the manager know we were here and I stopped to become distracted by a replica of Elvis' 1959 Cadillac.

"It's not an original, you know," he said from behind.

"Really?" I smirked, playfully punching him in the gut.

MINUTES LATER, we were one floor above the madness, overlooking a near acre of Hollywood paraphernalia.

"Has to be a tourist's wet dream, huh?" I asked the manager as a way to get the conversation started.

"And this is just *one* of our stores. We have two more: one about ten blocks away and another in The Valley."

"Good for you," I said, removing the statue from a pocket. "We're here to track this down."

Mr. Wong took a pair of glasses from the pocket of his pressed guayabera. After examining it for a tenth of a second, he said, "I'm afraid I won't be much help. That is, *if* you think you have something unique here."

"Why's that?" Stuart asked.

"Dime a dozen. You can get them *anywhere*. In fact," he said, motioning toward the front of the store. "See that huge LA neon sign? There are literally thousands of them stacked up that entire wall. And that's just *this* store. And just *my* chain. That doesn't count the rest of the guys in this city trying to sell the same crap. And certainly doesn't count *online* stores who import and sell these by the millions for every Oscar party in the free world."

We thanked Mr. Wong for his time, gave him our card—citing the standard *If anything comes up let us know*—then left.

Halfway back to the precinct, my cell rang. It was Captain Nelson.

"Detective Norelli."

"Of course it is. Who else would it be? Never mind. Find a shrink yet?"

I put him on speaker, so Stuart could enjoy it as well.

"Yes, sir. Actually, I did. Already been and I'd say—"

"Good, just wondering. Listen, I've got a person from *The Hollywood Mole*—a Ms. Everest—saying you two came in there guns blazing."

My stomach sank. "Sir, I can explain—"

"Said you interrupted their shit show—my words, not theirs—interrogating and maybe harassing one of the employees with no cause. That true?"

"Yes, the Director, Bobby Shapiro. He's our—"

"Good. Keep it up. And let me know when you're ready to put the hammer on him."

"Copy. In fact, we're about to—"

"Good talk. More to come."

Looking at my phone, I saw he was gone.

30

COIN FLIP

It was just before six when I left the station and before long I was deeply entrenched in Sunset Boulevard congestion. The air was thick with pollution and my patience was thin with frustration. Sitting in bumper-to-bumper was not my strong suit, so I flipped through radio stations, not settling on any one for very long, when my cell rang.

"Norelli."

"Hello, Detective. I want to report a crime."

"You'll need to..." I began, then looked at the number again. It seemed familiar.

"Pat. It's Steve Owen. Sorry if that was a bad joke. Angie gave me your number—"

"Steve! Oh my God," I laughed. "I thought you were....well, no worries. I'm glad you called."

"Look, Angie and I go way back and when she told me about you, I thought, what the heck, right?"

"Right. What the heck," I chuckled. "She's been a friend for a long time. And she's told me some things about you, too."

"Oh, shit," he laughed.

"No, no, it's all good."

"Well, since I'm batting a thousand, let me spring this idea on you. And I know it's kinda last minute, but what are you doing tonight?"

I thought, *Do I play hard to get?*

"Hello?"

"Just navigating a hairy intersection," I lied. "Actually, I'm just leaving work and was trying to decide on what to do for dinner."

"Perfect timing then. Listen, let me take you to dinner. I'm in The Valley. Where are you?"

"Oh, maybe halfway between my office in Hollywood and Century City. On the way up the canyon. I'd say—"

"Good. Let me interrupt. I'm just getting on the 405. I'll text you the place I have in mind as soon as we hang up. It's on the edge of Brentwood. Great burgers and even better cocktails. You won't be sorry."

I enjoyed the smile I found spreading across my face. "Well, then I'm all in."

"Great. You and I should get there about the same time. I'll meet you out front."

As soon as we rang off, the address appeared on my phone. I locked it into GPS and was cruising in the opposite direction in no time—anxious to see what Lady Luck had in store for me.

31

OPPOSITES DISTRACT

My father must have channeled boys early on because he got his wish for the first go-round. What he got in the second round, however, was a pretty tomboy with keen male skills who developed into a beautiful woman with solid female skills. I took a spare seven minutes to run my Camaro through a slow-moving and touchless car wash which gave me enough time to change from company clothes to something more attractive. As my car passed through the high-speed dryer, I rolled my pits and spritzed my neck.

Within minutes, I was pulling up to Father's Office on Montana, a Gastropub haven of craft burgers and beers. Scanning the street for parking, I spotted a guy I had to assume was Steve. He was hard to miss, standing in the middle of a prime parking spot and directly behind an enormous Ford F-450 Super-Duty 4x4.

Holding a cell with one hand, he waved off approaching cars with the other—obviously saving the parking spot for me—so I pulled in. As I got out, he took my hand.

"Hello, beautiful," he said, admiring my landscape.

"Hello, yourself," I said, repeating his gesture. "Angie didn't tell me you were this handsome."

"Don't know about all that, but I suppose I clean up okay. And she didn't tell me *you* were drop-dead gorgeous."

"Aw shucks."

Extending his arm for me, he stopped traffic in both directions as we crossed the street.

"A take-charge kinda guy. I like that."

"Whatever it takes."

TALKING to Steve Albert Owen was like visiting with an old friend. Our conversations covered the gamut—from raising children and surviving divorce to navigating single life while maneuvering our revered list of *non-negotiables.*

His non-negs, as we started calling them, were as follows: financially independent—he was not hip to supporting more mouths than necessary; a sense of humor—that seemed to cover a multitude of sins; able to keep up with his fervor—people who expected everything to come to them were of no interest. His last requirement was expected: physically fit and attractive.

We laughed about how I mirrored his non-negs and I added three more: no being intimidated by the heft of my job—it was my chosen profession; no harming or disrespecting me—been there, done that, and will not stand for it. My last requirement got a good laugh when I explained that whoever managed to get my attention must be able to keep up with me both at the bar and in bed.

I was pretty sure that gave him a bright green light to push things along.

It was interesting how perfectly comfortable I felt sharing my inner self with this stranger. Sure, I was attracted to his looks, but there was a vibe of self-confidence that quickly became extra attractive. Also, if I were to be honest with myself, I needed to be comfortable asking for exactly what I wanted. Given the power and position of my father, along with the domineering push of my mother—not to mention the narcissistic husband I was married to during my formative years—I had taken a backseat to *me* a long time ago. That felt like it was beginning to change, and I had Shay to thank for the push.

The first two Old Fashioned cocktails were delicious and worked quickly in helping ease the state of self-consciousness while greasing the wheels of horniness. The burgers were tasty and their adjoining two craft beers quickly became four. By the time our conversation got to the point of admitting I had come to a place where I was as equally interested in deep conversations as I was in deep orgasms, I knew a shift was in the making.

Shortly after, he waved down the waitress and paid the check.

"So, how about this," he said when we stepped into the cool night air. "My boat is twenty minutes from here. Why don't we head there for a nightcap?"

It sounded nice and the thought of his not coming to my place was spot on; however, driving to MDR then back home was a buzz kill—not to mention the fear of getting a DUI would certainly dampen the evening mood.

"Uh, that sounds like a plan. Just one thing—"

"I'm driving. You can't," he interrupted. "*And* I'll have you home by midnight."

Checking my watch, I seriously doubted I would be returning to my car.

"Sure," I grinned.

"Or, if things go well, you can crash with me and—"

"Uhhh...."

"Okay, I get it. Maybe that's not such a good idea. I'm breaking one of my *own* rules anyway."

"Which is?"

"I never bring a girl over on the first date," he laughed as we walked to our cars.

"Why?"

"I like to be the one to leave, depending on how things are going. And if they're at my place and things are, you know—"

Fuck it, I thought, pulling his arm in the direction of his truck.

WE MADE it to his place in a bit more than twenty minutes, but they went by like five. Passing through the neighborhood gates, we snagged a parking spot near the docks and were quickly down below. The boat was simple, handsome, and appeared efficient. Steve poured two short glasses of single malt Scotch older than my daughter, and we stretched out on a horseshoe-shaped couch.

"This is more like it, huh?" Steve asked, kicking off his shoes while removing mine. Setting aside his Scotch, he began rubbing my feet.

"Uh, yeah, and if you keep doing that," I nodded toward his handiwork, "You'll have a hard time getting rid of me."

"Mission accomplished," he winked.

"Do you spend this much attention on all your girls?"

Grinning, he said, "Actually? Never."

This could be a first. "I actually believe you."

It wasn't long before we were half naked and making out like high schoolers. It had been a long time since I was with a man who spent more time making sure I was being pleasured than the other way around—and it was pure pleasure.

Watching him tower over me was incredibly hot. The muscles in his arms and chest were solid and impressive, his eye contact intoxicating.

And if there were a trophy for his talents, he would have certainly won first prize because his tongue knew exactly what it was doing.

32

HOT DAMN

A n hour later, I was awakened by a distant gurgling noise. Alarmed, I quickly sat up in bed, trying to place it.

It was Steve, snoring.

"Holy shit, that's loud," I mumbled.

Grunting, he sat up as quickly as I did.

"What is it?" he slurred.

"You."

"Huh?"

"You were snoring so loud, I think you woke the fish."

"Funny," he said, sitting on the side of the bed, rubbing his face.

In my haze, I wasn't sure what to do next. Checking my watch, I saw it was way too late, and I felt caught in that space between rolling over to sleep off the booze and impending headache, or getting up and facing the music.

"Sorry. Guess I had more than I thought."

"Ditto," I said.

"I, uh, only snore when I get hammered."

"No biggie," I chuckled. "I do the same thing. Just maybe not quite as loud."

"Right," he smirked, checking his watch, then taking empty glasses to the sink. "Guess I should be getting you back."

I decided to go with it, taking the disruption as a sign. Besides I figured, if this had a chance of going anywhere, we would pick up where we left off. Getting dressed, I tried to retain levity.

"You know for such a big guy, it's a small boat, isn't it?"

"What?" he asked, whipping his head around and frowning.

"I mean, you have an enormous truck," I stammered, "A huge, you know," I nod toward his crotch. "But—"

"Did you say *small* boat?" he asked, not waiting for an answer. "You have any idea how much this thing cost?"

"Okay, that was…" I stuttered. "Sorry. I was kidding," I said, pushing him aside. Bending over to grab my panties, I must have pushed harder than I thought because he lost his balance and fell backwards over the edge of the couch.

Instinctively, he reached out to catch himself but inadvertently pushed me back—a move that caught me off guard, causing me to fall backwards. Spinning at the last second, I felt my cheek abruptly meet the corner of the dining table.

The timing could not have been planned—nor ended in a worse way.

"Fuck!" I shouted, falling to the floor. Reaching for my face, I saw blood and felt the swelling begin instantly.

"Holy shit!" he shouted, coming to my rescue. "I'm so sorry. Damn, I didn't realize—"

Pushing his hand away, I barked, "Can you get me a wet cloth? Maybe some ice?"

He immediately grabbed a damp towel from the sink. "That was stupid. And accidental. I'm truly sorry. Sometimes I…well, it was just a reaction."

My mind raced back to when my ex-husband Billy, on more than several occasions, "just had a reaction" with a backhand or a shove. It always ended up doing more damage than he had accidentally meant to cause. Invariably, his response included a reason why it happened but never an explanation why it wouldn't stop.

"I'm sure the swelling won't be too bad," I said, taking the compress from my cheek. "Right?"

His grimace said otherwise.

"That's not a good look!"

"Neither is that," he chuckled, trying to ease the tension.

"Now it's your turn to be funny?"

"Hold tight, I'll run to a neighbor's boat."

"No, seriously, it's—"

"Hold on. He's out of town and has plenty of ice. Besides, his is *bigger* than mine," he grinned. Before I could stop him, he was gone.

"Nice," I mumbled, shaking my head. "What dumb luck."

Waiting for him to return, I looked around. A frosted glass cupboard with a dangling, unlocked padlock caught my eye. Being a detective, I *had* to peek.

Inside was a Sig Sauer P227, .45ACP, a Glock 9MM, a Smith & Wesson .357 revolver, a P238 conceal-carry Sig, and an AR-15 on the top shelf. The ammunition was on the next shelf. And on the bottom shelf was an elaborate wooden box.

Curiosity being what it is, I opened the box.

"What the—" I whispered, looking at an assortment of straight razors. Several had bone handles; one, a titanium handle, and another, a pearl handle. All were bright and shiny except one that had an extra long blade covered in blood, lying atop a rag.

My mind raced to Meredith. I saw her neck and the pool of blood. My stomach tightened and my heart raced as my imagination kicked into hyper speed.

"Whatcha doing?" Steve asked behind me.

Startled, I shut the door and spun around. It was instinct but appeared silly. His look was stern, yet menacing.

"Sorry. I, uh, was looking for another towel," I said, removing the one from my cheek, showing him the bloody remains.

"Here," he fumbled, taking the towel from me and rinsing it in the sink. Ringing it out, he filled it with ice from a large plastic bag and handed it to me, following my glance back toward the cupboard. "They're all registered."

The sound of breaking glass several boats away broke the silence. While it startled me, Scott didn't flinch.

"I was in the Marines. Camp Pendleton. Old habits die hard—shit like that," he said, staring past me at nothing.

I acknowledged him with a nod.

"I like to keep heat nearby. Part of my prep for when the shit hits the fan."

Nodding again, I pushed the silence.

"And it will. Someday."

"Quite a collection of razors."

The awkward silence made me weary.

"My grandfather was a barber. His will left his collection of razors to my dad who always shaved with a straight razor until he got older. When his hands started to shake, he gave them to me."

I couldn't help but look at his thick beard.

"I use them. From time to time," he said, stroking his hairy chin.

My head was pounding, my cheek throbbing, and all I could think was, *I want to go home.*

"And the blood?"

"Huh?" he asked, looking clueless.

"On the razor? And the towel."

"Oh, yeah. I was gutting fish this morning. They're a *lot* sharper than the filet knife I dropped overboard. Goes through flesh like warm butter."

I instantly shuddered at the thought.

"Okay, I have to get home," I said, looking for my purse. When he grabbed it from the floor in the corner, I saw a scratch on the side of his neck—one I didn't recall seeing earlier.

"What happened here? Did I do that?" I asked, pointing at it.

Touching it, he said, "Nah. Damn cat."

"You don't have a cat."

His nervous chuckle felt odd. "The Manhattan Beach property I told you about? The one Angie wants me to fix for you?"

"Right."

"The last family bounced and left three cats behind. Evidently, one was hiding in a closet. So, when I went to pull the doors off, it jumped off the shelf and got me."

"I hate cats."

"Me, too. But they're gone now."

My mind flashed back to Meredith. I imagined her putting up a fight with her attacker.

"C'mon, why not sleep it off here? I'll take you back to the car first thing."

"No, that's fine, really."

"Hell, *earlier* than first thing—if you like."

"Nah, it's been fun. And interesting. But I need to be fresh. Got a stacked day tomorrow."

"Today, you mean."

"Right."

33

SWINGING DICKS

The 24 Hour Fitness was packed at such an early hour. Bobby Shapiro and his gym rat pal Chris Banyon spent nearly as much time gawking at girls as they did lifting the lead. With each plate added, their testosterone rose and their IQs dipped. Both men sweated and grunted as though the higher the volume the greater their strength.

After a particularly heavy lift where Bobby clean jerked 400 pounds, he goaded Chris to match it. Bobby had four inches in height and thirty-plus pounds of body mass over his partner, so Chris lost the lift because of insufficient strength but gained the attention of a woman across the room, thanks to his supermodel smile.

Taking a swallow from a stainless steel sports bottle, Chris said, "See that blonde across the room?"

Drinking from a plain gallon jug, Bobby said, "Mean the one in pink with the overdone tits and bunny tattoo on her left ankle? No, I don't see her."

"Hot as hell."

"Not bad."

"Not bad?" Chris snorted, "Like to deadlift her over my head and drop squat her on my face."

Bobby piled more weight on the rack, looked at her, then got up in Chris' face. "Never. Happen."

"Shit. Happens all the time."

"In your dreams maybe," Bobby said, tightening the ring collars on the bar, then taking his place beneath the stack.

"Whatever."

"C'mon, one more lift, a quick cool down, and if you're a good boy, I'll show you how it's done."

"You mean the deadlift, or…" Chris nodded toward her.

"Both."

———

THIRTY REPS and twenty minutes on a bike later, the two men were wiping themselves off with small towels and ogling a gaggle of beautiful women working out on a row of Pilates machines across the room.

"Okay, Mr. Universe," Chris said, punching Bobby's massive arm. "Show me the *Shapiro Magic*—that special sauce that has all the women aching for your junk."

Bobby looked at him like he was an idiot. "And you wonder why you can't get laid," he said, throwing his sweaty towel in Chris' face before walking across the room. Chris eagerly watched.

Less than three minutes had passed when Bobby returned, smirking at Chris the entire distance of the room.

"And?"

"392-6001."

"Shit! What'd you say?"

"My usual. And yes. We're grabbing drinks after work."

"Dammit," Chris shook his head. "She's hotter than balls."

"Even prettier up close."

"I don't get it. I'm better looking than you—"

"But you're a geek with no game. And I'm just the opposite."

———

CROSSING THE ENORMOUS PARKING LOT, they approached their cars. Bobby tapped the remote and his windows and convertible top silently lowered. Chris pointed his remote and his F-150 Raptor loudly double-beeped.

"That's the *other* reason you don't get the ladies, you bitch," Bobby said, tossing his bag in the front seat.

"Girls dig it, bro. 'Specially the *long* bed," Chris said, tossing his bag in the back.

"Keep telling yourself that." Bobby polished his sunglasses before putting them on. "I'm out. Punished you enough for one day."

Chris was pissed. First, he got beat in their lifting competition—for the umpteenth time—then he had to watch Bobby effortlessly snag another girl. And to finish it off, Bobby trash-talked his ride.

Knowing Bobby's weakness, he went in for the kill. "Hey, wanna win back that 15 grand you lost in poker last week?"

Bobby stopped and peered over his sunglasses. "Love to, you cheating prick."

"I didn't cheat. You just suck at poker, is all."

Bobby stared. Chris waited.

"What's the bet?"

"What's her name?" Chris nodded toward the club. "The girl."

"Elizabeth Conroy. Some hoity-toity socialite. It was a layup, dude."

Still pissed, Chris just stared.

"C'mon, what's the bet? I gotta get to work."

"Rough her up and get me pictures," Chris said through a cold stare. "And I'll give you the fifteen large back."

Bobby frowned. "I'm fucking whacked, dude, but you're insane," he snorted, starting to get in his car.

"All it takes is some nasty photos. And get as *whacked* as you want."

Chris had not spent the money he won from Bobby and had more than enough to cover any bet they made. His position at Blackridge Capital was solid and the Hedge Fund business was booming. Besides being a rising star, he also knew exactly how to make his money back—even *after* paying it to Bobby.

Chris understood several things about his warped friend. First, he did not like to lose—at anything. Second, he was a sick fuck with a demented sense of reality. Last, he knew Bobby would do anything to win—no matter the bet or what was at stake. His greed was deep and his ego enormous.

Bobby waved him off, got into his car, and started to pull away.

"Wait!" Chris shouted, running over to his window. "Make it video and I'll *double* the amount."

Bobby looked over the top of his shades, sneered, and said, "You're on," then peeled out of the driveway and disappeared from sight.

34

THREE WAY

Stuart and I arrived at Dr. Tercel's office within seconds of one another. He had labored the 405 from The Valley while I had flown through backroads via the canyons. He was wearing what looked to be a new suit—it was handsome. I was wearing what looked like a swollen cheek—it was ghastly.

"Holy shit," Stuart said as he climbed from his car.

"No doubt," I responded, taking my portfolio from the backseat.

"Just hope the other gal looks worse," he grinned.

"And I hope this won't get any more attention than that," I said, motioning for us to get a move on.

"Seriously, it looks like—"

"Can we save that for later? Today's meeting with Tercel is important, and you'll hear *all* about the liaison later. Promise."

"Copy that."

"By the way, nice suit. Job interview?"

"Funny. And no, the wife went shopping."

THE WAITING room was a nice respite from the noisy outdoors and the quiet music helped reduce stress. Knowing we had to push harder today in order to make some progress, I welcomed the calm before the storm.

Sitting at stoplights on my commute, I had checked emails on my phone. The Captain was making noises about tying up loose ends and finding solutions. I was sure he was getting heat from upstairs which meant the temperature was rising for us as well.

Shit, dude—we're just getting started, I thought, trying to quiet my monkey mind.

"Damn girl, this place is *faaanncy*," Stuart said, dragging the last word to a laughable length.

I smacked his thigh. The room was so quiet it seemed to echo.

"Ow."

"Stop it, or I'll give you something to whine about," I winked.

"See? You like that rough shit."

"You're insane."

As the door opened, Dr. Tercel greeted us with a warm smile and a friendly handshake. Pleasantries were shared as we settled into his office where coffee was served by an assistant I hadn't seen before. She was young, pretty, and disappeared quickly.

"Detective Norelli, what on earth happened to your cheek?" Tercel asked with genuine concern.

"Working out with a colleague. She kicked me in the face. Looks worse than it really is."

He let it go, so I smiled and turned to Stuart.

Before our meeting, we decided it'd be best if he led the discussions. Given I was currently Tercel's client, it made the most sense. Stuart's posture and my demeanor confirmed such to the Doctor.

"So, how may I be of service?" Tercel said, looking from me to Stuart.

"Well, it's pretty straight forward," Stuart began. "We're making our way to meet any and all people who knew Ms. Johansen. And today, we'd like to discuss your relationship with Meredith—both professionally and personally."

It felt different being on this side of the couch asking the therapist about his world, instead of his probing into mine.

"And before you begin," Stuart added, "Let me assure you that given the recent demise of your client, you can feel comfortable divulging any and all information you have that could potentially assist in our learning more about her."

Before Tercel could start, Stuart produced a document from his coat pocket. "And sorry to interrupt right after I begin, but I want you to feel confident we're abiding by all the rules."

Stuart stood, handing Tercel the document.

"I see that," Tercel said, reading the paper. "Not exactly a subpoena." He continued to read. "And gives you full access to my notes and her records."

Stuart nodded and smiled. It felt like a duel for a moment.

Another moment passed before Tercel placed the document in his desk drawer. "Looks to be in order. Now, Detective Brown, your parter tells me your person of interest—my client— committed suicide."

We both nod.

"However, my assumption—perhaps better stated, my *intuition* tells me you believe this is…otherwise? Is that safe to assume?"

"Personally, we believe it's a case of murder. However, we are required to expose every potential angle we can think of."

"Absolutely."

"There was a suicide note. Whether or not it was actually written and signed by her…is an entirely different thing."

"I see."

"Dr. Tercel, to that point, would you classify Ms. Johansen as clinically depressed?"

Tercel considered that for a long moment. "Actually, yes. I could easily say she was depressed. In fact, in just the last several months, I saw a downward spiral in her moods. She would cancel appointments, often at the last moment. Other times, she would volley between crying for much of a session and having outbursts of anger."

Stuart wrote in his pad.

"And don't get me wrong," he said, looking at both of us. "She was a lovely gal. Inside and out. Would do anything for anyone she met. She gave of her time, donated a great deal to a number of charities around the city—taking on several initiatives like the Children's Home, Pet Shelters, and Unwed Mothers. Helped so many people. It was beautiful to watch."

After a long silence, he wiped an eye and shook his head. "She was one of the good ones."

"How's that, Doctor?"

"You know how this town can be. Vapid. Empty. Lonely. Full of go-getters with hidden agendas. Others, not so hidden."

It was time I added to the mix. "Dr. Tercel, on a personal level, how did you feel about Meredith?"

He thought for another long moment, and adding a warm smile said, "When she came recommended to me by a mutual friend, she was at a place where she needed to work through some parental issues. Also at the time, she was having difficulty with a boyfriend. He was rough on her. Physically *and* mentally. So, we agreed to meet for several sessions."

He paused to open a thin leather portfolio off to the side, scan it, and then continued.

"I was just checking some notes I'd made in order to be prepared for our meeting. I took the liberty to double-check dates. She came to me the first of last year. I helped her for about five months, and we made quick progress in unlocking some buried issues. She was a driven person and a quick study."

I helped myself to water from a coffee table as Stuart flipped a page in his pad.

"It was shortly thereafter that, well, things shifted. She told me of her feelings for me—something that can happen between practitioner and patient. I told her there was no way we could see one another because I was her doctor. She became rather persistent. And to be frank, I believe she had worked out a good many of her issues. As I said, she was a very quick study."

Silence.

"So, when she told me she no longer wanted to see me as a patient, I finally agreed after a fair amount of pushback on my part."

I smiled and Stuart nodded then said, "And?"

"And I released her from my care. Sometime later, she sent me an email suggesting I ask her out. To dinner or drinks."

"Does that happen often? Between you and your patients?" he asked.

Tercel grinned. "As I said, it *can* happen. And *has* happened with a good many other practitioners. However, that's the *first* time it's ever happened to me. Frankly, I was surprised."

"And you felt she had *improved* enough to stop treatment?" I asked, nearly holding my breath.

Turning his body in my direction, he smiled. "Yes. I felt her progress was substantial. And she was well on her way. Not needing any more assistance. My primary focus was to help her work out some emotional scars from childhood. As an avid student, she had read a good many books which, I believe, helped expedite her..." he paused.

"Well, recovery sounds as though she had deep-seated clinical issues, when in fact, she just needed some gentle tweaking to her guidance system."

"Interesting," is all Stuart said.

"Yes, think of it like a software update to your GPS."

"Makes sense," I said.

"It was obvious—to everyone who met her—she was used to getting what she wanted. The drive and determination of that young woman was impressive. And convincing."

Stuart closed his pad and leaned forward. "And did it take a great deal of convincing for you to transition her from patient to someone with whom you could develop a relationship?"

Tercel frowned for just a second. "While I'm confident you're just doing your job asking the hard questions, let me assure you Detective, the convincing part wasn't about her mental health. It was about making sure she knew the difference between the services I gave her as a doctor…and the attributes I might bring to a healthy and loving relationship."

"And do you—" I began.

"Please excuse me a moment, Detective Norelli," he interrupted, "But I want to clarify something."

Turning back to Stuart, he said, "We went out perhaps a dozen or so times, but I quickly—rather, *we* quickly—realized there was too much difference between us. It wasn't as much about age—perhaps a decade between us—as it was about life *experience*."

I had heard this line before.

"She was obsessed with her documentary film. I mean, she had been reaching for an Oscar for more than a decade." He brushed a spec of lint from his slacks. "Frankly, I think it was I who grew tired of competing with her work."

As he looked out the window, Stuart and I exchanged looks. I glanced at my watch and Tercel stood to get bottled water from across the room. "I'm parched. May I get either of you something?"

"No, thank you," Stuart replied. "Actually, we're almost about done here. Perhaps another question or two and we'll be on our way."

"Take all the time you need. I'm here to help," Tercel said, returning to his chair.

"For the record, and as I said earlier, neither Detective Norelli nor I believe this was a suicide. Mainly because we have a problem believing a woman would cut her own throat. In that fashion. Cut wrists in a bathtub?

That's a different story. But then, who knows what goes on in the mind of someone who wants out?"

"Well put, Detective. And I see your reasoning. As you said, who knows what one will do when pushed too far?" Tercel said to the floor.

His somber expression felt genuine and hearing the opinions of a professional certainly gave me reason to consider things differently.

Looking up, he said, "Not only did Meredith foster deep resentment toward her father who was a drunk and abusive parent, but she also repeated similar patterns by searching for those same characteristics in her relationships."

"How's that?" I asked.

"What, specifically?"

Trying not to fidget, I said, "You mentioned repeating similar patterns. During our investigation, we've spoken with people who have witnessed similar behaviors. In fact, someone she was close to acted much like her father."

He quietly said, "Bobby Shapiro."

Stuart and I glanced at one another before he said, "We've spoken to him. He said he never hit her, but her coworkers say otherwise."

Silence for several moments before Tercel said, "Bobby has issues. He's full of aggression. And Meredith—while drawn to him—actually feared him."

"Do you think it's possible," I hesitated, "He drove her to it?"

"Do I believe she was capable of taking her own life? Yes. Is it possible Bobby was responsible?" Stopping, he stared at his hands—like he was choosing a response. Looking up, he said, "I don't know. And given I've seen him before, I really can't say because of doctor and patient privacy."

Scribbling, Stuart said, "Just one more question, Dr. Tercel. You mentioned emotional scars from childhood. Besides the abusive father, what else was there?"

Tercel replied, "Where do I begin?"

"Maybe a *Reader's Digest* version?" He smiled.

"Of course," Tercel cleared his throat. "I'd say Meredith had three major issues. An abusive father, low self esteem, and insecurity because of abandonment issues."

"We've all got our stuff," I said.

"You're right, Detective. And doing the best we can."

At that pause, Stuart gave a deliberate nod, smacked his thighs and stood. "Well, this has been good. You've been a tremendous help, Dr. Tercel."

Shaking hands, we headed toward the door.

"If there's anything else you need, please don't hesitate to reach out."

STUART and I didn't say anything until we got to the car. Across the top of the car he said, "Nice guy. Seems sincere. And I'm guessing as a patient, he probably makes you feel at ease."

I looked at him and started to say something but stopped.

"What?"

Looking back at the building, I said, "He is. On all counts. And my gut tells me…he really cared for her. Perhaps more than he's letting on."

"Probably. And you know what? I wouldn't blame him from what we've learned so far. Could you?"

Shaking my head, I smiled.

35

UNUSUAL SUSPECTS

S tuart dropped me off back at the precinct so that he could run home to check on a potential false alarm with his on-the-verge-of-delivering wife. Within minutes, I was knee-deep in phone slips that ran the gamut from copycat killers to wack-jobs starved for attention. I had been contemplating Meredith's calendar sprinkled with two-letter codes when McCloud pinged me to share a few extra surprises from one of her cell phones. Come to learn our well-educated, philanthropic broadcaster and filmmaker had a hefty Rolodex that revealed a veracious sexual appetite.

50 shades of Anastasia and Christian got nothing on Meredith.

Swiping through the digital rolodex, I came across a calendar named *Proposition 69*, and out of curiosity, googled all of the California propositions. Scanning the screen, I found a list that began with Proposition 51 about school bonds. 52 was the Medi-Cal Hospital Fee Program. 53 was about more bonds. 55 covered tax extensions. 56 was a cigarette tax to fund healthcare. I kept skimming until I got to 67 about a ban on single-use plastic bags.

There was no Proposition 69.

I suddenly realized the proposition was "code" for her sexual escapades—not the topic of an upcoming documentary film.

Position 69. Clever and clandestine—just like her Panic Room.

"The plot thickens, Miss Johansen," I mumbled to myself.

"What's that?" a voice said from behind.

I spun around to catch McCloud sitting at Stuart's desk performing fellatio on a sucker.

"What are you doing?" I asked.

"Sucking on a—"

"I see that freak. I mean—"

"Right. I wanted to hand deliver her laptop," he said, stroking the case like it was a purring kitten.

"You're crazy," I said, spinning back around to continue cracking the codes embedded in the same corner of each day of the month.

"Have you gotten to her clientele list? Or should I say *customer* list?"

Without turning around, I said, "Not yet."

"Copy that. Oh, and I couldn't crack the code on this laptop."

"What?" I asked, spinning around to see the laptop facing me. It was open and revealed a picture of Meredith, I assumed, wearing a long gossamer dress. Actually, it was more like an elaborate nightie and she was not in her bedroom. Instead, she was standing in front of a half dozen men—all of whom were wearing similar yet more masculine robes and devilish masks.

It looked to be taking place at what I assumed was Hugh Hefner's Playboy Mansion. Next to Meredith was a very tall and striking blond who I felt sure was Sharon Gladstone. She was dressed in a man's suit and tie; however, the suit was sheer and very sexy.

"Nice, right?" McCloud sneered. "There's hundreds, hell, *thousands* of photographs. And this one's tame."

"Thought you couldn't—"

"Really? There isn't a computer I can't hack."

"If you weren't underage, I'd kiss you."

"What?" he rattled his head. "I'm not."

The phone rang. I barked, "Norelli."

"False alarm. Janine's fine," Stuart sighed.

"Good."

"Yeah, except this being on the edge is driving me crazy."

I motioned for McCloud to wait one minute. He nodded, continuing to ogle more photos.

"Okay, just take your time. I've got it all under control."

I could hear his wife in the background.

"Hold on, baby. Be right there," he shouted to her before returning to me. He continued to prattle on at length about his exit strategy for when the baby arrived. I half-heartedly listened as my eyes fell on my list of two-letter codes: EN, GJ, TS, SH, DT, BS, BW, and SG.

I had not scoured the entire calendar but had at least covered the last several months. Only a few dates were without the two-letter codes.

"Before I bounce, whatcha working on?" he asked, snapping me back.

"Uh, something you'll be able to help me with. And completely enjoy," I said, looking over at McCloud who continued to eyeball soft porn on MJ's laptop. "I think you'll see it's simple to follow, especially given the names I've tracked down from social media, press, and such."

"Hit me."

"I'm emailing you a calendar right now. It contains a series of initials we got from MJ's cell phones, thanks to the mighty skills of our McCloud."

"I'm also sending photos. You can help me put faces to names, or rather, initials."

"Love me some puzzles."

"Coming your way. See ya," I said, disconnecting.

McCloud was happy to share the laptop but quickly explained about having to take it with him. I objected, but when he presented me with a thumb drive of her entire photo library, I let it ride. According to him, she should *not* have had personal photos on her company laptop, but frankly I didn't care.

My desk phone rang. It was the Captain calling to tell me I was taking too long in solving this case and how my brother would have solved it already. I told him I was *this close* and would get back to him the second something broke.

Next, McCloud and I headed out—me for a Coke and him for a choke. We had to discuss our agreement—the one where I asked him to help me with the situation my father had told me about. We referred to it as "NCA" (Nicky Confiscation Agreement). While he spent way too much time explaining the complexity of maneuvering said mission, I impressed upon him the complexity of my maneuvering his future.

He moved me to the front of his line.

THIRTY MINUTES LATER, I was back at our desks, printing out Stuart's email that had his immediate hits and added them to the cross-referenced information McCloud and I had created. With copious photos and personal emails, it didn't take long for us to finish deciphering the roster of Meredith's roosters. It was a Who's Who of local celebs—from notorious bad boy actors to entrepreneurial brainiacs, all of whom were extremely wealthy and decidedly naughty.

I called them *The Notorious 8*.

36

CRYSTAL PERSUASION

After some initial small talk, Angie and Dr. Tercel began with a recap of last week's appointment. She explained about how she had gone easy on the sauce—partially true. She shared how she was feeling stronger about sharing her opinions on matters of the heart—mostly true. And she discussed how her issues of controlling her rage when people bullied her were slowly disappearing—completely untrue. Dr. Tercel listened intently, smiling from time to time and, as always, helped her relax. Near the end of their 90-minute session, he scooted his chair forward several inches.

"Angie, you and I have been working together for *ten* years now. Can you believe it?"

"It's amazing, isn't it? And you've helped me so much."

"Thank you, but *you* have done all the hard work. And I'm so proud of you. I think that while you've made such dramatic inroads, there are still just a couple of tiny things left to work on. And I believe in my heart of hearts you're going to ace them. Like I said, you've done all the hard work, and I've laid much of the groundwork for what I believe is the next..." he paused to scratch his chin, then smiled. "Yes, the next chapter in this phase of our upcoming sessions. You're going to see that you will literally *soar* to new heights."

Her smile took on a childlike quality. Knowing her love language was words of affirmations—a methodology he learned in school—his encouragement would prepare her for future receptivity of deeper training.

"Thank you."

Patting her hand, he said, "With that said, I'd like to make a suggestion you're really going to like."

Walking to his credenza, he removed a small crystal attached to a thin chain and rejoined her by the couch.

"That's so beautiful. What is it?"

"It's a fine crystal—the purest on earth—but it's more than that. It's a conduit. Something for you to concentrate on while we discuss a couple of things before our session comes to a close."

"I'm all ears."

"Of course you are. And are you familiar with a practice called Hypnotherapy?"

Frowning, she said, "I've heard of hypnosis—"

"Hypnotherapy is basically hypnosis but easier to understand. It's completely safe and *very* effective in jumping over any last hurdles that may stand in one's way. Make sense?"

"I think so."

"Think of it this way," he smiled, "Say you're a smoker and you've tried everything: cold turkey, nicotine gum, and whatever else. Imagine being at your wits' end. You'd be willing to try anything to help kick that habit for good, right?"

"Absolutely. Oh…" she said with a glimmer of recognition, "You're thinking hypnotherapy may help my, uh, self-confidence and anger issues, right?"

"Exactly. And this is simply an effective tool to let's say *steer* your subconscious into working *with you* rather than against you. You're 100% in control, not going to do anything crazy. Moreover, there's no secret power anyone has over you."

"You'd never do that anyway."

"You're absolutely right. So, let's get started, and after a few minutes, trust me, you'll think you took a nap because you'll be so refreshed."

She was nearly giddy with enthusiasm and instinctively took a deep breath, rolled her head around to loosen her neck, and let out a long exhale.

"See? You're so intuitive. I was going to ask you to do that very thing. Now, just watch this crystal—as I swing it back and forth—and clear your mind—removing any and all thoughts you may have—just allowing you and me—to enter into this safe and sacred place—with no distractions— and nothing but peaceful harmony and loving, good thoughts."

Her shoulders relaxed as her hands fell limp in her lap.

37

RICH BOY

The *Notorious 8* covered the gamut of industries and nearly all had much less than six degrees of separation from the business of Hollywood. Given we faced a full day of hitting the streets, McCloud and I split up so Stuart and I could visit with our third potential suspect Elgin Nessbach. He was the founder of Sparke, the Solar Car empire.

Their factory was located in Pomona about 30 miles east of downtown Los Angeles. His company bought the Brackett Field Airport in La Verne, ten minutes north of downtown, and transformed the old airport into a state-of-the-art facility, complete with runways operating as test tracks and former hangars doubling as assembly lines and paint bays. While Pomona was much cheaper than LA—making the location a perfect economic fit for production— Nessbach's obsession with the sparkle of wealth and prestige placed his executive offices in the epicenter of downtown LA.

The Wilshire Grand Center, located in the Financial District, was not only the tallest building in LA but also the tenth tallest building in the United States—the perfect beacon to show off his global-reaching empire.

After getting approved by a front desk secretary, then passed to an executive secretary for a brief quiz, we finally met with Nessbach's personal assistant and were cleared for an interview.

Nessbach was on the other side of a 16-foot wall of glass, talking to what appeared to be a Board of Directors sitting at a table long enough to feed all three shifts of employees in our Hollywood Precinct.

"He only has 15 minutes, Detectives," Francine Beaumont—his personal assistant of ten years—said with little fanfare.

"Thank you," Stuart said, taking a seat in the oversized chair next to the oversized coffee table in the oversized lobby.

"Room's big enough to play football," I said quietly.

Ms. Beaumont excused herself with a tiny yet false smile, pivoted like a soldier, and entered the glass sanctuary. We both watched her perfectly shaped rear float across the room where she proceeded to stand—ramrod straight—awaiting her boss' next command.

"Really?" Stuart said, tossing his head toward an enormous oil painting of Nessbach on the wall.

"And with only a *hint* of Hitler," I grinned.

TWENTY MINUTES, two bottles of imported water, and one *Wired* magazine later—featuring none other than our next suspect—our Boy Wonder arrived. And I do mean boy.

Stuart and I learned there had to be more than a bit of overcompensation at work when one of the wealthiest men alive owns one of the most profitable world-renowned companies and locates it in one of the tallest buildings in the world.

Charming and handsome, Elgin Nessbach was shorter than I imagined. His eyes were closer together than photos portrayed, and he was easily the most self-aware person I had ever met. The result was a handsome narcissist with a short-man complex and the wherewithal to buy pretty much anything in the world.

"Helloooooooo, Detectives," he said, approaching us with outstretched arms and a welcoming smile reminiscent of an Evangelist. "Sorry to keep you both waiting. Lots to do when building an empire," he smiled, shaking our hands, then waving us to follow him.

We took our seats and, knowing our time was limited, got right to the point.

"Mr. Nessbach, we are here to—" I began.

"Elgin," he interrupted. "Please call me Elgin. No need to be formal. I'm happy to help in any way I can. I've done so much for the men and women in blue for the past several years."

"Good enough, Elgin," I said. "We're here to discuss your relationship with Ms. Meredith Johansen."

"Lovely gal. Really bright. Amazing talent," he said, nodding repeatedly. "Well, *had*."

"Right," Stuart politely smiled. "And what was your relationship?"

Elgin's expression looked like he had been asked to guess the circumference of Saturn.

"Well, it was on and off. And by that I mean we were off while the show was going well, but then were on when the numbers started to dip. And funding for her pet project wasn't coming in as quickly as she'd hoped. Also, she was a bit of a depressive. I think they call it manic."

"What makes you say that?" I asked.

Elgin made a roller coaster hand gesture with one hand, then whistled —making a spinning gesture to the side of his head with his other.

"Meaning?"

"Meaning just that. She was up and down, always emotional, always needing everything her way, and just—" he continued, pinching his thumb and index finger, "A wee bit crazy."

"And that didn't work for you?" Stuart asked.

"Does it work for anyone?" he said, making a stupid face. Looking at Stuart's hand, he continued, "Right, you're married, then you completely understand. Me? No thanks. No ball and chain here. Who needs to worry about losing half my money when life gets complicated?"

He looked at his watch, then to Ms. Beaumont who nodded.

"Are we about finished?" he asked.

Stuart ignored the question and looked at me.

"Elgin, did you ever hit Ms. Johansen?" I asked.

"WHAT? Absolutely not! I cared for her. Deeply. And as I said, she had many admirable qualities. Hell, my mother even adored her," he said, pinching his eyes at the bridge of his nose, then mumbling, "And she doesn't like anyone."

"So the three of you...had a relationship."

With slanted eyes, he said, "What are you implying, Detective?"

"Just asking if you three were close. As in, were you thinking of marrying her and asking for Mother's approval? Or were you perhaps—"

"I don't need my mother's approval, Detective," he interrupted. "I'm a very wealthy and powerful man and can do whatever, with whomever, and wherever I desire. To put it simply, when she learned I wouldn't be pushed around just because she wanted something from me—not my heart might I add—then I saw the writing on the wall and exited stage right."

My partner and I shared a glance.

Elgin must have taken the pause as a sign we were done and stood. "Now, if you'll excuse me."

Stuart pointed to the chair. "Sit down, Mr. Nessbach. Please. I have just another question or two and we will be on our way. Then you can return to doing, uh, all your *powerful* things," he said, flipping a page in his notebook.

Elgin snorted but obeyed.

"Where were you on Sunday night?"

Evidently, it was time to play the drama card again because he stared at the ceiling like the answer was spray painted up there. He methodically stroked his scant outline of a goatee.

"Let's see. Oscar night. Yes, I was hosting an Oscar party at my BelAir home."

Without looking up from his notes, Stuart said, "And I'm assuming someone can corroborate—"

"About 35 corroborations," he said, snapping his fingers toward his assistant. Without missing a beat, she opened the cover of an iPad, swiped the screen several times, and handed it to him.

"As you'll see from this invite list, it was a veritable *plethora* of celebrities," he gloated.

In the time it took Stuart and me to read the document, Ms. Beaumont had left the room, printed a copy, and returned.

With a smirk across his face as big as his ego, he said, "Anything else, Detectives?"

38

ROYAL BLUFF

Our time had run out, or better yet, the Elgin lead felt decidedly cold, so we returned to *The Hollywood Mole* where we would follow up with our favorite prime suspect.

Evidently, we arrived at the same time their show planning session was about to begin. I spotted Julia King, and as she was heading our way, it took her one second to recognize me, two seconds to make a plan of action, and another three seconds to whisper something to her assistant. I felt pretty sure her exit speech wouldn't take much longer than four seconds. Either way, I was prepared.

"That's the phoniest smile I've ever seen," I said from the corner of my mouth.

Stuart coughed, "*Bullshit.*"

Thankfully, she was not close enough to catch it, and within seconds she greeted me by taking an elbow and ever-so-slowly pushing me backwards toward the door.

"It's so nice to see you but we're just now heading into a really important meeting, one I can't miss nor be late for, so if you don't mind could you please pretty please either call me later come back later or leave whatever information you have or need from me with my assistant and thank you ever so much."

She literally said that in one breath. Although her smile was pleasant, her insincerity made me want to throw up.

"Ms. King, all I need is literally *fifteen seconds*. That's all, and I promise I'll be out of this building, in my car, and across town in a blink. Give me that and you'll never have to deal with me again."

"Really?" She said, genuinely shocked.

"This week, anyway."

Her fake smile instantly dissolved into a sad frown. She waved the small entourage following on her heels to go into the conference room, adding, "Start the opening bullshit, give me two minutes and I'll be there, but do *not* start without me."

Turning, she reapplied the same phony smile and waved Stuart and me over to the seating area. "Okay, fifteen seconds, huh? I'd like to see that."

I wanted to punch the snob right off her overdone face.

"Thank you. This is going to be super simple. Hell, it'll be the quickest decision you'll make today."

"Doubt that," she snipped.

I ignored her. "And I'll make it even easier by creating a multiple choice of only two options."

The heavy sigh that blew from her nicotine-laced lungs nearly knocked me over. I tried not to wince.

"Let's hear it."

"Choice A: Allow us to view the security footage from your building —to include the front, rear, and loading dock cameras covering the last ten days. Or, Choice B: We go to a judge who just so happens to be LA's most powerful judge—one who would *love* to help us out—and we'll return with a search warrant and shut this place down and take our sweet-ass time wasting your prime time by going through every piece of footage in this entire building," I responded with a smirk.

Watching blood vessels pulsate on either side of her temples made me happy. The flinching jaw sent me over the moon.

"Okay, fine. I'll have someone meet you here. Just give me twenty minutes and you'll—"

"Five. No telling what could *accidentally* happen in just twenty little minutes."

I could tell she wanted to punch me in the face—as much as I did her. I also knew we were walking a very thin rope, but Stuart felt it was smart to put two alpha females against one another.

"Fine. Five minutes. Now, I *must* get to this meeting. And my assistant told me you were also looking for Mr. Shapiro. Well, as much as you'd like to harass him, today won't work. He's on location in Malibu, directing a sit-down with, well, I'm not at liberty to say—except they're a very famous couple who steal the headlines all the time."

"Riveting, I'm sure," I snarked.

She ignored me. "You'll have to catch him another time."

"Oh, we'll make the time," I said to Stuart. "In fact, perhaps we'll head there after we finish here."

"Sounds like a plan," Stuart followed along.

I wasn't sure what her sudden look of fear was about, but I had my suspicions.

"So! Give us access to that footage, and I promise we'll be out in a blink. Girl Scout Promise," I said, holding up three fingers.

"Honor," she said, shaking her head and walking away.

"What?" I asked.

She stopped, spun, and said, "It's Girl Scout's *Honor*," then turned and left.

"That went well, huh?" Stuart said quietly, still facing the conference room and giving the eye to some of the dimmer bulbs in the group.

"Just glad she didn't go with Option B. Most judges would tell me to go fuck myself—for obvious reasons."

"And your Dad?" Stuart chuckled, "What'd he say?"

"Maybe not that. But close."

―――――――

As PROMISED, we were escorted to a production studio library where a short dork with long hair introduced us to a cold room with a wall of machines. He flew through a short list of Do's and Don'ts; then after a thorough, albeit speedy explanation pertaining to which dials to turn and which buttons not to push, he looked at our glazed eyes and said, "What the hell, I'll do it."

An hour later, and going back a full two weeks, we found nothing of any importance. In fact, the video we had seen earlier was nowhere to be found.

"Odd, huh?" Stuart asked.

"Convenient's a word I'd use."

"What say we head out and shake our next suspect's tree?"

"Nothing to lose; everything to gain."

39

HEIR JORDAN

Stuart and I headed to Century City to meet with our next suspect Grey Jordan, a life coach and motivational expert. His office was in a mid-rise tower in the shadow of the Westfield Shopping Center at the corner of Constellation Boulevard and Avenue of the Stars.

The office was handsome and understated. Walls were adorned with photos of him standing with former Presidents Ronald Reagan, Clinton, and Obama. In several, he shared the stage with the likes of Tony Robbins, Sir Richard Branson, and Deepak Chopra. Other photos showed him embraced by several single name personalities including Cher, Madonna, and Oprah. On another wall, bookshelves were covered with a wide array of self-help books, motivational mantras penned in glossy frames, and a variety of statues, awards, and plaques.

What instantly caught my attention was the smooth, nearly seductive way he approached us. He seemed to glide as he walked. His voice was as mellow as old Scotch, his skin the color of caramel, and his eyes a bright green.

This was also the first time I ever recalled seeing Stuart even slightly intimidated. While they were roughly the same height, it was obvious Grey was in much better shape. He also had a polish Stuart would never have. Conversely, I would bet dollars to donuts Grey did not have half the heart of my partner.

Grey immediately put the room at ease, asking his secretary to hold all calls before inviting us into his office. She took coffee orders, then disappeared with a pleasant smile.

"Please come in and make yourselves comfortable, Detectives," his baritone voice purred. "Let's sit over here and relax," he motioned.

Here was a cozy corner of low modern couches wrapped in soft leather and surrounded by oversized crystal lamps with black shades and soft light. The windows looked out onto Santa Monica Boulevard—nothing fancy, but lots of daylight. The vibe was sophisticated, and we made small talk while his secretary served us coffee in china cups, then disappeared again with a smile.

"Now, how may I be of service?" he asked, looking at us directly.

"We appreciate your time and will keep it short. We're investigating the murder of Meredith Johansen," Stuart said with a matter of fact tone.

Grey's forehead creased and his eyes narrowed in a display of minor shock.

"I thought it was...*suicide*," he whispered.

"That was the original report," I said, "However, thanks to new evidence, it's clearly a case of homicide."

Looking away, he said, "I see."

"Mr. Jordan, what was your relationship with Ms. Johansen?" Stuart asked.

Listening, I scanned the awards on the wall behind him.

"Please call me Grey. And it was amicable. Close, actually. She was a wonderful young woman and truthfully, I *really* cared for her. And to your point, we saw one another for a period of time."

I watched for emotional triggers as he wiped his eyes. Taking a deep breath, he forced a smile.

"How long would you say that was?" I asked. "And how recently?"

"We dated for about three months. The first time. Took a couple of months break because of our work schedules, then dated for another three month period shortly thereafter."

"And—"

"And that was...recently. In fact, the last time I saw her was about three weeks ago. We were at a benefit in West Hollywood to raise money for a suicide crisis center. It's a program developed by a renowned therapist here in town. Darius Tercel."

I tuned out for a split second, trying to place the event.

"Do you know Dr. Tercel?" Grey asked.

"We've met him several times," said Stuart.

"Then you know what a tremendous humanitarian, he is."

"Yes, and back to your periods of relationship, would you say Meredith could be described as more happy or sad?"

Grey's frown eased. "While she could drop into periods of melancholy, overall she was a surprisingly bright and upbeat woman—full of hope and enthusiasm."

"Would you describe her as being surprisingly dramatic in say... private spaces?" I asked.

This got a surprised look from both men.

"Guys, sometimes you have to cut to the chase when trying to solve a murder. If that sounded crass, please forgive me."

He suppressed a chuckle. "Detective, while I'm a big personality— more on stage than in life—I'm private and a pretty conservative guy. The bravado of self-help guru can often be a lot of self-promotion. That said, all my relationships, and there have been several, have tabloids referring to me as a playboy."

"Speaking of, I'm guessing it was Hugh Hefner's Mansion where you, Meredith, and a gaggle of half-naked Hollywood celebs gathered for... well, *whatever* it was."

"Yes, it was the Playboy Mansion. And it was...a little crazy. You may be interested to know her Grace Kelly appearance and demeanor wasn't the same woman I knew behind closed doors."

Stuart fidgeted and said, "Grey, we're not here to peel away your private life. What I think Detective Norelli may be getting at is perhaps Meredith had a promiscuity shared by many. And we are assuming *someone* didn't like that fact."

"Understood. And that's exactly what I meant. When I learned Meredith was sharing her talents with a number of men, well, it wasn't for me."

"But Grey—and forgive me for being so bold—isn't it true you've actually been linked to number of high profile celebrities who are, how do I put it—"

"Promiscuous troublemakers?"

"That's what I was getting at. In fact, weren't you recently accused of physical abuse to the rap star—"

"Bullshit!"

The outburst caught both of us off guard.

"Sorry," he blushed, adjusting his sleeves. "But frankly, it burns me up the way the *press* eats celebrities for breakfast. And their lies become the truth. Just because they report it."

Stuart and I stole a glance when he said, "We completely understand. And you're certainly not on trial here. We're simply looking into a short list of people who were involved with Meredith—in many different capacities."

Grey held up both hands. "Right, right. I understand. And I know you aren't. I just want to be sure you know everything."

"And we appreciate your candor, Grey," I said.

"Look, I enjoy turning it up, but the thought of her doing the same with many other men, well, frankly, I couldn't take it any longer." He stared at his hands. "I figured if I wasn't enough...it would be best to go our separate ways."

WE SPENT a short time climbing out from his private world, discussing his days with the Lakers. I could not help but mention reading somewhere about his nickname *50 Shades*. Fortunately, that gave us all a good laugh.

Catching Stuart eyeball his watch, I wrapped our conversation by asking his whereabouts on the night of the murder.

"I was speaking in Manhattan at a motivational event. It was just me and a few thousand people," he winked.

And with that we stood to leave. He gave us both a copy of his recent bestseller, *Start With Me: Uncovering the Real You in a False World*, and we made our way into the lobby where a poster caught my attention. It was the event he mentioned earlier. As Stuart was having him autograph his copy, I examined the poster.

"Excuse me, Grey, but didn't you say you were speaking at this event?" I asked, pointing to the poster. "Last weekend, right?"

He looked up from signing. "Correct."

"But that was a prior weekend—as in the one *before* this past weekend."

His expression went from pleasant smile to deep frown. "Oh, right. I'm sorry. It *was* last weekend. I travel so much—they all run together."

"Understandable," I smiled. "So, you were back here—"

"I got back here, what," he stopped, turning to his secretary who was entering the room.

With no expression, she said, "You returned late Sunday night because on Monday morning we had that luncheon with the Women's Coalition group, remember?"

He held her gaze for what felt like an uncomfortably long moment before he snapped his fingers. "It completely slipped my mind."

WE WERE EXITING the elevator into the garage when Stuart broke the silence. "I was digging the brother until you mentioned the discrepancy. Then...I don't know...something seemed to shift," he said, unlocking the car.

We got in and sat for a minute before I said, "Yeah, but does he strike you as a killer?"

"Doubtful. But then..." he tapped the book, "Sometimes people have to uncover the *real* you first—in this big ol' false world."

"*Word.*"

40

SONNY SIXPACK

In a city with more personal trainers per square mile than any other in the country, it was hard to find one who did not brag about a *secret sauce*, a *workout like none other*, or a *secret to unleash your inner beast*.

In Los Angeles, Sonny "Six-Pack" Hoffman was the #1 Personal Fitness Trainer for the past two years and he lived what he preached. At 48 but looking 38, the Hollywood legend got as much press about his constantly-denied nip-tucks as his near-perfect physique—6'0" and 195 pounds of perfectly sculpted muscle—made him the envy of nearly everyone his age. His clients were actors, studio execs, doctors, surgeons, therapists, bankers, and the like who all paid exorbitant membership fees both per year and per session.

We arrived at Sonny's home perched above Highway 1 in Malibu with a breathtaking view. Sitting squarely in one of the tiniest spots in the area above the Malibu Pier, The Surfrider Malibu, and Casa Escobar, his incredible place fostered pangs of envy in people.

Pulling up the long driveway, we saw the symbols of wealth: an enormous pool, tennis courts, a putting green and bocce ball court, and perfectly manicured lawns complete with organic gardens. Perhaps most impressive was the 180 degree view of the prime beachfront. The opposing 180 degree view of Pepperdine to the north and acres of unpopulated canyons to the south was equally stunning.

Getting out of the car, I tried not to drag my jaw on the perfectly granulated gravel driveway.

"Yeah, wow."

"No, shit," Stuart mumbled.

Across the driveway sat what appeared to be a studio and workout facility. A sign over the entrance read, *Temple of Fitness.* We would later learn it was the trademark for all Sonny Hoffman brands that included fitness, food, clothing, books, and TV shows.

Parked in the circular driveway was a candy-apple red 812 Ferrari. I couldn't help but gawk at what most gearheads knew was the highest performance car Ferrari ever made. The V-12 engine confirmed its moniker, *Superfast.*

Behind me I heard Stuart clear his throat and turned to see Sonny climbing out from his infinity edge pool. A shapely assistant was in tow, but I couldn't pry my eyes from his chiseled chest and abs.

I whispered, "Hello, gorgeous," as we approached him toweling off.

He reached out and shook my hand first. His crystal blue eyes sparkled as he said, "You must be Detective Norelli."

"Yes, it is. I mean, I am. Nice to meet you. Mr. Hoffman."

"Sonny, please," he smiled, holding my stare before turning to Stuart.

"And Detective Brown? Welcome to my temple of fitness."

We followed him toward an umbrella-covered table poolside. When the water stilled, I noticed how the letters S and H—painted with jewel-toned tiles on the bottom—overlapped to look like a dollar sign.

He insisted on us having a drink and, turning to his assistant, ordered an organic jasmine and ginger enhanced green tea for Stuart, and his signature *Clean Temple* for me.

"Let's hydrate your lovely skin with vital nutrients from apple, cucumber, green pepper, orange and aloe vera juice so you'll look and feel refreshed."

While we waited for our *Temple Restorations,* we made small talk about the neighborhood (pricey), proximity to the ocean (duh), and the length of the drive (insane).

As drinks arrived, I began. "Sonny, as I'm sure you've surmised by now, we're investigating the murder of Meredith Johansen and we—"

"Just tragic," he said, shaking his head in slow motion.

"Yes, it is. We've learned from many of our interviews what a talented woman she was."

"Only one of the very best. Kind, considerate, and beautiful with so much to offer," he said, pinching the end of his perfect nose.

"We have also found," I continued, "She was a very popular woman. And her calendar was filled with all sorts of events, from benefits and fundraisers to news and tabloid coverage."

"And don't forget the documentary she had been working on for I don't know how long," he said. "That was a significant accomplishment."

"Her same calendar was filled with a vast number of names—both men and women who we feel helped bring her vision to life," I said. "Among those influential people is *you.*"

"Yes," he smiled. "She was well liked by many."

Stuart stopped mid-sip. "More than just liked. I—rather *we,*" he tossed a chin toward me, "Think it's more like obsessed."

I leaned forward. "Would you share with us your relationship with Meredith?"

Placing his palms together like he was praying, he took a deep breath. "Yes, I was involved with her. She was among the best souls I've had the pleasure of meeting while living here."

"Living here," I waved toward the property, "Or here in Los Angeles?"

"Los Angeles. I've only been here for about five years," he said, looking skyward. "Yes, five actually, because it was when I first met Meredith. She had moved here from San Diego where she was a host on one of those magazine shows. We met at a function and I was instantly taken with her. What's the best way to say it? Her naïveté and seductiveness were magic," he smiled. "One might think they're two different things, but truly it's the synergistic combination of two personality traits that made her so alluring."

"We've heard a similar sentiment from others," Stuart said.

"I imagine so," he looked away.

"Where were you this past Sunday, Sonny?" I asked.

"Morning or evening," he said, turning to me with gentle eyes.

"Both," I smiled.

"Let's see. I had just returned from the Bay Area that morning. Caught an early flight after spending all day Friday in meetings. Most of the day Saturday was spent at a winery in Napa. I'm working on releasing an organic wine later this year. In fact, Meredith and I would often jump a quick flight for the weekend."

"When was that?" Stuart asked, flipping a page in his pad. "Or better yet, the last time you two made that trip?"

He picked up his phone and swiped several times. "Let's see, yes, just last weekend. I couldn't recall if it was last weekend or the one before. I wanted to get her opinion of a white grape we were considering. She loved white wine."

I held his gaze.

"Yes, last Friday. We went up early, spent some time in Mill Valley before heading up to Napa for the rest of the day on Saturday. We were on the second morning flight on Sunday."

Stuart asked, "And Sunday night?"

"Yes, I was actually here. Catching my breath and preparing for a hectic week. We have a new TV show I'm creating. So many details..." he trailed off.

"And was anyone with you?"

He was quiet for a moment. I couldn't read his face.

"No. Needed some time to recharge. Gather my thoughts and such," he smiled.

Stuart said, "So you were here. Alone."

A nod.

"Can anyone vouch for that?" I asked.

For the first time since we arrived, Sonny's face changed. It was not a full-blown frown, but certainly less placid.

"Well, since my three chocolate Labradoodles were at the Malibu Dog Spa, and my housekeeper has Sundays off, I decided to keep it chill here at TOF."

My eyebrows scrunched.

"Temple Of Fitness."

"As a couple, had you and Meredith been having any problems of late?" Stuart asked while I locked on his body language.

Sonny shifted from facing me to facing Stuart. "Not really. I mean, nothing more than, you know, the everyday things couples go through."

"Like what?" I asked.

He shifted back to face me. "You know, your schedule is crazy, but mine is crazier, can we do it my way just for now. Or, I know you're under a great deal of pressure, but don't take that angst out on me. Especially the kind that comes from her workplace and the people..." he fidgeted, "Some of them can be particularly troublesome."

"How's that?" I smiled.

He sighed. "There's one person—well, actually two—who seemed to know exactly how to push her buttons. Whereupon she would come to this nice zen space and just *vomit* angst, anger, and anxiety."

No one said anything.

"It got tiresome to be honest," he said quietly. Breathing heavier, he added, "And personally, I couldn't stand it. Her work was okay. At best. But she could have done *so* much better," he shook his head. "Higher quality."

Stuart and I held our collective breaths.

"I told her a year ago to dump that station and the *loser* of a boyfriend…Shapiro. What an idiot."

I couldn't help but grin. He caught it.

"What? You've met him?"

"Oh yeah, we've met. And you're right. Piece of work."

Stuart closed his notepad, drained the last of his drink, then wiped his mouth. "Well, Mr. Hoffman, we certainly appreciate your time."

Sonny stood. "Think nothing of it."

Stuart remained seated and said, "Just one more question before we go."

Sonny sat back down. "Sure, what is it?"

Clearing his throat, he said, "We have to ask everyone associated with Meredith the same thing, so, I'll ask you. Did you have *anything* to do with Meredith's recent demise?"

Sonny's face went dark. "Are you asking me, Detective Brown, if I *murdered* Meredith? Is that what you and Detective Norelli…" he said, turning his attention to me, "Are asking me? Someone who has done so much for people? For our community? Someone of my integrity who wants nothing more than to see people thrive and to live healthy, prosperous lives? Is that what you're asking me?"

"Sorry, but yes, that's exactly what I'm asking."

I smiled, "Please."

Letting out a big breath, he said, "No. I did not. I cared too deeply for her to ever bring her any harm," he said, making the sign of the cross. "May she rest in peace."

WALKING TO THE CAR, I cut a sideways glance to Stuart and smirked, "I didn't see him being Catholic."

"Yeah, I figured more of a Southern Baptist vibe," he grinned.

HEADING SOUTH ON HIGHWAY 1, I rolled down my window and let the ocean breeze fill my lungs and clear my head. Since we only had his word for it, we weren't eager to let him off the hook. However, given his reputation as a stand-up guy and a professional in the community who actually gave a great deal to people, we'd have to find more evidence. At the moment, he didn't *feel* right for it, but those are the ones I tended to keep an eye on.

"Did you see all the cameras around that spread," I asked Stuart.

"Yeah. I counted ten just along the part we had access to."

"Really? I had nine."

"Right, but did you see the tiny one in the umbrella just above our heads?"

"Your eye for detail trumps mine, partner."

He snorted, "Nah, yours is tight—that is when you're not undressing our suspects."

I whipped my head toward him, "I was NOT!"

"Yeah, keep telling yourself that," he chuckled. "No wonder you weren't in a hurry to leave."

"Whatever," I said, trying to hide a grin.

I thought it was the time to check in with McCloud, so I rang to ask if he'd check out Sonny's surveillance system. He asked if he needed to go there or could do it from the office. I suggested that he go to the garage, book an undercover van, and run out to Malibu to sniff around.

Less than ninety minutes later, he rang to tell me he had skimmed through the last several days of video and didn't find much. However, he had learned a few interesting facts about Sonny.

First, he loves to skinny dip late at night. Second, he enjoys a hearty session of masturbating in his four-person jacuzzi just before bed. Third, it appears Mr. Healthy Juice also enjoys a less-than-healthy Scotch just before bedtime.

While I was vicariously enjoying the behind-the-scenes secrets, I had other demands, so I asked him to cut to the chase and tell me what Sonny was doing on the night in question.

"It's crazy, but he was asleep in bed by 10 and literally didn't move until 6 the next morning."

"Okay then—"

"No. Norelli, I mean, I ran the video at hyper speed and he did not... move...a *single* muscle...for *eight* hours. It was weird."

Ringing off, I made a note to keep a special eye on Sonny.

41

FAMILY DRAMA

B ack at my desk, I sipped a coffee while flipping through Stuart's notes, cross referencing them with databases on my computer. Since the only person at *The Hollywood Mole* who would give us the time of day was Ms. Everest, I'd been on the phone working my sweet side with a vengeance, trying to see what else I could glean about our prime suspect.

Bobby Eugene Shapiro was not the nice Jewish young man his newer parents had hoped he would become. According to his rap sheet—literally longer than my arm—he had seen nothing but trouble in his relatively young life. It made me wonder what level of talent it took to get on the inside track. I had always heard the real players in Hollywood liked to work with people who were nice, kind, and on time. I doubted he fit any of those bills.

According to HR, he had been written up a handful of times since coming to work at *The Hollywood Mole* nearly four years ago. All reports were made by women. All counts were based on either sexual innuendo, sexual language, or double-entendre conversations—nothing physical, but certainly harassing. As I read the notes from two different HR reps, I noticed three of the four women—after follow-ups were completed—declined to make any comments.

Checking college records, I learned he and another young man, Stanley Jansen, were accused of raping a girl on campus during their hazing week. Charges were dropped when the girl came forward and went on record saying she consented to having sex with Bobby. Rumors were prominent that he was labeled "a wild man" while Jansen was known as an angry racist. Not only did Jansen lose his scholarship, but all NFL teams rescinded their tentative offers.

Legal sources close to Bobby said the initial report stated Anne Latimer was violently and repeatedly raped by the two named men and potentially two more; however, those additional names never made it into the records. One person with whom I made a connection, told me the other two young men went on to enjoy full-ride scholarships, eventually entering the world of professional sports.

The most intriguing find was how Bobby was adopted his junior year of high school. It was the adoptive father who was the good guy and the one who had greased paths for the man I see as a genuine Neanderthal. Bobby's birth father, on the other hand, ruled a troubled and eventually broken home.

"Whatcha working on?" Stuart asked, startling me as he entered. Sitting on the corner of my desk, he shoved a buttermilk biscuit into his mouth.

"Shapiro," I said with zero emotion.

I spun a folder in his direction. "Looks like our boy's a bad one. At least I understand his temper better now."

He began licking his fingers, "Yeah, but doesn't give him the right to hit a woman," he said.

"For real," I frowned.

"Never," he said.

Lick.

"Ever," he added.

Lick.

I added a printout copy of what I had discovered and handed it to him —along with a napkin.

Flipping through it, he whistled before slurping the end of his coffee. "Boy's got anger issues."

"No doubt."

"Bet your Doctor Tercel could help him get a handle."

"Not a bad idea," I shrugged.

The word *weapons* pinged the back of my mind, so I pulled up Google for a quick search. The browser picked up my location and instantly provided stores and clubs. One in particular caught my eye. It was a hunting store and club called Straight & Arrow. Reading further, I learned groups of people on both the Westside and The Valley—up near North-ridge and Valencia—met to share their passion for compound bows and hunting knives.

According to the article, it was a place for people who enjoyed "the silent kill."

Scanning images on the front page of their website, I found a large photograph and a long article on one of their elite members Bobby Shapiro who had been shooting compound bows for nearly a dozen years. In fact, it looked like he was an expert marksman with a long list of achievements. Reading on, I saw he was also an avid collector of hunting knives—and straight razors.

"Stuart, look at this," I said, turning the monitor.

"Okay, bows, arrows, knives…" he stopped. "Yup, there's our boy."

"Wild, huh?"

"And looks like he's a real marksman," he mumbled. "Look at that collection of blades."

"Yeah, a regular Daniel Boone," I stood to look over his shoulder.

Then my stomach tightened.

Taking over the mouse, I scrolled back up the page to find a photo of three men standing next to one another. According to the caption below, they were sharing bragging rights.

The headline read: *Local marksmen share their impressive collection of rare and antique blades.*

"Look," I whispered, tapping the screen. "That's the guy I went out with. The one who busted my face."

"You're kidding me."

"Steve Owen."

42

SUCK IT

The precinct office buzzed with ringing phones and murmuring voices in nearby cubicles. People came in and out of our area—their shoes echoing off the marble floors in the hallway—as Stuart and I stared at one another.

"A *second* blade collector?" he asked.

"Looks like it. And even though he busted me up on our first date, I was starting to like him."

Stuart stood and stretched, rolling his neck. "As far as I'm concerned? I think we have enough to bring him in."

"Who?"

"What do you mean, who?" He said, snapping his head toward me. "Who're you talking about?"

"Steve?"

"*No*, Bobby."

"Of course. Just a shame I'm going to have to bounce on Steve."

"Are you losing your mind?"

"Probably."

Stuart walked to a cubicle two desks over and took a lollipop from the corner of Josh Preston's desk. A note attached to the box read: *Suck it for a buck*. Taking the sucker and unwrapping it, Stuart tossed a single and Preston tossed him a nod, not looking up from his computer screen.

"Can you just keep it in your pants…" Stuart asked between licks as he returned. "At least long enough for us to get things in order?"

We laughed.

"You know he'll be coming back for more," he mumbled.

"Yeah, but maybe I've had it with the crazies, Stuart. Time I find a nice guy and—"

He gave me that look again. "Settle down?" He tried not to laugh.

Shaking my head, I punched him in the arm as I passed him. "We'll finish this in a minute. I gotta pee," I said, scooting down the hall.

"WHAT'S UP, MCCLOUD," I asked, entering his jam-packed office.

"S'up?" he said, glancing in my direction, but not changing his expression.

"Geez, you guys ever throw anything out?" I asked, looking at racks of research and a pile of files in the shared contractors' office.

Without looking up, he grunted, "Do I come into your home and tell you how to arrange your life?"

I plopped beside him like his new best friend. "Just wanted to see if you'd discovered anything that could shed new light on our story."

He let out a deep breath, pushed his glasses onto the top of his head, and spun his swivel chair in my direction.

"Let's see. If I recall, I cracked her cloud—giving you full access to her Mac account. Then I unlocked her phone—giving you full access to all her calendar and photos, which I seem to recall your saying was going to be extremely helpful."

"Absolutely. Thing is you told me you were going to actually *give* me the phone after you ran through the—as you said—proper channels."

I let that hang.

"Right," he said. "Guess I forgot."

"Or, *maybe* you were dragging your feet. Taking time to duplicate a few things? Maybe *sell* some of the photos to—I don't know—outside sources? Something like that?"

As hard as he tried, there was no hiding the look of fear that blanketed his face. He spun around, typed a few keys, then said, "Be right back."

Hearing him sprint down the hall, I took the opportunity to snoop. Moving his mouse, the monitor awoke; however, his screensaver came on, asking for a password. I took out my smartphone and snapped a photo of an open file. It had some names and addresses I recognized. Before I had the chance to look at anything else, I heard him running down the hall and, with just enough time to spin away, I pretended to be reading messages on my phone.

"Okay, first of all," he began, trying to catch his breath. "I did, uh, borrow some of the photos. I didn't think all that much about it being a big deal."

"But it's part of an *investigation*," I said, tapping an app on my phone.

"I know," he replied, lowering his voice and looking around. "It's just I don't get paid that much, and well, some of her photos could—especially given her current situation—literally pay off my school debt."

I understood where he was coming from and was sure if I were in his place, I might do similarly.

"Please don't say anything. I'll do *anything* to keep this job."

That's when an idea came to me.

"Detective?"

I looked away to let him sweat and added head shaking for good measure.

"Do you think we could, you know, keep this between you and me?"

"I don't know. This is some serious shit. You know what would happen if—"

"Yes, of course I do," he blurted, before lowering his voice. "I'd be bounced in an instant. And never be able to work with the LAPD again. Maybe not *any* law enforcement agency."

He was sweating now. Literally. A thin film formed on his forehead as he repeatedly licked his lips.

He was a good guy, had great promise, was smart as hell, and was driven like a machine. I felt for him. Plus, I knew we could work together.

"Do you realize this is one of the biggest cases to come along in a long time? I mean, it's a career changer—for *me*. I can't take any chances of something going wonky."

"Detective Norelli, it won't. Seriously, we can work something out. You know I do good work, have always played ball with you and Detective Brown, and love, I mean *loooove* my job. And there is no f'n way I can afford to get fired."

Knowing his anxiety was high, I was sure he would take any offer to keep his job.

"Okay. I have an idea. But it's going to take..." I crossed the room and closed the door. "It's going to take a ton of trust—on both of our parts."

BY THE TIME I returned to the office, Stuart had fully examined the Straight & Arrow website, contacted the owner, learned of the manufacturer of razors matching the one found in Meredith's hand, and made an appointment for us to meet with the owner. His nose was buried in his notepad when I returned.

"What tells me you were doing more than just peeing?" he asked, not looking up.

"I know we're partners, but isn't that just a bit *too* personal?" I asked, reapplying lip gloss.

"What were you doing...bugging McCloud?"

"How'd you—?"

"Find anything new?"

"Just photos and schedules and lots of juicy details," I said, taking a phone from my bag to wave it in his face.

He instantly snatched it. "When were you going to share?"

"I am. Right now."

He swiped the screen through dozens of photos, mumbling, "Kid's a genius." Scanning photos, he added, "And her? Truly beautiful."

43

STRAIGHT ARROW

The Straight & Arrow was an enormous sporting goods store in The Valley at the corner of Ventura and Sepulveda Boulevards. It sat in the shadow of Sherman Oaks Galleria and directly beneath the concrete spaghetti of the 405 and 101. The sign over the entrance read, *Largest Store on the West Coast for Bows, Blades, Arrows & Ammunition.*

The size and sound of the space was overwhelming.

"Looks like Cabela's had sex with Bass Pro Shop."

"You," Stuart grinned. "Didn't know you frequented those places."

"It's called having a father and a brother who loved hunting anything that moved. Who're we seeing, anyway?"

He checked his trusty pad.

"Jonathan Hubble."

"Copy that."

A buttoned-up kid with an enormous smile approached us with a badge that read, *Walter from Sioux City, Iowa.* He looked more like one of those Jehovah's Witnesses who trolled neighborhoods asking people if they knew where they went when they died.

To the Coroner, I used to say.

"Hello, Detectives. I'm Walter from—"

"Sioux City. We see that," I grinned. "I'm Detective Norelli. This is my partner, Detective Brown. You two spoke earlier today."

"Yes, of course. Mr. Hubble is expecting you. Right this way."

Three minutes—but feeling like three miles later—we entered the General Manager's office, a likewise unusually large and overly decorated room with all brands of non-ballistic weaponry. A wall of television screens monitored the showroom floor, loading docks, employees cafeteria, all entrances—front, back and sideways—as well as the rooftop.

"Welcome, Detectives, welcome. What can I do you for?" he asked, waving us to have a seat in the two oversized Adirondack chairs flanking a desk that appeared to be a fallen California redwood. It was the size of a picnic table.

"Is that real?" I pointed to an enormous compound bow hanging on the wall behind his desk.

"What's that, little lady?" Hubble said, spinning around to look. "Oh, that's what they call promotional *swag*. Eye candy, if you will. The one time it was fired, we launched an arrow 'bout the size of a javelin. It was a demonstration for one of our retailers in Northridge. Damn thing flew a quarter mile 'fore landing in a field. Took two men to remove it from the dirt. Mounted it up there the next day. Been there ever since."

"It's as big as a Mini Cooper," I chuckled.

"Yes ma'am," he said, busting a belly laugh, "It's a big'un, all right."

Stuart got us started, "Mr. Hubble, we're kinda short on time—"

"Hell's bells, Detectives, y'all call me Jonathan. And I understand. People say I talk too much. I'll shut up and let you get to asking your questions. Just know that I'm happy to help you in any way I can. So tell me then, what's on your mind? Go right ahead. Got all the time in the world for the men...and women," he nodded toward me, "In blue. Let's hear it."

"We're looking at a couple things," Stuart began, taking out his phone and pulling up some photos. "Do you know this man? We pulled it from your website."

Hubble looked intently, pursed his lips, and said, "I see that. Yessiree, that's Mr. Bobby Shapiro. Accepting an award, right here in our store. He's one of our biggest clients. Bought a *lot* of his toys from us. Big spender. Great shooter. And has one *helluva* collection."

"Would you say he's a responsible collector and marksman?" I asked.

"Absotootley. A fine example of our best customer. And a good man in the community too, you know. A director at that TV show, *Hollywood Mole*. Wife and I love that program. Never miss it."

"Mr. Hubble, see the fellow next to him," Stuart said. "Do you know him, too?"

"Yeah, he's some Real Estate Construction developer or such. Helluva nice guy, but can be kinda short—with people, that is, not stature. 'Cuz, as you can see, he's a *big* fella."

You have no idea. "Short like how?"

He squinted at me. "Um, edgy? Anxious? Not a lot of patience. Almost like he's always in a rush to be somewhere."

"Understood. But he's also a collector, right?"

"Oh yeah. You know, a good many clients do a heap of collecting. It's maybe a guy thing, Ma'am, but once you find something you like, you just keep collecting 'em. One may be pretty, but there's always another one that comes along that may be even prettier. And well, you gotta have that one too!"

Stuart shared a chuckle with the misogynistic asshole, and I only pretended to join in. While I heard what he was saying, I was having a hard time believing the Steve I was getting to know could be a killer. Yes, he was gruff sometimes, but I just took it as his personality, his upbringing, and maybe his time on the Force.

Either way, the verdict was still out—for everyone.

It was not that I was sensitive to innuendo or to guys who thought they were clever hiding messages in conversations, but more how many men I've known were testosterone-stacked neanderthals whose primary focus was beer, boobs, wings, and sports—not necessarily in that order.

Hubble must have suddenly disliked my vibe because his body language quietly shifted and he began wrapping things up.

"Well, I should get back to work," he said, slapping his thighs and standing.

Stuart stood and said, "Reason we came out here was to look into the death of a young woman who worked at the station you mentioned earlier. We're following any leads whatsoever."

"Holy moly, you mean Miss Johansen. Yeah, wife and I heard about that. Man, she was some kind of beautiful. What a sad state of affairs taking her own life like that," Hubble said.

"Actually, we're pretty sure she was murdered," I said with more intensity than I intended.

As Hubble and Stuart looked at me, Stuart said, "It's not *completely* official, but we are following leads. If there's anything you can think of, please don't hesitate to call," he said, handing him a card.

"One last thing, Mr. Hubble. I have a father and brother who collected guns their whole life. And I suppose they both have a knife or two. But are knives, and in this case razors, something all men collect?"

"Hell yes, Ms. Norelli. If it's a weapon and it's valuable, it's a collectible. And while some gents prefer guns or bows and arrows, others like the steel."

I nodded, stared, and said nothing else.

Hubble stood there with a dumb look and a slack jaw, mindlessly tapping Stuart's card before pushing a button on his desk and saying, "Okay, good 'nuff. I'll be in touch. As needed. Thanks for stopping in. We'll see ya'll now."

Walter from Iowa quietly arrived and waved for us to follow him.

"Thanks for your time," I said, extending my hand.

Hubble looked at my hand, up my entire torso to my face, then slowly shook my hand. Silent, he sat and buried his face in his work.

Just as I was about to leave, my eyes fell on a picture frame on his desk. It was a photo of Steve standing with a man I did not recognize and one I did: Tercel.

My stomach dropped, and at the moment I was about to speak, Hubble looked up and frowned. "If there's nothing else, Detective, I really must get back to it."

I pretended to smile, and left.

44

SECRET STASH

Between the new construction of Studio A and several back-to-back meetings with investors, Bobby gave his entire crew the rest of the day off. When the team left to nosh at Chin Chin in Sunset Plaza, he left to run several errands before noshing on something entirely different later in the day.

He pulled into a bank lot and parked under the shade of a large euca-lyptus tree, shutting off the engine to take a minute to catch his breath. The morning had begun with hot sex with a soft-porn actress named Tandy. They met at a bar the night before where she told him she wanted to get into *real* television. She was stunningly beautiful but profoundly stupid, so although a great workout in the sack, she would never win the Director's Assistant position.

Those activities were followed by a workout with his pal Chris Banyon who left him with an enticing challenge to win some large money. Bobby liked challenges because he liked to win, but he enjoyed beating people even more—especially an egomaniacal prick like Chris.

After the workout, he showed up early at work, tasked with directing an interview with a start-up genius who was opening a film studio in The Valley—North Hollywood, not Silicon. The punk had entirely too much money and wanted to show off by building a shrine-slash-studio for himself.

Next, Bobby sat in on a meeting with a team working on a retrospective on Meredith's life that would cover her growing up in a small town outside Madison, Wisconsin, before following her news career and dream of becoming the next Sophia Coppola. What would not be revealed was her dark sexual persona—something very few knew about.

He entered the massive bank and was greeted by a pleasant yet nondescript banker who led him to a private room where he was left to peruse the contents of an oversized safety deposit box. Opening it, he found an envelope full of Meredith photographs. They were duplicated on an enclosed thumb drive that could upend several low-life socialites with dark proclivities.

He enjoyed having tangible reminders of his dark escapades, so several Blu-ray DVDs held hours of prime video where he was both director and participant.

As much of a pervert as his pal Chris Banyon was, Bobby knew of one video that would return his money from their earlier wager. Additional information would also net a handsome sum from the right buyer—a perfect recipe for future blackmail.

Scenes of Meredith's naked body brought a rush of memories of their first meeting. He was a new director at *The Hollywood Mole*—she, a new on-air talent. Bobby saw in her what most people would quickly learn: her street smarts superseded her beauty pageant looks.

He flipped through another stack of equally naughty photos. The event was a trade for services at a late night gathering of rich, spoiled playboys. In fact, the Playboy Mansion had been leased for a three-day bender of booze, babes, coke, and cocks. Attendees paid $100,000 for the invite-only, free-for-all event in the true Hollywood tradition.

The last item in the safety deposit box held a tiny professional GoPro camera, a small tool that would yield large results.

He was about to wrap up when he saw a photo with three recognizable faces, all of whom were handsome and rich. That was when Bobby got an adrenaline-thumping idea.

The first was Patrick McEvoy, aka Pretty Boy Pat, a well-known celebrity chef and newest taste of the town since his TV show *Hot Chef* had become a smash hit. Bobby directed the entire season and developed a friendship with Patrick because of their shared passions for hunting and women.

The second candidate was Beverly Hills therapist Darius Tercel, a savior to LA's self-absorbed, star-studded community. Those in the know were familiar with his helping up-and-coming actors who had reached their own down-and-out status. When he got them green lit, or in Holly-wood terms "back on their feet," it made him a hero of studio execs.

The last guy was not a Hollywood star, but he was a notorious ladies' man. As a former Marine turned Real Estate & Land Developer, he bought and built or fixed and flipped many of the mansions of the Hollywood elite. Steve Owen held a top position in one of many Who's Who lists. He and Bobby were pals, having met at a competition event at Straight & Arrow. Owen had the looks of a killer and the reputation of a ball-breaker. Bobby liked him.

If the police got any closer to linking Bobby to Meredith's murder, any one of these three would become the perfect target for his Plan B.

45

SPEED RACER

Bobby's Porsche 911 clocked zero-to-90 in less than five seconds as the light turned green at the corner of Fairfax and Santa Monica Boulevards. Anyone looking sideways would have only seen a yellow blur.

He called Chris to tell him of a more devilish idea—he was all ears. Bobby said his video would top anything Chris had seen, but it would cost him big. Bobby could practically feel his friend's hot breath pant over the phone. Before ringing off, he told Chris to expect the hard-on of his life inside the next 24.

The next call was to his assistant, asking her to locate contact info for his three blackmail candidates and forward to his private dropbox—*not* his phone. She agreed, knowing he had the same kind of blackmail material on her and could end her career if he wanted.

Then he called his attorney Andrew Jacobitz in Century City. Bobby told him they needed to talk. When Jacobitz said he was pushed for time, Bobby reminded Jacobitz of his debt to Bobby and he quickly agreed to meet.

Hanging up, Bobby got a call from a friend inside *The Hollywood Mole* saying the cops were looking for him again. He dismissed the jolt of nerves, feeling confident in his new plan. However, he called Sharon Gladstone as a backup.

"Let's get together later."

"Can't," she said, "Got a new girlfriend."

"Already?"

"She's my backup plan. You know how flaky MJ could get."

Instantly bored of the small talk, he dropped a live wire. "I think the cops want me as their prime suspect."

Silence.

"Hello?"

"Well, you know I've got your back, Bobby. Hell, I'm as guilty as you are, so before you do anything stupid, please tell me first."

"I'm thinking about talking to them."

"What the fuck," she shouted so loudly he had to move the phone from his ear.

"Listen to the method of my madness," he growled.

"Bobby, seriously," she began to cry, "With your temper…maybe it's not such a good idea."

He wanted to believe her motives were pure, but he knew better. As much as he enjoyed using her—just as she used him—she was bat-shit crazy.

"You still there?"

"Yes," he said, pulling into the garage of the Century City parking deck. "I might *have* to go to the cops," he started. "The evidence—"

"FUCK, Bobby! Please tell me you're not!"

"Sharon, settle down. You'll be fine. Trust me." Fighting the urge to yell, he quietly said, "I gotta bounce."

As a valet handed him a ticket, a beautiful woman in a tight skirt exited a talent agency next door and entered the garage elevator.

"Bobby, let's go play," she purred. "I'll make it worth your while."

He became aroused at the thought of taking Sharon apart.

Her voice had an edge. "Been too long since we got *super* crazy."

She was hard to resist, but so was the skirt in front of him.

"Okay. I'll text you the place."

Hanging up, he stepped into the elevator, inhaling the woman's intoxicating perfume. She flipped her long auburn hair behind her neck in his direction. He examined the reflection of her full cleavage in the mirrored doors. As she pulled at her skirt, he looked down at the shape of her perfect ass.

He texted: *The Standard @ 7.*

The woman dabbed at the edges of her full lips, then turned just enough for their eyes to meet.

He smiled.

She turned.

Exiting, he typed: *Make it 8. Your place. Be ready for pain.*

46

HORNET NEST

Stuart and I were back at the office where I sat quietly at my desk. Between Meredith's murderer and Fat Frankie's threat to my father and our family, my mind was a whirling dervish. I pictured Fat Frankie lining us up on the living room couch and shooting us execution style or sneaking into our homes and whacking us in our sleep.

My nerves can't take this shit.

I texted McCloud: *Ready for that favor?*

In less than thirty seconds, a text appeared: *Who is this? Erase me, Fucker!*

Instantly, my office phone rang. It was from inside the building.

"What the fuck are you doing, Detective?"

"I'm trying to see if you're—"

"I know what you're *trying* to do. Just not on my *cell phone*. Meet me downstairs in five, between the food truck and the smoking section."

Right then, Stuart came around the corner.

"Yeah, okay. Just wanted to see if you're going to meet me for drinks later. Sure. Talk to you later," I said to nobody, hanging up and stretching my back.

"Steve back in the picture?"

I ran a quick list of people. "Nah, Angie. More ideas about places to live." Heading for the door, I said, "I gotta pee."

We had been together long enough to know when either one was bluffing. Maybe I was just getting paranoid. Either way, I walked toward the ladies' room—only to cut back down the hall to take the stairs.

Once outside, I spotted McCloud. He had already gotten served and was leaning against a picnic table next to the smokers, stuffing a burrito the size of a baseball mitt into his mouth.

"Smoke while you eat?" I smirked.

McCloud looked over to see two smokers chuffing away as hard as they could. He shrugged and kept cramming.

In between bites he managed to say, "Not any different than eating at a cookout."

The burrito was gone before I could decide whether I wanted a Diet Coke or the real thing.

"Hungry?" I asked.

"Not now," he said, trying unsuccessfully to suppress a belch. "Sorry to bust your nuts earlier, but c'mon, that was a bogus move."

"Just caught off guard, I guess."

"I get it. So, let's talk about this, um, elephant in the room," he chuckled. "See what I did there? Frankie, the fat guy—"

I stopped him with a stare. "Brilliant. And while you're being *Jimmy Fallon,* why don't you share how you're going to—"

"Yeah, about that."

"McCloud? Don't do or say *anything* that's gonna make me want to punch your skinny face."

"Geez," he frowned, "Wound tight?"

"If you were in my place you would be too."

The crowd was growing, so while I got my soft drink, he moved to the other end of the parking lot and lit up.

"Who still smokes?"

"I do," he said, exhaling a thick cloud.

"No wonder you're a buck-sixty-five. Listen, we can't waste more time on this. The hammer's coming and I do *not* want it falling on my fa... my family's head."

"It's okay," he nonchalantly grinned. "I know it's your dad you're protecting."

"Why do you say that?"

"Really? Besides the fact your father was the *only* robe who presided over the most *notorious* mob story in the past—what—*forty* years? And the *only* high-level judge I know who's on the way *out* while you're on the way *up*."

I looked away, trying to ignore his smugness.

"You're in a tricky spot, Detective. And he's in a sticky one. It took me all of 20 minutes," he lit a second cigarette with the first. "To figure *I* was the best guy to blackmail."

Shaking my head in disbelief. "Wait a second, you—"

"It's cool," he said holding up a hand. "I know the deal. And the shit I'm standing in. Plus, without me, you and your family won't be celebrating holidays."

This kid was cocky, but smart—the reason I cut him slack.

"And it's *Detective* Norelli."

I wanted to pat his chest for a wire.

"Copy that. And speaking of evidence," he said, producing a thumb drive from his pocket. "Call this a down payment."

I stared.

"Look, you know I'm in this for the long haul. So, I help you—you help me. This…" he said, sliding the drive into my jacket pocket, "This little something shows you I'm a team player. And all that happy horseshit."

"*Okaaaaay.*"

Rolling his eyes, he smirked, "I know exactly how I'm going to get what you need. This will help you get closer to solving your case. After all, sooner you solve this—sooner we can focus on other shit, right?"

"Something from Meredith?"

A nod. "And for the record, I have *perfect* access to the…" he looked around before lowering his voice. "*Party room.* I'm head of the *guest list* with keys to the *exhibit hall* which will be a *grand event* for your upcoming *celebration.*"

I couldn't help but smile because this kid had balls.

We were people watching for thirty seconds before I had run out of time and patience.

"Okay, I gotta go. Stuart'll be wondering where I am."

"Hey," he nodded to the taco truck. "Buy him a taco."

"Smart," I smiled, heading that way.

"True," he said, following me and leaving a trail of smoke in his wake.

As I abruptly stopped, he nearly bumped into me. "And put that damn thing out. Then quit. You've got a career in front of you and I'd hate to see you drown in your own lung butter."

"Shit, that's graphic."

"So is death."

47

ATTORNEY PRIVILEGE

S hapiro and Jacobitz sat facing one another, but both appeared focused on the impressive Century City view. The attorney's suite of offices was one floor below the monolithic talent agency whose name adorned the perimeter of the penthouse. The nearly two-story letters could be seen from most of Westside.

Jacobitz & Partners was the second largest legal group in SoCal, so when they needed an address that matched their stature, ICM—the former MGM Tower—was a solid choice.

"Helluva view, huh, Bobby?" Andrew asked.

"Peachy. Now, can we get back to the subject, or are you humping me so you can add another wing to your Malibu spread?"

Andrew let his minute smile serve more as an acknowledgement than an affirmation. Known as one of the most powerful litigators in LA and an unconscionable ball-breaker, Andrew hated the thought of some money-saturated, underrated director like Shapiro walking all over him. He had to keep his cool because he did not get to where he was by being an irrational hothead. Plus, he enjoyed how his client paid him a thousand dollars an hour for his precious time and profound talents.

"Sure. Back to business."

"Good," Bobby snapped.

"What they've got is circumstantial and only potentially admissible. But what you've got—"

"Is enough to redirect attention from me to another party," Bobby grinned.

They stared in silence before Andrew said, "Yes, you have the creativity. And I, the credibility."

Bobby let his shoulders drop. "Thought so. With the fucking heat on my back, it's got me looking in all directions."

"Understandable," Andrew said, walking to his desk. "I say you move forward with the plan just as you showed me." Swiping his iPad screen, he said, "And I'll make all the necessary arrangements. You made a smart move getting ahead of this thing."

"Not my first rodeo."

Leaving his attorney to do the dirty work, Bobby had some undercover work of his own to do.

Descending the tower, he fired a text to the gal he had seen earlier. He had grabbed her number as they went their separate ways.

The texts begin bouncing.

Bobby: *Make it 5:30. I'll come to you. What's your address?*

Within seconds, a response: *Pushy little puppy, huh?*

Bobby: *More like an eager beaver.*

In seconds, her address and gate code pinged his phone, along with a photo that made Bobby want to give her the ride of her life.

48

SHIT SHOW

B ack in the office, Stuart sipped a coffee while staring at his computer screen. Without a word, he pointed his forehead toward my desk. I took a seat and untwisted the string on the huge Interdepartment manilla envelope.

In the well-worn envelope was a smaller envelope marked CLASSI-FIED. I looked over to see Stuart bobbing his head like a kid ready to spill the answer to a quiz when it wasn't his turn. Opening the second envelope, I found Bobby's rap sheet with new pages. Skimming, I realized what we'd found earlier was just the tip of the iceberg.

"Holy freak, Stuart."

"Exactly. Look how far back the trail of that shit-bag goes," he said. "Start at the top."

My eyes fell on several dates. At Bobby's fourteenth birthday, his father was either coming off or climbing aboard a bender and gave his son a black eye and dislocated his wife's shoulder.

"First offense," I whispered.

Two years later, Dad showed up to his son's football game and proceeded to shout obscenities at Bobby and the team's coach. By the end of the game, Frank the father was completely shit-faced and picked a fight with the coach in the parking lot. Bobby's mother said something and Frank threw her to the ground, twisting her ankle in the process. Bobby stepped in only to get his nose broken before Frank went after the coach, swinging at him with a football helmet. He took out the man's two front teeth and the coach pressed charges. Later, however, the coach agreed to drop the charges with three conditions: Frank pays for all damages, agrees to 40 hours of community service, and lets his son pursue a football career.

I looked at Stuart.

"Keep going," he said. "It gets better."

Bobby's graduating year, Frank returned home after pulling an 18-month stint at Pleasant Valley State Prison for aggravated assault when he took a tire iron to a bodyshop mechanic over a bill dispute.

Frank pretended to make nice with the family until he polished off a fifth of vodka one day and went after his son with a baseball bat, taunting him about being too stupid for college. Things got complicated when his mother jumped in to break things up—resulting in her broken nose. Given Bobby had grown considerably since his father was in prison—thanks to weightlifting and steroids—he went after Frank with a blind fury, breaking his father's nose and his jaw in two places.

Adding insult to injury, Bobby shattered several bones in his own hand which ruined his chance of finishing the season as quarterback. Weeks later, after his parents' injuries healed, his mother asked for a divorce. Frank begged his wife for just one more chance, swearing he would change. Sadly, she agreed.

"You can't make this shit up," I said, shaking my head.

"Right?" Stuart said, "Be right back."

I kept reading.

Three months later and on the night before his high school graduation, Bobby's mother was hosting a party. Frank and a woman showed up under the influence of several substances. After Bobby's mother begged Frank to leave for good, an argument broke out. Frank went after his wife with a steak knife and Bobby stepped in. Frank was stabbed in the stomach and he bled out on the kitchen floor before the EMT arrived. Charges were dropped when Bobby's mother testified her son was acting in self-defense.

Bobby walked, and his mother eventually recovered.

As I finished, Stuart returned with two fresh coffees.

"Pretty f'd up, huh?"

"Yeah," I said, taking coffee. "Apple didn't fall far."

"Well, before you get all warm and fuzzy on our guy," he said, "Here's something else."

He flipped open his notepad.

"Christmas that same year, his mother was killed in an auto accident on the way to work. The other driver died and his family sued Bobby—not sure the reason, but it was deemed his mother's fault. His parents never had insurance, so Bobby couldn't pay off the mortgage and it was foreclosed. He ended up having no career in football because of the injury—thanks to his dad. His life had become a shit show, so he left town and moved here to live with a cousin who happened to be a television director. He's been in showbiz ever since."

"Damn," I sighed. Something felt wonky, so I flipped through the file. "Last name's Shapiro, but his father and mother's name—"

"Jackson," he nods. "According to a counselor I spoke with, he wanted to forget his past so badly he changed his name to his cousin's last name."

"Odd."

"Maybe."

"Certainly helps us understand his state of mind better, I suppose."

"You mean his having a Grade-A clusterfuck of an adolescence?"

"Yeah," I nodded. "Do you suppose it really *was* only self-defense?"

"Would it matter?"

"Good point. And no."

After a long exhale, I said, "Well, how about seeing if we can cheer ourselves up with another potential suspect."

Stuart grinned, "Thought you'd never ask."

49

PEARL NECKLACE

B obby showed up at Elizabeth's condo in Brentwood and was about to knock when she opened the door with the presentation of a suburban housewife at Halloween. Her long sheer dress was black and left nothing to the imagination. Bobby admired the tiny black panties and matching push-up that enhanced her perfect body. She was more magnificent than he had even imagined.

"Well, are you going to just stand there gawking?"

Fifty minutes, four cocktails, several lines of coke, and a handful of orgasms between the two of them later, Elizabeth and Bobby were lying in a pile of sweat-soaked sheets in her king-sized playpen, complete with leather straps, handcuffs, and more. Both were on their backs catching their breath and laughing at the randomness of their hookup.

"Bet you don't do this everyday," Bobby said.

"And you would lose that bet, Bobby," she giggled. "Or, is it Robert? Or just *Bob*."

"It's whatever you want to call me, Elizabeth. Or, is it Beth? Or just *Lizzy*."

They laughed as she climbed on top of him.

"All aboard the Bobby train," she said, rubbing back and forth along his crotch.

"Choo…fuckin'…choo," he grinned.

"Well, what do we have here, Mr. Cocky?"

"What's it look like, Professor Pussy?"

She moaned, "Ready for another go round?"

"Sure," he said, getting started. "And do you really do this every day? To complete strangers?"

"I'm what's known as a sex addict," she purred. "I can't help myself."

He growled, "You're a bad little girl, aren't you?" His smile dissolved as his grip increased.

"Bobby, you're hurting me."

Thrusting harder, he said, "I know, but you like it."

"Actually, I don't," she whimpered. "Please stop!"

"I can't," he growled.

Her legs were going numb from his grip. "Wh—Why not?"

"Because I'm what's known…as a *sex addict*."

"Bobby, you're really hurting."

In one swift move, he lifted her in the air and flipped her on her back —straddling her while pinning both arms.

"Remember when you said you liked—what did you call it—*erotic asphyxiation*? You do know this game doesn't always end with you simply gasping for air, right?"

Her eyes widened and her breathing increased. "That was before," she whined. "Now you're *really* hurting me."

Her eyes flicked toward the nightstand.

He followed her look.

"What's that? Another sex toy you haven't showed me?"

She shook her head.

"I thought we'd seen them all."

Leaning over to open the drawer, he ignited with anger.

"What the fuck do we have here?" He growled, slowly removing a handgun with two fingers. "You didn't answer my question."

As he released her arms, she shook them, trying to regain circulation. "It's a gun, Bobby. What do you think it is? Now, get the fuck off of me," she barked. "You ignorant *Neanderthal*."

His expression turned ice-cold. "I know what it is. That's *not* the question."

She licked her lips. "What?"

"The question about erotic asphyxiation." Dropping the gun, he wrapped both hands around her neck. "Like this!"

She kicked violently.

He squeezed harder.

She continued kicking until she could no longer move.

Looking up and down her beautiful, motionless body, he said, "Where's all that passion now, my little *sex addict?*"

———

SHOWERED AND DRESSED, Bobby put on his watch and buttoned his sleeves, all the while surveying the room.

He put the handgun in his jacket and wiped everything down.

Next, he picked up his cell phone and stopped the camera from recording before changing it to photo mode.

Putting straps around her wrists and ankles, he attached them to her neck, then tied them off to the bed. Placing something in the palm of her hand, he stepped back for a final photo.

"Seems like a lot of work to get yourself off," he sneered.

At the door, he blew a kiss and left.

———

VIOLENTLY GASPING for air moments later, Elizabeth coughed and spewed a mouthful of bloody spit. She had to dislocate her shoulder in order to free herself from Bobby's contraption and, screaming in pain, briefly lost her vision.

Several tortuous minutes later, she was free and rubbing her wrists and ankles. Terrified, she sat on the bed, fighting to regain her composure.

Suddenly, her eyes shot to a bookcase on the other side of the room.

Gingerly easing off the bed, she crossed the room.

Moving aside several plants, she retrieved the hidden camera and turned off the recorder.

"Two can play your game, *Bobby*," she whispered.

50

SKIN FLIX

S tuart and I were on our way to meet our next suspect Thomas Showalter, aka Tommy Showoffer. He was not only one of the youngest CEOs in town but also one of the most successful studio executives in all of Hollywood—thanks to his enormously successful online porn channel, Skinflix.

According to recent stats, the porn industry was worth more than $100 billion a year, and the United States accounted for no less than fifteen percent of that market. Showalter had gotten in the game early, combining life savings with an expertise of using a handy-cam. Merge that savvy with the cash from several horn-dog venture capitalists, and they were off to the races. Setting up fast websites and cheap cameras with starving actors proved to be a winning combo and made Tommy and his team wealthy beyond their dreams.

Dressing more like a '70s pimp than a studio exec, Tommy was flashy. Even his car, a lipstick-red $2.5 million Pagani Huayra, was over the top.

Tommy *Showoffer* fit.

Their offices and studios were housed in an enormous warehouse in the San Fernando Valley on the border between Reseda and Northridge, an area known as the epicenter of porn. It was also home to the devastating 1994 earthquake. While news sources referred to the shaker as the Northridge earthquake, locals knew the real quake epicenter was located in Reseda.

What made its location poetic was the family community of Reseda. With fifteen public schools and five private ones, alongside dozens of Mom & Pop managed strip malls, Skinflix was the business that drove a handsome slice of those billions into Reseda's backyards.

We arrived at the Skinflix offices at lunchtime and were greeted by a receptionist named Candy who enthusiastically shared with us how lucky we were to spend time with Tommy because he was often traveling the world to find new channels of distribution for his first-class smut.

Today was special, as employees, cast, and crew were on hand to celebrate his thirty-first birthday. She invited us into an enormous dining area where 200-plus gathered around an enormous phallic-shaped birthday cake—complete with two big balls and shaved chocolate for hair.

Classy, I thought, shooting a glance at my partner.

After watching the group celebrate their boss for a good four minutes, they returned to work while Stuart and I joined Tommy in his office that overlooked an enormous maze of offices, studios, and edit bays.

We took our seats in front of his desk—a huge slab of white marble set atop four Roman columns. Tommy started to light a cigarette, but seeing our matching frowns, he returned it to a drawer.

"Okay, what's on your nasty little minds?" he sneered.

"Thank you for your time, Mr. Showalter, and as your receptionist told you, we're here about Meredith Johansen. Do you think she was a supporter of your business?" I asked.

Looking away, he pursed his lips. "Good question. I'm not sure she was as big a *supporter* as she liked what it provided her—by way of me. And for the record, she was good at it."

"You mean, she was good at supporting you for what you provided her or good at performing for your camera?"

The cat just ate the canary.

"You're good, Detective. And I'd say both. Which is kinda what I said. She saw the benefit and didn't argue. Hell, I gave her the downpayment for her house as a gift. And I used her in one of my early films, back when she was new to town."

"Really?" Stuart added, scribbling in his notepad. "How did she feel from the standpoint of integrity? And what I mean is because of the *news* she covered."

"News?" he laughed. "Tabloid bullshit! And she knew it."

"She was also a filmmaker," I said.

"And who do you think funded that little *hobby*?"

"So, you gifted her the down and funded her documentary—"

He held up a hand to stop me. "Not all—just seed money."

"How much?" I asked.

"A hundred," he said, removing a pack of nicotine gum from his desk.

Stuart leaned in. "And the house?"

"Five hundred," he said, putting two pieces in his mouth.

"So, 600K total?" I clarified with a nod.

He shook his head nonchalantly.

"And she repaid you…," I said.

He grinned but said nothing.

"But you have, what, a thousand actresses who'd do it for—"

"The attention? Yes."

"But if she's making a good living as an anchor and following her dream of filmmaking—"

"Same hundred-year-old story, Detectives," he smiled at both of us.

"To be famous," Stuart said.

Tommy touched the tip of his nose. "She wanted to be a *Staaaaaar*. And the only way she could really set herself apart was her favorite flavor of stardom," he grinned.

"And what flavor was that?" I smiled.

"S & M."

"Same story," Stuart began. "Fresh off-the-farm girl rolls into town searching for her place in Hollywood."

"Right. Look, we all know how *50 Shades* turned up the heat—pun intended—on that whole scene. And while the Dark Web has a much darker version of all that shit, her interest was in boundary pushing and attention getting. Besides, being a bit of a twisted Nelly, she had a fair amount of bats in her attic."

Stuart wrote something down.

"And the people she hung out with? 'Specially that *Director* she's been fucking. Along with a half-dozen others."

We remained silent.

"Well, it doesn't take a brain surgeon to figure out someone, somewhere was going to go too far," he fidgeted.

"Speaking of—are you among those half-dozen others?" I asked.

"Let's just say I primed the pump. Saw her need. Fueled the desire. Then moved on." Tommy flicked his tongue between the inside of his cheeks. "Detectives, I hope this has been helpful. And thanks for celebrating my birthday, but I really must get back to work. You should come to my house in the Hills. I'll have my receptionist give you the details."

He stood while we remained sitting.

"What?"

"Just one more question, Tommy," Stuart said, motioning for him to sit. "Where were you on Oscar night?"

"And with whom?" I added.

He took a deep breath and sat. "I was hosting a small party at my house. Several close friends and a couple of employees, all watching the show. And comparing it to *our* awards show."

"Which is?" I asked.

"The AVN Awards. Adult Video News. It's three weeks before the Oscars. Very similar glamour. Just fewer clothes," he giggled.

"I want to back up, Tommy," I said. "So you were entertaining friends, but had you seen Meredith that night?"

He shook his head side to side.

"When was the last time you saw her? Alive."

He looked away. "One day, early last week."

"Why?"

"Like I said, we had dated," Tommy began. "It didn't really work for me. We broke up but stayed friends. We often had brunch together—we loved the cabanas at the Beverly Hills Hotel. You know, eat, drink, and get merry."

I leaned forward. "Can you think of anyone who would want to kill her?"

"Maybe." He chewed the inside of his mouth. "I mean, if the reason was revenge."

"What?" Stuart asked.

"Who?" I added.

He turned to Stuart. "Everybody has a button they don't want pushed. And Meredith, for all her kindness, not only knew everyone's buttons but would push them—often relentlessly—in order to get what she wanted."

Then, he faced me. "As for whom? I can think of at least three."

"Go on."

Holding up a finger, "Bobby Shapiro. Those two knew how to cook one another's nerves. Always arguing. Plus, everyone knows Shapiro's a raging lunatic. Between the steroids and her depression? Hell, it was an insanity cocktail from the get-go."

He held up a second finger. "Sharon Gladstone. I don't know which bitch is crazier. They used to be roomies, and let's just say they shared it all—the good, the bad, *and* the ugly. Look, we all shared a piece of Sharon at one time or another, but damn, MJ was always holding something over Sharon's head. If it wasn't real estate or men, it was who could get more *work done* to look better—if you know what I mean. Again, a constant, dysfunctional soup of neurosis."

He raised a third finger. "And me!"

Stuart and I looked at one another.

"She and I got involved in some, uh, arguments over footage she wanted to use in her documentary. Stuff that could've gotten a lot of people in trouble. When I asked her not to use it, she held it ransom. Anyhow, I threatened her—sorry to admit—and she threatened me back."

Silence.

"But I *promise* you, on a stack of bibles, I did NOT kill her!"

51

SHREWD AWAKENING

As Bobby put on his shoes, Dr. Tercel poured a cup of tea for both of them. He watched Bobby closely while slowly dipping a tea bag in and out of his own cup.

"Thanks for seeing me, Doc. Guess I just needed…you know, some guidance."

"Of course, Bobby. That's what I'm here for."

"Yeah, but you gotta help me, Doc. My anger's getting out of hand. Sometimes, I don't even know who I am when I'm with the ladies, ya know?"

"I understand," Tercel gently smiled. "Anger is a powerful force."

"I know I've got issues—big surprise—but this sexual addiction thing you've told me I have is getting, or gotten…out of control."

Tercel raised an eyebrow.

"And now the cops want me some kind of bad. I've talked to my attorney, and we feel—well, he feels pretty confident what they have is circumstantial. Thing is…" he stopped to take a sip of tea, grimaced, then set it down.

"What is it, Bobby?"

After a long beat, he leaned close. "Fact is, Doc, I've been bull-shittin' you. Pretty much the whole time."

Tercel sat expressionless.

"Yeah, this isn't working. Better yet, *you're* not working."

"What?"

"This whole dog and pony show of yours. Not digging it. Might've helped your girl, but not me."

Tercel frowned.

"Besides, I'm the one who won't be working if I don't figure out a way to fix this thing."

Tercel relaxed his shoulders, attempting to send a comforting message to his patient. "We can discuss anything you need."

"What I need is you to help me figure out how to handle the heat."

"Bobby, what *exactly* do you mean?"

"Really, Doc? My jail record. Death of my father. C'mon, all the shit I've done? And Meredith?"

They locked stares.

"With our patient-doctor privilege thing—the police come knocking, you can't share anything I say in these meetings, right?"

"That's correct," Tercel calmly replied.

"Right. So, I have an idea. You can call it an ultimatum but that sounds so heavy, you know, between friends like us. What I need is for you to help me to get removed from the eye-line of Detectives Norelli and Brown." He licked his lips and took a slow breath. "Or else."

"Bobby, I'm confused. What do you mean handle the heat? And what do you mean, *or else*?"

Bobby's eyes suddenly appeared lifeless. "I'll hand the video over to them."

Clearly confused, he said, "What video?"

"Don't play stupid, Doc. You have too many initials behind your name for that."

Tercel remained expressionless.

"I don't want my face smeared all over those shitty tabloid shows."

Tercel grinned. "Like the one you work for?"

"I *have* to. It's my *job*. Doesn't mean I enjoy having my personal life fed to the public."

"Spoken like a true closeted addict."

"So what? I am. And so are you," Bobby spat.

Tercel shook his head in disbelief. "Not really. And besides, we're talking about you, not me."

Bobby stood and went to the window. "You going to help me or what?"

Tercel waited a long moment. "I will."

Bobby watched the hazy sunshine cast irregular shadows outside the window. A similar shadow seemed to fall over his face. "I have an excuse," Bobby mumbled.

"How's that?"

"My father was a mean, drunk, son-of-a-bitch," Bobby whispered.

Tercel joined him at the window. "I suppose I do, too."

Bobby's chuckle fell short. "Yeah, right. And how do you figure that?"

"My mother was a mean drunk of a bitch."

Bobby managed a crooked grin. "We're a couple of sick puppies, huh?"

A long beat of silence before Tercel said, "You hated your father, so you killed him. Perhaps I had a similar hatred."

Bobby's head whipped toward Tercel. Through a squint, Bobby said, "You told me she killed herself."

"She did," Tercel replied, shifting his attention from outdoors to Bobby. "You know what your gift was Bobby?"

He shook his head.

"Besides a reason? You had *control*."

"What do you mean?"

"You could leave," Tercel said. "I couldn't."

"Bullshit," Bobby snapped.

"You were a man. I was…still a boy."

Bobby looked down, wrinkling his brow.

Tercel patted Bobby's shoulder. "Today was a good session. I'm glad you came in to talk with me. You've continued to make *remarkable* progress."

Bobby's expression was part peaceful, part confused.

"C'mon, Bobby, let me walk you to your car."

In the parking lot, they stood next to Bobby's car, studying one another's expressions before Bobby got into his car and started it, then rolled down the window.

"It was good to see you, Bobby. I'm proud of you. And the work you've done."

Looking up at Tercel, Bobby allowed a tiny smirk to punctuate his dead stare.

"Yeah, not sure what else to say, Doc, so….guess I won't."

52

TURN ABOUT

B obby redlined his Porsche through every gear and every block as he made his way to Sharon's house in the hills. His testosterone was also redlining while he envisioned his last sexual escapade. Nervous energy, rushing endorphins, and pure fear coursed through his body at breakneck speed. Adding cocaine to the mix did not help.

"Not so sure Doc helped me all that much," he mumbled.

His eyes shot back and forth as he weaved in and out of traffic.

"How did I let that woman get me so jacked up?" he asked aloud.

His mind was in overdrive—his paranoia, accelerating.

"And how did I let it get that far?" he asked, nearly shouting.

He needed to slow down before he crashed and burned.

Panicked, he mumbled, "What if someone saw me leave?"

Bobby would be at Sharon's in less than twenty minutes and he could not let her see him this way. It would throw her into a fit and she was already wound tightly enough for both of them.

The light at the corner of Sunset and Beverly Glen Boulevard turned yellow. He checked his speedometer and considered trying to beat it, but in the blink it took him to eyeball the rearview, he spotted a police motorcycle in the distance.

Quickly downshifting, he was able to avoid slamming his brakes and slowly pulled to the light. Taking a deep breath, he checked both the rear and side mirrors—his eyes flitting back and forth between the cop and his dash. When the light turned green, he pulled away and instantly heard the chirp of a siren.

Looking in his rearview, he saw the flash of red and blue as the cop came from behind a car.

Bobby pulled through the intersection, then to the curb. Glancing at the floorboard, he saw the black handle of the .38 peek from his jacket pocket. He checked the mirror. The officer dismounted and was walking toward him. He folded the jacket over, quickly putting the gun out of sight. As he sat up, he peeked at the side mirror just as the officer placed his hand atop his gun. Bobby let out a deep breath.

Approaching, the Beverly Hills Police Officer's name tag read: *Taggert*.

"License and registration, please."

"Yes, Officer."

Bobby learned long ago, when in sticky situations like this, it was best to be polite and say as little as necessary.

Taking the two pieces of information, Taggert said, "Be right back."

Flipping down the vanity mirror, Bobby checked his nose for coke, wiped his brow, then downed a bottle of water.

Two minutes became four.

Four became eight.

He texted Sharon: *Running behind. Hang tight.*

Eight minutes become ten.

Sharon texted: *No worries. Not going anywhere.*

Ten minutes becomes fifteen.

Bobby's eyes flicked from his watch to the rearview, then to his surroundings, back to the cop, and finally back to his watch. He felt like a sitting duck and did not want to be seen by anyone. The coke was wearing off, a headache was closing in, and his patience was waning. However, he knew better than to make sudden moves or get out of his car.

According to his pricey timepiece, twenty-two minutes had passed when Officer Taggert returned.

"Where are we Officer Taggert?" Bobby asked politely.

Taggert eyeballed him for several long cool seconds.

"Mr. Shapiro, I've written you a citation for speeding. I spotted you several lights back when you stomped on it. Clocked you doing 66 in a 45. That's not cool. And frankly, plenty dangerous."

Bobby wanted to punch the guy but held tight. "Yes, sir. You're right. And I apologize."

"Officially, I'd say your speed was well over 70, but if I did that, I'd have your license and you'd be walking home. So, I'm giving you a break."

He took a slow breath and said, "Thank you."

"I'm also citing you for reckless driving."

"What?"

"For passing a stopped school bus four blocks back. You passed as his blinkers came on."

He could feel himself flush but held steady. "Yes, sir."

"Lastly, I'm adding negligence because you appeared to be texting while driving."

"But Officer Taggert, I wasn't."

The officer did not budge.

"Besides, it's not illegal to text."

"Isn't it?" Taggert frowned.

Bobby stopped.

"What's the big hurry?"

"I'm, uh, late for a production meeting," he lied.

"Uh huh. Must be an important one. What are you some big-time director?"

Bobby wondered if the Officer recognized him. "Yes, actually I direct the—"

"The ticket will be $1475, minus court costs. We'll see you in court on the date circled," Taggert said, handing him the ticket before walking away.

Maybe it was the raging testosterone or the drugs and booze wearing off—or maybe his feeling disregarded. Either way, Bobby could not help himself.

"Don't you think—" he shouted out the window to Taggert's back, "You could cut me some slack?"

Officer Taggert stopped, slowly turned, and walked back to Bobby's car.

Leaning forward and staring a hole through Bobby, Taggert said, "What I think is you're a reckless guy. And given this is the end of my day, I'm *trying* to go easy on you. So, what do you say we leave it there. Good?"

"Yes, sir. You're right. Good idea."

"Trust me, it could've been worse," he said, walking away. "Have a nice day," he said over his shoulder.

Waiting until he was well out of earshot, Bobby spat, "Could've been worse for *you,* asshole!"

53

BEFORE

Twenty minutes earlier—

Officer Taggert stood next to his bike, just behind Bobby's car. Taking out a cell phone, he dialed a number. Waiting to connect, he watched Bobby's watched eyes flick between his rear view and side mirrors.

"Norelli."

"Detective Norelli, this is LAPD Officer Taggert. I wanted to give you a heads up."

"What's that?"

Taggert continued to eyeball the back of Shapiro's twitching head. "I heard about the Johansen murder," he said. "Damn sad."

"Yes, it was. How did—"

"We were neighbors. She lived a handful of blocks away from me. Small world, huh?"

"No doubt."

"Thing is, I heard through the grapevine you had that TV director Shapiro in your sights."

"Yeah, actually he's our prime suspect. But my partner and I are having a hard time finding him."

"Well, I know where he is."

"Really? Where's that?"

"Sittin' about twenty yards in front of me. Just pulled him over for speeding."

"Driving a school-bus yellow Porsche 911?"

"The same."

"And you're—"

"At Sunset and Beverly Glen Boulevards. Writing him up. You want, I could drag my feet."

The phone went silent for a moment.

"Detective?"

"Sorry, just talking to my partner. That'd be great. Thing is—"

"Might spook him, huh?" He watched Bobby continue to fidget. "True."

"We're 15, maybe 20, away."

"Norelli?"

"Yes?"

"Tell you what…"

54

AFTER

B obby slowly pulled away from the curb, merging into traffic and heading eastbound.

"That turned out well," Stuart said as I pulled from a curb across the street, heading westbound.

Making a U-turn, we passed a smiling Officer Taggert. He nodded, touching his helmet visor. I returned a nod and a smile.

Passing the Beverly Hills Hotel, I said, "Yes, it did. I'd say someone is looking out for us."

"You bet, partner," Stuart said, eyeballing the legendary hotel. "You know, I've lived here my whole life and never even seen that place. Maybe I'll take Janine there after the baby comes. Ya know, a little adult getaway," he winked.

"You only live once."

Bobby hung a left onto North Beverly. I wanted to keep a safe distance without getting caught by the upcoming light, so I got up on the car bumper in front of me. Squeezing through the amber and onto the other side of the light, the driver flipped me off as he turned left onto Lexington.

"So..." Stuart said, tapping the dash, "Left on Beverly or right on Coldwater? Quick, before this clown turns. Winner gets the next beer."

"Coldwater," I said.

"Bever..."

Bobby shot up Coldwater Canyon.

"Shit," he mumbled. "Did he make us?"

"Was wondering the same. Hey, just thought of something. Do me a favor and see where Sharon Gladstone lives."

"Huh?"

"Well, think about it…"

"Ah, yes," he grinned.

―――――――

AT THE TOP OF COLDWATER, we hit Mulholland Drive. I knew if we didn't hang back far enough, Bobby would see us as he made the switchback onto Mulholland, so I pulled into a random driveway and parked.

"2711 Bowmont Drive," Stuart said. "Just up ahead."

Fortunately, two cars separated us, but I could easily see his car. Since I had no idea how long the street was that he just turned onto, I hung back again.

Stuart double-checked his phone. "Bowmont's to the right."

I saw Bobby's car crest the hill just before disappearing.

Pulling Stuart's phone closer, I pointed, "Guessing that's a short street, so I'll park at this overlook and give him a few minutes to, you know, make plans and such."

"Right," he smiled. "And such."

Five minutes later, we pulled into the driveway, blocked his car, and gave them several more minutes while we planned next steps.

55

BOBBY TRAP

W here have you been, Bobby? I rang your phone," Sharon whimpered.

Bobby entered the room with his arms wide, looking as though he had not a care in the world. And while he looked disheveled, she was dolled up like Saturday night. That is, *if* Saturday night included a see-through robe, mink slippers, and a one-piece sheer nightie. He took her by the waist and picked her up like an oversized doll.

"I know. I'm sorry, baby, but I got caught up at work. You know how it is—ratings season and all."

She whispered, "It's been too long."

"I'm here now."

IN THE BEDROOM, Sharon was riding Bobby like a cowgirl on a bucking bronco. They were both drenched in sweat.

Sharon whispered, "Choke me."

They continued toward the mountaintop.

"Choke me," Sharon said louder.

The room became hotter by the minutes as did his torturous anger.

"C'mon, you *Neanderthal* fuck-toy. Stop being a pussy and choke me!"

Just then, something clicked in Bobby's head. Lifting her with his hips, he grabbed her waist and dropped her onto the bed like a rag doll.

With heaving chest and blushing face, she twisted his nipples and gasped, "C'mon, you bad little boy, fuck the life outta me!"

Wrapping both hands around her neck, he squeezed. She writhed at first, but then quickly panicked. She struck out at him, but he was too strong.

Getting weaker by the second, she tried pounding his chest.

Suddenly, someone pounded on the front door, "POLICE, OPEN UP!"

BOBBY AND SHARON sat next to one another on an oversized couch. The contrast of the elegant living room with their disheveled appearance—in the light of day and by two detectives—was entertaining.

She was wearing most of a robe—he, only pants.

Stuart and I stood across the room.

"I know it sounds silly, but it's not what it looks like," she said, lighting a cigarette.

"Really, Sharon? Because judging by the bruising on your neck," I said, "And the scratches on your back, Bobby, I'd say it went well beyond foreplay."

"But that's what it was. Just play," Bobby snarled, "And *none* of your fucking business."

I looked to Stuart, who said, "Thing is, Bobby, it *is* our business. Because we're taking you downtown to discuss the murder of Meredith Johansen."

Bobby stood quickly and yelled, "Fuck you! You've got NOTHING to pin that on me!"

I was startled as his explosive outburst and touched the top of my gun.

Stuart did the same and said, "Actually, we do, so let's go, Bobby."

He didn't budge.

"Put on a shirt," Stuart added, removing handcuffs from his belt. "Or I'll be happy to use these."

We knew because of his size, things could get ugly fast. So I tried a more subtle approach. "C'mon, Bobby, let's not *any* of us do anything crazy. You heard him. Let's go. And quietly, okay?"

He looked to Sharon and smiled, then turned back to us and said, "Fine, but I want to speak to my attorney."

"No problem," said Stuart.

ON THE WAY to the car, I took out a copy of the Miranda Rights and read them to him. When I was finished and we were standing by the car, I asked, "Mind if I look inside your car?"

While the look on his face read, *Hell No,* he said, "Got nothing to hide."

As I approached the car, his smirk disappeared. "Uh, no. You can't."

I punctuated his outburst with a dramatic exhale. "See, Bobby," I began, "You were doing just fine, but now you have to act like a big man. But here's the thing, you can make this easy and we'll be on our way to the station, or you can make this difficult and...well, blah-de-blah."

"The fuck I care you have to work harder."

"What she's not saying is," Stuart said. "You say 'yes,' everything will be easy breezy. We'll take a quick look, then head in, ask a few questions, and you'll be on your way. But, if you wanna be a hard-ass and make us go to the DA and eventually a judge, well, you can see how complicated it could get."

His expression went from confusion to complacency. "It's all yours," he said, leaning against our car.

"Good choice," I said with a plastic smile. On the floorboard, I found a jacket and opened it. Using a hand towel with a 24 Hour Fitness logo, I picked up a .38 revolver. "What's this, Bobby?"

As hard as he tried, he couldn't hide the look. "S'not mine. Belongs to a friend. She wants me to keep it until she gets more confident with her shooting—which I'm teaching her to do."

"Right."

Getting a nod from Stuart, I leaned back in and pushed aside an over-sized gym bag. That was when I saw something that caught my breath.

I turned back to Bobby who was giving me a look, then nodded for Stuart to join me. He leaned in to investigate while Bobby and I engaged in a stare down. Sharon stood very close to him, mumbling something I couldn't hear.

"What have we here, Director Boy?" Stuart said, taking a large baggie and raising it in the air.

Inside were several dozen small, golden Oscar statuettes.

56

BIG FOOT

Booking Bobby was going to feel particularly good for many reasons. Maybe because it was my first big case—one not influenced by my brother or steered by my father. Maybe it was because Captain Nelson was throwing me a Hail Mary, trying to keep me from self-destruction. In the end, it would be our work at bringing a murderer to justice that would be remembered—and hopefully rewarded.

What I couldn't figure out for the life of me was why I was still feeling anxious despite making the collar.

I thought about this while staring at Bobby through a two-way mirror as he sat at a table in the interrogation room. Stuart joined me with two cups of jet black coffee and a folder under his arm.

"Smells like burnt oven mitts and is stronger than asphalt, but it's something," he said, handing me a styrofoam cup.

I took a sniff and dropped it in a trashcan.

He handed me a folder. "Take a look."

Stuart had run the record on the gun. Bobby was not lying. It was registered to an Elizabeth Conroy who lived on Bundy Drive, just off Sunset Boulevard in Brentwood.

Quickly scanning, I read aloud, "Conroy works as a Physician's Assistant at Ronald Reagan UCLA Medical Center…bought the gun from —" I looked up to find Stuart grinning. "Straight & Arrow? And the circle of coincidences just keep coming."

"Wacky, right?"

"According to the report," I continued, "A Richard Moffett, salesperson on duty at the time, said she purchased it within the past six months, paid cash, and has been attending night classes alongside our boy."

"I say we talk with her." I handed him the folder. "Something could turn up."

He held up a hand. "No, read the last page. Blue tab."

I turned to find a purchase order on *The Hollywood Mole* letterhead for 1,000 tiny plastic golden Oscar statuettes.

"Shit."

"Truly."

I dropped my head and sighed. "Well, at least he doesn't know we have this," I said tapping the folder against my palm.

My phone rang. I was about to silence it when I looked at the screen and answered, "What's up Jackie?"

"Hey, Pat. Got something. Hasn't been the easiest, what with the Santa Ana winds kicking up…"

"Jackie, sorry to interrupt, but we just brought in—"

"Bobby Shapiro?"

My eyes shot to Stuart. "Yeah, he's in the interrogation room right now, why?"

"That's why I'm calling. We have a boot print from the scene."

"Yeah?"

"Tell me, can you see him now?"

"Yeah," I said, putting the phone on speaker. "He's not twenty feet away."

"Does he have big feet?" she asked.

Looking through the glass, I checked under the table. His legs were stretched out—like he had all the time in the world.

"Yeah, they're big," I answered, then asked Stuart, "What size boot does he wear?"

Stuart looked. "I'm a 13. He's got to be at least a 14, maybe 15. Nice boots, too."

"14, maybe 15," I said to Jackie. "And fancy, according to Stuart."

"That helps. The print's a size 15. Has a lugged rubber sole and a rounded toe, but a square heel."

We look at one another, then eyeballed Bobby's boots.

"Hey, Jackie, it's Stuart. Was the sole newer or worn? And can you shoot me a picture?"

"Not brand new, but certainly not old. And of course. Give me a couple minutes."

He gave a thumbs up and I said, "This is perfect timing, Jackie. Shoot it to us and we'll get back in touch. Thanks."

As Stuart opened the door for us, I said, "Let's shake that boy's tree."

"LET ME GUESS. You found out I wasn't lying about the gun," Bobby said quietly, looking at his reflection in the glass. "And that I'm a part-time instructor at the Straight & Arrow."

"Yeah, yeah, we learned all that," Stuart said, looking at his notes instead of Bobby and continuing to stand while I took a chair.

"And those Oscar trinkets were for a commercial shoot I was doing in Malibu last week. Big deal."

I was surprised he was being so chatty. And laid back. Either way, we would let him continue. Suspects' nervous energy often got them talking and often tripping.

"Bobby, you're right. We found all that. Unfortunately, not much led us to you," I lied with a pleasant smile.

Standing at the edge of the table, Stuart said, "I got to hand one thing to you, Bobby," taking a silk hankie from his breast pocket, then polishing his glasses. "You are one sharp dressed man. The TV business must be good."

"People judge you by your clothes," Shapiro said plainly.

Returning his glasses to his face, he opened the folder without looking up. "The suit makes the man."

"And your physique," he said.

"Especially in this town."

Stuart took a seat, accidentally kicking Bobby's feet. "Sorry, bro. My feet are always getting in the way," he said, looking under the table, "I thought my feet were big."

Frowning, Bobby looked under the table.

"Nice kicks," Stuart said. "Gucci?"

"Berluti. From Paris," he sneered. "Gucci's are for pimps."

Stuart whistled, "Damn. Half my month's salary."

"Look, can we get this fashion show over? You and I both know everything has checked out, so what the hell am I still doing here?"

I began tapping the table. "Bobby, do you recall when Detective Brown and I approached you at your job?"

He stared at me, saying nothing.

"Right. And you recall when I said there was an easy way to do this and a hard way. And you just stared at the both of us acting like a douche —kinda like you're doing now."

Still quiet, he turned to stare at the mirrored wall behind us.

"Well, we tried to be amenable then, but after we spoke with several of your coworkers—nearly all of whom had very little, if *anything,* nice to say about you—we started to get the picture. Then we checked the surveillance footage of your workplace and saw you hit—rather violently —not one, but two of your coworkers."

He whipped his head toward me for an instant, caught himself, then returned his attention to his staring spot.

"It could have been just one. But I'm *certain* you've hit more. Especially Meredith."

He snorted.

"Bet you're wondering where you slipped up, right?"

Without looking at me, a faint grin appeared. "You got *zip.*"

Opening a folder, I pretended to read—for a long, slow minute. "We know you were with her the night of the murder. You were directing the Oscars and had spent a lot of time with her in rehearsals. Arguing." I continued looking at my notes, "According to *several* eyewitnesses."

"Whatever. I was directing the fucking show and she was one of the contenders."

"We know you were on and off again for the past several months even though she had been seeing a new boy."

Nothing.

"And we have a confirmation by her therapist…"

His focus shifted for a split second. I cut a look to Stuart from the corner of my eye.

Stuart grinned. "Yeah, seems Dr. Tercel said you two had a very…," he paused to flip through his notepad. "He used the phrase *complicated relationship.* Something about it being, let me see, fraught with anxiety and periodic estrangement."

Still nothing.

"Is that, like, psychobabble for *gay*?"

Bobby's nostrils flared and his jaw clenched, but he didn't move.

"The depth of the cut to her neck?" I said, "Nobody, and I mean *nobody* believes she killed herself."

More of nothing.

"But with your strength, anger, and blind jealousy of seeing her with all those other men. Geez, that must've driven you mad."

"No *way* she could off herself like that. But *you* could. A huge outdoorsman like you. Easy, right?"

His nostrils flared again, but he was not biting.

"There are plenty of big, sharp tools for a chicken-shit *Neanderthal* like you to do a job like that."

"Hell, you can find straight razors like that anywhere on the internet. It wasn't ME!"

No one said a word.

No one made a move.

The silence was deafening.

I leaned forward several inches and quietly said, "Bobby, neither of us said anything about a straight razor."

Slamming his fists on the table, he shouted, "I want my attorney!"

57

FOUL BALLS

Stuart and I had taken the necessary precautions well before we followed and approached Bobby. In fact, not thirty minutes before we got the call from Officer Taggert, we were discussing our need for an arrest warrant.

Imagine our surprise when Taggert laid a huge gift in our laps.

Bobby would appear before the court and be charged with no less than a $1,000,000 bond. I was pretty sure his attorney wouldn't be able to do much better. And since murder is a felony and he could easily flee, the judge would make the bond as painful as possible.

The bad news for Bobby was that he lived under the shroud of a checkered past and a precarious present. And when factored in with the additional allegations against him by the HR department at *The Hollywood Mole,* he was in deep. The good news—which may or may not play in his favor—is that he was a seasoned director with a solid reputation in the industry. He also had a powerful and well-respected stepfather in the business.

One hitch in the giddy-up was the tiny, yet supremely significant element: Reasonable Doubt.

Back at our desks, Stuart and I breathed a metaphorical sigh of relief. He smiled at me like he had just won the lottery. I felt differently. I was happy to have Shapiro in custody, but the whole story wouldn't actually be over until he was locked up.

"Is it just me, or does it feel like a good time for a cocktail?" Stuart said, licking his lips.

I was just about to agree when I saw Captain Nelson barreling down the hall toward us.

Stuart saw my expression and said, "What?"

"Too late," I whispered as Nelson approached.

"Children, please tell me you're putting this puppy to bed," Nelson barked before sipping coffee.

"Yes, sir," I began, "We have him awaiting arraignment and bail should be posted immediately. As for evidence—"

"Wait!" Captain Nelson held up his hand. "Just tell me if it'll stick."

"Sir?" Stuart asked.

He sighed. "Will it stick?"

"Yes, sir," I said. "We have a boot print that's, well, pretty sure to match, *several* testimonies from various sources who absolutely confirm his violent behavior, a renowned therapist who will provide solid confirmation as to our accusations, and we have video of several of his violent outbursts."

"And more recently," Stuart added, "We arrived at his home to find him nearly strangling a woman to death."

Nelson held up a hand in Stuart's face. "Yeah, got all that. What I'd rather know is this," he said, sitting on the corner of my desk. "What do *you* think, Norelli?"

"Sir?"

"I mean, it's *your* case. First big break and all. Chance to show you got the goods. Do you?"

"Sir, exactly what Stuart said, we have a great deal of evidence, plus a few extras that lead us—"

"What extras?"

As I looked to Stuart, he held up a bag. "These."

"I'm not blind, Detective Brown, and while I'm sure they're just like the one found in Ms. Johansen's hand, it could be a plant in any one of several directions, or a coincidence."

"I don't believe in—"

"I know you don't believe in coincidences, Norelli," he mocked. "Neither do I. Nor do I believe in the Easter Bunny. And I certainly don't think it was suicide—as I said from the get-go. But what I do believe is this." he said, tossing his empty cup in the trash. "One: Forget the statues. Two:

Match the f'n boot to him. Three: Be sure his therapist is a lock *and* will say so on the stand. By the way, who is he?"

"Dr. Darius Tercel."

He stopped and stared at me. "As in—"

I nod.

"Well, super-fucking-duper. That'll either be a great coo, or—"

"A coincidence, I know, but hear me out, it *will* work to our advantage. Stuart and I have met with him and feel extremely confident—"

Waving me off, he stood and headed for the door, saying over his shoulder, "Just make sure you get me something *concrete*, Norelli!"

58

BABY LEAVE

A bout that drink…" I said, trying to catch my mental breath from Nelson's tirade. Stuart and I were numb. We felt *this close*, yet potentially still so far away.

Once the demise of Bobby hit the press, more employees contacted us, confirming his violent behavior, and more than a couple were happy to rat him out—but only under the umbrella of anonymity.

We began re-running facts in hopes of finding something we might've missed. Just as we were getting in the groove, Stuart's cell pinged.

Looking at the screen, he read and swallowed hard. "9-1-1. Oh, shit."

"What?"

The color in his face drained. "That's the first sign."

"Of?"

"Things to—"

The phone rang.

"Come," he finished, looking at the screen and licking his lips with a nervous smack. "Hello? Yeah, uh huh, oh shit. Okay, right. Yes, I'm on my way. See you—what? The office. Oh, you mean—uh huh, oh shit. Okay, right. I'll just meet you…hello?" He stared at the screen. "She hung up."

"Well?"

"Huh?"

"Well? From all the *uh-huhs* and *oh shits* and *yeah, rights,* I'd said you were—"

"Having a BABY!" he shouted. Standing up, he began frantically looking around. "Where in the hell?"

"What?"

"My keys!"

I pointed to the desk in front of him. "Right. Okay. Oh shit. I gotta' get going."

Several coworkers within earshot stood and clapped. He quickly bowed, then ran down the hall. I followed behind.

By the time I was outside, he was already in his car and starting toward the exit. Slamming the brakes, he reversed much too fast and screeched at the end of the sidewalk where I had made my way.

He rolled down the window. "Sorry, Pat. Just kinda overwhelmed, ya know?"

Tearing up, I said, "I know, partner. Get the hell outta here and go be with your wife!"

"Thanks! I'll call later." He tore out and instantly disappeared.

"Stuart's a Daddy!"

59

DEEP SLEEP

As happy an occasion as it was, the timing of Stuart's maternity leave couldn't have come at a worse time. We were fine-tooth combing clues, and I was left without the net of my partner. At my desk, I stared at my notes thumbtacked on the wall. Several ideas began bouncing around my head like balls on a racquetball court.

The boot cast, the statuettes—despite what Captain said—the common denominator of Tercel, and my personal dangling participle called Fat Frankie. The boot seemed obvious. The statuette was a perfect calling card. And while it was obvious I liked Dr. Tercel—being the caring man who was helping me navigate mental speed bumps, plus the fact he was well-liked and had an impeccable reputation—he remained mysterious.

And that mystery made me oddly nervous.

Had he been married? Children? What schools did he attend?

Tossing my notebook aside, I googled his name and instantly found his websites along with several newspaper articles about his work. There were links to articles about his appearance on local news shows, plus several hits where he had accepted awards for a wide variety of honors. I also learned about his starting a suicide prevention foundation.

Next, I kept the search the same but switched to images and I saw Tercel posing for many of the awards I had read about. There were other pictures of him attending sporting events as well as many photos of him with a variety of beautiful women attending glamorous Hollywood functions. One in particular caught my eye—The Oscars, just days ago.

I was about to move on when a headline got my attention: *Dr. Darius Tercel hasn't missed an Oscar in 40 years.* In another, *Dr. Tercel shares his passion for the quintessential awards show.*

Many of the top articles originated in tabloids or local shows, so I began tracking him to older Oscar shows. That led me to scan the Best Pictures and their respective years. I found a different article but with a similar theme that stated he had attended every premiere since he was *born.* That led me to even more photos of him with a different woman at every Oscar show.

There he was in 1976, wrapped in a blanket and held by a woman I assumed was his mother. A weary looking man stood next to her. The old *Hollywood Reporter* article featured a "People To Watch" section.

It read: *Genevieve Turkel, an up and coming starlet in her own right, joins thousands of adoring fans for the Oscars at the Dorothy Chandler Pavilion in Hollywood. This year's enormous hit film is 'One Flew Over The Cuckoo's Nest,' starring Jack Nicholson. Mrs. Turkel is seen here with husband, horror movie actor Dwight Turkel, happy to be celebrating with their ten-week old son, Darius. Genevieve said, 'If my son is going to follow along in his parents' footsteps, he better start networking now.'*

I caught myself smiling, knowing the therapist I sat across from was the same baby in this photo. Already I knew things about the doctor I hadn't known before. His parents were—or still are—Hollywood actors, he is a huge movie buff, and it appears he has been quite the ladies' man.

Scanning other Oscar years, I came to *Terms of Endearment* and reminisced where I was when it won in 1983.

Five years old is where I was.

I was about to close the window when a headline caught my attention: *Young Starlet, Genevieve Turkel, Starring in the B movies, 'Creature from the Deep Black Sea,' 'Hot Women in Cold Cells,' and 'Beast from Terror Town' was found dead in her Bel Air home early this morning. Authorities report it as suicide. Following a celebration at the Oscars at the Dorothy Chandler...*

I stopped reading but continued shaking my head. I found it hard to believe in one moment Darius' mother was celebrating a once-in-a-lifetime event and in the next was ending her own life. I searched to find a picture of Darius. There he was handsomely dressed in a tuxedo and backstage as his mother's date.

What the hell?

As much as I wanted to call Stuart, he had his hands full and it could wait until morning. There was a great little coffee shop just around the corner, so I headed out.

Twenty minutes, two coffees, and a cheese danish in hand later, I was back at my desk. The only noises in the precinct came from someone typing in one corner and a television playing local news in another one. Second shift was well under way and I kept moving.

Within minutes I was logged into our Homicide database, typed in Genevieve's last name, and added the parameters of "suicide" and "Bel Air" for cross-reference purposes. Seconds later, I was reading her autopsy. The cause of death was an overdose of booze and valium.

"There's a recipe for a deep sleep," I mumbled to no one. Opening an attachment, I saw a photo of the suicide note. It appeared to be a woman's handwriting: *Dear Darius, I am so sorry to have left you, but I simply cannot go on any longer. The days have grown dark and I feel it will be better if I sleep. I'm sorry. All My Love, Mom.*

I read it a second time, thinking it would make more sense. No such luck. Having lived with a shrink in my former life and growing up with a mother who relied on what she called "Mother's Little Helper," I knew how mixing prescriptions with alcohol could be dangerous.

What if she didn't mix them?

As my mind returned to Darius, I couldn't imagine how that incident must have single-handedly devastated him. I also wondered how it affected him later in life and how it affected his father's career.

I googled Dwight Turkel and up came Wikipedia with a picture and a short bio: *Dwight David Turkel (October 3, 1950 - April 26, 1984), an American actor who starred in the cult films, 'Dawn of Evil,' 'Twisted Mother,' and 'Swamp Children,' died of an apparent suicide following a long bout of depression. He leaves behind....*

"What?" I barked, slamming the desk, then mumbled, "Fifteen years old and both parents are dead from *suicide?*"

I created another search in the database and within minutes had a hit. Someone discovered Dwight with a gunshot wound to the head. I opened a photo attachment of the typewritten suicide note: *Dear Genevieve and Darius, I am so sorry, but I hate not being able to find work. Perhaps I'm not cut out for this. Genevieve, I am devastated you no longer want me. It's more than I can take. Please forgive me, Darius. Love, Dad.*

My head was spinning as I considered his father died when he was ten and his mother when he was fifteen.

No wonder he became a shrink.

60

REASONABLE DOUBT

I don't give a shit *what* it takes, just that you *fix* this. And I don't mean tomorrow. I mean NOW!" Bobby shouted over the phone at his attorney.

Andrew Jacobitz has been his attorney for nearly a decade and the only man Bobby had ever known to stick by him during all the HR shit he had marched through over the years. Furthermore, Andrew was one of only three people who knew the real story behind the death of Bobby's father—what the court had called: Justifiable Homicide.

Bobby continued to rant about all the things he and Andrew had covered a dozen times inside the past month. And Andrew let him spew.

When authorities accused Bobby of premeditated murder in his father's death, Jacobitz went into action, and to that end, did exactly what the law required of him. He objectively proved beyond all reasonable doubt that the victim, aka Bobby's father, intended to commit life-threatening violence to Bobby and his mother. His father's homicide was legally ruled "blameless and distinct from the less stringent criteria authorizing deadly force in stand your ground rulings."

In other words: Bobby walked.

Andrew continued to endure Bobby's vitriolic rage, holding the receiver from his ear and interjecting an occasional "Right" or "I understand" in order to keep the clown going. After all, he was on the clock and watching the digital meter on his phone tick the minutes.

About the only thing Andrew had difficulty tolerating—more than potential clients complaining about his astronomical hourly rate, more than current clients whining about how everything took so long, and more than past clients dragging their feet on past payments—was people yelling at him. His mother yelled at him as a child, his father yelled at him as a teenager, his ex-wife yelled at him during the tough years, his current wife yelled at him when she did not get her way, and now one of his best clients was yelling at him.

He despised it.

As Bobby droned on about the system being unfair, judging a man on circumstances and not evidence, Andrew really wanted to fire Bobby and be done with him. And the more Bobby whined about the cops walking in on his sexual playground and demanding to search the premises without any warrants, Andrew wished he could silence the noise.

But he would neither fire nor silence Bobby because by the time this case went to trial—knowing what he knew the detectives had uncovered, how the press continued to hover, and the visibility of all the lovers—he would have made so much money he would not be able to count it all.

"Are you listening, ya fuckin' Jew?"

And what Bobby heard: CLICK.

When Bobby instantly rang back, Andrew had his secretary tell Bobby to call back in twenty minutes. After Andrew figured his client had cooled off, he took the call.

"Hi, Bobby," he said before his client could speak a word, "If you yell one more time, I will not only hang up on you *again*, but I will walk the fuck away, never to speak to you again. Are we clear?"

"Yes."

"Good. Now, let's talk about what's next. Like civilized human beings."

AN HOUR LATER, Bobby left the conversation satisfied that Andrew would do everything in his power to get most, if not all, of the charges dropped. As for Bobby's one million dollar bail—Andrew explained it was just the price of doing business. As much as Bobby hated it, he understood how the system worked. Besides, he knew how to get that money back and had no intention of telling Andrew any of those plans.

Andrew, on the other hand, had plans of his own. His proverbial chess pieces were on the board and he began moving those figures into play. He surmised that between the relationships he had cultivated over the past three decades, along with the invaluable litany of favors he had accrued in his favor bank, he would not only have Bobby exonerated as a free man but would also be free from the Neanderthal's disgusting behavior—once and for all.

Considering his next move, Andrew told his secretary to hold all calls, then sequestered himself in his office. Choosing to disregard both the landline and his cell, he took a burner from a locked drawer. He often used untraceable cell phones for "under the radar business," only to toss them into an industrial shredder afterwards.

He dialed, spoke to a secretary, and was connected within seconds.

"Judge Norelli."

"Hi Samuel, it's Andrew Jacobitz. How are you?"

"Fine, thanks. What's on your mind, Andrew?"

"I won't keep you long, just wanted to discuss something that affects us both."

"Okay."

"Let's just say we share a problem that needs solving—one that shares a common denominator."

Andrew heard the Judge take a deep breath. "Just a second."

Next, he heard a muffled conversation followed by silence and checked to see he still had a connection. "Okay, you have my undivided."

"Good. I'll cut to the chase. I believe I have a solution to a particularly *sticky* situation you find yourself in."

"Get in line," he snorted. "You have any idea how many *sticky* situations I find myself in on any given month?"

"I'm sure."

"But I'll play along. What, pray tell, could this one be?"

"I can make your…*mob situation*…disappear. "

A long silence followed.

Andrew wondered if he had been disconnected again or if the one-off phone was short on minutes. He heard a click, then Samuel said, "Okay."

"What was that?" Andrew asked.

"Switched to a private line," Norelli said quietly. "How'd you know about that?"

Andrew grinned. "It's my job to know *a lot more* than anyone else. You know how many people your daughter's department has sent away over the past several years? People *I* represented?"

"Of course I do. I helped groom her."

Andrew shook his head. "That same daughter is cooking some plan to help you out, right?"

More silence.

"Okay, I get it—silence speaks volumes. But you have to know I have people on the inside," Andrew said. "And playing both sides."

"Uh huh."

"And several happen to owe me big."

"Who?" Norelli asked.

"Yeah, right. Look, we've known one another a long time, and even though we don't see eye to eye—"

"On *many* things," Norelli interrupted.

"However, we *do* agree on several key things."

"Like?"

"Like your daughter is too smart to get nicked because of your mistakes."

"Sad. But I agree."

Andrew knew he had to be careful. "You don't want to put this play into motion right before you retire. It could go all sorts of sideways. You have, what, 40 years of impeccable service—only to finish with a single yet major mark on your legacy?"

"That would never be forgotten."

"Agreed."

"So, what's on your mind, Jacobitz? You're not a non-profit. Hell, you're barely a nice guy."

"I'll ignore that," he said, taking a deep breath. "I have a case that's going to get a lot of attention soon."

"Bobby Shapiro?" the Judge said with a smile in his voice.

"Exactly. He's innocent and—"

"And you're high."

"Save it, Judge. And for the record, you should've set that bail higher —would've made a nice going away gift."

"Hey, before you—"

"Keep your robe on. You and I both stand to lose if we're not careful. And it's not like you don't already know, but we *both* have much to gain. If we keep our heads on straight."

"Enough of the cloak and dagger, Jacobitz, whaddya got?"

Smiling, Andrew said, "I see where your kids get their smart mouths."

"Yeah, you should meet their mother."

61

SWIRLING DERVISH

As I sat across from Dr. Tercel, I was a mixed bag of emotions, intentions, and who knew what else. Staring at my hands, I looked up to find Tercel smiling.

"You seem a bit fidgety today."

"Yeah, lots going on. But really, it's just the usual."

"Usual is good, right?"

Nodding, I kept moving. "Thanks for keeping this appointment. Stuart and I had plans to follow up with you, but he got called away to baby duty."

"I'm happy for him. He'll make a good father."

Figuring it was best to simply jump in, I said, "So, I was reading last night—research and such—and saw that your father committed suicide… when you were just ten years old."

I hadn't known Tercel long, but the reaction I just witnessed felt like heartbreak. His eyes fell to his lap where he uncharacteristically began wringing his hands.

"I'm sorry," I said quietly, "I shouldn't have—"

"No, no, it's fine. But this is your time, not mine," he said, "Please continue with—"

"No, Dr. Tercel, this is important. Please tell me what you felt, what you must have gone through. Helping me understand you…will help me understand me."

"That was a long time ago," he nervously smiled, crossing the room for a glass of water. "I was ten and he was my hero. It was late winter—maybe early spring." He stopped to look out the window. "It was just after the Oscars. Both my parents were actors, so I never missed a chance to attend. In fact," he chuckled, "I've never missed an Oscars in 42 years."

Having just learned that, I felt we shared a secret.

Returning to his seat, he handed me a glass. "Please continue."

"I had come home from playing with some neighborhood friends. Riding my bike into the driveway, I saw the garage door open. It was *always* closed, especially when Dad's car was parked in it—as it was at the time. Which was odd. Anyway, as I approached the garage, I saw broken glass on the passenger side of the garage floor. First thing that went through my mind was that we had been robbed."

Taking a sip, he whispered, "That's when I saw him."

I didn't move a muscle.

"His head was thrown back and cocked to one side, laying against the headrest. A portion of the right side of his face—right about the temple," he said, touching the area, "Was...gone. The gun was still in his left hand. In his lap. Evidently, the caliber was large enough to go through both his head and the passenger window." He stopped to dab the corner of his eyes, "Sorry."

"I can't imagine."

We were silent for several moments before I spoke. "Can I ask you something?"

"Yes," he said, straightening his posture.

"Was there a note?"

He released a long breath before nodding an affirmative.

"It seems like a silly question, but how did you get through that? "

"No, it isn't. Everyone needs to understand our coping mechanisms." He took another sip, then set aside his glass. "How? Slowly. And not very nicely."

He went on to discuss the note, telling me it was typed on an old Smith Corona his father kept in his home office. As he revealed more, I asked more. He continued to answer.

We discussed the obvious impetus for setting up his Save Yourself Foundation—a non-profit that raised millions to help people recovering from attempted suicide, and he shared how successful it had grown. He went on to speak about how his mother used to berate his father—about how he was a lousy actor and would never amount to anything. That pushed his father to withdraw and eventually his social drinking became everyday drinking.

"The yelling turned into throwing and eventually into hitting. But hardest of all? Was how Mother emasculated him. After he was gone, she started her own downward spiral into depression—taking pills to sleep, pills to wake, and still others to cope with depression. She exacerbated the situation by mixing with alcohol," Tercel said quietly.

Something in our conversation triggered an old memory about my ex-husband, and before long I was sharing how he began to morph into another sort of person during grad school as his obsession about learning the inner workings of the mind seemed to overshadow anything else—including me.

"It's as though his studies became him. Or, the other way around."

Tercel's expression was intense. "That's often the case, especially in clinical psychology. Call it getting too close or digging too deep...I'm not sure, but it happens. And to more people than you would think. In fact, and I hesitate to share this for fear of going too deep, but while attending grad school, a study partner of mine...did that very thing."

"What do you mean?"

"Often, while studying a particular field—in this case suicide—students can get obsessed with trying to learn what makes someone take his or her own life. How far down a rabbit hole does one go? And what are the impulses to take us, or rather anyone, that far?"

For a moment, he seemed to disappear.

"Doctor?"

"Sorry, I was just recalling my study partner. She had tendencies toward that dilemma. The whole time I knew her. She spent so much time in research and trying to fix her screwed up childhood..." he trailed off.

"And?"

With barely a whisper, he said, "She hanged herself."

Without thinking, I sucked in my breath, covering my mouth.

"Sorry," he smiled nervously. "I think we've drilled deep enough for one day."

"Are you kidding? I completely understand. And I feel for you."

"Excuse me for a half second," he said, disappearing behind a wall next to his beverage counter.

I glanced at the books on his shelves: *Metaphysics, Hypnoanalysis, Pharmaceuticals, Suicide, Death & Dying,* and *Transactional Analysis.*

Seconds later, he was back in his chair. "Sorry. Looks like we have a few more minutes, and let's *please* spend that remaining time on *you*."

"Vulnerability breeds intimacy," I said without thinking. "Uh, what I meant was—"

"You're actually blushing, Detective," he laughed. "I find it honest. And thoroughly refreshing."

Sharing the laugh, I gathered my things but remained seated. "Dr. Tercel, before I go, I need to ask about a client. And I understand the doctor-patient privilege aspect, but we're so very close with this investigation, and I need your help navigating it."

"Okay."

"When did you first sense Bobby needed your help? As a patient."

"You know I can't address—"

"Yes, I understand. However, he's accused of her murder, and while delicate, you could potentially help us with the case."

His expression showed struggle.

"Tell me this, and it's a simple yes or no answer. In your professional opinion, do you think he has suicidal tendencies."

Squinting, his eyebrows pinched as he sighed, "I'm just not comfortable with this."

"Let's try this. What if you were to pass me on the street and we were to discuss—"

"But we wouldn't."

"But if you did."

"But why is that important?"

"Because I need to know," I said, leaning forward. "Okay, let's just say you knew he had an emotionally charged past."

"Yes," he said, clearing his throat. "And a troublesome present."

"Right. Common knowledge."

"And it wouldn't surprise me," he said with a nervous smile, "That *if* things continue as they are, he could *possibly* be prone to such."

"Thank you," I smiled.

"Speaking merely as a *professional*."

I was about to speak when he added, "But then, isn't everyone prone? To the possibility?"

"Are we?"

"Of course."

"And isn't it good to come to terms with our feelings?" I asked.

"You're starting to sound like me," he grinned.

"That's good, right?"

He chuckled, "Is it?"

We laughed.

Gathering my things, I walked to the door and stopped at his beverage service to throw away my cup when I absently noticed something in the trash can. Before I could process it, his hand on my arm turned me toward him.

"By the way, today's session is on the house."

"Absolutely not."

Standing closer than usual, I could smell his cologne. The musk was alluring.

"I insist. After all, we spent more time talking about me, which is *not* the reason you're here."

I suddenly felt warmer than before. "Uh, but that's not part of—"

"Please," he said, taking my hand, "Trust me when I say, I get paid very well for my time. And I can certainly comp an occasional session."

I WAS several blocks down Santa Monica Boulevard when I realized my mind was wandering. Passing Cedar-Sinai Medical Center on Beverly, I thought about Stuart—wondering how he and Janine were getting along with a newborn. Skirting Fairfax and landing on Melrose, I recalled how Shay and I would spend weekends shopping for hip clothes when she was in high school.

As curiosity tapped the back of my mind, I needed an answer, so I dialed Tercel's number.

He answered within a ring, "Dr. Tercel."

"Hi, Doc, it's Norelli. Sorry to bother, but I have just one quick question. Got a second?"

"Sure, what is it?"

"I'm certain you mentioned it, but what school did you attend? Just curious to see if you and my ex were at the same school at the same time."

After a beat, he said, "I received my Undergrad in Clinical Psychology from San Diego State, then my Masters in Mental Health Counseling from USFCA."

"San Francisco? Nice," I said. "Yeah, he went to SFSU."

"Good school."

"Yeah, but no USF."

USF was private and SFS was a commuter school. One was pricey and prestigious—the other, cheap and charming.

"But actually?" Tercel said, "It's all about how you use it; especially *where* you do your training. I hate to be rude, but my next client just arrived. Do you—"

"Sorry, and of course. You get to it. Thanks for your time."

Ringing off, I considered his schools. They were legit. And the degrees, earned. I knew from past experience the hours they put in were no joke. I should know, my ex was rarely around in the later years.

But back then, he spent most of his extracurricular hours studying *someone* else.

62

EVIDENCE SCHMEVIDENCE

Attorney Jacobitz leaned against the window, watching all the worker ants scurry about their workdays, wondering if they had any idea of how their lives would play out.

"My client did not kill that anchor—he loved her," Andrew said. "He's just damn crazy."

It was up to Judge Norelli to make the next move.

"Yeah, but I've seen and heard more than enough evidence."

"Schmevidence," Andrew said. "It's all circumstantial and you know it —or *will* know it soon enough. Let him ride. Hell, at the very worst, give him six months of soft time. Put the fear of God in him. Or, slap him with a *ton* of community service—which I promise he will gladly do. And here's another thought; have him pay damages to the family. He can afford it."

Norelli liked that idea. Families often suffered the most while bene-fiting the least.

"He won't be able to go back to the network," Norelli said.

"Doubt that'll break his heart. Especially with his girlfriend commit-ting suicide—"

"*Murder*," Norelli said.

"No, that's what I'm saying. There *is* enough to make it suicide."

More silence. Andrew waited.

"Thing is…it's my daughter. And she—"

"Sorry to interrupt, Judge. I know she's got a lot to prove, but she can catch the next one."

"She isn't one to fold," said Norelli.

"Not fold. Just *slide*."

"Not much for letting things slide either."

"Just like her old man."

"What can I say? Taught my kids to fight for what's right."

"Then again…" he held the pause like a freeze-frame. "We're having *this* conversation, right?"

"Right," he said quietly.

"Look, I'm sure you taught your kids the difference. But the thing is, right sometimes becomes wrong."

"No, wrong is always wrong," Norelli said sternly.

"Maybe so. But you and I both know these are different days. Hell, your son's in the epicenter of the world where deals—just like this one— get done everyday, right *or* wrong."

"Keep him out of this," Norelli growled. "This is *our* agreement. Nobody else has to—hell, nobody else *can* know."

"Fair enough. And just to refresh, you let him walk, I'll help you out. Simple as that."

"What's your plan?

Andrew shifted. "Is it true you've been having conversations with Fat Frankie?"

"Are you kidding me?"

"Like I said."

"Alright already—you've got eyes everywhere. Yes, I did, why?"

"Just trying to drive home the fact I can handle this."

"This what? Just to be sure we're on the same page."

Now, Andrew was growing impatient. "The thing Nicky needs to disappear."

"Yeah?"

"I can do that."

"Personally?"

"Are you fuckin' kiddin' me, Judge? I got a secretary who practically wipes my ass for me. No dirt happens within a zip code of me. So, no not me personally, but trust me, it'll get done. Disappear. Voila!"

The Judge chuckled. "Who says that anymore?"

"Says what?"

"Viola."

"I do."

"I see that."

"So?"

"So, what?" Judge Norelli asked impatiently.

"So, do we have a deal?"

"You'll make this go away—which will keep my family *completely* safe from here on out—and all I have to do—"

"For Chrissake, don't say it out loud!" Andrew blurted.

He was within ten yards of scoring a touchdown; up until now, it could be called conjecture.

Finally, his partner-in-crime released the deciding sigh, "Yes."

Andrew asked, "Is that a yes, yes, or—"

"It's a yes!"

"Good."

"Good."

———

THE NEXT DAY Bobby was free on bail but not allowed to venture outside the city limits. The first thing he did was go into work to talk to his boss. When he showed up to odd glances—Julia King being the first—he was not thrilled to find coworkers eyeballing him like he was a convict. He let her know things were going to be fine.

"Really?" She frowned. "How?"

"Yes, and first of all," Bobby said, sneering at coworkers through the glass of her office, "I did *not* kill Meredith. No matter what you heard or will hear."

"I know that. I saw the way you looked at her. And as sappy as it sounds, it was the closest thing I've seen to love since I moved to this fucking town."

Bobby looked at her with an expression she had not seen before—it made her feel sorry for the big lug.

"I don't know how *she* felt, but I could see in your eyes it was the real deal."

"And as much as we had our troubles, I'd have done anything for her. Which is why I'm going to kill the *fuckwad* who killed her," he growled through gritted teeth.

"So, suicide's not even—"

He shook his head. "I have a pretty solid idea who did it. Just a matter of putting the pieces into place so that *when* he trips up, he'll basically fuck himself in the ass."

Another frown. "Do you *have* to sound like such a Neander—"

"Don't fucking say it!"

63

GONE FISHING

Returning to the precinct, I instinctively looked for Stuart's car, then realized he was likely changing an umpteenth diaper of the day. Back at my desk, I set aside a coffee, opened Meredith's file, and logged into my computer.

Last night, I had fallen asleep going through Tercel's websites—both the practice and his suicide foundation. They were informative, but I was exhausted. Much of the psychology of suicide was drier than I had imagined. I was having a tough time staying awake until I made an interesting, yet macabre, discovery.

Come to find out, there were more ways people killed themselves than I had ever imagined. The list I came across—"The Most Lethal Methods of Suicide"—listed the number of suicides by methods. Published in 1995, 291 lay persons and 10 forensic pathologists rated the lethality, time, and agony for 28 methods of suicide for 4,117 cases of completed suicides in Los Angeles County during the period from 1988-1991.

The number one choice by all three parameters was a shotgun to the head. That was different from a *gun*shot to the head, rated number three. Rounding out the top ten: cyanide, explosives, hit by a train, jumping from a great height, hanging, and car crash. The oddest methods included: household toxins, asphyxiation by plastic bag, or setting oneself on fire. By the time I got to wrists cutting and drug overdosing, I had all the suicide ideas I would ever need.

Needing to change my mental scenery, I grabbed my mug and went to the lunchroom for a fresh cup.

En route, I texted Stuart: *Hey Big Daddy, how's Mom & baby? I need your help. Call when you can.*

Pouring a fresh cup, I thought of Bobby.

What if he killed her then staged it to look like a suicide?

Back at my desk, I thought of Tercel.

How must it feel to spend your whole life wondering if you weren't enough to stick around for?

Trying to imagine that pain, I scanned my notes again—noting how it was ten years later when his college study partner killed herself.

And how bad must you hate life to hang yourself?

Looking into Bobby's past for the umpteenth time, I ran across a page of notes from several of his teachers. Comments revealed he had a terrible temper, was always getting into fights, and was suspended a number of times for hitting his classmates with a variety of props from baseball bats and hockey sticks to golf clubs and football helmets. And when he was not taking his anger out in sports, he was expelled from school for putting a classmate in the hospital with a hunting knife he carried.

According to one file, he severed a major artery in the kid's leg in a fight over a girl. Lucky for him, the school nurse who had served as an army medic was on duty and saved the kid's life. Self-defense was what saved Bobby because the kid was twice his size and with three times the violent offenses as Bobby.

I closed the file and put my feet up on the desk, letting my mind free fall. It bounced from one of Meredith's coworkers to another, lighting up my brain like an arcade pinball machine. Their faces came back to me— one after the next—and their stories all told the same thing: Bobby was a bully and had a bad temper, but he loved the girl.

Without Stuart, I didn't have someone to discuss what I may or may not have missed, so I revisited my *Notorious 8* list taped to the file cabinet next to my desk. Eight people had a relationship of some sort with Meredith—whether for months or years. All eight were in calendars across all her devices and described as *meetings*. Some were semi-regular; others were *very* regular.

The heading read: Initials, Name, and Gauge, followed by a grade of 1-8 from the lowest to highest probability.

EN: Elgin Nessbach. Doubtful: 2

GJ: Grey Jordan. Questionable: 6

TS: Tommy Showalter. Possible: 7
SH: Sonny Hoffman. Unlikely: 4
BP: Bruce Panneck. No exposure: 0
DT: Darius Tercel. Hard to imagine: 3
SG: Sharon Gladstone. Accomplice: 8
BS: Bobby Shapiro. Hell yes: 9+

Captain Nelson ambled in the office by my desk while I was knee-deep in contemplation.

"Norelli, is this heaven?" he chuckled.

"No, it's Iowa," I played along. "Good movie."

"*Field of Dreams*. My fave. Seriously, were you here all night? Or out partying then thought you'd come in for..." he stopped, leaning over for a sniff. "Hell, you smell pretty. You were in here *fresh*."

"Captain, I'm just—"

"No, wait. I meant to say," he said, looking around, "Thank you for coming in, Detective Norelli. It's a pleasure seeing someone work as diligently as you."

I looked at him like he was insane.

"Don't want any 'me-too bullshit,' you know," he whispered. "And get bounced on *improper conduct* in the workplace so near to retirement."

I shook my head, trying to play along. "All good, sir. How may I help you?"

"When were you going to tell me Bobby was released on bail?"

"I thought you knew. I'm sure if—"

"Fucking with you, Norelli."

"Of course, sir."

"But we do have enough to get him convicted, right?"

"Yes."

"But not *really*, right Norelli?" he said, leaning closer. "Just wondering if, you know, he had any ideas of scooting out."

"Always a possibility, sir."

"Everything's a possibility. What I'd like to *gently* suggest is that you keep a very strategic eye on him."

"Sir, are you—"

"Just saying," he said, pointing to the ceiling. "The sooner you wrap it, the better. For you and me."

He started to walk away, stopped and looked around, then returned. "Norelli, can I ask you something?"

Without waiting for an answer, he sat in Stuart's chair, sliding closer to me. "You know—hell, everyone knows—I'm close to pulling the pin. And well, I would prefer to go out with—you know—a bang. Well, anything, just so it's BIG. *Comprende?*"

"Si," I smiled.

He squinted. "Being a smart-ass, are you, Norelli?"

"Kind of."

He allowed a tiny smirk. "Well, get to it then."

"Trying, Sir," I planted a phony smile. "Diligently."

"And you're doing a heck of a job," he said, slapping my thigh. "I'll be in my office. Carry on."

I wasn't exactly sure what he was up to, but I had enough time in uniform to know how the system worked and how the chances of things getting solved narrowed quickly if they dragged on too long.

Next came a text from Stuart: *Hey, girl. Knee-deep in baby poop, scrambling to finish Honey-do's. Give me 30?*

Smiling, I responded: *Do what you must.*

I pulled up Tommy Showalter's website. It was a veritable *soup* of sex. Anything and everything imaginable was there.

Next, I tried to quiet my mind—which worked for all of fifteen seconds, so I sent another text to Stuart: *Hey, partner. Not waiting. I'm coming over.*

Grabbing my things, I flipped a sign outside my cubicle that read: GONE FISHING.

64

HEAD GAMES

Bobby had a newfound freedom—one he did not even know he needed. Sure, he had to dig into his 401K to post bail, but he figured maybe they were right—it was the price of doing business. The first thing he did after reading the riot act to his attorney was putting his next plan into play. While he would not get his million back, he could get repaid by setting up the guy who had made his life a living hell. If his cards were played right, he figured a book deal about the story behind the madness would be made. Plus, he imagined being asked to direct the film.

Bobby had gone without a shave for several days and decided to clean himself up. After a hot shower he checked the time and considered whether to make a move now or wait until later. Weighing the odds, he chose night. Besides, now would be a good time to get other matters out of the way as he thought of all the material he had on his friends. He had spent years acquiring and storing the dirt just in case he got in a tight spot.

He had the most material on his gym pal Chris, a Class A pervert who was known for nothing being off limits—as long as the women were hot and naked and the action was kinky and dangerous. Videos were better than photos, and he was willing to gamble on anything if it got him tuned up. He would be the easiest to frame.

Tercel was an easy pin because Bobby was around him a lot during Meredith's treatment days and had learned a great deal from Tercel. Bobby imagined what a twisted little fuck he had to be; after all, he figured that doctors of the mind were most likely to be the sickest of all patients. Given Tercel's high profile, it could prove to work against Bobby, but he did not care—Tercel moved to the top of his list.

Next, he imagined a nut who was wound tighter than tight. Steve Owen, the eager beaver from his hunting and self-defense workshops, was a guy who seemed level-headed on the surface, but Bobby could see him going nuts on a parking lot of people.

That made him consider the most volatile tool of all: Sharon—hot as balls, smart enough to concoct a murder, and manipulative enough to command the right assistance. His only hesitation with her: he did not like the thought of losing the second hottest booty call of all, even if she was batshit-crazy. The fact she had a hard-on for both balls *and* broads made her a wild card.

Thinking about who he could irrevocably fuck, his mind next went to Julia King. He knew she would be easy to frame since she hated Meredith so much and everyone knew it.

In the end, his smartest move would be one of his two closest connections: Gladstone or Tercel. Tercel had a method. As a doctor, he could prescribe drugs—getting patients to do things they would not ordinarily do —and he was loaded. Gladstone, on the other hand, was an "Insider," was also well-funded, and could get investors to fund projects they ordinarily would never consider supporting.

Both could *Pay to Play*, so he flipped a mental coin.

65

UNKNOWN CALLER

On the drive to Stuart's home, my phone rang. Thinking it was Jackie, I answered without looking at the screen.

"What's up, *biooooootch*!"

"Now *that's* a greeting. Hello, Detective Norelli."

Shit. "Hi, Dr. Tercel. Sorry about that. I was just…I thought—"

"No worries," he laughed. "And I won't keep you. Just need to ask you a quick question."

"Shoot."

"As much as I hate to do this—and rarely ever do—could we possibly postpone our next appointment? If we could push it off just two days, but at the same time, it would help me tremendously."

"Sure, that's fine. Everything okay?"

"Thank you. And yes. I've been asked—unfortunately at the last minute—to speak at a symposium in San Jose tomorrow. It's part of an adjunct program to my alma mater and their key speaker had a death in the family. They asked if I could assist."

"Understood. And no worries. I have plenty of work, especially with a partner on leave."

We were about to sign off when I took a stab at an impulse. "Dr. Tercel, may I ask you one quick question?"

"Sure."

"Have you ever been married?"

There was just enough silence and I felt awkward.

"Yes, her name was Clare. She was a lovely gal."

I caught myself smiling, trying to imagine what she must have been like. "Wait. Was?"

"Well, we weren't *actually* married, but we'd been together for so long. Then, right when she got pregnant, we made it official."

I was waiting for the next sentence. "Dr. Tercel?"

"Sorry. I was just remembering how in love we were."

"What happened?"

"The short story? I was launching my practice while she was planning the wedding—and getting more pregnant by the day," he chuckled. "Then, a week before her thirty-first birthday, we couldn't find a heartbeat. And she...miscarried."

My heart sank, "I'm truly sorry. Did you find—"

"No, just that his heart stopped beating."

A little boy. I wanted to cry.

"It crushed us. And...she dove into a *deep* depression."

"Dr. Tercel, I'm so sorry. I can't imagine."

"I'm sure you didn't ask for all that," he exhaled deeply. "That's why I haven't married. Or had children. Too much pain."

"I get it."

"Now you know why I'm a shrink," he nervously chuckled.

"I get it."

"Well, I really must go. And thank you again for working with me. I don't like changing appointments, but this is quite important."

Tossing my phone onto the seat, I shook my head.

Holy shit that was depressing.

I cranked the stereo and hoped Led Zeppelin's "Rock and Roll" would distract me from wanting to lie down in the middle of oncoming traffic on the 405.

66

COLLATERAL DAMAGE

Bobby showed up at Tercel's office fifteen minutes before the Doctor's last appointment ended. Sitting in the parking lot, he ran down the way he would present his scheme for both his Plan A and Plan B.

Tercel was his Plan A.

Knowing Tercel as long as he had, Bobby was aware of the unique way the doctor could play with a person's head. It often appeared Tercel was one step ahead, which always pissed off Bobby. He knew it was education and technique that set them apart. However, Bobby was much bigger and way stronger.

Taking a long swig of his post-workout drink—a mixture of caffeine, creatine, and benzedrine—Bobby gained his focus. He suddenly saw the light in Tercel's office go dark and felt a rush of adrenaline course through his body as he got out of the car.

Within seconds, Tercel exited the building and made his way across the parking lot straight toward Bobby's car parked right next to his own car. Tercel's eyes were fixated on his phone screen, so he did not see Bobby until he was several feet away.

Looking up, he was clearly startled. "Oh, hello, Bobby. Long time no see. How are you?"

"Good, thanks. You?"

He thought he saw a flash of fear cross Tercel's eyes when he looked around the parking lot that was emptying as the daylight was fading.

"Good, just in a bit of a hurry. A dinner appointment. But always have time for you. Is there something you need?"

"Actually there is. I've thought it over and came to a very *significant* conclusion."

With raised eyebrows, Tercel smiled. "Okay."

"I need you to do me a favor."

Calmly, "What's that?"

Bobby responded in a matter-of-fact tone, "I need you to take the fall for Meredith's murder."

67

TURNING POINT

Two men. One parking lot. A dozen ways things could go south.
Both stared at one another. Any shred of civility had vanished like yesterday's smog.

Tercel frowned. "Excuse me?"

Standing taller, looking tougher, Bobby smirked, "You heard me. You made the mess. You clean it up."

Suddenly, Tercel broke out laughing.

Squinting, Bobby clenched his jaw.

Tercel was laughing so hard, he had to set down his briefcase and wipe his eyes with a handkerchief.

"Oh, Bobby, you are *too* funny. That's the hardest I've laughed in a long time," his said, catching his breath. "Thank you. I so needed that."

Bobby thought he felt his chemical rush begin to fade. He kept staring, waiting for Tercel to squirm.

"First of all, dude? You're insane. Second, you know how it all went down. And third, you know exactly how it *will* go down next. You're going to the authorities and admit you killed Meredith. Hell, tell them it was an accident. Tell them you didn't mean for things to go as far as they did…that you…didn't know your own strength."

Regaining his composure, Tercel neatly folded and put away his handkerchief, then adjusted his coat sleeves, releasing a satisfying breath. He looked around before checking his watch, then started toward the driver side of his car.

"As fun as it has been catching up with you, Bobby—not to mention your providing a much needed laugh at the end of an exhausting day—I must bid you adieu and ask we continue this conversation..." he hesitated while opening the rear door, dropping his case on the seat. "Never."

Still smiling, he removed his sport coat and hung it on a hook in the back.

"We've had some good times," Bobby growled. "You, me, Meredith, Sharon. Some of the best. But those *good* times are gone. And the *bad* times are just around the corner. The degree of badness is up to you. So, if you'll—"

"Wait!" Tercel barked, throwing Bobby off balance.

"If you *think* for one minute you're going to come to my place of business and *threaten* me with your passive-aggressive and *maniacal* attitude...with an idea so *preposterous*, I can't *begin* to fathom just how *ridiculous* you are, well my friend, you've got another thing coming."

With each exaggerated word, he had taken a step closer to Bobby so that by the time he finished, they were nearly toe to toe.

Bobby had never seen this side of the gentle doctor, but he was neither scared nor threatened. In fact, as his anger began to erode, he wondered if he had overreacted.

Tercel released a short breath and smiled. "I'll tell you what, Bobby. I'll show you I'm an okay guy—which you already know," he said, checking his watch for the third time. "However, I'm completely late and you know how I deplore tardiness. That said, I'm going to leave but will gladly swing by your home later tonight as I'll be on that side of town, anyway..."

He opened the car door.

"Or, we can meet back here if you like. Either way, it's no problem. Just give me, let's say two hours and change? At that time, we can sit down and discuss this matter further like the gentlemen we are. Is that fair?"

With a faint sigh, Bobby's shoulders dropped.

"Yeah, I guess that's fair." Checking his watch, he said, "I'll hit the gym. For *another* workout. And see you at my place in a couple hours."

"Say, 8? 8:30? That work for you, Bobby?"

"That'll work."

"Good. See you then."

He got in and buckled up. With a wink and nod, he pulled away.

Watching his car leave the parking lot, Bobby shook his head and snorted, "Smooth little son-of-a-*bitch*."

BOBBY WAS HALFWAY to the gym when he dialed Sharon's phone. After four rings, a message picked up: *Hi, it's Sharon. You know what to do. I'll ring you back when I can.*

After the beep, he said, "Hey Sharon, it's me. Call me when you get this. I need to talk to you about that thing you did for me the other day. I may have a change of plans. Anyhow, just ring me, okay? Thanks. Love ya."

Minutes later, he arrived at the Hollywood 24 Hour Fitness, got out, and tossed the valet his keys.

"Hey Chip, I'll be done in 45. Keep it up front?"

"You got it, boss."

Bobby slid him a $20 and headed inside.

Chip had already parked the car and was greeting another client when Bobby's cell phone—tucked in the middle console—rang.

Halfway through the third ring, it stopped.

68

PALM JOB

Tercel and Sharon sat in the back of The Palm, a Beverly Hills mainstay, staring at one another like newlyweds. He sipped a rich Italian Barolo while she nursed an oversized Gin Martini. With one shoe off, her bare toes were inspecting his shin, looking to bypass a sock for some skin.

"I noticed you were on the phone when I showed up," he smiled. "Who were you talking to?"

"Just a client," she said, leaning closer. "So, how was your day?"

"Interesting. And full. Yours?"

"Splendid. We have a new show arriving next week. A modern retrospective. Andy Warhol's early work, along with a handsome smattering of Lichtenstein."

Tercel watched her take a healthy sip of her drink, then fiddle with the olive.

"That's impressive. Love Warhol."

She continued to suck the oversized olive—pulling it in and out between her full lips.

"Remember when you and Meredith were getting all *hot 'n sticky* that weekend the four of us decided a trip to New York on July 4th weekend was a good idea?"

Confused by the instant trip down memory lane, he played along. "We must've been crazy. But thank God we moved the party to the Hamptons," he chuckled.

"Ah, the Hamptons….*dahling*."

Sucking the olive one more time, she dramatically swallowed it.

"You are *such* a tease," he smiled.

She moaned.

Leaning in, he whispered, "And recall how you were in the arms of—"

Playfully slapping his hand, she pouted, "Don't remind me. Bobby Can't-Miss-A-Workout Shapiro!"

When he checked his watch, she brought her face closer. "What are you doing?"

"What? Just checking the time. I've got to—"

"To what? Blow me off? And for *whoooom*? Another date?"

He enjoyed watching her feign hurt. But he also knew she preferred Bobby's maniacal, marathon-length sexual escapades.

"It's business, love."

"For *him*?" She pulled back. "Of all people." Pouting, she took the phone from her purse and swiped the screen. "Speak of the devil, he's called several times."

Tercel checked his phone. A text read: *Running 20 late. Back doors open if you beat me there.*

She put away her phone and adjusted her blouse to reveal more cleavage. "What is it, baby?"

"He and I just need to put a few things to rest," he said, waving to the bartender for another round. "That's all. Nothing major," he said, leaning closer—running a finger along the silhouette of her breasts. "But not before you and I enjoy another cocktail."

Her body heat was present, but her body language distant.

"Love, what's on your mind?"

Sighing heavily, she slurred, "I'm sure I should tell you."

He took her hand in his. "You can tell me anything."

"True. But maybe I shouldn't tell *this*," she said, looking away. "You love me, right?"

"You know I do."

Turning back, she said, "More than Bobby?"

"Yes, I love you more than I love Bobby," he chuckled.

Frowning, she touched his face. "You should know what's on his mind."

His stomach tightened. "We don't have secrets, Sharon. Never have, never will. And we've always been honest with one another, right?"

The bartender delivered two more drinks, then quietly disappeared. Tercel held up his glass, they touched rims, and she took a large sip.

"That's what lovers do," he whispered.

"But Meredith was your real lover," she pouted.

He gently placed a finger against her lips. "Stop, Sharon. My body may have been with her, but my heart has always been with you. You know that."

"I do," she smiled.

"So, what is it you want to share with me about our dear friend?"

She looked into her drink as though searching for an answer. "He's talking about...turning the video into those Detectives."

Stone-faced silence was followed by a long, hidden exhale. "That's unfortunate."

"I think he'll do it. He's been pretty wiggy lately. More so than usual," she giggled.

"He has, hasn't he? Do you know where it is now?"

A tiny nod. A short sip.

Reaching into her purse, she removed a small GoPro camera and slid it across the table.

"That's it?"

"Yes."

"*That*...has the footage?" He whispered.

Another nod.

"And it's nowhere else?"

She shook her head.

"And he doesn't have a backup copy?"

"I know, right? I mean, he's all Mr. TV 'n shit," she slurred. "Something about not having the right adapter or something to copy it. I dunno. Said all he could focus on was putting it someplace safe."

"Which was?"

"A safety deposit box at his bank."

Deep breath. "How did you get it and...what were *you* going to do with it?"

Appearing nervous, she looked around. "He asked me to get it, so I did. And I don't know...give it to the Detectives?"

His chest tightened. "That was excellent thinking on your part, my love. A very smart idea."

His bright teeth cheated an authentic smile.

"Thank you," her head bobbled.

"And personally, I think giving it to me was an even *better* idea. Thank you for trusting me."

She watched as he put it in his pocket. "What are you going to do with it?"

Nonchalantly, he asked, "Did you see what was on it?"

Fear flashed across her eyes. "No, he wanted me to. And I started to, but just couldn't."

"But he told you what was on there, yes?"

A slow nod, before she turned away. "You're making me nervous," she frowned, "Like I've done something wrong."

Tercel gently pulled her chin toward him. Kissing her cheek, he whispered, "I'm sorry, that was not my intent. I wouldn't do anything to harm you. Everything is fine, Love. Seriously. Not a single thing to worry about."

He kissed her passionately.

Pulling apart, she smiled. "I love you."

"And I love you," he said, nodding to the bartender. "And as much as I truly hate to do this—I've got to scoot."

While he paid the tab, she gathered her things.

At her car, she pulled him close, nibbled his earlobe, and whispered, "You'll be sorry you're going to miss a *long, hot, soapy* bubble bath with your girl."

"Perhaps we could…prolong the wait? And please, let me call you a cab," he said, taking the keys from her hand.

Suddenly feeling hopeful for a happy ending, she straightened up. "Don't be silly. You know I can handle my cocktails. I was just all warm and fuzzy," she said, taking her keys back. "You run along and I'll do the same. Just text me when…or if…you'd like to get soapy with your girl," she added, winking.

Without waiting, she got in her car and drove away, tossing a wave out the window.

69

HELLA BIG

Lost in thought, Angie drove the curvy canyon roads, listening to jazz on the radio while enjoying the cool night air fragrant with eucalyptus and orange blossom. She had received a phone call before leaving the office and knew she had to see Sharon before getting home. Since her office was close to Sharon's home, the quick stop would make for a friendly visit and a quick bit of business.

SHARON WAS in the master running a hot bath, sipping a glass of wine, and nearing a hot soak when the doorbell rang. Startled, she turned off the water and went to the front of the house.

"Hello, Angie," she said, opening the door. "What a...pleasant surprise."

"Hi, Sharon. I'm so sorry to barge in, and I do hope it isn't an inconvenient time, but I was on my way home—passing right by your neighborhood—and just *had* to stop by. It's important and simply *could not* wait. I'll be gone in a *New York* minute."

Sharon's unease settled at the mention of her hometown.

"Sure, come in," she smiled, motioning for Angie to enter. "I was about to take a bubble bath then maybe fall asleep in front of a movie, but I'm always up for a visit from a friend."

Walking to the bar, she refreshed her glass and took out another. "Can I get you a glass? It's quite tasty."

Portfolio in hand, Angie followed along. "Maybe just one little glass, but only if it's not a problem."

"Are you kidding? Drinking with a girlfriend on a school night? Doesn't get much better, right? By the way, how's the real estate business?"

"Business is exceptionally good," she smiled, taking out several papers. "In fact, it's the very reason for my *rude* interruption."

"Really?" Sharon smiled with a frown, handing Angie a glass. "What do you have there?"

"I have an extremely handsome offer for your home."

Another confused expression. "But it isn't on the market. I love this home and frankly, I have no intention of selling. You do know it's a one-of-a-kind Eichler. With a restoration that took me *years*."

"I do, I do—"

"In fact," Sharon chuckled, "I don't think I'll ever move."

"Well," Angie said, lifting her glass for a toast, "That's why they call this a...*Make Me Move* offer."

70

BABY MONITOR

Within minutes I was basking in the Stuart vibe, thankful I had a partner with whom I could share anything. We sat in his man cave and the juxtaposition of this enormous man holding a tiny baby was quite the sight.

"Man," I grinned ear to ear, "That looks good on you."

"Yeah, I gotta say, she's awesome."

Waving both hands, I said, "C'mon, Aunt Patty needs some baby love."

Handing his baby daughter over, he crossed to the mini-fridge for two cold beers and before he could ask, I answered, "After the day I've had? Hell to the yes."

STUART WANTED MORE information on the remaining *Notorious 8* potential suspects, so I drilled down. Sharing notes, we had a close match. He favored Nessbach more than I did and believed Jordan was less of a threat —especially after having met him. When it came to Showalter, he leaned more in his direction than I did. Finally between the two of us, it came down to Gladstone, Shapiro, and Tercel.

"I know it looks the most like Bobby's the guy, but I gotta tell you— my gut isn't feeling a hundred-percent."

He tossed his chin for me to continue.

"And you know I love me some Dr. Tercel—both for what he's done for me and for what I had *hoped* him to be."

"But you also said Sharon Gladstone has qualities for being a perfect fit."

"Agreed."

"Hey, before we keep going, are you as hungry as I am?"

"Yes, I don't think I had more than a rice cake and almond butter at my desk, uh, whenever ago."

"Good. Follow me."

WITHIN MINUTES, we were standing inside a local Mexican dive ordering fresh fish tacos. Snagging a couple of beers, we grabbed a corner booth while we waited.

"Let me show you what else I found while you were laying around watching Dr. Phil," I winked.

"Oh, shut the hell up," he laughed.

"So, how about Tercel's father, the actor turning telescope demonstrator?"

"What?"

"Yeah, little known fact," I began, "Couldn't make it as an actor but liked staring at a different kind of star, so he picked up a gig at the Griffith Observatory. He began as a janitor, then worked his way up to telescope guru while bit parts got fewer and SAG checks stopped coming. He turned to the bottle, his wife tired of the nonsense, they split over *irreconcilables*, and one day their son comes home to find father with a .38 slug through his temple. Messed him up pretty good. He sets off on a journey to—my words not his—find the reason for Pop's suicide."

"Okay, so Tercel's *ten* at the time?"

Swigging, I nodded and turned a page. "Five years later, Genevieve *Turkel*, a promising actress whose son is her date, decides its lights out on —get this—the night of the *Oscars*."

"NO!" he smacked my hand. "Don't even—"

"Yep, the next morning he finds Mom facedown before heading to school."

Stuart buried his face in both hands, "Poor kid."

"For certain," I said, lifting his head. "However, don't feel *too* badly until you hear what's next."

His eyes widened, "It gets worse?"

With raised eyebrows, I said, "Yeah, back to Genevieve. It was an OD on sleeping pills 'n booze. Nothing like a classic Hollywood exit, but something else—"

Just then, the guy at the counter called Stuart's name.

"Wait!" he said, grabbing the takeout and dropping $20. "We're heading back to the cave. Gotta put this up on the big board."

"Good, because you ain't seen nothing yet!"

71

NICE RACK

Located in a prestigious Los Angeles neighborhood near Pacific Palisades, Bobby's estate was surrounded by tall hedges and equipped with a solid gate that made seeing into the compound nearly impossible. Given the gate was open when Tercel arrived, he entered and circled the enormous fountain, parking behind Bobby's Porsche. Approaching Bobby's car, he touched the hood to see if it was still warm —it was.

At the massive front door of the modern home, he rang the doorbell. Bobby arrived in seconds with an easy smile and awash in a cloud of overdone cologne.

"Hello, Bobby."

"Hey, Doc, come on in," he waved. "Game won't start for a while, so why don't you let me get you a drink. What's your poison?"

Scanning the enormous bar, he spotted several bottles of Scotch. "Looks like you're a Scotch man, Bobby. I'll have what you're having."

"Perfect. I am, and you'll like it." On the way to the bar, Bobby tripped. "Whoops," he laughed. "Yeah, so I started without you."

Chuckling, Tercel was distracted by an enormous rack which held an impressive array of compound bows and knives on a trophy wall. He stopped to admire.

"Didn't know you were a fan, Doc," Bobby said, pouring drinks and watching Tercel.

"Well, I may not know much about these, but I do love the hunt."

Bobby handed him a drink. They raised glasses and took a sip, then Bobby took down one of his largest compound bows and handed it to his guest. "Feel how light this one is."

Tercel set down his glass and bounced the bow in the air. "Amazing."

"Especially considering the pull strength. And the freakin' *speed* once it leaves the rest."

"Rest?"

"Here," he pointed. "Where the arrow rests just before launch."

"Intimidating," Tercel said, handing it back to him.

"Not really. Once you get used to it," he winked. "And dangerous as *hell*."

They took another sip and then turned their attention to the 80-inch television where ESPN was muted.

After a minute of watching in silence, Bobby said, "So, let's pick up where we left off earlier. We can make it short and sweet as I'm sure you have plans. Besides, the game'll start soon and I doubt it's your cup of tea."

"Sounds like a plan," Tercel said, finishing his drink. Setting the empty glass on a nearby table, he reached into his breast pocket. "Here's something I'm certain will interest you."

In the next moment, Bobby's expression turned priceless.

"How did you get that?" Bobby frowned, "I hid it away in—"

"Perhaps not the *safest* of places," he grinned. "Guess she doesn't trust you, Bobby. Which is exactly what you should've been doing with me all along. Why go behind my back? We're friends, aren't we?"

Bobby was speechless.

Tercel said, "Aren't you in the business of shooting and editing trash like this to extort people?"

Bobby said nothing and Tercel noticed how Bobby's breathing increased while his eyes did not leave the camera.

"And yet you didn't even create a backup copy."

After a heavy sigh, he took a hefty swig. "I know. That was stupid. I just didn't take the time. Been a lot of shit happening."

Handing the camera to Bobby, he said, "You really shouldn't have trusted her, Bobby. She was, and is, in a situation well below her pay grade."

Bobby looked at the camera like it was a rare coin. Then a smile slowly spread across his tanned face.

"Yeah, but looks like I have it now, doesn't it, Doc?"

"Yes, you do. And you know why, Bobby? Because I trust you. And as you can see, you can't trust Sharon. But then, Bobby, you never could. Don't you know that? That's what I've been trying to tell you. You can't trust these women. You can enjoy them—for what they can do for you— but truly, they're merely here for your pleasure."

They stared at one another, motionless.

Bobby's brow tightened and his shoulders relaxed. "Bitch."

"But soon this will all be over and life will return to normal," Tercel said, glancing at the TV.

Bobby's snorted, "Normal? What the fuck, Doc. I'm only out on *bail*. I'm going to trial for *murder*. There's no normal in that!"

Emotionless, Tercel looked at Bobby. "They can't touch you. It's a ruse, Bobby. Besides, one of my clients, Detective Norelli—"

"What?"

Tercel was enjoying watching Bobby spin. "Yes. Didn't you know I'm seeing her? Several times a week."

"As a patient?"

"Yes, but that's not important now. You just need to know the things I'm hearing on the *inside*. They don't have anything on you. Trust me. Next month this time? All a distant memory."

Bobby looked at the camera in his hand. His eyes darted around the room. "Why should I trust you?"

Tercel stepped closer. "Because you know I'm a man of my word. And because frankly, what other choice do you have?"

"Plenty."

Although Bobby stood six inches taller and packed an extra 40 pounds of solid muscle, Tercel was not intimidated. He knew Bobby's Achilles heel.

"Have I ever lied to you?"

Bobby hesitated before shaking his head.

"Have I ever done *anything* to hurt you? No. In fact, I've done nothing but help you. Right?"

A nod.

"And show you the love and respect you never had before. Right, Bobby?"

Another nod.

Placing a hand on Bobby' shoulder, Tercel lowered his voice. "Then you know, as a man of my word, I want to help you. Just as I always have. You know that I believe in you, Bobby, right?"

A tiny smile of acknowledgement and matching nod.

"We both know you didn't kill Meredith. Heck, you'd never hurt a single hair on her beautiful head, would you, Bobby?"

A tear fought to crowd his vision.

"That's right. You loved her, Bobby. She was your *soulmate*. You would've done anything for her, right?"

He rubbed an eye.

"We both know Sharon's the real culprit. She was the one who couldn't take Meredith having all the limelight. All the glory. Sharon—the power-hitter from New York—wanted to be the Queen of LA. Not Meredith the farm girl from Wisconsin. We both know Sharon's jealousy got the best of her. She had to have it all. End the competition. And the nightmare from which she couldn't wake. Let's be honest. She got tired of being second fiddle to you, to me, and to all the beautiful people in Hollywood, right, Bobby? That's when she took matters into her own hands. By killing Meredith."

Bobby's wide eyes relaxed. Then, a scant nod.

"Exactly. I'm glad we understand one another. It's good when friends trust one another. And isn't it good to know all the noise that happened before will actually be seen for what it is? False. And Sharon will take the fall for what happened to Meredith. Not you."

Bobby finally managed a smile.

"Good. Now, hand me your glass and let me pour a drink to celebrate our friendship, okay Bobby?"

"Sounds good."

Motioning for Bobby to watch the game, Tercel refreshed their drinks while watching Bobby in the mirror over the bar.

He returned with a toast.

"Cheers to my friend, Bobby Shapiro. May you continue to be happy and prosperous for years to come. *And* cheers to the true mastermind of it all, our girl, Sharon Gladstone."

"Hell, yeah," Bobby said, clinking his guest's glass. "Cheers to that bat-shit crazy *bitch*!"

72

MONEY SHOT

Sharon stood frozen in place, staring at her new best friend. "Holy shit, that's an enormous number. That's *double* what I paid," Sharon said.

Angie smiled, "I know."

"No, actually maybe *more* than what I paid for the house *and* renovation!"

"I know," she smiled as they broke out in loud laughter.

"Look, Sharon, I'll find you another Eichler. Or a Mies Van der Rohe, or Saarinen, or a Gehry—"

"But nothing quite like...*this*," Sharon said, waving her hand like a magic wand.

Seeing Sharon was both tipsy and excited, Angie held up an empty glass. "Mind if I have just a *tiny* splash? Then I'm on my way. Promise!"

"Absolutely..." she slurred, making her way to the bar. "Hell, this is amazing. I had no idea and can't even imagine who in their right mind—"

"It doesn't matter, does it, Sharon? They saw what you've created and wanted it for their own."

Returning to her drinking partner, Sharon nearly spilled the glass when she handed it over. "Sorry. I'm just so taken aback. Who was it? Who *is* it —that wants my home?"

"They prefer to remain anonymous. But trust me when I say, they're a fan of what you've created and are willing to act quickly. With *cash.*"

"What? That's a *lot* of cash, Angie," Sharon slurred again. "A *helluva* lot."

They clinked glasses.

"Indeed. And we can close this entire deal before the end of the week. And you, my friend, will be one of the—hell—*the* wealthiest women I know!" Angie laughed.

"I suppose for that amount of money I *can* find another place for all my things," she said, sloppily motioning to her furniture.

Angie took a document and a pen from her portfolio and placed them on the dining room table. "All I need from you is your signature on this one document, and I'll handle all the rest."

Sharon was having a challenge focusing, so she crossed the room for a pair of glasses. Angie took that moment to pour more wine.

"What's the document say? Well, the gist of it anyway?"

"Just that you will accept the offer, agree to a cash deal, and vacate the premises within 30 days."

Sharon began to sign, then stopped in mid-signature. "Wait, 30 days? How can I find a place in that amount of time?"

Angie patted Sharon's hand. "Because I'm here to help. That's what I do. And if we need more time, I can make that happen. The buyer understands the abrupt nature of his transaction and can be flexible. Just leave it to Angie. Oh, and don't forget, you have *three days* to turn this down... just in case you so choose," she smiled. "How's that sound?"

Releasing a heavy sigh, Sharon's shoulders sagged. "That's... fantastic."

"Are you okay?"

"Maybe a little too much wine," she said, finishing the signature. "And perhaps not enough to eat," she mumbled. "So, if you don't mind, I think I'll excuse myself to a hot bath and call it a night."

"Of course. I'll get out of your hair," Angie said, gathering her things before leaving. "I'll talk to you later!"

73

DEEP DIVE

Back at Stuart's man cave, we continued deciphering the madness while dipping our tacos in mole sauce. I opened another two beers and began laying all my accumulated sticky notes out on the coffee table.

"I've been wanting to break this bad boy in for some time," Stuart said, adjusting the angle of the oversized whiteboard. "Okay, what else ya got?"

Kicking off my shoes, I took a sip of beer and slid him two police reports concerning Tercel's parents. As he attached them to the board, I removed my next file and joined him, gesturing for him to take a seat.

"Okay, news flash. I just learned my doctor had an ex-wife."

"Ooooookay."

"Right, because it just didn't seem like a guy this smart, this handsome, and this educated wouldn't have a wife," I said, flipping through my papers. "Clare Bernard was 31. He had just launched the practice he still runs today. They were together for two years, and in fact, they were celebrating their anniversary when he asked her to marry him."

Mesmerized, Stuart took a sip and nodded.

"Actually, let me back up. They were together for two years and she was pregnant. However, she had a miscarriage right around the time of their anniversary. According to the police report, she had been suffering depression and was under a doctor's care. So, on the night of her thirty-first birthday, they'd gone out to dinner and then returned home. He proceeded to work in his library while she went out for ice cream. On the way back from the store, she stopped at the Colorado Street Bridge in Pasadena—"

"Your hometown."

"Yes, which is how I was able to go one layer deeper," I winked. "It was sometime around 11:30 p.m. when she jumped off the bridge."

He involuntarily gasped, then froze in place.

"Fortunately, a Robert Pierson was out walking his dog very close to where she landed. He heard a thud and moments later found her."

Shaking his head, Stuart sighed.

"Here's where the pieces—while foggy—need your help."

"Shit's tragic," he shook his head. "Okay, shoot."

"Two witnesses were quoted as saying they saw a pleasant couple celebrating at the Arroyo Chop House when an argument broke out. There was some shouting by the man, followed by the woman crying. Shortly thereafter, they left. This was a little after nine. Two and a half hours later they're home and he's working—said the officers who received the call. According to Officers Newcomb and McCoy, Tercel reported that she left some time around eleven because she wanted some ice cream."

"Just for curiosity, let me pull up a map on my laptop and connect it to the overhead."

Seconds later, it was displayed on the board.

"There's the Chop House on South Arroyo Parkway," I said. "Right in the heart of Pasadena."

"Copy that. And here's the Colorado Street Bridge," Stuart said, pointing to the map.

"Thing is, they live *well north* of Pasadena in the quiet and well-to-do hood of Altadena. That's at least 20 minutes away—in the *opposite direction* of the Colorado Street Bridge."

Stuart's eyebrows raised before dropping into a deep frown. "Whatcha talkin' bout Willis?"

"Exactly," I chuckled.

"So why do they have dinner in downtown, drive north 20 or so to home, and then she drives back south—"

"*When* there are no less than a *dozen* ice-cream shops, grocery stores, neighborhood markets and such within blocks of their house."

"Why that bridge? Why jump?"

"The bridge is famous for jumpers. Why it's called, 'Suicide Bridge.' Freakin' violent way to go."

Stuart's eyes shifted. "Wait, take me back to the police report," he said, reaching for my notes. "Is there evidence of violence, any bruising to her..." he stopped. "Well, that would be pretty tough to find dropping—"

"150 feet."

"Fifteen stories," he mumbled.

"Yeah, no one survives that."

"Autopsy report?"

I pulled a sheet. "Not pretty."

He took it, disregarded the photo, and read aloud, "Between her face, hands and...you'd never see prior damage."

"Okay. So, they went to dinner and got into a fight. Don't know why, not important. They go home, he works late, she heads out for dessert. She never came home. Funeral's a few days later. He goes back to work. Life returns to normal—whatever that is. Open and shut."

"Okay."

"This is, or rather *was*, the weakest link in my chain so far. Until I started looking at dates."

"Like?" he asked.

I placed a grid on the board with everything in blocks and cross-referenced dates. "Okay, follow along. Father died when Tercel was 10. It's 1986. Mother died when he was 15. Five years later. It's 1991."

"Right."

"Fast forward to 2011. Tercel's now 35 when his 31-year old wife dies."

We looked at one another. He said, "Go on.

"So, I'm talking to Tercel in a recent appointment and, for whatever reason, he opens up to me—something he rarely does—and proceeds to tell me about a girl in his Psych class at SDSU. As part of their work, they're studying *suicide*."

"And?"

"And in their third semester together—"

"No," he said, cocking his head.

"Yes."

"What?"

"They're romantically involved. At least that's what I surmised from their yearbook, along with a short conversation I had with their Psych professor." Opening my notes, I continued, "Dr. Jack Carr said they spent all their time together—classes, labs, internships, thesis papers. Always together and at the same facilities. Get this...even for target practice."

His eyebrows shot up. "You mean...," he mimes putting a gun to his head.

I nod. He shook.

"She killed herself three weeks before graduation."

"What the..." he trailed off, staring at the floor.

I was just about to continue when he snapped his fingers. "Wait, what year is it?"

"1996. He was 20."

Stuart frowned.

"I'll come back to this, but let me jump ahead a second. It'll help you. Hang with me."

He rubbed his hands together like they were cold. "Rock it, baby."

"Knowing his undergrad was in Clinical Psych, I asked where he went to grad school."

"Where?"

"USFCA, a nice San Francisco *private* school."

"Copy that."

"So, there he is studying Mental Health Counseling in San Francisco, far away from San Diego or Los Angeles where he's been since grad school—"

"Besides Pasadena, but yeah, it's, uh, never mind...continue."

"Okay, thesis work is intense. Hours are long. But you still have to have a social life, right?"

A nod.

"And so he's dating this gal, Stephanie Oliver. Beautiful—I saw some pictures. Smart—her grades were amazing. And maybe just a...*little bit* cray-cray. Lots of girls are. But one day she—"

Stuart started shaking his head early. "No fuckin' way!"

"Yes. Way."

His head whipped toward the board. "By hanging herself? What year?"

"2006. He's 30 now."

He slapped his hands together and yelled, "Fuck," pointing to the board. "Every five years! Almost, anyway."

"And *that's* when the *coincidences* started messing with my head. Remember I said a second ago, remind me to come back?"

"Yeah."

"So, back to 1996. And Rebecca Cheswick."

"Stop one second," he said. "Sorry, but I gotta pee like a racehorse."

"Do it."

While Stuart went to the bathroom, I realized my phone had been silenced for a better part of the day, so I checked messages.

I replayed the first phone message: *Hi, Detective Norelli, it's Sharon Gladstone from the Getty. I, uh, wanted to speak with you...about something that, I don't know, could be helpful. I'm sorry, I know I sound scattered. Uh, I'll try you again tomorrow. Perhaps we could meet up for a coffee. Or even a lunch here at the Getty. You'd be my guest. Okay, gotta go. Thanks.*

I considered calling her now but, looking at my watch, decided it was too late and made a note to call her first thing.

The next message was Shay. I smiled hearing her voice: *Hi, Momma Bear. It's your little cub. Hope you're doing well. I'm good. Life is good. All is well. Just wanted to call and say I love you. And having a great time here with Dad. Looking into the school stuff and such. Anyway, I'm babbling. I'll try you later. Or, you can call me. Tomorrow. Not urgent, okay? I love you. Bye.*

I was still smiling when I saw Stuart kissing his little girl. Janine and I exchanged waves as I pushed play for the next message: *Hi, Detective Norelli. McCloud here. I, uh, have some stuff you may want to see and all. I can be reached at—hell—you know how to reach me. Just call when you can. Thanks.*

Waiting for Stuart to return, I ended playback and read the last text. It was from Dr. Tercel:

"Thanks for shifting. I owe you."

74

HANDY WORK

Tercel stood across the room admiring his handiwork. Bobby sat on his king-size bed, completely naked and strapped to the massive headboard. At the foot of the bed was an elaborate setup that included Bobby's favorite compound bow anchored in a repair stand. The bow was loaded with an arrow—its razor tip and fiberglass shaft pointed directly at his heart. Because of the way Bobby was strapped to the bed, there was no way he could move from the path of the oncoming arrow.

Tercel had taken great care in orchestrating the setup. The arrow was placed in the rest where it gently, yet firmly, held a poisoned arrow ready to launch. The poison tip was only a precautionary back-up plan. That way, in the off chance the trajectory was not *exactly* precise, the arrow had enough poison to drop a buffalo. The pull string was attached to a reverse pulley whereby the pull was dependent upon the strength—or in this case, the fatigue of a man's grip. Given the torque was between 75 and 100 pounds pull, it was likely Bobby's hand would give out long before his core strength.

He had given Bobby just enough Fentanyl to knock him out while he set the stage. He also had an ammonia capsule to wake him when the time was right. Knowing the lethargy his muscles would experience because of the drugs and Scotch, he knew Bobby's hand would no doubt give out more quickly than usual.

While taking photos, Tercel hummed, "*Straight to the heart and you're to blame, you gave love a bad name.*" When he was finished, he snapped a capsule and awakened the sleeping giant.

"Here, hold this" he said, placing the line to the rig in Bobby's hand.

He was confident Bobby would instinctively take it—which he did. Feeling the tension, Bobby instantly responded as expected.

The look of horror on Bobby's face was worth the price of admission.

"Hey, buddy. How you feeling?"

Bobby was groggy, but he had enough presence of mind to hold tight and keep still. He looked from Tercel to his own hand.

"My guess is you'll last, I don't know—five, maybe ten minutes? More or less. I would've saved you the trouble and me the time, but it seemed like a good idea to let you...you know, take yourself out. Or, as the case will be, have Sharon take you out."

Confused and terrified, Bobby stared at him.

"I'd say by that expression you're wondering something," he said with a mocking voice, "What does my pal the Doctor mean...Sharon taking me out? She's not here," he laughed. Catching his breath, he added, "But she will be."

"You are a sick motherfucker," Bobby growled as his hand quivered and eyes widened.

"Oh my," Tercel mocked, "Your strength may not be as strong as expected." He pulled a chair to the foot of the bed. "Guess you won't be needing this after all," he chuckled, shaking the GoPro in the air. Pushing record, he set it on a nearby nightstand, then took a seat. "Yeah, seems silly going through all those motions, but I needed you to buy the whole thing."

Bobby's breathing was heavy, but he did not budge an inch.

"Yeah, the look on your face?" he continued with the mocking voice, "Did Doc really intend to give me that video? Yeah, no. How about this: Did Doc really hypnotize me all those times in his office? Uh, yeah. And you know what? You are, or rather—soon to be—*were* one of my *very* best students. You always went under quickly, always followed directions precisely, and never remembered a thing. Tell me I'm wrong. The only one better than you is my girl, Angie. Now *there's* a straight-A student."

"You son of a *bitch*," he spat—his eyes, bulging with fear. "You'll burn for this!"

Nodding, he said, "Yeah," then dramatically shook his head and added, "I don't think so."

Bobby's breathing increased.

"As you can imagine—knowing my attention to detail—I've thought of pretty much everything. It's what I do."

"You fucking *FUCK*!" He swallowed hard, making his hand shake. Watching the compound bow shimmy, he caught himself.

"You may want to save your energy, Bobby."

Suddenly, there was a knock at the front door.

Startled, Tercel leaned forward and frowned. "Were you expecting someone?"

"Of course not, you fucking maniac!" Bobby spat, trying with all his might to control himself.

As he left for the other room, Bobby stared at the bow. After a moment, he heard a familiar woman's voice. His eyes darted from the compound bow to the doorway as sweat streamed down his face.

"Look who's paying us a surprise visit, Bobby. An old friend of yours," Tercel said, entering the room and holding a woman's hand—her body, just out of view. "And such very good timing."

Elizabeth Conroy popped her head in the room and sang, "*Hello, Bobby, Oh Hello, Bobby...*" Seeing the getup, she gasped, "Holy Shit!"

Tercel clapped.

Gathering herself, Elizabeth got closer to the bed and raised a pair of handcuffs in the air. Enjoying Bobby's confusing stare, she purred, "Remember these, Fuck-face?"

"The fuck?" He squeaked. "I thought you were—"

"Yeah, not quite. But you came pretty fucking close," she shouted, lunging toward the bed.

The move startled Bobby and he nearly lost his grip.

Tercel quickly stepped in. "Hold on, Elizabeth. Bobby and I were just in the middle of, how shall I say, a very delicate conversation. Perhaps you'd like to watch?"

She admired the setup. "My, my, this is quite something you have here, Bobby," she purred, looking at his privates. "Seems to have changed your perspective, yes?"

"You fucking bitch," he spat. "I should've held on longer. Made sure I finished the fucking job!"

Tercel crossed the room and pulled out a chair for her. "May I offer you a ringside seat?"

"Why, thank you," she smiled, looking around. "Perhaps a cocktail, too?"

"Of course. Where *are* my manners?"

Seconds later, he returned with a hefty pour of Bourbon. They clinked glasses and sipped.

"Now, where were we?" Tercel asked, setting down his glass and returning to the side of the bed.

"If you and I were on equal ground, I'd crush you with my bare hands," Bobby grunted.

"Yeah, but that's not going to happen, is it Bobby?"

His hand trembled. The bow shook.

His eyes widened. The string wobbled.

His breathing increased. The sweat flowed.

"Any last words, Bobby?"

"Yeah, WHY?" he screamed. "You're an insane fucking nut job," his voice quivered—eyes shifting rapidly back and forth between the bow and his opponent.

Tercel glanced back at Elizabeth who blew Bobby a kiss.

Sweat ran into Bobby's eyes. After several beats, he growled, "You're a greedy prick, Doc!"

"Really? Seems you're the greedy one, Bobby. You had Meredith, but I was the one who really wanted her. You did nothing but mistreat her where I gave her nothing but kindness—in my office *and* her bedroom."

He stopped to watch Bobby absorb the truth.

"But you had to *beat* her to get your way. And all she wanted was to love you. Then you got her pregnant and you didn't even know it was *yours*!" Tercel shouted. "As far as we know," he laughed.

Bobby's hand trembled as sweat dripped from his forehead into his eyes.

"Frankly? I think it was mine."

Bobby frowned.

"Or was it Grey's? Or Tommy's," he smirked, turning to Elizabeth. "Hell, so many were tapping that fountain of youth, it was hard to know."

The color was rapidly draining from Bobby's face.

"I wanted her all to myself. More than Sharon. More than anyone. And *you* had her right in the palm of your hand," he said, looking at Bobby's hand—now white from fatigue.

Grunting, Bobby tried to steady himself. He was obviously losing.

"So tell me, Bobby, how do you see this movie ending? You're the director, after all."

Bobby's eyes bugged when his hand trembled and his grip loosened.

Just then the rig shook and the bow released.

THWAT!

Launching at 300 feet per second, the arrow fully penetrated Bobby's heart, pinning him into the headboard.

"Holy *Shit*!" Elizabeth shrieked.

Seconds later, Bobby's last breath escaped and his head dropped.

"Aaaaaand that's a wrap!" Tercel laughed, spinning toward Elizabeth.

Her face was a mixture of terror and passion. "*That*...was fucking intense!"

"And so was the video of you two," he grinned, waving toward Bobby. "I saw it on his phone."

With a wicked sneer, she cooed, "You liked?"

"Just what the doctor ordered," he said, bouncing his eyebrows.

She circled her lips with her tongue.

"Now, how about you and I pick up where you and the late Mr. Shapiro left off?"

75

DARK UNDERBELLY

L ooking at me sideways when he returned, Stuart said, "You okay?"
       "Yeah, just got some messages that…well, I'll share in a second,
but I wanna wrap this up," I said, distracted from the last text.

Opening another beer, he waved for me to continue. "Okay, so we
were talking about Rebecca Cheswick. The one who shot herself."

"Right," I said. "1996. The autopsy said she died from a gunshot
wound to the head. Her temple to be exact. She had been renting an
upstairs garage apartment from an elderly couple. The gun was found in
the front seat of her car in the garage, exactly like—"

"Tercel's father."

"Exactly. Let's jump back to the hanging and the girl he was
dating—"

"Stephanie Oliver," he nodded.

"Right. So in the report she was found hanging from a pipe in the
basement of her home. The autopsy said she was choked."

"Makes sense. Wait, how'd you—"

"I did an internship with a local office while the ex was in school. I
made friends with a wacky cat by the name of Seth. Worked in the
morgue. We traded favors—professional, of course. Anyhow, I spent a few
hours with him the other day catching up. And asking questions."

Cocking his head to the side, Stuart scratched his two-day growth.
"Okay, it was a hanging, but I thought you said she was *choked*."

"Right. Except her trachea and voice box were not crushed—as would be the case in a hanging. Especially given the distance she dropped, along with her weight. She was a big-boned girl."

"So?"

"So, she *could* have been choked, even 'accidentally,' and then placed in that noose…"

"To *look* like a suicide," he mumbled.

"Bingo."

Stuart returned to the grid. "Okay, for the sake of argument, let's say there's a—call it a five-year pattern. I see a couple potential holes."

"True, but I also haven't finished," I grinned playfully.

"Okay, then allow me to shut the F up."

I crossed the room to snag a bottle of water from the fridge and downed it.

"This is huge, Pat. Nice work."

"I should mention that while it's, as you put it 'nice work,' it doesn't actually prove anything. Factually. But the *patterns*? That's where the magic lies."

"Show me the magic."

"All right. Everything up until his graduate work can be explained. Mostly. In one way or the other. Also, the early deaths all made sense, and the later deaths took place outside LA. Well, except the *almost*-wife."

"Gimme a minute," he said, eyeballing his laptop, the map, and his notes. "Okay, locked and loaded."

"Good," I said, "Because here comes the last link I have. It's 2016 and it's been five years since his wife died. His practice is thriving, and I'm going to guess—time to start dating again. So, who would a handsome, super successful 40 year old bachelor with a thriving practice want to date?"

"Me? A supermodel."

"Ding, ding. That would be the super tall, super beautiful, super model Natasha Teresa Campbell. She's two-thirds his age and the talk of the town."

"Wait, I know her. About the time everyone wanted to go by one name, she had *three*."

"That's right. Plus, she had a trifecta of bad habits."

"Really."

"Sex, drugs, *and* rock'n roll."

"The American dream."

"Sex," I said, holding up a single finger. "As in appeared in several films, thanks to our pal, Tommy Showalter."

"Copy that."

"Drugs." I held up a second finger. "As in heroin and coke."

"Shit."

"And rock 'n roll." I added a third finger. "As in spreading it wide for many A-list talents."

"Oh boy. And her connection to our Doctor?"

"They dated—big surprise—but only after he *treated* her for depression. It didn't last though because she was seeing several guys at the same time. That's the rumor, anyway."

"And her demise?"

"OD. Found in a Venice Beach Hostel."

"Classy way to go."

"You bet. Hard to pin this one—again because of multiple partners and...," I stopped to hand him the police report. "Dr. Tercel was on a flight to Vegas. And around the time she was found by the maid—he was already speaking at a conference. Timeline's close; you make the call."

"Hot damn, girl. And look," he said, pointing to the overhead grid, "Every five years like clockwork. Except, what—2006?"

"Yeah," I mumbled. "But it felt so much more—"

"Norelli, you kidding me?" Leaning forward, he said, "This is *solid* detective work. I'm proud. And Nelson's *got* to be thrilled."

I said nothing, pulling all the paperwork together.

"What are you *not* saying?"

"Thank you for being proud."

"Why haven't you told the boss?"

"I needed your input. Your advice. And your sign off."

"Whoa, whoa, girl. You have my input. My advice is to push forward. Time's of the essence—especially with Bobby released on bail. As for signing off? I'll be there, front and center. In fact, Janine doesn't know it yet, but I'm coming back tomorrow."

"No, Stuart, you have to—"

"No, *you* wait. I don't *have* to do anything except be sure we nail the murderer's ass to the wall. WE are partners. And WE have a job to do. Janine understands that. Seriously, I am back *tomorrow*. Period. And I'm talking to the Captain about pulling four 10's. Same amount of work— more time with my girls."

Smiling, I gave him a hug.

"In the meantime…" I said, brushing away a tear, "First thing tomorrow I'll get extra coverage for Shapiro and Gladstone. They're the last pieces of the puzzle that will pull this whole thing together."

76

BLOOD BATH

Angie patiently waited in her car, sipping a bottle of water and listening to the sounds of the evening. When all but one of Sharon's lights went out, she sent a text to Dr. Tercel: *The deal is signed. Just waiting for approval.*

He was weaving through one of many prestigious neighborhoods when his phone pinged. He slowed to a curb, read, and replied: *Thank you. Give me ten.*

Angie knew enough to keep communication neutral and to a minimum. And Tercel appreciated her for following directions so well.

In minutes, he pulled up to Sharon's house, spotted Angie's car, and parked in the driveway.

"Hello, Angie. Good to see you. How are you feeling?" he asked calmly.

"I'm good. Nice to see you, too."

"And how is our friend, Sharon?"

"Besides ecstatic with the incredible offer, she was all but passed out when I said goodnight. We had several glasses of wine and she was going to soak in the tub before heading to bed."

"Good, Angie. Thank you for taking care of this. As I said, my clients —actually my friends in Palm Springs—saw this house when they were in town and just had to have it."

"I know they'll love it."

"You've had a long day. Why don't you head home and get some rest? There will be a *very* handsome commission for you soon."

"Thank you. And good idea, I'm tired," she said, starting the car. "What are you going to do?"

"I'll just peek my head in and say hello—*if* she's not asleep already. Then I'm heading home. It's been a long day for me as well. Now, get some rest and we'll have a session in a couple days."

"Thanks, will do."

As Angie put the car into gear, Tercel put his hand on the door. "Oh, before you go, do you have the contract?"

"Yes, of course," she chuckled. Reaching to the seat beside her, she handed it to him. "Almost forgot."

He slid it into his jacket and softly patted her arm. "Thank you again, Angie. You're a good friend. Don't forget to call my phone the *moment* you get home. I wouldn't be able to sleep tonight if I don't hear your voice, telling me you were home safe and sound. Promise?"

"Promise," she smiled, then pulled away.

Before long, she would be sound asleep with no recollection of her whereabouts between their last call and crawling into bed.

Quietly, he took a case from his trunk and approached the house. Walking around back to the sunroom—knowing Sharon never locked it— he gently opened the sliding door. "Sharon?" he called out, "Are you home?"

Nothing.

Inside, he passed through the kitchen and the dining room, and then entered the master bedroom suite where he found Sharon passed out in the tub.

Making sure she was completely out, he reached over and turned on the warm water. Next, he opened the case and removed Bobby's compound bow and placed her left hand on the bow, establishing solid prints.

As the water neared the top of the tub, he turned it off and replaced the bow in its case. Next, he rolled up one sleeve, then reached into his jacket and removed a razor.

He first sliced through a femoral artery in one thigh, then the other. Next, he lifted one wrist and sliced the vein vertically, making sure to keep the spurting blood inside the tub. Placing her arm in the warm bath, he did the same procedure with her other arm.

Drying off his arm with a towel before rolling down his sleeve, he looked around to make sure he had not touched anything but the faucet that he wiped down. Then, retrieving his smartphone, he took several well-framed shots.

Finally, he removed a letter from his jacket and placed it on the night-stand in the bedroom and left.

77

NIGHT NIGHT

Heading home after a great work session with Stuart, I pulled out my phone and sent a voice text to Shay: *Hey, baby girl. Been a long day. About to crash. If you need me, I've got 20 free, or we can talk over coffee in the morning. Love you.*

The next voice text was for McCloud: *Hey, got your message. I'm toast. Let's chat at 8AM. G'night.*

The next voice text went to Stuart: *Thanks for today. We're almost there. Love you, dude.*

I had another fifteen before I hit the canyon, so I cranked one out to Dad: *Hey Pops, just checking in. Not to worry, I'm on it. Let's connect before EOD tomorrow. Miss and love you and Mom.*

Hanging a right onto Beverly Canyon and heading up into the hills with my windows rolled down, I enjoyed the fragrant cool air while Van Morrison's "Someone like You" played on the stereo.

As my mind turned to Steve, I realized I had let too much time go between booty calls, so I sent a voice text: *Hey there. Big apologies for being AWOL. Don't mean to. Give me the rest of this week and I'll make it up to you. Promise. Big hugs, Naughty Norelli.*

Inside about two minutes, a text returned: *No worries. Glad you're catching bad guys. Save time for me and I'll be the one making it up to you. Sleep tight. Stevo*

"He's turned out to be a sweet one," I whispered to the night.

Making my way up the last of the curves to home, I ran a mental laundry list of things I had to do first thing in the morning.

Suddenly, a deer leapt across the road and, before disappearing, managed to kick the front end of my car with his hind leg—catching my headlight in the process. I instantly downshifted my nerves and car, trying not to slam my breaks.

While I felt sure the animal would be fine, I wasn't sure the same could be said for my ride. And as much as that chapped me, I knew it could've been worse.

Cresting the hill, I saw the lights of my humble cottage and let out a sigh of relief.

Within minutes, I was lost in a hot bath.

———

TWENTY MINUTES LATER, all the lights in the house were out and the neighborhood was silent, except for a dog barking in the distance and the sound of a red-eye overhead, heading east.

Another ten minutes passed before a figure, dressed in all black, got out of a car and silently crossed the street to Norelli's house.

Creeping up the driveway—along the backside of the house and away from the motion-sensor lights—the figure stopped at the corner between a hedge and her car. Next, they crouched low, making their way alongside the car before scooting under it.

As a car approached, the figure stopped moving long enough for the swath of headlights to pass.

Within several minutes, they reversed their moves with precision, pausing a beat at each point, and silently returned to the car.

Rolling down the hill, they waited until out of sight of Norelli's house before turning on the headlights, then disappeared into the night.

78

SWITCH BACK

B efore the morning sun broke the horizon, I was running along one of the many crests of Mulholland, doing my best to keep my tummy tucked and fanny fit without having to resort to doing the same under anesthesia.

Climbing my driveway, I was now ready to face the damage from last night's deer crossing. While not as bad as I had suspected, it wasn't pretty, and given I was fairly OCD, I simply couldn't let it go the week without having it fixed.

Inside, I spent several minutes stretching while I contemplated whether to take it to the dealer or hit up Jackie's brother who had a body shop in The Valley. For now, I had a shower, an Americano, and a mother-daughter phone call in my immediate future.

Stuart rang. "S'up partner? Feeling on your game?"

"How about *ahead* of it. You?"

"Just helping Janine with the tiny one, then I'll meet you at the station."

"Okay. Gotta run my car to the shop for some body work, but I should hit the office at the same time."

"Wait, what happened?"

"Nothing big. Hit a deer on the way home last night."

"That's what you get for living in the country," he laughed.

"Funny."

"Wait, I'll pick you up. We'll be together all day anyway. Plus, we can pull double duty in the car."

After texting Jackie for her brother's number, I got ready. There was a chance I might see Steve tonight after work, so I put on the extra spiff.

Within forty minutes, I walked out to find Stuart leaning against my car eating a donut. He stopped shoving sugar and looked at me.

"What?" I smiled. "Never seen a detective before?"

"Not one as fine as you, Detective Norelli," he winked.

Jackie's brother, Jésus, was going to take my car to his shop later, so I left the keys inside the fender.

AN HOUR LATER, Jésus had retrieved the damaged car and was making his way along Mulholland. Traffic had eased up and he was driving faster than he probably should have been. Having just passed Dona Pegita Drive, he hit a straight-away and punched it, smiling as the horses got up to gallop.

He was about to hit a wicked switchback—locally referred to as Snake Bite—when he realized he had waited 50 yards too long before downshifting. Seeing he was also going too fast, he reached for the short stick to downshift and hit the brakes—too hard.

He felt the brake pedal drop to the floor.

Making matters worse, he was in the center of the switchback and an oncoming truck was six inches over the double line. He had to make a snap decision.

Instantly, he knew it was the wrong one because there was no guardrail to stop him. Cutting the wheel, he slid through the loose gravel and was instantly airborne.

For the next three to four seconds, he was flying—and not on a plane.

Nope, Jésus No-Relation-To-Christ Corazon was piloting a Camaro ZL1 650-hp toward Mother Earth that was appearing entirely too fast.

Make that: approaching the side of a house—embedded in the side of a mountain—next to a kidney-shaped pool—too fast.

ONE OF THE benefits of working with the LAPD was I had friends all over the place. Also, one of the best things I ever bought for my car was a gizmo called Carlock. The smartphone app alerted my phone if my car was tampered with, stolen, or wrecked. And in a city like LA, it was easy to see why I might need it.

Stuart and I were sitting at our desks having coffee when my Carlock pinged: *YOUR CAR IS IN TROUBLE.*

Before I could get my head around why my car would be in trouble—given it had just been picked up by my professional, friend-of-the-family *mechanic*—my phone rang.

"Detective Norelli," I answered with hesitation.

"Hi Detective. This is Officer Scott Denton, LAPD. Your car's been involved in an accident and the driver wanted me to call you right away."

The look on my face must have told Stuart a shitstorm was brewing because both of his hands were in the air as he whispered, "What's up?"

I motioned for him to wait. "Officer Denton, is it? What happened?"

"Your friend, Jésus Corazon, was maneuvering Mulholland—my guess much too fast—when he, let's say *misjudged* a curve, dodged an oncoming vehicle and, well—"

"Well, what?"

"Jumped the curve and crashed your car."

My heart sank, "But he's okay, right?"

"Couple of nasty scratches. Looks like a broken arm, but all in all, he'll be okay."

"Good, good."

"Yeah, that's the good news. I mean, if he were a smart driver, my guess is it'd be next to impossible to do a better job of landing on—"

"My car, Officer Denton?"

"Yeah, pretty much toast, Detective. He took off the front end when he caught a tree on the way down. Luckily, that broke his fall. Well, that and the edge of the pool. Which leads me to—"

"Yes?"

"It's on the bottom of that pool."

"Shit."

"The guys are fishing it out now."

We wrapped the call by discussing which hospital Jésus had been taken to and confirming that my car would be taken to his garage. I hung up and shared the story with Stuart.

We stared at one another before I said, "Well, thank Christ he's okay."

Stuart looked at me. "That's just rude."

We laughed. Then the heft of what could be behind the accident hit us.

My head said, *Fat Frankie* as Stuart said, "Are you thinking—"

"No coincidence."

Suddenly, I felt an overwhelming need to speed things up, so Stuart and I grabbed our notes from yesterday's debrief and started hammering.

"Let's revisit that call I got from Sharon. She sounded distraught. Wanted to show me something I'd find *helpful*."

"That's easy," Stuart said, flipping open his pad, then dialing a number.

"Hello, this is Detective Brown, LAPD. My partner and I, Detective Norelli met Ms. Gladstone recently and, oh, that's right, we did meet. Nice to meet you again. Certainly, is she in?"

He shook his head. "Wait, let me put you on speaker."

Engaging the speaker, he continued, "Is that unusual?"

"Yes, it is. She's an early bird. Arrives earlier than most and works later than everyone. Pretty much every day like clockwork. But we haven't heard a word from her and her phone is never outside her reach."

"Hi, it's Detective Norelli. Is there anything else—I don't know—*strange* in her behavior lately?"

After a long hesitation, she said, "Well, truth be told, she has been on edge lately. More than usual. And maybe that's just me being a paranoid assistant, but, I don't know...maybe not."

As Stuart rang off, I said, "Let's head her way and then swing by Bobby's place after that to chat with him."

Grabbing another donut, Stuart winked, "I'll drive."

79

FUNNING GAMES

We arrived at Sharon's home to find her car in the driveway but got no answer when we knocked on her front door. After several more minutes, we circled the house; me, in one direction, and Stuart, the other. We simultaneously arrived at the back entrance to find the door unlocked.

I called out her name.

Nothing.

Giving one another a nod, we slowly moved through the house room by room. Then, we smelled it: the unmistakable fragrance of death. Approaching the master bedroom, we knew what we would find. Sharon had been soaking for quite a while.

"Holy shit," we said simultaneously.

Without skipping a beat, Stuart dialed Jackie. She answered on the second ring, telling us she could arrive in twenty because she was wrapping a job nearby. He texted her the address as a backup, then stepped across the patio to call HQ.

In the meantime, I retraced my steps to the kitchen area. Finding two empty wine bottles, but no evidence of struggle, I kept looking. Nothing was out of the ordinary until I ended up back in the master bedroom—this time not chasing the smell.

Propped up against a crystal lamp on the nightstand, an apparent suicide note was ready for an audience. Taking out tweezers, I picked it up and placed it in an evidence bag. Looking outside, I saw Stuart was still on the phone, so I pulled up Bobby's address, punched it into my smartphone, then rang *The Hollywood Mole.*

"Okay, thanks," Stuart said, re-entering the house. "How about we call—"

I turned my phone so he could see: Calling SHAPIRO.

"Wish I'd thought of that."

"Hi, this is Detective Norelli. May I speak with your HR department? Yes, a Ms. *Everest.* Like the mountain," I winked.

A voice mumbled something and I instantly heard on-hold music. While we waited, I motioned toward the door, making a face like I was about to vomit.

Outside, I took deep breaths. "*This* is when I wish I smoked."

"Why? It's a nasty habit."

"But I wouldn't have to smell *that.*"

"*Hello*?" Ms. Everest's voice whined.

Putting us on speaker, I greeted her kindly and reintroduced ourselves before asking, "Has Bobby been around since he was released?"

"Yes. He stopped in to tell Ms. King he was innocent, then came to me for his check."

Stuart and I bounced back and forth asking if he had been acting unusual, if there were any new reports of improper conduct, and if there was anything else she could tell us. Getting zero additional assistance, we rang off and called the one place she told us he went every day after work: the gym.

After being connected to a variety of operators, we finally reached the Valet Department where we learned that even though Bobby was there every day, he had not been in recently.

Just then Jackie arrived.

"Nice to see you girl," I said with a hug.

"You, too—considering the circumstances," she said, giving Stuart a fist bump.

Entering the living room, she whistled at the digs. As we made our way through the house, she frowned, waving at the air. When we stopped at the door to the master bath, she said, "And the hits just keep coming."

"Listen to this," I said, reading Sharon's note. *It was time for the madness to stop. Meredith took so much from me. Her life was all I had left to take from her. And when Bobby told me he was going to turn us all*

*in, I had to stop him. As crazy as this sounds, I couldn't handle the guilt.
I'm sorry Mom & Dad, Love, Sharon.*

Looking at one another we frowned, collectively shaking our heads.

Stuart mumbled, "I don't think so."

Jackie said, "Eso es una locura."

Stuart raised his eyebrows.

Grinning, she said, "That shit's crazy."

"Yeah, as in *total* bullshit," I said.

Within minutes, the room felt like a flash mob. One moment it was deathly quiet and in the next one, it was lit up like Grand Central Station. There was a full forensics crew setting up in one corner and some tall guy in a suit none of us knew in the other.

"Why all the fuss..." I said, before Stuart pressed a finger to his lips and waved me outside. Jackie nodded and kept working.

Outside, Stuart said, "My hunch? Internal Affairs. And like before, someone higher than us wants this looked into. Faster than usual."

Or to watch how I'm handling this case.

Stuart texted Jackie: *Heading to Shapiro's. Touch base shortly.*

80

DEEP DIVE

I t was not long before we were pulling up to Bobby's house. The gate was open, his car was there, and all looked normal—but felt hinky. Walking toward the front door, I stopped to touch the engine hood of his car—it was cold.

Stuart rang the doorbell and we waited.

Nothing.

He rang again.

Still nothing.

He knocked and tried the door, but since it was locked, we started around the house in opposite directions.

After knocking on the back door, we entered through a sliding door to find a large and handsome living room that was certainly a guy's place. The TV was on to a sports channel with the volume muted. Most of the lights were on, and there were empty bottles and glasses scattered about like a party had taken place.

Stuart called out his name a couple times.

Nothing.

We drew our guns and continued moving through the house, splitting up to cover more space in less time. Nothing was in the front of the home. We met at the master bedroom where our questions were answered.

Lying on the floor next to Bobby's bed was a massive compound bow —just like the ones we saw at the Straight & Arrow. There was also an arrow straight through a very dead Bobby. His head was slumped over and his eyes were still open with a frozen expression.

"Shit," Stuart said, holstering his gun.

"Someone got right to the point," I said without thinking.

He deadpanned to me and said, "There's something you don't see every day."

"You mean went out as the hunted instead of the hunter?"

"Right. Okay, let's run this before we call it in to Jackie *or* the Captain."

"Copy that."

Stuart backed up to examine the whole room and we both scanned the room for a suicide note.

Coming up empty, Stuart smirked. "Can this get any weirder?"

Stuart made his way through into what looked to be an office while I ended up in another master bedroom.

I involuntarily gasped. "Stuart?" I shouted. "It just got weirder."

He quickly appeared in the door and said, "Wow."

"Wow" was a woman in her early to mid 30's. She was blonde, beautiful, and quite dead—tied up in the middle of a large, modern four-poster bed.

"What the hell?" he whispered. "And who do you suppose this is?"

I circled the opposite side to observe the elaborate contraption. "Whatever happened to just good old fashioned sex?"

The woman was hog tied and on her knees, her wrists bound together behind her back then tied to her ankles—all with silk scarves. Another several scarves were tied together, wrapped around her neck, then looped over and tied off to a metal bar overhead. Obviously, the complex contraption was orchestrated so that the more the victim struggled, the closer they came to their ultimate demise.

"I've seen this in bondage videos but never in person," Stuart mumbled.

"Doesn't look all that sexy if you ask me."

With all the bindings, it was anyone's guess whether her being blue was due to the loss of circulation, the length of time in that position, or both. Either way, Jackie would know.

Stuart had a quizzical expression. "You think sex got outta hand and he freaked or—"

"No," I said, shaking my head. "Our guy wouldn't freak. Whoever's behind this made it look exactly like what he *wanted* it to look."

Stuart mumbled, "Too tidy."

"Entirely."

Back in Bobby's room, Stuart walked around the bed several times, examining the elaborate set up. "I'm guessing they haven't been dead that long."

Nodding, I had a thought circling my head like a trapped bird.

"Just for the sake of argument—which is how it's *supposed* to look— let's say Sharon came here, killed him, and then drove all the way back home to kill herself." I looked back toward the other room. "But was she done *before* Bobby? I mean, she'd have to have been, right?"

"Perhaps. Or, maybe, like you're noodling now, Sharon walked in on their kinky and in a jealous rage killed her then…" he trailed off.

"Maybe. But just to think outside the box, what if she's doing a two-for-one?"

"Huh?"

I paced the room. "As in, you've come this far, got nothing to lose, and go out in a blaze of glory."

"Hmm…"

"And like I said, our guy wants us to do exactly what we're doing— trying to make sense of the chaos, when in reality—"

Snapping his fingers, he said, "That's where my money is."

I motioned for Stuart to join me outside. After a deep inhale I said, "You know what this is."

"What?"

"Variety."

"*Splain.*"

"Remember the variety of methods? In our earlier conversation?"

He nodded.

"Sometime ago…someone found his father dead…and imagined that if a person wanted to get rid of someone…he'd stage a suicide," I said— adrenaline surging.

"Like your list," he responded like a bobblehead. "So, the span of time keeps you out of view and the variety becomes the calling card."

"Yes, and maybe even along with the way the bodies are *posed*."

Staring at one another, I said, "And all we have to do is catch him before his *next* pose."

81

SHE SAID

I got a voicemail from my insurance company saying they wanted me to call them, but I had little patience for that and I wanted to see the car now. Cranking through Hollywood and jumping onto the 101, we would be in The Valley in a blink.

Just about the time I began fantasizing about the next car I would get, McCloud sent a text saying he heard the news and wanted the dish. Then, just as we descended into Studio City, Jackie pinged to say "The Suit" was indeed Internal Affairs and wanted to see my report before anyone else. I thanked her, saying they could all get in line.

Blocks from the shop, I saw Dad had left a voicemail, so I listened to a message about them already having an offer on the house.

"Well, that's great timing," I mumbled.

Stuart had been following the barrage of incoming messages the whole way but didn't say anything.

With a sigh I whined, "Can I join your maternity sabbatical?"

STANDING in the bay of the hot, noisy, grease-stained body shop, I nearly cried when I saw my baby. She was a scratched and tangled, wet and twisted hunk of steel on a tow truck.

Stuart wrapped his arm around me. "She didn't feel a thing."

An enormous and fully tatted employee eyeballed us for much-too-long before shuffling our way.

"Looks like a long stretch of hard time," I mumbled before he was within earshot.

"And then some."

Approaching, I read his oval name badge. Mongo stood a half foot taller than my already tall partner. He smelled like the inside of an oil pan and had unusually kind eyes.

Removing a sweaty bandana, he asked, "Can I help you?"

Showing our badges, I said, "Detectives Norelli and Brown. We're friends of Jésus. Here to see about that car," I pointed.

His hardened and expressionless face morphed into a huge smile, revealing a row of white teeth. Front and off center was a big gold cap with the letter "M" adorned in sparkling stones.

"Any friend of Jésus is a friend of mine," he said, extending a huge, filthy hand. I bypassed the grease and instead shared a fist bump. We made small talk about the condition of Jésus before getting down to business where I explained my relation to Jackie and how my car was originally set to get here.

"Big reason for coming right away was to see *why* the car lost the brakes."

With a wink and a lopsided grin, he said, "Let's take a peek and see what we can learn, Ms. Detective."

Within minutes, Mongo and his team had the car unloaded from the truck and lifted high on a rack where we were all looking at her belly underneath the car.

"Oh, shit. Yeah, not good. Look at this, Ms. Detective," he said, shoving his head in between parts I never knew existed. "The brake lines were cut. Whoever did this cut the line just enough so after a short drive and a couple good pumps, they'd give out."

I whimpered, "What the fuck!"

Mongo grinned. "What *she* said."

82

PLAN SEE

E vidently news of our multiple finds had quickly spread because we returned to the precinct with applauds from a handful of officers. We gave nods like we were receiving an award. On the way to my cubicle, I tossed an In & Out burger bag in the trash and noticed a blinking red light on my desk phone.

Turning to Stuart, I said, "Since when did we—"

"New phone system. Put in overnight," a rookie named Rogers said, handing us both a notice. I tossed mine in the trash. Stuart scanned his.

"Heard it was coming," he mumbled. "They're referring to it as 'Call Management' or something, so we can't ignore the messages."

"Mission accomplished."

Stuart grabbed a cup from his desk and tossed his head toward the canteen. While he went for coffee, I went for the phone, punched keys, and listened to a message from Sharon: *Detective Norelli, I've been trying to get ahold of you. I have something you really should have. It's, um, a video that shows, well, stuff...you need to see. I don't want to say much more until—I've got to go.*

Just before she disconnected, I heard her say, "Hi handsome." She sounded off her game and maybe drunk. The noise in the background sounded like a restaurant.

The timestamp said it was received at 6:17 p.m. last night.

The machine blinked another light. I pushed play: *Hello, Detective. IF you're hearing this, you've no doubt survived to live another day. Life has a way of changing in the blink of an eye, doesn't it? Stay tuned...for more surprises ahead.*

My skin crawled like a thousand spiders. The voice was heavily disguised—like I had heard in movies. It was unnerving, but the message was even creepier. The timestamp read 12:04 a.m.

Who was that, and change how?

Stuart returned with two cups. Handing me one, he stared. "Uh oh, what's wrong?"

"Just listen." I put it on speaker.

Watching him, I tried to recall the last time I saw Sharon. After hearing both messages, he said, "*That* is too damn freaky."

I took a long, deep breath and said, "Time to make our move."

LATER THAT NIGHT in downtown Los Angeles, we all gathered at the secluded watering hole Conundrum on 6th Street. Stuart got a hall pass from Janine. Steve hanged his hammer for the day and drove up from Marina del Rey. Jackie put the morgue on hold and made the shortest commute from Echo Park. And McCloud joined us from The Valley.

An old-flame-turned-good-friend, Gabe King, owned the joint. Wounded by an IED in Afghanistan, Gabe returned home to open a handsome speakeasy in the tradition of old Hollywood. He was built like a brick furnace and sported a beard that even Grizzly Adams would envy. While he didn't look like he would own a classy joint like this, Gabe said he wanted to do something completely different when he returned to the States. So, after rounding-up cash from friends and family, he launched the club and never looked back. Gabe came to our table and met all the players, and after quickly learning what everybody did for a living and what each person lived to do, he bought the group a round.

After dinner, we covered the finer details about our mission, explaining how we wanted to keep things quiet, push through the bureaucracy, and run the operation "off the books."

Given our suspected mastermind was behind a long series of murders and had remained undetected for decades—not to mention he was a formidable foe who should not be taken lightly—we wasted little time orchestrating our next steps and put "Plan C" into play.

83

WRONG NUMBER

The next morning, both the *LA Times* and *LA Daily News* released the Bobby Shapiro story. Their bold headlines were sure to sell.

LA Times: TV DIRECTOR BOBBY SHAPIRO AND GETTY ART CURATOR SHARON GLADSTONE FOUND DEAD

LA Daily News: LOCAL CELEB DIRECTOR SHAPIRO ENDS MYSTERY WITH DOUBLE-MURDER/SUICIDE

I sat at my desk reading both articles and realized it was the first time in my career I recalled seeing my name in print. I had to admit it was cool. My brother was always in the press; it helped he had the heft of both my father and Captain Nelson—his boss at one time—to boost his ratings. Once again, the Norelli name was synonymous with crime fighting in Southern California.

When I read a headline from another news source, I rolled my eyes, feeling sure they would be running their own "investigation."

The Hollywood Mole: STAR DIRECTOR BOBBY SHAPIRO FOUND DEAD IN MALIBU HOME: EX-GIRLFRIEND IS SUSPECT

My basking in the momentary glory was interrupted by a barrage of texts. First, my mother who rarely texts wrote: *So proud of my girl. Let's celebrate soon!*

My never-texting father said: *You done good, Darcy! xo, Dad.*

Shay wrote: *Nice work, Momma Bear. See you soon. Big Love!*

Steve texted: *"Bravo, Detective Superwoman. I'd say some cele-brating is in our future."*

The office phone rang. "Detective Norelli," I answered.

"Hello, Detective Norelli," the same disguised voice from before began. "How's that spotlight feeling about now?"

Here come the spiders.

"Feels good, doesn't it?" the garbled voice continued.

"Let me guess. Could this be the *real* killer?"

A warbled chuckle.

"That's very good, Detective. What's next? After you're done taking a bow in the limelight?"

"Excuse me?"

"Do your fucking job and catch the *real* killer!"

CLICK.

I sat in shock for a solid three minutes until my monkey mind was interrupted by my cell phone. I was relieved it was Stuart.

"Morning, Detective First Grade."

I could hear his mile-wide smile across the phone.

"Hello, Stuart."

"Uh oh, you have that tone. And you're using my proper name. What's wrong?"

"Ummm, I just got the most unnerving call. Give me a second while I figure out this new system. I think I can replay recorded incoming calls."

I figured it out, then played it back.

When it was done, I said, "Weird, huh?"

Stuart said, "Recall the conversation with our friends at the bar?"

"Which one?"

"The a-b-c conversation? About his being bored, wanting to get caught, or—"

"Right?"

"Looks like he wants two out of three—bored *and* wants to get caught."

We discussed the way we chose to release the story. As much as Captain Nelson didn't like misleading information, we both knew he wanted the mystery solved now and would likely agree with our take on the situation.

"Do you feel the timeline might be shorter than we originally thought?"

"Yeah, I was thinking about that last night," I said. "When I couldn't get to sleep."

"You thinking about making a push?"

"If it is him, then, it is what it is. And he's going to do what he's going to do."

I heard a suppressed chuckle. "Could you stop with the philosophical bullshit? Too early in the day."

A belly laugh suddenly felt good.

"Copy that. I say instead of waiting for his next move, we make ours. And push *all* his buttons."

"That's my girl."

He hung up and I began the setup.

First, I rang Dr. Tercel's office, asking the secretary if he was in. She said he was with a client and would be for another hour. I asked her to tell him I had an "emotional emergency" and to call me at his first opportunity.

Next, I texted McCloud an address, telling him we needed to shorten our gap by stepping up the process. A quick reply confirmed such.

Finally, I texted Jackie asking her to call me as soon as she could.

Needing some fresh air, I walked out back to where the taco trucks parked. Snagging a short Americano and a bench under a tree, I tried to calm my nerves.

Our plan would force the situation by creating our own trigger. And there was one thing Stuart and I knew: *all* suspects left clues *somewhere*— and more often than not, they were inside their own home.

My mission was simple: find a way into Dr. Tercel's home.

84

OFF CENTER

Given the trap needed to be set and I was the perfect bait, I put on my best and arrived at Dr. Tercel's home. I arrived early, hoping to catch him off guard. I wanted to be sure my crew—traveling a distance behind—would be able to get into place without attracting too much attention. We also didn't want to get there at the same time.

Just as I approached the front door, Tercel opened it.

Smiling, he took my hand and kissed it. "Hello, Patricia. You look amazing."

I did a curtsey—something I was pretty sure I'd never done in my life —and did my best to coo. "Thank you, Darius. You're pretty fetching yourself."

He waved me in, adding, "And early too, I see."

"It was the excitement, I suppose."

"Nice to see you out of uniform."

"And you, away from the confines of your office."

"Indeed."

I was wearing my favorite red dress—a stunning color and material that left very little to the imagination. I could practically feel him undress me as I entered the majestic foyer.

"Your home is spectacular."

"Thank you," he smiled, motioning for me to enter the large formal living room.

After pouring two glasses of champagne from the handsome bar, he conducted a lengthy tour of the entire home. We talked and laughed non-stop for nearly an hour, sharing stories of past loves and current hobbies, sprinkled with inspirational insights, favorite books, and films. We didn't speak about work—neither his nor mine—until the murder case snuck its way into the conversation during a momentary lull.

"How did you know Bobby Shapiro was the killer?" he casually asked.

I couldn't help my expression and felt certain he assumed he had crushed the magic of the moment. He tried to change the shift by showing me his impressive art collection.

"Not to change the subject," I said.

"But to change the subject," he grinned.

"I'll get back to that, but tell me, how were you able to acquire such an impressive collection of art?" I gawked at the art. "Several feel... familiar."

"Sharon Gladstone was instrumental in helping me curate such a grand collection. And they should be familiar. There's an original Warhol," he pointed across the room. "A Peter Max and an Edward Hopper on this wall," he continued. "And a favorite of mine is right here," he said, sliding his hand alongside an oversized frame.

"Lichtenstein," we said simultaneously.

That created an honest laugh.

"Amazing. And beautiful." I genuinely enjoyed the art and the light pouring in the room made for an overall serenity in his beautiful home.

"But most impressive is the Rembrandt—there, on the far wall. Certainly, the most expensive."

Walking over, I went to touch the signature.

"BOO!" he shouted.

I jumped and, without thinking, instantly broke into nervous laughter.

Still laughing, he said, "You know who you looked like right there at that very moment?"

"Who?"

"Julia Roberts in *Pretty Woman*."

"What?" Embarrassed, I said, "That's hilarious!"

Laughing, he kissed my cheek. "Please excuse me just a moment. Then, we'll have one more drink before heading out for dinner. Sound good?"

With a nod, I flashed a bright smile. "Sounds perfect."

"Good. Be right back."

As he disappeared, so did my smile.

Reaching in my purse, I removed my phone and sent a group text to Stuart, Steve, Jackie, and McCloud: *Get into position.*

After a beat, my phone silently pinged *Copy* from everyone in the group.

I returned the phone to my clutch and rushed to decide what came next. Call it experience, a wild guess, or an educated hunch, but for some reason—given his luxurious tastes—I decided to do a quick search of the room. I wasn't sure what to look for, but perhaps a secret panel, an odd switch, or just about anything that would provide some resemblance of a clue.

There wasn't enough time to scour the house, so I went with where I was standing. All the walls were completely smooth and covered only with meticulously placed priceless art. The only fixtures were the recessed lights in the ceiling.

Scanning the floor, I spotted a square pattern different from the rest. What caught my eye, amidst all the smooth symmetrical lines of the hardwood floors, was what looked to be a panel. I bent over and pushed. It clicked open, revealing two simple buttons: one was red; the other, blue. I pushed the red one and the lights dimmed.

Suddenly, a toilet flushed down the hall.

Quickly, I clicked the blue button. Each piece of art slowly and silently slid aside, revealing entirely different framed art beneath.

Stepping closer, I involuntarily gasped, completely caught off guard with the discovery.

85

BIG REVEAL

Frozen in place—visually devouring each of the hideous photographs —I heard footsteps coming down the hall. One older photo was black and white, slightly out of focus. It was a woman who appeared to be in her late 30s, lying on a bed in a peculiar pose. Pills were scattered on the bed beside her, an empty bottle on the nightstand.

Footsteps continued echoing down the hallway.

Another photo showed a heavy-set woman hanging from the end of a rope. Her mouth was open and her eyes bulging as she stared at the ceiling. I was mesmerized by another gruesome photo displaying a woman facedown on a city street, her head partially split open.

Tercel entered the room just as my eyes came to rest on another piece of "alternative art." He cleared his throat, breaking my concentration.

I spun around and said, "Are these…all the…murders?"

Expressionless, he remained silent.

I couldn't help but turn back and stare at a black and white photo of a man sitting in the front seat of an old car. The photograph was taken outside the shattered passenger window, revealing a large missing chunk from the man's head.

Without turning, I asked, "Is that your father?"

"You really shouldn't have, Patricia," he sighed, slowly shaking his head in disappointment. "We were off to such a great start."

As I stepped farther away from him and closer to the art, my eyes fell on another piece.

"Meredith," I whispered, recognizing the Marilyn Monroe pose and slit throat. The photo was black and white with the exception of blood, hand-tinted a deep red to match her lips. Its ethereal quality resembled an X-ray.

"She, like you, had so much potential to be loved by me."

His footsteps slowly approached, but I was locked on the images.

"They're all so haunting," I whispered.

"Why did you have to rush things, Patricia? We had such a lovely and *seductive* future ahead."

Turning, I saw a photograph of Bobby over Tercel's left shoulder, an arrow anchored him to a headboard. The over-processed colors created a psychedelic feel.

"My beautiful and intelligent Patricia."

When I turned back to him, our eyes met—but they were not the eyes I had revealed my innermost secrets to these past weeks. They appeared darker and more distant as though looking straight through me.

86

SURROUND SOUND

Outside Tercel's home, Stuart and Jackie—both dressed in all black—were fifteen feet from the master bedroom windows, tucked within two enormous spruce pines. Jackie was wearing a 9mm and Stuart, a 45mm. Both weapons were holstered but unsnapped.

They had wireless transmitters in their ears and were able to communicate with Steve and McCloud on Tercel's street two houses down. Their setup was a Cable TV van. Between the high-intensity microphone embedded in a satellite dish atop the van and wireless microphones attached to both the art gallery and master bedroom windows, McCloud was recording everything.

There were only two hitches so far.

First, there was an intermittent pulse—every twenty to thirty-seconds—that created a momentary static. It lasted long enough not only to create anxiety for a handful of seconds but also to cause the recording to miss some words along the way.

"Blocking device," McCloud mumbled. "Who knew?"

There was a second hitch. About twenty minutes ago, the only direct communication with Norelli's phone had completely vanished and that meant they were without a "Go" signal. It was not the biggest obstacle because they still had Stuart's and Jackie's eyeballs on the back of the house.

The plan was to wait until they heard Norelli use the trigger word:

Decoy. Otherwise, they would go with a visual if needed. Norelli's plan had been to enter, snoop, and pass intel—and the crew would then enter while the couple was out to dinner.

Somewhere during their gallery showing, something shifted.

According to Stuart, Norelli was now naked and bound to a bed in the master bedroom.

"Do you have enough of a confession to bust his nut?" Stuart whispered to McCloud.

"Maybe," McCloud replied. "Mostly."

"Are you ready to move?" Steve asked.

"Almost," Stuart whispered. "Stand by."

He looked at Jackie. "You good?"

"Ready to clock that *polla.*"

Stuart knew enough Spanish to know she meant *cock.*

87

AIR SUPPLY

S pending several weeks with Norelli in therapy, Dr. Tercel had quickly learned about several characteristics that made her the exemplary pupil and perfect candidate for his latest "suicide device."

She was beautiful, extremely headstrong, knew how to use the assets she had, and longed for the approval and acceptance of men. This was likely due to having to work for the love and attention of her father. He had ascertained that Norelli's status as a tomboy at an early age was a response to a need to fit in and be treated as an equal. Living in the shadow of her brother taught her to use any device available to compete in a man's world—not to mention she was a bit of a control freak.

Norelli was outstretched on an oversized 1835 William IV four-poster bed. The red velvet draping above her head was a striking contrast to her fair and naked body. Both her hands and feet were bound with silk kimono sashes. Her arms were spread wide and tied to the head of the bed. Her legs were close together and attached to the footboard. Her mouth was gagged with another kimono sash.

Tercel was not sure which half of Norelli's naked body was more attractive—or seductive. He stood at the foot of the bed admiring her striking figure. His plans were to turn the evening's particular pose into his most epic—creating a dramatic *Suicide Tour de Force*.

It would leave those who discovered her—breathless.

He had taken a luxurious time getting showered and shaved, using his immaculate preparation as the backdrop of luring his client into his bedroom. Having spent days, if not weeks, imagining the encounter, he was electrified with anticipation.

He was wearing Prada charcoal slacks, a black cashmere turtleneck, and black boots. His handsome and shiny Cartier watch vibrated at the top of the hour.

Staring at Norelli created an instant and eager arousal. "I admire how you arrived nearly an hour early for our date," he said. "No doubt hoping to throw me off balance."

She struggled to no avail.

He smiled without conscience.

"Little did you know I was prepared for your doing that, having planted that very seed of thought just hours ago. You don't even recall our quick little phone call, do you?"

Her confused expression gave him the answer.

"No, I don't suppose so," he smiled. "I've used that little trick on you so many times."

Taking his smartphone from a pocket, he swiped the screen until a video of his big smile appeared. He walked to the side of the bed and turned it so she could see. Norelli saw herself sitting across from him in his office. He was speaking quietly and with a specific cadence. Her eyes slowly closed. He turned the camera around to show his face as he mouthed, *Watch this.*

She watched with wide, panicked eyes, not recalling the scene she was witnessing.

He watched as a frown creased her forehead. "You don't remember that, do you?"

Years of studying hypnotherapy had paid off. Knowing how much practice, patience, and persuasion it required, Tercel was proud of himself because he had mastered all three.

"You know, the most-prized guinea pig in my stable has been Angie. She was among my first patients and had the most to gain, but she also had the weakest defense. Meredith was second and the patient upon which I based most of my sexual experiments. Knowing her tendency toward the more perverse, I gave her plenty of opportunities to prove she was a most exceptional student. And now, you."

He admired his latest display of art perched on his bed.

Then in a flash of anger, she exploded into a vitriolic rage. Gasping, she tried with all her might to kick him.

"Does that mean you don't want to be added to my magnificent art collection?"

Putting away his phone, Tercel crossed the room, picked up a professional camera, and began taking several pictures.

"These will act as the…*before* photos," he sneered.

88

TRUE CONFESSION

"I thought we could have a nice life together," he smiled. "You have everything I want and all I need. And I could have given you everything you dreamed possible. My biggest gift to you would have been the love of a good man based on unconditional love. Unlike your father."

With my appendages and mouth bound, all I could do was watch.

Frowning, he said, "And Steve? Well, it would have been oh so easy to have taken his place. He's weak. Just like Shapiro was."

Writhing back and forth, I fought the bonds that held me, and as much as I wanted to scream, the strips of silk muffled my efforts.

Tercel walked over and removed the gag.

Breathing hard and fast, I whispered, "Thank you, Darius. Seriously. And I really am sorry. Please believe me."

His expression showed a flicker of confusion.

"You don't mean it," he casually said, tossing the gag on the bed. "It was all perfectly planned and executed, Patricia. Bobby takes the fall and it is all sewn up. Or Sharon, if the wind blew in that direction. Either way, it was a delicious plan: a quarrel ends in a standoff where two lovers die. And the nightmare—as you said—would be *Case Closed*."

"I know," I whimpered. "I was so stupid. And I'm sorry. I really am, Darius. Please believe me." I couldn't get a read on his expression. "What can I do to make you believe me?"

"We were having a good time," he said, shaking his head. "Until you made it all go to hell!"

"What happened, Darius? Please help me understand you better."

He became silent for several minutes and walked to the window, staring out at the city lights.

"Hollywood, where all your dreams come true," he snorted. "Yeah, fuck that."

As he was lost in thought, I looked toward the wall of windows, searching for any sign of my team.

"The Oscars show was over..." he began in a low voice. "And we left early because Meredith wanted to party. And why not? She'd just had a lifetime dream come true. I can't imagine what it must have felt like winning an Oscar. But there were spoilsports among us."

"What do you mean?"

"Bobby was pissed because he wasn't getting his way, which only made her bitchy, and she caved. So, our famous Hollywood foursome left and drove to Bobby's to party—where we did for a while. That was until Meredith pulled a hissy fit saying she wanted to take the party to her home. She sweetened the pot by saying she had all sorts of tasty drugs for those who wanted them. And plenty of sex all night. Needless to say, that got *everyone's* attention."

Still staring out at the growing dusk, Tercel shook his head like he was listening to someone.

"I said I'd play along, and Sharon—who was hammered the most—agreed. And fickle Bobby? Well, whatever MJ wanted, he did. So, we went to Meredith's and partied well into the night."

"What happened then, Darius? Tell me, please."

His expression remained blank as he stared out the window.

"Sometime during the party, Meredith who was drunk *and* high—a rarity for her—blurts out she's pregnant with Bobby's baby. Sharon was happy, Bobby was surprised as hell, and I *tried* to be the good sport. Deep down, I was pissed."

When he paused, I was distracted by movement outside the window. My eyes flicked to him to make sure he hadn't seen me.

"We partied until about 2ish, I guess. Well, until everyone passed out."

He whipped his head toward me and said, "Why am I telling you all this? I'm the shrink here."

"Darius, please continue. I mean, why not—you know so much about me. It's plain to see we have a connection—whatever that is, and—"

"Maybe it's time," he mumbled. Just as he started to pace, he dialed his cell phone.

"Hi, Angie? It's Dr. Tercel," he said with a calm, measured voice. "How are you?" He looked at me, then turned his back. "Good, good. Sorry to bother you, but remember what you and I talked about the other day? About my mother's house? Yes, good of you to remember. And the other place in Malibu? Yes. Please move forward with that, will you? What? Oh, yes, immediately. In fact, write up the paperwork tonight and I'll meet you first thing in the morning. Yes, we'll dial it all in. Shouldn't take long. Okay, thank you. Bye, Angie."

Ringing off, he came to the side of the bed. Using the back of his hand, he softly brushed along the side of one breast, then the other, and then up along my neck. His gentle touch came to rest on the side of my cheek.

"You are so beautiful, Patricia. I want you all to myself."

I snuggled to his hand and whispered, "You can have me. All to yourself. Just like you said. It's all done and there's nothing left to say," I smiled.

"Almost." His eyes turned cold again and he walked away.

"Tell me the rest of it. Just between us. Like you said, it's case closed. I just want to understand you."

"Why not?" He smiled, methodically tying knots into the middle of kimono sashes. "It must have been about 3 a.m. when I left Sharon's room. We had made love before she passed out, and I was feeling good and very horny for Meredith, so I went to her room—where she and Bobby were—and woke him up, telling him to join Sharon."

"And?"

He looked up at me and grinned. "The four of us often did that. We'd make homemade porn on weekends. Just crazy shit. We had agreed to share earlier in the night, so he obliged. Well, that and some of my *hypno-magic*," he winked.

"Getting into bed, I woke her and told her the baby was mine. She didn't appear surprised and actually seemed happy. We made love until... until we passed out."

I was losing sensation in my hands and I saw my feet were turning blue. "Darius, could you please be a love and untie me? I can't feel my hands or my feet. They hurt."

"You'll just try and do something stupid."

"No, I promise, Darius. Please?"

He looked around as though he had misplaced something and then left the room.

Looking at the window, I saw no movement.

Tercel returned with a black leather satchel. "I can't quite decide which plan I want to go forward with, but since I called Angie and that play is in motion, maybe I should just..." he looked at me with cold eyes and continued, "As they say, cut my losses and move on."

He removed a length of rope, some zip ties, handcuffs, and another scarf, then displayed them across the bed.

"Darius, please finish the story. After that, you can do with me as you wish. But I *need* to know the truth."

He looked at me as though considering it.

"And laugh if you must, but I suppose it's the detective in me."

A smile sneaked up from the corner of his mouth.

"And if your secret has to die with me—that is, *if* you don't want to have me as your own—so be it. You can toss me aside like all the others."

Judging from his reaction, I assumed my plea brightened his spirits because he smiled and started neatly arranging the items side by side.

"I don't suppose there's any real harm in that. After all, you're a detective and I'm a doctor. We have a moral obligation to our respective professions."

He untied my wrists first, allowing me to rub the circulation back into them, then did the same with my ankles. Next, he placed heavy zip ties on my wrists. Apparently pleased, he sat on the side of the bed.

"The one mistake I made that night was not knowing just how much of a sex addict Bobby was. I mean, he had taken steroids forever, but he often was jacked up on speed, sometimes coke, and on a rare occasion, meth. That beast had the biggest cock I'd ever seen on a man. Mine's large, but his was like...let's just say he was sporting a non-stop hard-on that night.

"What I didn't learn until later—under hypnosis—was that he had awakened in the night and snuck into Meredith's panic room that had a two-way mirror. That was where he watched Meredith and me for who knows how long? When I woke up later, I was still fixated on her being *pregnant* with that *idiot's* kid!"

He got up and returned to the window where he seemed lost for a minute. I whispered, "Go on. Of all people, I won't hold anything against you. We built our relationship on trust, right?"

After a long sigh and a short nod, he continued. "I suppose when we started making love again we must have made some noise. I think the speaker in the panic room must've been on and awakened Bobby, who—by the way—loved watching us. Anyhow, it was later when I learned he had been filming us through the glass with his GoPro…"

He trailed off and I remained motionless.

"Somewhere along the way, I guess Bobby freaked. Then, sometime between then and when I went for a shower, he must have grabbed Sharon and snuck out together. *That* must have been the sound I heard."

His expression turned angry. "It wasn't until later he told me about the video and how he was planning to use it against me."

"Darius, is that why Sharon called me?"

Whipping his head toward me, his expression shifted as though I had just appeared. "What?"

"Is that why Sharon called me recently?"

"I suppose," he stared.

"And isn't it good knowing you can share your deepest secrets with me? Just like I've shared with you?"

His smile slowly dissolved.

"It wasn't supposed to end that way, Patricia. After all the pushing boundaries…I guess we just got crazy. And spun out. But when I learned Meredith was pregnant by that…*Neanderthal*, I couldn't bear the thought."

"I can understand why you'd be so angry, Darius."

After a long moment, he quietly said, "Somewhere along the way a switch got flipped…in all of us."

* * *

"Heads up," Stuart whispered into his mic. "I don't have eyes on Norelli. I repeat, no eyes on Norelli. Looks like Darius moved her to another room."

"Copy that," Steve replied. "I'm moving out. I'll travel along the South side of the house. Repeat: moving to the *South* side of the house."

Stuart said, "Copy. I'll move north. Jackie will cover the East and remain in the trees. Repeat: Stuart moving *North*. Jackie covers *East*."

"Copy," Steve said, climbing out of the van.

McCloud chimed in, "And I'm staying locked in the van."

89

INSIDE OUT

W hy Tercel suddenly decided to move me to another room, I had no idea, but he gave me a robe and secured me to a chair that faced French doors looking out onto a courtyard. Across the room, he pressed a button under the lip of his desk and a paneled wall slowly opened, revealing a bank of large television monitors.

At least if anything happens, I'll see it first.

I surmised the top eight monitors were connected to cameras pointed in all directions, providing a 360-degree view of the entire property. The next eight covered the front gate and front door, the kitchen door, both the outside and inside of the four-car garage as well as the courtyard I was facing that included the patio just outside the master. The final camera was high up in a palm tree on a corner of the property.

"When I went to the bathroom earlier, I checked all the cameras," Tercel sneered. "That's when I saw your partner in the trees just outside my bedroom. I also spotted their van parked on the street. And knowing working vans are not allowed in the neighborhood after 5 o'clock, plus the fact no one lives next door, *and* I know the gentleman across the street who, like myself, has satellite, it was easy to see the phony play."

He reached in his desk drawer and said, "On the upside, it looks like your team came prepared."

Removing a black Sig Sauer P229 and a large hypodermic needle full of a yellow fluid, he grinned, "As did I."

My blood ran cold.

"Darius, can I ask just one more question?"

He shook his head.

"I need to know if you killed every one of those people."

He stopped and frowned. "What people?"

"Let's start with your father."

"Heavens no! He was my idol. My hero. I would never hurt him."

"But your mother—"

Whipping his head in my direction, he shouted, "She was a tormenting *bitch*!" His voice bounced off the tall ceiling. "She was never happy. Always nagging my father. And eventually drove him to his death."

Staring at the wall of screens, he mumbled, "Good riddance."

"But all those others. You must have—"

"STOP! That's the past, Patricia. We're in the present," he sighed deeply. "Time to move on."

Just then, I saw motion outside my peripheral vision.

"Now where was I?" he asked, approaching the screens. "No one can get on or off the property without my being able to see them. And these," he nodded toward the gun and needle, "will be the two things that help me get away without a hitch."

For the first time, I didn't see a way out. My heart sank as my pulse ignited.

"Here's what we're going to do," he said, stepping behind me to roll the chair across the floor. "You're going to be my security blanket. They won't shoot at me for fear of hitting you. Also, I have this tasty little cocktail of sodium thiopental, pentobarbital, and pancuronium bromide— otherwise known as a lethal injection. I won't bore you with what each ingredient does, just suffice to say it only takes one small injection and within 30 seconds you're dead."

As brave as I thought I was, I wasn't. "Why are you doing this, Darius?"

"That's a good question, Patricia. Perhaps because even though the case is closed, you know as well as I do your people...and *you*...won't let it rest. You have a reason you must bring me down. And frankly, I can't let you."

"I understand how you feel. And honestly, you *can* get away with this, Darius. I'm serious."

"Please excuse my language, Patricia, but you're full of shit."

"The one piece of the equation that *must* remain intact is me. You kill a cop in Los Angeles? They'll turn the earth upside down to fry you—especially when both my father and brother get involved."

"I know who your family is."

"So, what do you—"

"STOP! If I thought you really cared for me, and would actually be with me, I'd do anything, and I mean *anything* in the entire world, to make that happen."

His expression seemed part scared boy, part desperate man. In the strangest and most inexplicable way, I felt drawn to him.

"But you don't. And I can't," his eyes turned cold. "Because it won't work."

He placed the gun in the small of his back, secured the syringe in his left hand, picked up what appeared to be an oversized house phone, and rolled me into the center of the hallway.

From the new vantage point, we were both able to see the front and back doors as well as the courtyard and kitchen entrances—all the while still being able to see the bank of monitors in his office. He pushed a button on the phone, and as he spoke, the loudspeakers in the four corners of the house came alive.

"Hello, friends, and welcome to my home. I can see each and every one of you right now—no matter your specific location. So please, wait right where you are for further instructions. Thank you."

"WHAT A FUCKER!" McCloud barked from inside the van.

He was sure he had calculated everything and this situation made him nervous—and he did not like being nervous—especially with his boss in the crosshairs and his ass in a sling.

"No shit!" Steve shouted into his microphone.

He was not used to making mistakes—never in the service and never at work. Rarely did he make mistakes in his personal life because it felt like weakness. And at the moment, Steve was feeling extremely weak.

"What the *hell*!" Stuart whispered loudly.

He knew a good deal of the success or failure of this mission rested on his shoulders. And he was damned and determined to make things right— for Pat, for his team, and for himself.

"*Puto bloque de gallo,*" Jackie growled into her mic.

Stuart turned toward her.

"Fucking cock block," she said with a tight grin.

She was protective of her family and friends, and if any of them were ever in danger, all bets were off.

With minutes ticking, nerves wracking, palms sweating, and Norelli in way-too-deep, the team knew they had to kick things into high gear.

Having served in Afghanistan, Steve saw it as a no-brainer. "We need to barge the door, give him a 'tap-tap, tap," and save the girl," he blurted to the group.

Jackie pictured her brother and was enraged. "Mierda!"

Stuart felt the heft of the situation and shouted into the microphone, "No one is going to die on my watch!"

McCloud mumbled, "I should've chosen a different van."

90

TICK TOCK

Opening the secret compartment in the floor where he stored more than enough incriminating evidence to put him away for eight life-times, Tercel removed a Go-Bag that contained money, passports, a ring of keys, a burner phone, and a device that looked like a remote control.

Dialing a burner phone, he said, "It's me. Open the garage, leave the keys, and walk away. Do it right now. Got it? Now go!"

Hanging up, he removed the SIM card, walked down the hall to the powder room, and flushed it down the toilet.

Back in the middle of the hall, he stared at me with a half-cocked grin.

"This is where things can get sticky or go smoothly. Your call. Follow my rules and you go free. Do that and all of you will be talking about your close call over cold beers by midnight."

He leaned over to kiss me, but I turned my face at the last second, giving him my cheek. After hesitating, he kissed it.

"Have it your way," he said, pressing the button on his speaker phone. "Okay, people, listen up. I want you all to remain calm. If you do, every-thing will turn out okay. Stuart, you and your lady friend, come out of the trees and enter through the back door. You on the side of the house, and you in the van, both of you enter through the front door. Do as I say and Norelli will be safe. If not, it won't be good."

He turned and pointed the phone at my face. "Assure them you're safe and then tell them that if they make any stupid moves, you'll be dead before you hit the ground."

He placed the phone in front of my mouth.

"Guys, like he said, come in, and when you enter, place your guns on the floor and slide them to the center of the hallway. And please…don't be a hero."

Within 30 seconds, the front and rear doors slowly opened simultaneously. Each person carried a gun by two fingers and then followed precise instructions.

"Very good. Now, each of you—do you see this syringe nearly piercing Detective Norelli's neck?" he barked. "All it takes is an ounce of pressure and she's dead. And this gun in my other hand? Will shoot each of you. Trust me. I'm not afraid to kill all of you."

"You'll burn for this Tercel," Stuart growled.

"Perhaps. But unlikely," he said, pointing to a door at the end of the hall. "Now, each of you go to that door…slowly…and line up in a single file."

They did as he said, but at the last moment, Steve leapt toward Tercel who—without hesitating or moving the syringe—shot him in the leg.

"Shit!" Steve fell to the floor, writhing in pain. Blood spurted from his wound.

"The hero just had to do something stupid. Oh so very predictable," he said. Shaking his head, he turned the gun toward Jackie. "Please grab a hand towel from that powder room, tear it into strips, and wrap your boy's leg. Now!"

Jackie followed directions and got him bandaged in a blink.

"Good. Now, this next step is easy, but important. I need all of you to get in there." Turning to Steve, he added, "Including you, *hero*!"

McCloud, closest to the door, opened it.

"It won't bite. It's only an elevator," he smirked. No one moved, so he shouted, "Get inside!"

They moved instantly.

"Good, and the moment you're in, pull that lever. It's just a safety device to keep the door from opening during its descent. You'll be safe. But just to be extra safe on my end, and you'll have to trust me, I'm going to keep Norelli with me."

I noticed Tercel had changed from using my first name to using my last.

"Please don't be a hero or she will die. I guarantee you." He turned to me. "Do you trust me? Well, as much as you can?"

"Yes."

"Good, then assure them."

"Go ahead," I nodded toward the elevator. "You'll be okay. He won't hurt me."

"You're just going to push one button and go down one flight. Right into the wine cellar," he said. "As soon as I'm away, I'll ring the phone down there and give you the emergency code. You'll be up and out and home in time for dinner. By the way, there's no exit down there, so save your energy."

Pushing a button, Tercel closed the door and the engine whirred for several seconds before stopping.

Something didn't seem right. I whipped my head toward him. "What just happened?"

Grinning, he stepped aside. "That's the tricky part. There *is* a wine cellar. And as you saw, it *is* an elevator. However, they're currently half way between this floor and the basement."

"And?"

"That wouldn't ordinarily be a problem. However, as an extra precaution, I've suspended them between the two floors. And it's in an airlock— meaning they have maybe an hour before they suffocate to death."

"You son of a bitch!" I screamed, struggling to get free. "You said it was safe. And told me to—"

"Calm down, Patricia. They'll be okay, *if* you play along."

"Tell me what will happen, Darius. NOW!"

"Well, first—and I wish we could've done this so much differently, but we can't—I'm going to leave and lock the doors behind me, thus making it impossible for you to get out," he said, placing the syringe at my neck.

I instantly began to sweat.

"Mainly because you're going to take a nice…long…nap."

"No, Darius, *please*. I've done everything you've said—"

"Your friends will be safe, soon enough. I've hidden a phone in a floor panel, and when I'm away, I'll ring it, give them a code to unlock the elevator, and all will be fine."

"But you said—"

"I know, love," he said, kissing me on the mouth. "I said a lot of things —many of which were *mostly* true."

"Darius, please, isn't there *any* way we can work this out?"

He only grinned.

"Please don't kill me," I whimpered.

"Enjoy your nap."

"Please, Darius. I'll do *anything*..."

"I'm sure you would," he said, inserting the needle into my neck and pressing the plunger.

91

GREAT ESCAPE

Inside the elevator, all four listened and heard nothing. Looking at one another, their expressions showed fear.

"We're stuck between floors," Stuart said. "And if I'm not mistaken—"

"What?" Jackie said with wide eyes.

"Nothing," he said, looking at the floor.

Now panicked, Jackie screamed, "WHAT?"

McCoy sighed. "Probably an airlock."

Her eyes opened wider, "Wh-which means?"

Steve chimed in, "Means we only have so much air."

"Holy shit," Jackie whimpered, sliding down the wall. "What a *shitty* way to go."

They looked at one another.

Stuart looked at the only two buttons—*Foyer* and *Cellar*—then clenched his jaw.

No windows.

No handles.

No vents.

The floor and ceiling appeared smooth. But there was something that looked like a phone panel on the elevator wall. He yanked it open.

It held an emergency phone—unplugged.

There was a speaker inside the panel but no way to speak.

He slammed his fists on the elevator door. "Dammit!"

UPSTAIRS, Tercel waited to be sure Norelli was out cold and grinned at the distraction of their banging inside the elevator. Taking a knife, he cut the zip ties, lost the robe, and carried her into the bedroom.

Carefully positioning her, he tweaked her placement for the ultimate picture before clicking a series of shots.

Taking several steps back, he admired his handiwork, swelling with thoughts. "There'll be another time for all that," he whispered, turning off his camera.

Stopping at the door, he blew a kiss, then returned to the foyer and gathered his things.

As soon as he was outside, he used the remote to open the garage, pushed another button to lock every door in the house, then pressed the last button whereupon the front gate opened.

Entering the garage, he tossed his bag on the seat, got in, and pulled to the end of the driveway, stopping to look back at the house one last time.

"Thanks for the memories, Mum," he whispered.

AFTER HE HAD TRAVELED a number of blocks, he pulled into another driveway, keyed a code, and watched the gate open.

Around the back of the house, he entered the middle of three bays and parked. Taking out several stacks of hundreds, he tossed them and the keys onto the front seat, then closed the garage.

In the next bay, he got into a new Cadillac STS and drove away.

92

DOUBLE TAKE

Nearly two hours later, I was propped up in a hospital bed, still groggy from the hypodermic cocktail Tercel gave me.

"Situation could've ended differently, partner," Stuart said, holding my hand.

"No doubt," I said with a scratchy voice and a foggy head.

Jackie stood guard at the foot of my bed, shaking her head, "Damn straight. Thought we were all going to die in that freakin' elevator."

"But we didn't, thanks to Mr. Gadget figuring out a way to hack that elevator," Stuart grinned.

Adjusting the pillows to get more comfortable, I said, "Where is he anyway?"

"Who, my new hero?" Jackie smiled. "Downstairs waiting to see how Steve's doing."

"Yeah, just about the time he figured it out," Stuart said, "Tercel did exactly what he said he would. Literally at the 60 minute mark, the phone rang and we got the code. It wasn't him, but someone else who gave it to us."

The drugs were wearing off and I was uncomfortably antsy. "Speaking of Steve, I need to see him. C'mon, let's get outta here," I said, throwing the covers aside. But as I stood, the room spun, I wobbled, and Stuart caught me while Jackie pushed me back into bed.

"Not yet," she said. "Doc said you need observation time. No telling what all was in that syringe."

"Okay," I said, lying back down. "But Steve. Is he okay?"

"Yes, still in the ER, but should be out shortly," Stuart smiled. "Lost a lot of blood, but he'll be okay."

"Won't be running marathons anytime soon, but I doubt it'll stop him from taking care of you," Jackie winked.

There was a tap at the door, followed by a familiar face. "Baby Girl," Samuel whispered as he came in for a hug.

"So good to see you, Dad."

"You okay?"

I gave a nod as he kissed my cheek. "All good."

"Now, I want you to listen to the Doctors and don't try to get back to it too fast, Detective *First Grade*," he smiled.

"Thank you, and I won't." Not wanting to let go of his hand, I said, "Anything more about—"

"We'll talk later," he winked. "But rest assured...it's *all* good."

"Speaking of good news," Stuart said, "We have more than enough crime scene photos of *all* the killings."

I forced a smile.

"The bad news? So far we don't have any actual...*solid* evidence that links those photos to him—or the murders."

"What?" I shouted loud enough that everyone jumped.

"Not yet, anyway. And theoretically, he *could've* purchased those photos from any sick bastard—say from the Dark Web."

"You're shitting me."

"I shit you not."

"But what about the recordings? McCloud was—"

Shaking his head, Stuart stopped me in mid-sentence. "There was more than enough static and interruption in them to complicate matters. Basically, he jammed us," he shook his head. "That equipment? State-of-the-art."

I let out a desperate sigh.

"And..." he stared at his hands, "Even with the recordings, he doesn't *actually* confess too much of anything. Just that they all partied."

My expression must have been sad because they all stared at me.

Stuart said, "I know. It's f'd up."

A knock at the door distracted us as Captain Nelson entered. "How the hell are ya, Norelli?" he barked, entering the room like he was late for the party. "You okay?"

"Pretty good, Captain. Ready to find this maniac."

Nodding acknowledgements to Dad, Stuart, and Jackie, he approached and patted my leg. "Yeah, about that. We've got a statewide APB out, covering all modes of transpo, but you know how it is—a city this size... and *his* resources."

"Yeah," I mumbled.

"Not promising," he shrugged. "Not right now, anyway."

I could feel heat rise in my chest. "How could I have been so—"

"Whoa, now," Stuart interrupted.

"Yeah, stop it, Norelli," Captain Nelson added, "Without your instincts, we wouldn't be here knowing who the real killer was. We'll get him. Rather...*you'll* get him. 'Cause you know as well as I do...he'll screw up somewhere and you'll be there to bring him down."

While I knew he was trying to make me feel better, I wasn't sure I completely bought it. "Thanks, Captain."

"Captain's right, Pat. This team'll find him," Stuart said, bumping my fist.

Slapping his hands together, Captain said, "Now, get better and we'll see you in a day or two." He patted my leg like a good puppy, then started to leave. At the door, he turned back. "Just kidding, take whatever time you need. And Detective Norelli?"

"Yes, sir?"

"You did good. I'm proud of you," he smiled, then looked at the team. "We all are."

With that, he was gone.

Dad, Stuart, and Jackie looked at one another before Stuart said, "Is that like the first time he ever—"

"Pretty much," I smiled.

STUART AND JACKIE left at the same time a nurse arrived to give me a pill to help me sleep. Now that we were alone, Dad stayed for another twenty minutes, peppering the conversation with details of how a *business connection*—he actually used air-quotes—helped him put Nicky the Crusher away. Because of a "special arrangement" he would only have to serve three *soft* years—not life—and in exchange, the Judge and family would not suffer any further complications. From what I recall, they called it "the price of doing business."

After several hugs and a kiss, he said he was taking Mom out for dinner to celebrate a handsome full-price offer on the house—thanks to an anonymous buyer from Palm Springs.

As soon as the door shut behind him, the meds must have kicked in because I was instantly out cold.

93

KNOCK KNOCK

W hen I awoke, the sky was dark and the halls quiet. Since I was without my phone—a casualty lost in the shuffle—I felt completely alone.

Lying there, I watched the twinkling lights of West Hollywood as my mind drifted to my last moments with Dr. Darius Tercel.

"Not sure if I should call him Doctor any longer," I mumbled.

Just then, the door slowly opened and a man's hand holding a small bouquet of red tulips slowly extended beyond the door and seemed to float in mid-air.

Still groggy, I squeaked out, "Hello?"

Next, the arm was followed by a body.

"Hello, Patricia," Tercel said with an enormous smile. "How are you feeling?"

My stomach bottomed out and my heart began racing—as evidenced by the beeping monitor overhead. In that instant, I was torn between outright fear and odd attraction.

With a dry mouth, I said, "Hello, Darius."

"I love it when you call me by my first name," he said, approaching my bed. "Your mind is probably racing with all sorts of questions, isn't it?"

He placed the flowers in my lap and took my hand.

"Yes, actually."

"It's good to see you," he said, taking my hand and kissing it.

"What are you—doing here?"

"Checking on you. And to say how sorry I am for having left you so quickly. But you see, I couldn't stay."

He was so close I could smell his cologne. It was woodsy and manly and alluring.

He slowly leaned down to kiss my cheek.

At the last second, I turned and our lips met.

We kissed—gentle at first—then our tongues passionately entangled.

KNOCK, KNOCK!

EPILOGUE

I awoke instantly. Looking around, I realized I was still in my hospital bed and it appeared to be just before sunset. Another double knock at the door startled me again. Disoriented and a bit panicked, I answered.

"Hello?"

Watching the door open, a young orderly entered, carrying a bunch of flowers and a small package under his arm.

"Detective Norelli," he asked, confirming my name from a note in his free hand.

"Yes?"

"Sorry to bother you, but these were delivered by a man who asked that I deliver them immediately. I'm guessing official police work?"

Confused—either by the dream or the drugs—I wondered if he was asking or stating.

"Was he a police officer? Was he in uniform? What did he look like? Did he give a name?"

He fumbled, "Uh, no, I don't think he was an officer. Well, he wasn't wearing a uniform. He was kinda tall and fit looking. Handsome, I guess."

He stopped. I stared.

"And?"

"Oh, um, what was the last thing you asked?"

"A name?"

"Just a first, I'm guessing."

I raised my eyebrows.

"Oh, right." Looking down at his notes, the orderly responded, "He said to tell you it was from Darius."

Suddenly, it felt as though my head had been shaken like a glass snow globe. And the snow inside was tiny bits of facts mixed with lucid dreams.

It took me another minute to shift from dream to reality.

Clearly uncomfortable, the young man looked around before placing the flowers in a water pitcher on a nearby stand. Handing me the package, he said, "I'll see that you get a fresh pitcher of water. I work downstairs. In the gift shop. Have a good night."

After the door closed, I stared at the package. Pulling the tab open, I slowly removed the book: *Men Are From Mars, Women Are From Venus* by John Gray.

"You've got to be kidding," I said aloud.

Removing the dust jacket, I discovered a different well-marked book: *Hypnoanalysis* by Lewis R. Wolberg.

A chewed yellow Ticonderoga pencil marked a dog-eared page.

I began reading the highlighted section:

In some patients, particularly compulsive neurotics, it may be advisable to induce the patient deeply during the first session. Compulsive patients are often impressed with the changes occurring in themselves and, not knowing what to expect next, cannot marshal their hypnosis the first time, but thereafter knowing what to expect, they can resist. Once in a deep trance, post-hypnotic suggestions may be made that will cause them to enter into a much deeper, manageable state.

"What?" I mumbled, staring at the book while half-expecting it to answer.

Turning to the front, I found an elegantly handsome *Thank You* note tucked into the seam. My name was handwritten on the front in fountain pen ink. Opening it, I read:

My Dear Patricia,

I hope you enjoy the flowers and this book. The "secret powers" within have served me well over the years.

You must know how much I enjoyed our time together and am sad because it was much too short. I trust you learned things about yourself as you are an exceptional patient—so quick to learn, so willing to dive deeply. That spirit of teachableness is hard to come by.

I feel certain that in time, you will come to see how much you will have adapted to ideas of which you had no conscious awareness. Be prepared for all sorts of revelations!

Speaking of which, if you find yourself needing a good therapist to handle your PTSD, I can make an excellent recommendation. He's a good listener and even makes house calls (wink).

In the meantime, I am moving far from the grasp of you and your coworkers. Guess that will make me an unsolved case, won't it? However, I'm certain you will have plenty of other cases which will require your attention. Your Captain is bound to be impressed with his star protégé.

By the way, as a parting gift I lent a hand in one of your business matters—the one between you, your father, and some persons of ill repute. Let's just say I have friends in odd places, and your friend will no longer be a problem, and your father can retire with a clear conscience and your family can rest easy. Seems as though Nicky the Crusher didn't like prison and had an extreme case of claustrophobia and hanged himself. Tragic, isn't it?

Until we speak again, may you find great success as a First Grade Detective and know that you will always be First Class in my book.

I hope your father enjoys retirement, your daughter enjoys school, and you and Steve have fun together. Sorry about his leg.

If you fancy a getaway, be sure to look me up. I'll be the tanned surfer walking the golden, sun-kissed beaches of Australia looking for the one true love who got away.

All my love, Darius

Letting out a long breath, I allowed my emotional mind to battle my monkey mind, knowing it would be important for me to find a way to come to terms with knowing innocent people died at the hand of a psychopath. And while I don't know why the maniac chose not to take my life, I'm grateful he didn't.

Lastly, I wasn't sure what was in store for me, but I felt he had awakened something in me that I wouldn't understand for some time.

After several moments, my body finally relaxed and my anxiety drifted away like the day's diminishing light. In that serene moment between being awake and asleep, I was confident I had given it my all. However, I also knew I would spend a long time hoping for a second chance to find Darius and beat him at his own game.

Thank you for reading The Poser.
I had fun creating Detective Pat Norelli and look forward to you reading her next adventure in the sequel, The Impostor. In the meantime, stop by my website davidetemple.com and drop me a note.
I'd love to keep in touch with you.
David

THE IMPOSTOR: SNEAK PEEK

Detective Patricia Norelli thought she'd left her most brutal case behind.

She was wrong.

In this follow-up to *The Poser*, the ghost of Dr. Darius Tercel won't stay buried—and when an old friend turns up dead, Norelli is forced to confront the one killer she never stopped fearing.

What follows is the opening of *The Impostor*, now available exclusively on Amazon.

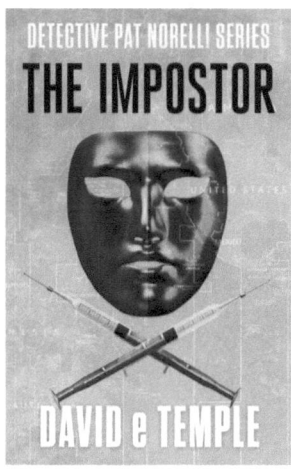

THE IMPOSTOR

CHAPTER ONE

Palm Desert, California—

Norelli's eyes flick back and forth beneath closed lids.

Pinched in permanent frown, her forehead is dotted with beads of sweat. Erratic breathing and twitches punctuate her tanned face. Struggling to get free, she twists in one direction, then another.

Her mind pushes aside a myriad of haunting images when her eyes suddenly snap open. The only light in the dark room comes from a blue glow illuminating a familiar face.

What?

"More bad dreams, Patricia?" a man's voice croaks.

She remains motionless, wondering if she is lost in a nightmare or awaking to another one.

Suddenly, a flash, and she is momentarily blinded.

"Nice," the low voice whispers. "Another trophy for my collection."

She slowly reaches under her pillow.

Shit.

Struggling to gain her bearings, she works at slowing her breath, then stretches toward the bedside lamp. Her finger finds the switch. With a turn, she lights the room.

"Morning, love," Darius smiles, squinting at the light.

Dressed in black from head to toe, he looks calm and resembles a burglar—but he is neither. His nervous eyes belie his steady demeanor.

Looking down at her feet, she sees familiar strips of silk cloth binding her ankles to the footboard. Her sweat-covered naked body lures him to sneak glimpses.

"Dreams still tormenting you?"

"What are you doing here?" She asks, scanning the room. His eyes follow.

"Just tying up loose ends," he says, tightening his grip on her ankles with his left hand while sliding the smartphone into his back pocket with his right hand.

She writhes to get loose, but his grip is a vise.

Her eyes widen as he removes a syringe from his jacket pocket—a shock wave of fear shoots through her body.

Removing a plastic cap from the end of the needle with his teeth, he spits it on the floor. "One could say I'm putting a period at the end of a long sentence."

"You're insane, Darius!" "Perhaps."

"And why in the hell risk your freedom for—"

"Hah," he blurts. "What freedom? You'll likely never stop chasing me."

She is losing circulation and patience. "Not likely," she says, glaring at him. "Certain."

"*Riiiiiight,*" he says, pointing the syringe between her first and second toes. "When they find you, they'll assume you had a heart attack. That will be correct because your heart will suffer enough drugs to drop a charging bull—or a raging *Bobby,*" he cackles.

With each passing moment, her fear increases.

His staring eyes are glowing. "You wouldn't believe how much I shot into that neanderthal. But then again, you saw the results, didn't you?"

As she tries to sit up, he yanks at her bonds. "Stop! You should know by now fighting me will only make it worse."

Frozen in place, Norelli hears her pounding heartbeat.

"Play along," he growls, "and in moments you'll return to your fitful slumber."

Stuck between terror and bravery, she doesn't see a way out. "Darius, please, I won't follow you," she whimpers. "I promise.

And I can forget you— like it never happened. Seriously."

Sympathy dissolves from his face as he tightens his grip and inserts the needle. When the plunger reaches the bottom, a wave of nauseous heat instantly courses through her legs, racing upwards toward her torso, igniting every vein in her body.

As the drug hits her beating heart, it explodes.

THE IMPOSTOR

CHAPTER TWO

I spring up in bed, gasping for breath, trying to gain my bearings.

What the hell?

A slice of sunshine between blackout curtains splits the darkness. Reaching for the nightstand lamp, I light up the room and see the covers twisted around my ankles at the foot of the bed. My sheets are soaked with sweat.

It's gotta be a hundred degrees.

I look up.

Why isn't the fan on?

With my eyes trying to adjust, I look to the curtains; they're still.

AC's off.

Catching my breath, I try to quiet my monkey mind.

I'm losing it.

Suddenly, a noise down the hall breaks the silence. Kicking off the covers, I reach under the pillow, remove my service weapon, slip on a nightie, and approach the door.

Easing it open, I listen. Nothing.

Why isn't the pool fountain running?

Even though the sun has yet to crack the horizon, there is enough light to see down the hall.

Approaching my parent's room, I stop to listen.

Heavy breathing.

Padding down the marble corridor, I scan the rooms along the way. Peering out to the pool, I see nothing out of the ordinary.

Suddenly, I hear metal hit something. I freeze, quietly chamber a round, and slowly approach the mudroom that separates the kitchen from the garage entrance. Approaching the garage, I lean close to the door and squint a listen.

Nothing.

Taking a deep breath, I point my gun at eye level and count: *Three, two, one.*

Kicking the door open, I crouch low. "Police! Hold it right there!"

ACKNOWLEDGMENTS

This story began as a spark on a winter night in 1994. I wrote the opening scene in less than twenty minutes, then set it aside for nearly twenty-three years. Life intervened—moves, a marriage, losses, and lessons—until one day my partner, now my wife, Tammy, said simply, *This is the book you're meant to write.* She was right.

The manuscript that followed took more than two years to complete and went through its own transformation along the way—135,000 words down to its fighting weight at 88,000. The process tested me, reshaped me, and reminded me why I love storytelling.

There are three people I want to thank.

First, my sister, Barbara Ann. Long before I believed this could be more than a hobby, you did. That faith has carried me farther than you know. Thank you, Sis.

Second, Don Winslow—whose work I deeply admire—thank you for the generosity you showed a stranger during a conversation at Warwick's bookstore in La Jolla. Your simple advice stays with me: *If you love to write, keep writing. And never give up.* Thank you, Don.

And finally, my wife, Tammy. Your belief in me never wavers. Your love, patience, and steady encouragement make all of this possible. Every page I write is stronger because of you.

To the reader—thank you for choosing this book. Because of you, I get to keep doing the work I love. If this story stayed with you, I'd be grateful if you shared your thoughts in a review on your favorite platform.

With appreciation,
David

David e Temple spent the first chapter of his life talking to millions of strangers in the dark. As a major-market radio host, he worked in New York, Los Angeles, Chicago, Detroit, Philadelphia, Norfolk, and Charlotte, and was heard nationwide on Westwood One and Armed Forces Radio. Along the way, he built a parallel career as a nationally recognized voice-over artist. He also holds a master's degree in Broadcast Management—an education in both the art and the business of storytelling.

After decades in radio, Temple walked away from the comfort of the studio and threw himself into film. He wrote his first novel, *Discovering Grace*, then adapted it into the feature film *Chasing Grace*. Serving as writer, director, producer, and actor, he raised the financing, built the team, and brought the project to life. The film was acquired by Word Entertainment/Curb Films and went on to stream on Netflix and Hallmark. It now lives on Amazon Prime, reaching audiences in more than 100 countries.

In what he calls his *Chapter Three,* Temple is all-in on crime, mystery, and psychological suspense—just like his upcoming thriller *Dark Hunger* (February 2026). Imagine: Shawshank Redemption meets Hannibal.

When asked what comes next, he doesn't hesitate: to keep writing sharp, character-driven stories with the hope of seeing them come alive on television or film. And if one of those stories happens to feature a radio host who can't quite outrun his past, he won't be surprised.

David lives in North County San Diego with his wife, Tammy. Learn more at DavideTemple.com.

www.ingramcontent.com/pod-product-compliance
Lightning Source LLC
Chambersburg PA
CBHW051948240626
47153CB00005B/1679